Jean Saunders began her career as a writer of short stories in 1965. Since then she has published many novels and over 600 short stories, under various pseudonyms, in both Britain and America. She has also written two books in the Allison & Busby Writers' Guides series – *The Craft of Writing Romance* and *Writing Step By Step*. A member of the Romantic Novelists Association and the West Country Writers Association, she lectures widely and takes an active part in writers' groups and conferences. She is also a committee member of the Writers' Summer School. She is married and writes full time at her West Country home.

By the same author

All in the April Morning

Non Fiction

The Craft of Writing Romance
Writing Step By Step

JEAN SAUNDERS

The Bannister Girls

Grafton

This Grafton edition published 1997
by Diamond Books
An imprint of HarperCollins*Publishers*
77-85 Fulham Palace Rd
Hammersmith, London W6 8JB

First Published in Great Britain by
W H Allen 1990

ISBN 0 261 67002 6

Printed and bound in Great Britain by Caledonian

Chapter 1

The girls from the old pickle factory, now patriotically changed over to munitions, swore colourfully in the sudden downpour of rain glossing the streets as smoothly as sugar icing on a bun. Angel Bannister tried not to notice their jostling as she splashed along in her high-button boots, trying to avoid the puddles. The cold March wind had freshened, whipping against her cheeks and catching her breath.

Her skirt clung to her ankles as her overnight bag slipped in her grasp, and she wrenched off her sodden gloves and thrust them into the bag. She had already lost her silk scarf somewhere. The munitions girls glanced her way, dismissed her as posh, and disappeared into the dark alleyways.

Being posh wasn't helping Angel to get a taxi-cab that evening, and she felt her temper rise as one and then another trundled by, ignoring her frantic waving.

The London streets were congested with people caught out by the storm, as horse-drawn traffic, trams and private motors all tried to converge into spaces seemingly too small for them.

The tram Angel had boarded to take her home had broken down, and she felt as stranded as a fish out of water. On that dismal night, it seemed as though all the cab drivers were either blind, or preferred to pick up groups of passengers, rather than one slight figure who looked as if she was more used to riding in a Rolls-Royce than a hired vehicle.

She almost threw herself into the road to catch a driver's attention as the dimmed lights of a cab loomed up in front of her. He must have noticed her . . . and then a hand hauled her roughly back to the pavement.

'Are you trying to get yourself killed?'

Angel glowered up into the face of the young man in uniform. Her eyes were just level with his breast badge, the initials RFC held in the outstretched wings of a swift. So he belonged to the dashing Royal Flying Corps . . . but she was too incensed at losing the precious cab to waste more than a momentary interest. Her green eyes flashed at him.

'I'm trying to get home, and you've just lost me the only cab that looked like stopping in the last fifteen minutes!'

She heard a high-pitched snigger, and realised there were two other people hovering behind the man.

'We're all trying to get home, ducks – or trying to get away from it, if you get my meanin'!'

Angel glanced at the girl who spoke. Her face was bright with make-up, the eyes startlingly outlined, the lipstick the new vibrant orange known as Tango. The fingernails were lacquered to match, and she clung possessively to the arm of a second man, wearing the dull khaki of a soldier's uniform.

Beside the girl, in her flashy plum coloured costume and matching hat, Angel felt annoyingly dowdy despite her beautifully cut grey wool coat. Her own fair hair, expensively shaped and waved at a chic Mayfair salon, suddenly seemed faded by comparison with the other girl's bleached blonde locks.

Angel was furious for even noticing. The girl was a type that her mother would label immediately. She was a tart, one of those who seemed to have emerged like a butterfly from a chrysalis with the advent of the war to end all wars.

'Take no notice of Dolly, Miss. It seems like everyone's trying to get up West tonight.'

The girl's soldier companion grinned as he spoke, openly admiring of Angel's sophisticated appearance. No matter how ruffled she became, the exclusive girls' college insistence on keeping one's chin held high and one's shoulders held down, gave her the air of being able to handle any situation.

A taxi-cab slowed down as the driver saw four people on the kerbside. Angel felt a moment's annoyance. A man in uniform could get anything he wanted these days. The war with the Kaiser made heroes of them all, whether or not they had even seen a battlefield.

Angel leapt towards the cab, grasping the door handle at the same time as the Flying Corps officer. His fingers fastened over hers. She glared into his face, seeing it now at very close quarters.

It wasn't strictly good-looking, but it was a face full of character. The eyes were dark, holding the attention, the nose slightly crooked, the unsmiling mouth a little harsh. Oh yes, at any other time or place, she might have been interested. Now, all she wanted was to get away from him.

'You'll let a lady have first choice of a cab, I'm sure,' she said pointedly.

'Not on an evening like this, I won't,' he said calmly and unbelievably. Angel's mouth dropped open, unused to such boorish manners. By his manner and uniform she guessed that he was an officer, but he was certainly no gentleman.

'Oh, let's all get in the cab!' Dolly had lost all her patience. 'We can drop Madam off somewhere. We'll miss the show if we waste any more time.'

'I doubt if we're going in the same direction, and I've no intention of being left with your fare –' Angel began.

The cab driver settled it.

'I don't give a monkey's where any of yer goes, but if one of yer don't get in my bleedin' cab in the next ten seconds, I'm driving off and that's flat.'

The airman turned the door handle while Angel was still holding on to it, and bundled her inside in front of him.

Her mother would have a blue fit if she knew the way this lout was manhandling her, Angel thought angrily. She looked at him out of the corner of her eyes as the other two climbed into the cab and the soldier rattled off the name of some club up West. The airman's face was dark enough to be almost swarthy, especially with the sheen of rain on it.

He had a strong, very masculine jawline, and was undoubtedly a man used to getting his own way. Angel felt an unexpected little shiver run through her, as keen as a premonition.

He was as unlike the young men who were vetted before visiting her parents' town house, and even more boringly, those who arrived as guests when they all went down to the country, as it was possible to be.

The men her parents considered prospective suitors were generally fair-haired and chinless. Some peered at her through monocles as though she too were up for inspection despite her impeccable background. Many had titles or the expectation of titles. All were as deadly dull as the man her elder sister Louise had married, the Honourable Stanley Crabb.

Since Angel was just eighteen, the urgency of finding a suitable husband for her wasn't yet her mother's sole occupation. She was the youngest of the three pretty Bannister girls, and Lady Bannister was still seething at the way her middle daughter, Ellen, had joined ranks with those abominable suffragette women just over a year ago.

Finally, when Ellen had wanted to leave home and move into some appalling south London house with a group of them, her mother had merely washed her hands of her.

Dear Louise had conformed so admirably, and Lady Bannister just assumed that in due course Angel would do the same. A youngest daughter was normally so pliant . . . unfortunately, while fretting so much over the fortunes of the older two, Angel's growing independence had gone completely unnoticed.

Lady Bannister was frequently heard to say in all the best

London circles that a suitable marriage was such a blessing for one's daughters.

Even though in these impossible wartime days, one was forced to rub shoulders with the most frightful and unlikely people . . . but it would all be over soon, even if it hadn't been over by Christmas. Everybody said so.

Angel felt the warmth of the Flying Corps officer's body against hers, as the four of them squeezed into the back of the taxi-cab. The aroma of Dolly's cheap scent and the peculiar damp smell of wool from the servicemen's uniforms, mingled with the stuffiness of the cab, gave Angel an odd sense of claustrophobia.

It was difficult to breathe, but she had no intention of admitting any distress. The sooner she got out of here, the better, but there was a long way to go before they reached Hampstead. She would sit very still until the others got out, and then give her own address to the cabbie.

It was soon clear that the Flying Corps officer had other ideas. She realised that he hadn't stopped watching her from the minute they all got into the cab. There was still enough of the dying daylight to see, and slowly she turned to look at him as though compelled to do so. It was on the tip of her tongue to snub him, when his next words startled her.

'You have the most perfect profile I've ever seen. If you ever have your portrait painted, be sure and pose against a dark background, with side lighting to accentuate the curves and shadows –'

In the midst of her astonishment, Angel registered his slight accent for the first time. It was obviously European. French, perhaps. What was a Frenchman doing in the Royal Flying Corps at the beginning of the war . . .? Her thoughts were becoming confused.

It was the lengthy stare that did it. It was so . . . so bourgeois . . . so *outrageous*. It wasn't the way an English gentleman appraised a lady . . . a sensation akin to a flame ran through her.

Dolly giggled again, and the soldier chuckled, his boyish face alight with good humour. He leaned towards Angel.

'Don't mind Jacques, Miss. We're all ships that pass in the night here, but he told me and Dolly that he dabbled with the old oils in civvy street, and sees every pretty girl as his model. He don't mean any harm.'

'Shut up, Reg. If you don't know what you're talking about, it's best to keep quiet.' The officer spoke bluntly.

He studied Angel's face again, until she felt the blood fill her cheeks, and her skin begin to tingle. She wasn't used to such a prolonged stare. It was partly sexual, partly objective. She wasn't sure which part insulted her more.

'Do you think you'll know me if you see me again?'

She was annoyed her own voice sounded less assured than usual. The man gave a low laugh that seemed to start deep in his chest. Against him, in the close proximity of the cab, Angel could feel the vibration of that laugh.

'I would know you anywhere, *chérie*,' his voice dropped an octave, and now she was certain he was French. The endearment alone gave him away, but more than the words, it was the way he said them. That shiveringly seductive way he made the moment an intimate one, as if they were the only two people in the world, instead of being crushed together in the warm dampness of a London taxi-cab.

Angel forced herself to look away. The man was uncouth. He was the absolute opposite of what her mother would call a 'proper companion'. She acknowledged the small surge of rebellion at the thought. Lately, it had become more and more attractive to do the least of what her mother expected of her . . .

She was aware that Dolly and Reg were whispering furiously together. They glanced her way, and Dolly dug Reg in the ribs, making him grunt.

'If you've got nothing special to do, Miss, why don't you

come to the show at Beezer's with us? Jacques here has taken a shine to you, so how about it?'

She stared at him. She wasn't used to being offered or accepting such casual invitations. This afternoon's excursion to visit Margot Lacey, an old school friend, had taken weeks of organisation, and assurances that it was perfectly all right for her to stay the night at Margot's home.

Only to find that her friend had begun suffering badly with a sudden chill, and was feeling decidedly unsociable. They had both decided to curtail the visit, which was why Angel was making the journey home after all. She clutched her small overnight bag as though it were a lifeline.

'I think the young lady has other plans,' Jacques said lazily. She looked at him. He surprised her again. She would have expected him to jump at the soldier's suggestion and try to persuade her . . . she looked away quickly, her cheeks heated.

'Who or what is Beezer's?' She asked the other two.

'It ain't your cup o' tea, I bet.' Dolly spoke up. 'Sorry I mentioned it now. It's a club, see, and they have a show there. Dancing girls, and a singer or two, and a comic. I daresay the jokes 'ould be too vulgar for your delicate ears!'

'Do I look as though I was born yesterday?' Angel whipped at her, and guessed that compared with Dolly's sort of worldliness, she probably was.

She felt a hand cover hers. Felt the warm flesh of it, and the small caress of the fingers. The saliva seemed to dry in her throat. Was she going to be accosted? Or worse? What was wrong with her to be so unnerved, for heaven's sake!

But the old conventions were too firmly steeped in her mind, and the foolishness of getting into this situation began to alarm her . . .

'Why not come with us?' Jacques said now. 'If my manners have offended you, I apologise. But your company would do me honour, and these two would stop searching for a "friend" for me. I would see that you were put into a cab at the end of the evening, and guarantee that you come to no harm.'

His personality seemed to change with the ease of a chameleon. He could be the charming continental, or unpredictable, or just plain objectionable. Angel wavered. She shouldn't entertain the idea for a moment. She should tell them to get out of this cab the minute they reached Beezer's Club, whatever it was, and tell the cabbie to take her straight home. A voice from the driving seat floated back to them.

'Go on, ducks. Give yerself a birthday. Tain't every night a birdman invites yer out on the town!'

The others laughed at the cabbie's turn of phrase. Angel saw how the laughter lightened the officer's face. The hard line of his mouth softened, little lines fanned out from the corners of his eyes . . . and her heart was suddenly racing.

Why not? The little devil inside her asked. Why not take a chance for once, instead of having her life so irritatingly ordered? Didn't she always wish that something exciting could happen to her? And what harm could come of it? Despite her earlier misgivings, she was undeniably intrigued by Jacques whoever-he-was . . .

'Got to get back to Mummy, have yer?' Dolly said, when she didn't answer immediately. 'Never mind, Jax. We'll find somebody once we get to Beezer's –'

Angel felt the squeeze on her fingers again, as though the man was willing her to go with them. She snatched her hand away. She was capable of making up her own mind.

She thought swiftly. No one was expecting her home tonight. It wouldn't matter how late she arrived. It wouldn't be the first time she had sneaked indoors while everyone slept. She spoke sweetly to Dolly.

'I'll think about it. It might be fun to go slumming.'

Dolly's eyes flashed furiously, as Angel knew they would. She wasn't normally such a snob, but Dolly had the knack of putting her back up. Angel spoke directly to Jacques, and knew that her voice sounded somewhat breathless.

'You meant what you said? You'll find me a cab the minute I ask you to?'

'You have my word on it.'

Angel leaned back in the cab, with a strange feeling of launching herself into the unknown. Perhaps a little like the birdmen of the Flying Corps must feel when they soared into the sky in their flimsy wooden machines . . .

'All right. Why not? It'll be a lark,' she said recklessly, and far more coolly than she felt.

It was quite dark by the time the taxi-cab stopped, after what seemed an interminably long ride. They had presumably arrived at Beezer's Club. To Angel's dismay, she realised it was in Soho, to which would go yet another black mark against this evening's excursion.

The streets, dimmed by government decree, gave no indication of what was behind the stark sign swinging sadly in the rain above a steep flight of steps leading towards a cellar. Angel couldn't help thinking she was being extremely foolhardy as the Flying Corps officer held on tightly to her arm, while Reg paid the cabbie. As the vehicle trundled off into the night, Angel felt sudden panic.

'Having second thoughts?' Jacques said in her ear. 'I promise you this is not an abduction, though I can think of no more delightful companion if it was.'

Before she could answer, she was being hustled down the flight of steps and out of the rain. Once at the bottom, the four of them squashed tightly together until an outer door was closed before an inner one could be opened. As soon as it was, Angel realised why.

The contrast was stunning. Outside, all was gloom and depression. Here at Beezer's, the gaslights popped and flickered and made dazzling reflections of the glitteringly smart dresses worn by the women. They were mostly young, their hair rigidly waved, arms clattering with bracelets, mouths scarlet or orange. Their feet tapped gaily in a whirl of dancing on the tiny dance floor as their male companions swung them around to the music of a heavily-perspiring band. Without exception, all the men were in uniform, and several Union flags waved like banners across the top of the stage at the rear of the room.

'A uniform is your entry ticket,' Jacques spoke loudly against the noise. 'Though they do expect you to pay up as well!'

'You must let me pay my share –' Angel began at once, reaching into her bag. Jacques pushed her hand away.

'Don't be so modern,' he grinned. 'No Frenchman would let his lady pay for herself.'

Angel allowed the girl at the paying desk to take her coat and hat and the overnight bag, and give her a ticket in return, for her to reclaim them later. She saw Jacques' eyes take in the shiny white silk blouse that rippled against her figure, the perfect little cameo brooch at the high neckline that had been her parents' eighteenth birthday present to her, and the elegant grey wool skirt that matched her coat.

The rest of the women in the room might be dressed up like peacocks, but Angel Bannister outshone them all with her style and class. Jacques de Ville felt more drawn to her than to any other woman he had known in his life, and it had little to do with the fact that from the moment he had seen her, he had ached to paint her.

A man held up one finger to them to indicate that there was a table available for the officer and his party. As Angel followed Jacques, with Dolly and Reg right behind her, weaving their way in and out of the crush of people, she felt a little shimmer at his words. His lady? It was another of his preposterous comments, but one which had undoubtedly made her heart beat faster.

'We got here just in time,' Dolly hissed, as they took their seats, and the flickering gaslights were lowered one by one. 'Any later, and we'd have missed the start of the show.'

The couples on the dance floor dispersed like ghostly figures silhouetted against the brightness of the stage. A troupe of dancing girls came on, kicking their legs high to the wild applause of the uniformed men and their companions.

The dancers wore bright pink satin shorts and blouses that didn't quite reach the waist, so that every time they moved an intriguing little expanse of flesh was revealed. On their heads they wore a froth of matching pink feathers, and their mouths were identical glossy pink bows of colour. Their bosoms bounded joyfully with every kick, to the rousing cheers of the onlookers. At the end of the dance, the band played a burst of a patriotic song of the moment, and the girls pirouetted slowly, each one saluting and dropping down on one knee, before they all scrambled up and kicked their way sideways offstage.

'How d'you like it, me lady?' Dolly leaned across the table to leer at Angel.

'It's marvellous! I've never seen anything like it!'

Dolly looked taken aback at Angel's obvious enthusiasm. At first, her eyes had watered in the heavy smoky atmosphere, worse than any London pea-souper, but she had quickly got used to it, and revelled in the unusual evening.

'You really mean it, don't you?' Jacques said with pleasure. 'You look a different girl from the one who was so cross at not finding a cab!'

Angel laughed, perfectly relaxed. She felt different too. She felt – uninhibited, for the first time in her life. Even on her most defiant jaunts away from home, she had never felt quite this buoyant, and she couldn't explain why. She didn't want to explain, or to question it. In that instant, she identified totally with these people here, desperately enjoying themselves today, because none of them knew what tomorrow might bring.

'You don't even know my name,' she said suddenly, remembering her manners. 'It's Angel – Angel Bannister –'

'*Angel*! What a bleedin' name to go to bed with!' Dolly

shrieked. Reg leaned across the table.

'I had a mate who worked for a bigwig called Sir Fred Bannister in Yorkshire once. Bastard of a bloke, he was too. Only came visiting his factory once or twice a year to see they wasn't shirking, and spent the rest of his time in his posh house in London or his country estate in Somerset.'

Dolly was watching Angel's face.

'You'd better stop going on about 'im, Reg. Looks like our Angel's heard of 'im too.'

'He's my father,' she said calmly. 'And he's not such a bastard when you get to know him, Reg. It all depends on who he's dealing with.'

'*Touché!*' Jacques murmured with a smile. 'So we have someone important amongst us, do we?'

'No. Just another human being.'

She spoke smartly. It always made her squirm when she sensed inverted snobbery. Besides, somehow it didn't sit well on Jacques whoever-he-was. She asked him outright.

'Just another Flying Corps officer,' he replied in the same vein. 'Though my full name is Captain Jacques de Ville.'

'An' I'm Dolly Dilkes, an' this 'ere's Reg Porter, so now we all know each other, let's watch the show!' Dolly said, bored with all this formality. She and Reg had only taken Jax under their wing for the evening, so to speak, when he'd looked lost and lonely, and she was already half regretting it.

One of the dancing girls walked slowly across the stage carrying a large cardboard placard, announcing that the next act would be Miss Eliza Kent, the Songbird of the South.

'Ooh, she's lovely,' Dolly sighed. 'She always makes me want to cry.'

'Well, don't cry too much, or that black stuff will be running all over your face,' Reg grinned, as she flapped her heavy eyelashes at him for effect.

Miss Eliza Kent was small and waiflike, dressed in a long gown and a wide flowered hat that almost dwarfed her. But her voice was pure and powerful, tugging at the heartstrings from the moment she opened her mouth to sing of heartache and suffering, and ending with more inspiring songs spawned by the war, urging everyone to join in with her. They did so lustily, with tears in their eyes, or huskily through working throats.

'. . . and we'll never see our Johnny,
no, no, never again . . .
now he's gone to join his brothers
and the glo-o-ry . . .'

Amid roars of applause and whistling, Miss Eliza Kent bowed low, promising to sing for them all again for the finale of the show.

'I'm not sure I can stand another bout of slush and sentiment,' Jacques muttered to Angel.

'Where's your patriotism?' She grinned back. 'Can't you see how much they all love this vicarious suffering? The war's only been going for seven months. Think of all the work it's giving to songwriters and musicians!'

'That's very upper class cynicism, Miss Bannister!' Jacques mocked her.

'Yes. I'm sorry. I shouldn't have said it –'

'Why not? Why shouldn't we say what we think as long as we're not giving away state secrets? We might all be dead tomorrow, and we spend half our lives saying what we don't mean to people we don't care about.'

They looked at one another. It was a strangely charged moment. Just as quickly, they looked away. It was as if they had each glimpsed a secret truth that neither was prepared to acknowledge yet.

Chapter 2

The sleazy comic was next on stage. His jokes were daring and risqué. Dolly squealed with laughter and clung to Reg, who laughed just as heartily. When the anecdotes poked lavatorial fun at Kaiser Bill and his balloons, the laughter grew noisier, but Angel had to admit that the man's coarseness slightly diminished the horror of the threatened Zeppelin air raids.

All the same, she was glad when the comic finished his act and the jugglers came on, to be followed by a fire-eater, who drew gasps of disbelief from the audience.

'Enjoying your slumming, are yer, lady?' Dolly asked archly, as Angel laughingly wiped a film of beer froth from her upper lip at Jacques' instruction.

'It's not bad!' Angel said airily. 'It's a change from the way I usually spend my evenings, but you know what they say about a change being as good as a rest.'

'And how do you usually spend your evenings?' Jacques asked. 'You're a bit of a mystery lady, Angel.'

'Am I? You mean, because I was plucked out of the darkness and pushed into a London taxi-cab without proper introduction?' She taunted lightly. 'I know nothing about you, either, except your name and present occupation!'

'Isn't that all we know of most people? We only know what little we choose to give of ourselves.'

Angel felt herself warm to him. She liked a man who thought beyond the obvious. 'How perceptive you are. Not many people bother to analyse it so accurately. But you're quite right. And we put on a different face to everyone we meet, too. Like donning a mask at a masquerade ball.'

'Now you're being the perceptive one –'

A sudden shushing all around them stopped any further conversation, to Angel's annoyance. Jacques de Ville was definitely the most interesting man she had encountered for a very long time. Vastly more intelligent than some of the so-called intellectuals her parents invited to the house. Jacques was intelligent in a basic, vital way, not merely with the educated claptrap waffled by some of the young men down from university.

They sat through the pseudo-ballerina's performance, the woman teetering about on her points in a ghastly rendition of Swan Lake. Angel tried not to remember the exquisite performance given by the Royal Ballet at Covent Garden.

Next there was a ridiculous travesty of the Oxford and Cambridge boat race, so sadly terminated for the duration – that awful, doom-laden phrase that was bandied about so often now. Two teams of young men wearing huge dark blue or light blue scarves and caps, sat at opposite ends of the stage behind card cut-outs of the university boats, supposedly pulling on their oars, and singing the most hideous songs composed for the occasion.

> '. . . we'll pull till we burst,
> and we'll get our end in first,
> and we'll thumb at the accurs'd
> other fe-e-llows . . .'

'A bit different to the real thing, Angel,' Jacques said during the obligatory clapping.

'You've seen it then? Have you lived in England?'

He smiled. 'My mother was English, and I had an English education, although my family home is near Bordeaux in France.'

'Oh!' she said softly.

She dearly wanted to ask him more, but the Songbird of the South was coming back on stage to give a final rendition of a rousing ditty to stir all hearts. When it was over, she turned to Jacques once more.

'Has your home suffered at the hands of the Germans?'

'Not my home. But when one's country is under threat, then we all suffer.' He spoke with a dignity that touched her more than a long sorrowful dissertation on the evils of war.

'Come on, Jax. Don't get all morbid!' Dolly leaned forward, and a waft of her Californian Poppy scent enveloped them all. 'Why don't you and Angel have a dance, same as Reg and me?'

They realised that now the stage show was over, the gaslights were popping into life once more. Dolly dragged at Reg's arm, and frantically beckoned the other two to join them.

'We'll get no peace until we do,' Jacques grinned. 'May I have this dance, Miss Bannister?'

'With pleasure, Monsieur de Ville.'

She replied with as much grace as if this was a society occasion, instead of some anonymous little cellar club, temporarily safe from the German air raids. She went into his arms as the band changed its tune for a dreamy slow two-step as more couples merged onto the floor. There was not much space to move, and the dancing was little more than a slow shuffle to the music.

It was very different from the dances Angel attended with her parents. No gentleman would dare to hold a lady so close, and nor would she lean her head against his shoulder quite so brazenly. But every serviceman in that crowded room held the girl in his arms as though for the last time, and the feeling transmitted itself very forcibly to Angel Bannister. She could feel the thud of Jacques' heart against her body, and it echoed the beat of her own. She could feel his breath on her cheek, and the sudden sweet touch of his lips on her hair.

'I wish this night never had to end.'

He spoke abruptly, and Angel recognised the low throb of desire in his voice. 'I wish I could hold you for ever, *chérie*, because I'm so afraid that when I let you go, I shall never see you again.'

'Don't say that,' she whispered. 'It sounds so final.'

He gave a short mirthless laugh.

'Don't you know that's the way we're trained to think these days? Make the most of your leaves, chaps, because it will probably be your last!' He put on a mock British accent as he said the words.

'Are you on leave?'

'Why else would I be savouring every minute of this evening with a beautiful lady?'

The words seemed to float between them. The music played on, the dancers all around them moved back and forth across their vision, and they noticed none of it. Their footsteps slowed, until they were hardly moving, just holding each other in the middle of the dance floor.

'I think I should be getting home,' Angel murmured in sudden fright. 'You promised to get me a cab, Jacques.'

'Of course. We'll go at once.'

He steered her through the crowd, waving good-bye to Dolly and Reg, who gave them the thumbs up sign and danced on. Angel retrieved her coat and hat and overnight bag. Everything was being done in reverse. They would leave the club, being careful not to let any light shine outside to alert any enemy aircraft in the skies. They would climb the steep steps to the street. Jacques would put her into a taxi-cab, and the odds were that she would never see him again.

They stood outside, suddenly awkward with one another. The rain had stopped, and the March wind had dropped to no more than a crisp breeze. Angel shivered all the same.

'Do you really have to go home right away?' Jacques' voice was rich and deep. It wasn't trying to persuade her, but it was as if, like her, he was reluctant for this evening to end.

'I don't have to,' she said slowly. She looked up at him.

'Shall we walk for a while, or is too cold for you?'

'Of course not. I mean, no, it's not too cold, and yes, I'd like to walk.' Why did she suddenly feel so tongue-tied, so gauche and young, where minutes before she had felt so sophisticated and so much in control?

Jacques took the small overnight bag from her hand, and tucked her hand in his arm protectively. She could feel the warmth of him against her, and as she saw him smile in the dim light to which she was quickly becoming accustomed, she felt a new mood take hold of her, a kind of recklessness.

'Where shall we walk?' she asked. 'It sounds perfectly ridiculous, but I've rarely walked in London at night before, and never without my parents or a suitable chaperon!'

'Am I not a suitable chaperon for you, *chérie*?' His arm squeezed her to his side. 'You will always be safe with me.'

'I know.' She answered as gravely as if she had known him always. It was almost ludicrous to be walking through the dark London streets, going nowhere, in an area she didn't know.

And yet to feel as if there was a sweet inevitability about everything that was happening tonight. Their footsteps led them to one of London's small green parks, with its surround of wrought iron resembling black lace in the wisps of evening mist. They sat close together on a bench, and Jacques' arm slid around Angel's shoulders.

'If only we had more time.' Jacques spoke with an odd note of despair in his voice, as the sounds of London alternately loomed or receded all around them. 'Like everyone else in this bloody war, we have so little time –'

As he stopped abruptly, she glanced up at his strong profile, the breeze ruffling his dark hair, and she felt her heartbeat quicken. What he left unsaid was that they had so little time to be together . . .

'Tell me how long you've been with the Royal Flying

Corps,' she said huskily in the new awareness between them that was almost brittle.

'Seven months. But for the last six weeks I've been on pilot training. It's what I always wanted, of course, only now I've found something that I want even more.'

He looked at her. His fingers traced the soft curve of her cheek, and Angel held her breath. The hum of the late night London traffic was all around them, but she was only conscious of her own heartbeats, and Jacques' voice.

Angel trembled, not needing to be clairvoyant to know that Jacques would now be piloting one of the flimsy little flying machines on the dangerous missions over France.

'Does your leave last much longer?' She couldn't trust herself to say anything more than prosaic words at that moment. She couldn't even remember if he had already told her. It was all happening too soon . . . too frighteningly soon . . .

'Just tonight.'

From the disciplined flatness of his voice, Angel knew he didn't say it as some kind of emotional blackmail. She had asked the question, and the answer seemed to yawn like a chasm between them. Just tonight. And after that . . .?

'Jacques, I think perhaps I had better go –' she heard her own faint voice, and the hint of panic in it. He caressed her hands with his fingertips.

'If that's what you wish, I'll find you a cab at once, *chérie*. I promised you that. What *I* want, more than anything in the world, is to take you back to my hotel. Scream if it shocks you, but I can't bear to see you go. I don't want to spend the rest of the night alone with just the memory of you.'

Her mouth was too dry for her to speak. Her pulses raced. She knew exactly what Jacques' words implied. And oh, she wanted it too . . . she wanted *him*, in a way that was totally new and elating and awesome to her . . .

'I'm not in the habit of screaming,' she whispered, her answer in the tightening of her fingers against his as she spoke, and his arms closed around her, enveloping her. She felt as though she was discovering an age-old truth. How long, after all, did it take to fall in love?

They spoke very little in the cab that took them to the Hotel Portland where Jacques had a room for the night. And if this was seduction, Angel was very much aware that she was allowing it to happen. No one was forcing her, even though it was everything her mother had ever warned her against, and everything her sisters would despise.

Louise would be scandalised; Ellen would say scornfully that she'd always known that eventually Angel wouldn't be able to let a man keep his hands off her.

Once they were inside Jacques' room, he pulled across the heavy curtains and turned up the gaslight, and the room was bathed in a soft warm glow that hid the meanness of the decor and the basic furnishings. It wasn't the Ritz, but it wasn't the Ritz they were seeking.

Jacques put her overnight bag onto a chair, and gently unfastened her coat, tossing her hat after it. She seemed too numbed to say anything now. She was here, in a hotel bedroom with a stranger she had known for less than a day, and the enormity of it all was only just beginning to strike her.

The desperately bright tomorrow-we-die atmosphere among the servicemen and the painted girls at the club; the unaccustomed taste of beer in that thick, smoke-filled room; the charisma of the man with her now, so different from the rest . . . all of it turning her into a totally different person from the Angel Bannister who revelled in a lark with her chums, but who had never done anything like this before.

Some of her friends had spoken daringly of losing their virginity even before they left college, but to Angel, it had always seemed the most precious part of oneself, and not to be given away lightly.

Jacques took her in his arms. His eyes were understanding, as he looked into hers, seeing them wide and dark with sudden fright. He touched his mouth to hers without urgency or passion.

'Don't be afraid of me, Angel. Whatever happens will be because you want it to happen. You're so – so vulnerable – and innocent –'

She gave a tremulous smile.

'That's because I *am* innocent.' She blushed as she said the words, hoping he would understand. How absurd to blush when admitting that she wasn't a woman of the world, but as virginal as the first winter snow.

She was eighteen years old, barely out of college, and compared with Dolly Dilkes, as naïve as a newborn babe.

'Do you think I imagined anything different?' Jacques said. 'I felt that you were the woman of my heart from the moment I met you. I would give you the earth if I could. But for now, I can only give you myself – if you want me.'

His words were caring, his meaning crystal clear. He could be a rogue, or a man bowled over by his emotions. She had no way of knowing which. But her heart leapt at the sensuality in his voice, and the blood seemed to flow faster in her body at his nearness. She had known a few lacklustre suitors, but none had ever spoken to her in this way. None had ever aroused a matching desire in her . . .

The arch young men of her acquaintance were stilted in their English compliments. They didn't touch all her senses the way this man did. But now that the moment was here, did she *want* him, in the way he meant? Did she, in Biblical terms, want *carnal knowledge* of him?

The rigid words of her college religious instruction classes swam through her mind. Outdated, unrealistic, and some said ridiculous in these harsh days of 1915, and yet . . . and yet . . .

Angel swallowed at the importance of the decision. Jacques took her hand and led her to the window. Before they reached it, he turned out the gaslight so that they were in darkness. He pulled back the curtains and moonlight bathed the room. Beyond the window, the outlines of buildings and spires were softly grey against the rich navy blue of the sky. The branches of a lone tree sighed and whispered in the wind.

'When this war is over, Angel, you and I will come back to this very room and look out on the lights of London. That much I promise.'

When they arrived, she had seen his kit bag on the floor. There was little else scattered about. It was as if he had packed everything away in that small bag for his last night. It had promised to be a sterile night. But now they had each other . . .

The war seemed very far away from that snug little bedroom at the Hotel Portland. They didn't put on the light again. They undressed by moonlight, to gaze at one another and wonder at the beauty God had given them.

The preliminaries were sensually sweet as they lay together between the cold sheets, but it was more than the crisp cotton fabric that made Angel shiver.

She was a romantic, and these were moments that should be heralded with trumpet sounds and church bells . . . and then all the vague euphoric notions of her tender years evaporated as she felt the hard warmth of Jacques' body invade her own.

The first small sharp pain was followed by a glorious acceptance. This was what her body had been made for, what all her emotions had been awaiting. This was love.

'My beautiful Angel,' Jacques breathed her name against her skin. 'You are truly my perfect woman. In case I should forget to tell you in the next hundred years we shall spend together, remember that I told you tonight.'

His face on her own was damp with passion as he moved against her. His words exalted and humbled her.

'You expect us to spend a hundred years together, then?'

she asked tremulously, wanting to hear him say that this was truly forever.

'No. I should have said eternity,' he whispered in her ear, his lips tugging gently at her ear lobe.

Angel was overwhelmed by him. If this was continental charm, then Jacques had an abundance of it. If it was false, she didn't want to be told. She never even considered it in those precious stolen hours before the dawn of another grey March morning.

Angel awoke slowly. She was cold. It seemed only minutes before that she had been so warm, so safe. She had been wrapped in someone's arms, and had gone to sleep cocooned against his body. She had become a woman in every sense of the word. She knew now what fulfilment meant . . .

Her eyes flew open, and in an instant she knew that she didn't want to turn her head in that icy little bedroom. Nor to reach out her hand to encounter nothing but the cold pillow beside her. For a fraction of a moment more, she refused to believe what her mind told her, that Jacques had already gone . . .

But she had to believe it. She turned so quickly, her neck cricked. The bed was empty except for herself. She lay as if frozen, then forced herself to look around the room. There was no kit bag, no few personal belongings on the dressing table, nothing to say that Jacques de Ville had ever been there, or ever existed. Angel felt a sob tear at her throat. It was unbelievable. It was a cruel nightmare . . .

She slid out of bed, and felt a swift shame at seeing her own naked body. She reached for her clothes with shaking hands, and then she saw the note placed carefully on top of them. She ripped it open.

'My Angel, I know you'll be unhappy when you awake alone. I have to leave very early, and you and I found something too beautiful last night to spoil with tears and good-byes. When these anxious days are over I promise you we will meet again. We have a special date at a certain window.

Yours always, Jacques.'

Angel pressed the note to her lips, feeling the tears start to her eyes. Then just as quickly, a burning anger swept through her. How dare he do this! How dare he treat her as if she were weak enough to fall apart at having to say good-bye? She was no longer a child. Women said good-bye to their men every day of the year in wartime . . .

Angel realised to her shame that she had never even thought of it before. It hadn't touched her own life until now.

War was something that was happening in France, except for the nuisance of the air raids and the restrictions on lighting, and the forebodings of food shortages and the like . . . and she thought it slightly comic that even her pompous brother-in-law Stanley spoke vaguely about taking up an army commission.

Apart from that, her mother held knitting afternoons for the soldiers and her father complained, and said grimly that it was bound to get worse before it got better, the logic of which Angel found completely incomprehensible. The war hadn't affected Angel Bannister at all – until now.

'You bastard, Jacques de Ville!'

She spoke aloud through her pain, partly because it helped to use the forbidden word, and partly because it relieved her anguish at the thought that he had run out on her. Was she stronger than he, after all, because she had been able to face this parting and he hadn't?

If such thoughts had occurred to her at all during the hours she had spent in his arms, it was only with a feeling of pride at giving her man a talisman to take to war.

In leaving her alone, Jacques had managed to shatter all such noble ideals. Instead, she felt cheap – as cheap as Dolly Dilkes, who had undoubtedly spent the night with Reg Porter. The comparison didn't make Angel any happier.

Despite Jacques' note, which hinted of a shared future, she was ashamed of just being here, in a room which would probably make her mother faint with horror.

A sudden rapping on the door made her jump with alarm, and sent her heart racing. She snatched up the bedcover and pulled it round herself. She inched open the door to see the face of a maid outside, armed with clean sheets. The woman's eyes seemed to see all that had gone on in the room last night, and Angel had never felt so humiliated.

'The gent from this room paid up yesterday, and I've got to clean the room, Miss.'

Her voice implied that she'd seen this situation too many times to feel shock, but could still feel superior to the little tarts who went back to a serviceman's room for a night's pleasure and a few shillings payment. Angel's cheeks burned.

'I'll be leaving soon,' she said stiffly. 'Didn't my – husband mention that I would be staying a little later?'

The woman grinned, her eyes roaming past Angel's agonised face, to the expensive clothes on the chair. She shrugged. It took all sorts, and just because a girl wore flash clothes it didn't mean she couldn't open her legs to a good-looking man. And that tall dark bloke with the funny little accent had been handsome enough to make all the young hotel maids look twice.

'No, your *husband* didn't, Miss. I'll be back in half an hour then. The room's needed again, see?'

'I'll be gone by then,' Angel snapped, and slammed the door in the woman's face.

She stared at it tremblingly for several seconds. She was demoralised by that woman. She felt like a whore.

She flinched from the very sound of the word in her head, dressing as fast as she could. Her hands were so clammy they refused to fasten buttons, and she couldn't think properly.

Yesterday seemed decades away. She had grown up more in a single night than in the past eighteen years. She had lain with a man and seen the derision in a hotel maid's eyes. Without intending to, she had deceived her parents. She had fully intended going straight home early last evening. Instead . . .

Angel's throat felt suddenly thick. It was all spoiled. All the tender loving feelings between her and Jacques had evaporated, and no matter how hard she tried, she couldn't get them back. She wanted desperately to recapture every moment, to remember every word he had said . . . and failed. Perhaps this too, was a part of growing up, Angel thought bitterly. Nothing stayed as lovely as you thought it would. Everything faded.

She left the small hotel without a second glance, uncomfortably aware of the nudges between the receptionist and the maid as she went. Her knuckles were taut as she gripped the handle of her overnight bag. She felt stifled by their looks, and yet part of her could identify with them completely. Yesterday, she too would have thought a girl who went to bed with a stranger was no less than a shameless hussy.

Outside, the air was crisp and cold, but Angel welcomed its clean sharp touch on her skin. Her wool coat had a fur collar, and she pulled it up around her face, burying her chin in its softness. She was suddenly disorientated. Not by her muddled emotions now, or even her surroundings, but by the time of day.

It was too early in the morning to go home. Her mother would be suspicious if she supposedly arrived home from Margot Lacey's home so early. She must wait until at least mid-morning before making her appearance at the Bannister house.

At the end of the narrow street, she saw a small café, and went inside it to order tea and breakfast. She didn't feel like eating, but it helped to pass the time, even though the fare was meagre, the surroundings none too clean.

She saw a taxi-cab as soon as she left the café, and began to run for it, waving her hand. *A lady never runs for anything*, the tutors at college had instructed sternly. *A lady remains cool and dignified at all times* . . . a swift vision of herself and Jacques de Ville surged through her mind. Locked together in an abandonment of pleasure . . . hearts beating together, bodies pulsing in ecstasy . . .

'Do you want this cab or not, Miss?' A voice said irritably. 'I ain't got all day to wait while you're dreaming.'

Angel jumped. She hardly remembered reaching the vehicle, nor standing beside it with her hand on the door handle. Her eyes misted for a moment, remembering the clasp of another hand over hers, on another taxi-cab . . . she shook herself angrily, feeling that she must be in the grip of some madness to be behaving like a lovesick shopgirl.

'Can you take me to Hampstead?' she said jerkily.

The cabbie's eyes narrowed. This one looked as though she could pay for the journey, but she'd just come from a narrow back street, and it never hurt to be certain.

'Can you afford it, Miss? Hampstead's a good way off –'

'Naturally,' Angel snapped. 'Will you take me or won't you? I can easily call another cab.'

The man leaned over at that and opened the door. He wasn't losing this easy ticket.

'What's the address?' he asked, as Angel slid inside.

His practised eyes assessed her through his mirror. What a corker, he thought. Eyes like emeralds, and hair in that rich blonde colour that wasn't fake. And probably a shapely figure beneath the fancy grey coat. She had held it up out of the rain puddles as she'd run to his cab, and he'd glimpsed a pair of neat ankles encased in expensive looking boots. Yes, he'd get his money all right.

She gave the address quickly. It would be a relief to get home now. She was cold and miserable, and the thought of getting into a hot bath was becoming more attractive every minute. She must make up some tale as to why she hadn't had a bath before leaving Margot's house . . .

Angel bit her lip. Fairy tales to offset some girlish prank was one thing, but the necessary lies were increasing by the minute. How could one illicit night become so complicated! She wondered fleetingly how anyone could be bothered to make a habit of it. She remembered Jacques' seductive voice, warm against her skin, and knew only too well.

He had asked for her address so that he could find her again, and the request had made her feel so alive, so very wanted . . . Now, she felt cold and betrayed, doubting that she would ever hear from him again . . . and heaven help her if her parents ever found out where she had really been last night.

Chapter 3

Sir Fred Bannister had inherited his title from his father, and the fact had always been a source of irritation to him. Not that he despised any of the advantages that wealth and position gave him. But Sir Fred was a rarity in his circle. He believed in the personal pride of the self-made man, and since his family business had been handed to him on a platter, that personal striving had been denied him.

Of course, he could simply have turned his back on the textile business and gone into something new and adventurous, but marriage to the daughter of an old Etonian had stopped any such Socialist ideas. Clemence was staunchly Establishment-bred, and since Fred had so badly wanted to marry her in the sweet heyday of his youth, he had simply succumbed and allowed her to rule his life as well as his heart.

Only with his workers in his thriving mill in Yorkshire, did he really assert himself in the way he felt that a man should. Thus, he had the reputation of being dictatorial, a façade which his employees would have been astonished to see disappear as soon as he entered his own front door.

The plain truth was that Fred was completely dictated to by his household of women, except on the rare occasions when the lot of them went too far. At those times, he would roar like a British bulldog, and insist on getting his own way. The women knew when to recognise those times. Apart from that, it just wasn't worth the worry of dealing with three independent daughters who were more than any man could decently control, and the most harmonious way was to leave it all to Clemence.

She was a dear old thing, of course. She was all that a wife should be, especially in Clemence's own eyes. She presided at his table and gave dinner parties that had been the toast of the town until the new posters to save food for the war effort had put an end to half of them. Clemence had also taken to organising knitting parties with some of the old biddies Sir Fred privately loathed. He referred to them secretly as the pearls and lorgnette brigade.

Clemence was now heavily into Good Works. She had dutifully produced three daughters and decided long ago that that was enough, and had put aside that part of their married life. There was no likelihood of a son now to carry on the business. There was no hanky-panky after lights out, either. And if Fred didn't have a nice little lady friend tucked away in a Yorkshire village, which made his frequent visits North extremely convenient, he was sure he would have gone mad or blind long ago.

He was driving back to Hampstead in his comfortable Daimler motor that March morning, after an especially satisfying night with Harriet. She made his life worthwhile, he thought with pleasure. Harriet . . . and his three girls . . . his thoughts were on them as he hummed a little ditty, twirling his moustache in the little habit he had when he was pleased with life, as he drove back to town and thought about his daughters.

Louise . . . she was her mother's girl, if ever he saw one. Louise was handsome and clever, and would presumably give him a grandson or two in time. Ellen had brains too, although Fred wished that she would utilise them in some other way than by joining these radical women who tied themselves to railings and made damn nuisances of themselves.

Thank God she hadn't joined these damned suffragettes

until long after the appalling stupidity of the one who had thrown herself under the King's horse at the races. What earthly good had that done for any of them, except to make them seem utterly irresponsible?

Fred could still sympathise with Ellen's inclinations even if Clemence could not. Why should she be content with the trappings of her upper class background if she didn't want to be? What was the point of having money if you didn't have the freedom to do what you liked with it?

Then there was Angel . . . Fred's mouth broke into a smile. Angel was the darling of his heart. He had named her himself, to Clemence's intense irritation, when she'd promised him that the third child would be a son, and said recklessly that he could give him any name he chose.

The baby had been another girl, and to appease Fred's disappointment with Him Above who might think him an ungrateful sod, he'd called her Angel. And an angel she had turned out to be, growing more beautiful from her very first day. Golden-haired and green-eyed, Fred wondered how an old buffer like himself had ever fathered such a sweetheart. That he definitely had done, was unquestionable. Clemence simply didn't have it in her to be unfaithful. It just wasn't done . . .

Fred steered the car into the gravel driveway of his elegant Hampstead mansion, knowing that Clemence would be hovering behind the curtains, ready with a glass of sherry in her hand to welcome him. The predictability of the woman was sometimes stifling . . .

He left the car outside the front door for the chauffeur to put away. On his jaunts to Yorkshire he always drove himself, ostensibly for the need to keep up his driving practise, in reality for the convenience of his secret visits to Harriet.

A maid opened the door before he could get out his key. One of these days he'd beat her to it, he thought with grim humour. Before he could register that her face was unusually flushed, he heard the uproar from the drawing room.

'What the blazes is happening!'

He strode across to the room and flung open the door. His daughter Ellen was standing in the centre of the floor screaming at her mother like a fishwife.

'You say nothing when Louise marries that slimy oaf of hers, Mother! You let Angel stay out all night, but when I ask you a perfectly reasonable question, you flatly refuse!'

'I don't consider a request to fill Meadowcroft with your unspeakable friends to be a reasonable question, Ellen!' Clemence snapped, her normally refined features scarlet.

'I'm not intending to fill the house –'

'But that's how it begins, isn't it? I'm sorry, Ellen, but I've told you before what I think of these people. They're a danger to decent society –'

Ellen's square face was almost beautiful in its anger.

'Mother, you're a fool,' she raged. 'Can't you see that the movement cannot fail? Women will fulfil their role in society, and suffragettes will go down in history as pioneers of the future. They already have, but you're too stubborn and too snobbish to see it or admit it. This war is proving the need for self-reliant women. They're already working alongside men in ways unheard of a short while ago. Why do you persist in shutting your eyes to it, Mother!'

Fred decided that his daughter had gone too far.

'You will apologise at once, Ellen,' he snapped. 'Anyone who is uncouth enough to call her mother a fool has no place in this house.'

'I don't need your help in this matter, Fred –' Clemence snapped back, and Ellen turned on him at once.

'You don't understand, Dad. I only want to take Rose Morton down to Meadowcroft for a week or two –'

'Who or what is Rose Morton?' Fred ignored his wife's annoyance at his intervention in her domestic affairs.

'She's a good friend of mine,' Ellen almost choked. 'And

contrary to what you and Mother think of my choice of women friends, Rose was married to a young man who volunteered for service at the beginning of the war. He's been killed in France, and she needs somewhere quiet to get over the shock of it, Dad. Meadowcroft is just the haven she needs.'

Her voice was thick with grief as she finished. She didn't really expect them to understand. Nobody understood her or her motives. They didn't even try. She wasn't like the rest, but she wasn't a freak either.

Fred looked at her, stiff and proud in her sensible tweed skirt, her arms tightly crossed over her small high breasts, and gave a small sigh. Clemence saw him waver, and spoke sharply.

'Don't give in to her, Frederick. I'm sorry for the woman, but it doesn't change my views. And Ellen, please don't call your father Dad. You know how I hate it.'

Ellen looked at her mother speechlessly for a moment, and then rushed towards the door.

'You see how impossible she is, *Father*? I can't even talk to her sensibly. She's a prig, and I hate her!'

'Ellen, come back here at once!' Fred roared after her, but it was too late. The drawing room door rocked on its hinges as Ellen banged through it, and Clemence rounded on her husband.

'You never could control her! Now see what you've done!'

Fred stared at her. He had done nothing at all as far as he could see, and Clemence had certainly never wanted his help in bringing up their daughters. He was still wondering how to deal with this situation, when he heard the slam of a taxi-cab door outside the house.

He felt a sliver of relief, remembering that Angel had been to see that nice college chum of hers. Angel would soon fill the house with laughter again, telling them all about her visit. He poured himself the glass of sherry his wife had overlooked, noting that his hands were quite damp with all this upset, and depended on Angel's presence to lighten the atmosphere.

The minute she appeared, Fred sensed that there was something different about her. He couldn't tell what it was. He only knew that his best girl was in a heightened state of mind, and it wasn't merely from the excitement of a visit with a friend. As though Clemence sensed it too, his wife began to be unusually persistent in her questions about Angel's evening.

Wanting to get away, Angel leaned against the door in a most ungainly fashion that had Clemence tightening her lips. Her father thought that even in such a pose, Angel was still an enchanting sight. She was a picture in that lovely coat cut from the finest grey wool from his own mill. It complemented her flawless complexion and beautiful green eyes, as deep as gems this morning. He cleared his throat.

'Come on, old girl. Tell us what you and Margot got up to, and cheer your mother up,' Fred said encouragingly.

It was as though he had set light to a torch that suddenly burst into flames. Clemence's face burned with anger.

'She can't do that, Frederick, because she wasn't with Margot Lacey last night!'

Angel reeled as though she had been hit by a cold hard slap in the face. Indeed, her mother looked as if she would dearly like to do just that to her.

'What d'you mean?' Fred demanded. 'Of course she was with Margot. It was all arranged. She's got her overnight bag in her hand, so where else would she have been?'

'That's exactly what I want to know,' Clemence snapped.

They both looked at Angel. She felt so cold she knew that her face must be devoid of colour, and she wondered with alarm if she was going to faint. What in heaven's name had alerted her mother? It was impossible that she knew. She was bluffing.

'I don't know what you mean, Mother. Margot and I spent half the night gossiping, and I'm deadly tired. All I want is a hot bath, and to feel human again –'

'You're not going anywhere until I have an explanation,' Clemence snapped as Angel tried desperately to make her escape.

'An explanation of what?' Angel's heart hammered sickeningly at the sudden doubt on her father's face.

What would he say if he knew that her mother's intuition was right, and that she had spent a night of ecstasy and wonder that she couldn't forget, however little it had meant to Jacques.

'Margot's mother telephoned this morning,' Clemence said crisply. 'You left your scarf at the house. She also said how sorry she was that Margot had got this wretched chill, and that she hoped you got home safely before dark.'

'Well, Angel?' Fred knew he had better say something, though somehow he already knew. Not often given a sixth sense feeling, this time it was different.

He recognised now the look he had seen on his daughter's face, and his parental anger was tempered by something he couldn't explain. A sympathy, perhaps, that he could never share with his wife, because his own clandestine and loving association with Harriet gave him the same secret glow he had seen on Angel's face. Yet it had been obvious to him too, that she was not happy. Whatever had happened last night had been monumental, and Fred could only guess at what that was. And far from scandalising him, as it was clearly doing to Clemence, he felt an extraordinary tenderness for his youngest child.

'Well, my darling girl?' he said more gently.

Angel threw out her hands as if seeking help.

'All right. Margot had a chill, and I had trouble finding a cab when the tram broke down and there was a small hotel nearby. It seemed safer to stay there than risk coming home in the dark. That's all – except to say I'm sorry.'

The words sounded inane, even to herself. They gave away nothing of the wonderful night that was fast becoming no more than a lovely dream. She wanted to hold on to the dream, but suddenly Jacques' face was no longer so clear to her, and it made her want to weep.

She had truly believed herself to be in love, and she didn't want to lose the love and feel the shame.

'Was it beyond you to telephone us to let us know what had happened?' Clemence demanded.

'There didn't seem any point. You would only have worried. It was better you thought I was safe at Margot's.' She spoke defensively, but her faint hope that they would accept the explanation calmly was soon dashed.

'No point?' Clemence cried out in outrage. 'Is that how little you consider your parents? You were alone in London when those terrible Zeppelins might have dropped bombs on the very hotel where you were staying, and we would never have known! Is this how you repay us for allowing you to stay out all night? I assure you, young lady, it will be the last time. And your father may accept your ridiculous tale about a tram breaking down, but I do not. I'm not at all satisfied with your explanation. And the fact that you chose to lie to us makes me despair even more of all the money we threw away on your education.'

'I'm not lying about staying at a respectable hotel!'

Angel felt the furious tears start to her eyes. That part of it was certainly true. The night that had ended there had begun by her need to stand in the rain looking for a taxi-cab. That had led to Jacques de Ville pulling her back from the street . . . and more. Her throat ached with tears, remembering.

'I think you had better take that hot bath, and leave your mother and me to discuss it, Angel,' Fred spoke in a troubled voice. Clemence rounded on him.

'Don't be weak about this, Frederick. I know Angel can do no wrong in your eyes, but this time she's gone too far. She's out of control, and she must be punished for it.'

'Mother! I'm eighteen years old!' Angel said, incensed. 'I'm not a schoolgirl. Girls of my age are married with babies, or doing honest war work.'

'Well, if you think you're going to work in one of those dreadful munition factories, you can think again,' Clemence said. 'I'm not having one of my daughters called a canary because her skin's stained yellow with that ghastly stuff they put into the shells.'

'TNT,' Fred said mildly. 'I never thought to hear you being so unpatriotic, my dear –'

'I don't care what the stuff's called, and you know very well I do whatever I can for the war effort, Fred!' Clemence's face was brilliant now. 'My knitting circles are gaining support every week, and I'm going to join the groups who dispense tea and soup at the railway stations for the wounded soldiers. Angel can help me in those things from now on.'

'There are plenty of other ways I can be useful,' she said quickly, thankful that for the moment at least, her mother's attention seemed to have wandered from the disgrace of last night. 'I could be a nurse, or learn to drive an ambulance. I don't really think your knitting ladies would want me around them, Mother –'

And she could think of nothing more absolutely boring . . .

'But the returning soldiers undoubtedly would,' Fred put in, trying to ease the tension with a quick smile. 'It would brighten their day to see a pretty girl pouring tea for them –'

'We'll think about that later,' Clemence said coldly. 'But you can forget any nonsense about becoming a nurse, Angel. Go and have that bath. Your father and I have got to talk.'

Angel and Fred exchanged brief sympathetic glances before she slipped thankfully out of the room, and went upstairs. On the landing above, Ellen's astonished face was watching her, and clearly she had heard every word. Ellen was blotchy with tears, but her admiration for Angel was evident.

'I say, did you really stay at an hotel last night, old girl? What a lark!'

Angel bit her lip. They were the very words she had used to Jacques, and it seemed like centuries ago.

'Yes, I did. But I don't want to talk about it, thank-you very much.' She went to push past her sister, but Ellen caught at her arm, her voice lowered into a conspiratorial whisper.

'Oh Angel, don't go all huffy on me. What was he like?'

Angel stared at her. They didn't always get on together, and she had never thought Ellen particularly perceptive. And she had no intention of sharing her secret with Ellen or anyone else.

'Don't be stupid. If you were listening, then you heard what I said. The tram broke down and I got scared, that's all. It seemed safer to stay in town.'

'It's such a long way, of course!' Ellen didn't believe her for a second. 'Anyway, never mind all that. Did you mean what you said, about joining something?'

Angel pushed past her on the landing. 'If you mean, am I going to join your lot, then forget it. Some of those strident women make me sick.'

'They're not all like that. You haven't met Rose –' To Angel's horror, Ellen's square face suddenly crumpled. The vague suspicion of something 'not quite nice' about some of those women flared into her mind. Oh no, not Ellen . . .

Her sister's next words were a relief, quickly squashed as she heard the tearful story.

'You missed out on my big scene with the parents, Angel. All I want is for Rose to have a few weeks at Meadowcroft to get over her husband's death. He was blown to bits in France. Can you imagine that? She got a cold little letter from the War Office, and that was all. As far as they're concerned, Gunner Ronnie Morton no longer exists, and his poor widow can go hang.'

'I'm so sorry, Ellen.' Angel didn't know what else to say. It sounded too ghastly.

That was what war did to people. Tore them apart, made

widows of young women on the brink of life, cut down virile young men . . . a frisson of gladness for last night swept through her, despite the pain of it all. She had known love. For a little while it had been perfect. And whether Jacques de Ville had been a rogue or not, she had sent him off to war happy. It was the only thing she had to cling on to now.

Ellen sniffed. 'Oh well, it was what I expected of the parents. They think we're all queer, but it's simply not true. All we want is the right to be recognised as people. We exist, Angel. Women have always played their part in history, and someday they'll know our worth.'

'Ellen, I'm sure you're right, but please don't give me a political lecture right now. I want a bath, and then I have to face the music again.' She tried desperately to get away.

'All right. But I'll make a bargain with you. I'll stick up for your right to a bit of independence if you'll back me in getting Rose to stay at Meadowcroft.'

She held out her hand and Angel took it solemnly. It wouldn't make a scrap of difference if their mother had made up her mind, and she really didn't care whether Rose Morton stayed at Meadowcroft or not. It meant nothing to her. Except . . .

The memory of Ellen's terse words about her friend's husband stayed in Angel's mind while she soaped herself in a hot bath. Gunner Ronnie Morton, blown to bits in France . . . she never knew him, but the poignancy of those stark words wouldn't leave her. How awful. How simply and terribly awful. It could have been Jacques de Ville . . .

The words slid into her mind before she could stop them, and a sob tightened her throat. She couldn't forget him. He had been the most important person in her life. The man to whom a woman gave herself was surely that. They were bound together by something deeper than blood, stronger than hate.

She looked down at her own breasts, silky white with suds, and remembered Jacques' mouth on them, and it had been the first time a man had touched them. She felt a tingling in them at the memory. She remembered with an almost exquisite bittersweet pain the moments when the warm secret part of her had opened up to him like a flower blossoming in the sun, and in remembering, she felt the dampness of tears on her cheeks.

It had been so beautiful. It had been love. Angel was sure of that. And love was like eternity. Intangible, but undeniable. It never ended, even after death. Rose Morton, whoever she was, was proof of that. Angel swallowed back the tears and let the bath water run out.

By the time she was ready to go downstairs again, she wore a sensible frock of grey-green stripes with a big floppy bow at the neck, and her hair was brushed out into a golden sheen. She was extremely nervous at seeing her parents again. Her mother's discovery had been a terrible shock, even though she knew little of what had really happened.

But Angel realised that a pact with Ellen might be useful. They could present a solid front if need be. And why not agree to help the poor woman whose husband had been killed? In doing so, Angel cherished a strange hope that her good deed might repay her in Jacques de Ville's safe deliverance. She sent up a little prayer to that effect.

Fred was finding the problem of two rebel daughters a little too much to take all at once. Clemence was not normally a nagging wife. She had had no need of it over the years, since Fred had always given in to her. But now Clemence was insisting on his support, and he was very much afraid he was finding her a bore. For God's sake, why not let Ellen and her friend go down to Meadowcroft? At least they would know where Ellen was. And what more could they say to Angel but to reprimand her and tell her to behave herself in future?

What was done was done, and unless the girl had got herself in trouble, then no harm was done. Fred suddenly went cold at the thought, and refused to think about it. There was no point in meeting that kind of trouble halfway.

'Are you going to give me your support or not, Fred? You seem to be in a world of your own these days. I think you should stop going to Yorkshire so often. You're not as young as you were, and these long journeys do tire you out. Either that, or let Charles drive you as he's paid to do.'

Fred became alert at once.

'Nonsense. I'm perfectly capable of driving myself anywhere I want to go,' he said tartly. 'Besides, how would you get in and out of town without Charles driving you in the Sunbeam? I'd much rather leave you in his capable hands, old girl, than have you in and out of taxi-cabs all the time. One hears such odd things at times about the driver fellows.'

He didn't need to look at her face to know that she would agree with him instantly. Clemence really was a dreadful snob. She had passed it down to their eldest daughter, Louise, and sometimes the two of them were insufferable. At least his other girls were more down to earth, even if one of them had progressive ideas, and the other one was growing up and away from him at the same time.

He felt a swift sorrow, knowing that it was bound to happen, and in his heart he wouldn't want to stop it. But Angel was no longer his little girl. In one swift exchange of glances earlier that day, he had seen that she was a woman.

And later that afternoon, two things happened that were to make the decision for the future crystal clear.

Chapter 4

Louise Bannister Crabb drove herself to her parents' house that same afternoon, braking the car with a screech of tyres that could only forebode bad news. Louise was normally a sedate and slightly nervous driver, and her husband Stanley rarely agreed to her taking out the car alone.

Fred frequently compared the two of them with Siamese twins rather than husband and wife. He doubted that the Hon. Stanley did much in the marital bedding department either, but if Louise was anything like her mother, she wouldn't be too bothered on that account.

He and Clemence were ostensibly reading the daily newspapers, each still wondering what to do about Ellen and Angel, when Louise burst in on them like a whirlwind.

'Stanley's volunteered!' Her eyes were brilliant, her voice as shocked as that of a spoilt child deprived of its favourite plaything. Which on reflection, Fred thought, was exactly what she was.

Clemence jumped up at once, and put her arms round her eldest daughter.

'Oh, darling, how wonderful. You must be very proud!'

Louise looked furious.

'Mother, I thought you'd understand! Oh well, yes, I suppose I am a bit proud. I mean, King and Country, and all that. But I want him home! I don't want him in the trenches in France or wherever it is they're sending them –'

'But darling, he'll be an officer, surely? He'll be in some

command or other. They won't put such a clever and well-connected young man in any danger!'

Fred wanted to fetch up. He listened to the two of them, extolling the virtues of his inept son-in-law, whose qualifications for brilliance centred mainly around his father's money, horse breeding in his Hertfordshire home, and putting his horses to stud.

Which was possibly why he seemed to have no energy for what Fred suspected was an infrequent sex life of his own.

'Is there anyone we can talk to about it, Mummy? Do you know anyone, Daddy?'

'No, I do not,' Fred said shortly. 'If Stanley's volunteered, then it's the finest day's work of his life, and it's not up to us to interfere and make him seem a Mummy's boy.'

'Really, Fred,' Clemence said sharply, as Louise began to wail in a most undignified manner.

'But I shall be all alone!'

'Of course you won't, darling,' Clemence said soothingly. 'You'll move right back here with us, won't she, Frederick? Your old room is the same as when you left it.'

Fred groaned inwardly. They were two of a kind. He loved them both, but together they would be insufferable.

'Perhaps Louise would rather stay in her own home,' he said as casually as he could.

She shook her head vigorously.

'I hate the smell of horses all the time. I can stand it when Stanley's there, because he loves them so much, but it will be perfectly beastly without him. But London's so dangerous now, isn't it? Everyone says so.'

'You mean all these country experts who know everything about the city, do you?' her father retorted. 'Perhaps you'd better go down to Meadowcroft with Ellen and her friend, then.'

'Nothing's been decided about that yet,' Clemence said sharply.

'If you all think London's so dangerous, and you don't

like the idea of Meadowcroft, we could always go north to Yorkshire. It would be handy for me for the mill –' and for Harriet too, Fred thought, though knowing he was on perfectly safe ground.

If there was one place Clemence hated it was cold and windy Yorkshire, as she called it. She knew nothing of its beauties, the rolling dales and clean fresh moors . . . and it was as well that she knew nothing of Harriet either . . .

'Thank-you, Fred,' Clemence said tightly. 'You know very well that if we go anywhere at all, it will be to Meadowcroft.'

Fred congratulated himself on trapping her so neatly.

Louise had a faraway look in her eyes.

'Meadowcroft. It's so lovely there, and I haven't seen it for simply ages. I don't have to decide right away, do I?'

She dithered as usual. For a young married woman of twenty-four, she took an interminable time to make up her mind about anything, Fred realised. She relied on someone else to do her thinking whenever she could, which was probably why she was so hot and bothered about Stanley volunteering. Neither of the other two girls was so indecisive. Ellen knew exactly what she wanted to do, and Angel . . . Angel always said she could make a snap decision whenever something felt right.

There was a tap on the drawing room door while Fred was still ruminating over whether or not something had felt very right to Angel last night.

One of the maids bobbed a curtsey, her eyes bright with speculation. In her arms she held a great sheaf of spring flowers enclosed in tissue paper. Printed all over the tissue was the name of Simone's, London's most exclusive florist. The bouquet consisted of tiny white mignonette and freesias, budding jonquils and tiny, outrageously expensive hot-house forced pink tea roses. They were all bound together with a flamboyant pink ribbon, and there was a card attached.

'Someone's just delivered these for Miss Angel, m'lady,' the maid said excitedly. 'They came in a big florist's van, ever so posh –'

'Thank-you, Sophie,' Clemence said irritably. She took the flowers from the girl's hand, looking immediately at the card. She gave a strangled gasp.

'To my Angel,' she read out. 'Until we see the lights of London together.'

'Is that all? No signature?' Fred demanded as she stopped.

'None,' Clemence said furiously. 'Now will you believe me when I say that something's got to be done about that girl, Frederick?'

'I say. Has Angel got a beau?' Louise forgot her troubles for a second and stared at the flowers.

Stanley was a darling, but he usually forgot the little niceties of life, leaving things like birthdays and anniversaries for his secretary to remind him, and often to make the necessary purchases. Louise's envy of Angel soared.

'That's just what I'd like to know.' Clemence told Louise rapidly what little they knew of Angel's movements of the previous night, while Louise's eyes grew round as she listened. There was nothing of the rebel in Louise, but all the same, she could suddenly identify with the excitement Angel must have felt, unexpectedly having the freedom to do as she wished for one night in her life, and being daring enough to act on it.

'Is she in her room? Shall I take the flowers up to her?' Louise said eagerly, dying to find out more.

'Certainly not. I want to see her face when she reads the card,' Clemence said. 'You may call her down, Louise, but please don't mention the flowers.'

Dutifully, Louise left the room. Fred hid a little sigh. If Clemence told Louise to throw herself off Tower Bridge, she would probably do it without question. There must be a happy medium somewhere between the cloying obedience of one daughter, and the out-and-out contrariness of another. And Ellen, his middle girl, was certainly not it.

Angel and Ellen were talking together when Louise went upstairs, and the three girls came into the drawing room together. They were not often here en masse, and as if for the first time since they had grown up, Fred was struck by the differences and yet the similarities in them.

Louise stood above the other two by a few inches, though none of them could be called tall. They were all fair, with Angel having the softest honey-coloured hair of all. They all had Clemence's green eyes. In shape, they were very different.

Louise was going to be matronly very soon if she didn't watch her diet. Ellen was almost tubular in shape, while Angel had curves in all the right places. Fred cleared his throat. He had no doubt at all that many young men would find Angel irresistible before too long.

Without saying a word, Clemence handed Angel the sheaf of flowers, and Angel took them automatically, her eyes puzzled. She read the note, and felt her face flood with colour.

And suddenly nothing else mattered in the world but that Jacques had cared enough to send her flowers. He hadn't quite abandoned her as she had thought. She knew that he'd had to report back to his squadron early. Perhaps after all, he simply couldn't bear to say good-bye . . .

'Does that answer all your questions, Frederick?'

Angel heard her mother's accusing voice as though through a mist of joy.

'Until we see the lights of London together . . .' it spoke of continuity, of finding one another again no matter how war and circumstances parted them . . . or time, or space . . .

Fred took a quick glance around. Ellen sat sullenly after her initial interest in Angel's gift, still smarting over her mother's refusal to let Rose Morton go to Meadowcroft with her. Louise was still hot-faced over her husband's apparent determination to prove that he wasn't as spineless as he looked. Clemence was stiff with righteous indignation, and Angel looked as though she had just glimpsed heaven.

Fred asserted himself, knowing that it was time to act like the master in his own house.

'I have my own answer. We shall all go down to Meadowcroft for the duration.'

He ignored his wife's gasp of annoyance, and Angel's startled exclamation. He went on doggedly in a voice they all knew. When Fred had made up his mind, nothing would change it. He held up his hand for silence, though he didn't really need to.

'We have already established that London is becoming a dangerous place, with the risk of the Zeppelin raids and the strange characters roaming the city these days.' He avoided Angel's eyes. 'With Stanley volunteering, Louise will be all alone in that great barn of a house –'

'Except for a score of servants,' Ellen muttered.

'So she'll be glad of her family's company. It will certainly ease her mother's mind if Angel comes down to the country, away from the risks of the city, and as for Ellen's friend, I see no reason at all why we can't offer hospitality to her if we're all going to be living there. We'll shut this house up and move down wholesale as soon as possible.'

Clemence and Angel were still gaping at him as Ellen leapt towards him and threw her arms around his neck in an unusual burst of exuberance.

'I say, Dad, that's jolly sporting of you! Thanks a million. Rose will be so bucked. I'll get off now and tell her. I'll bring her along tomorrow to meet you all, shall I?'

'Oh, of course. Bring her to tea,' Clemence found her voice, and oozed sarcasm. 'Bring the entire suffragette movement with you, if you wish!'

Ellen didn't take the bait. Instead, she grinned at her mother and blew her a kiss on her way out.

'No thanks, Mother. You wouldn't want an army invading

the house. And I promise you there's enough of them to qualify for the name! See you all tomorrow, then – oh, and don't forget that Rose is in mourning, will you?'

Her voice sobered as she went through the door, and the little group in the drawing room felt suddenly uncomfortable. They hadn't had to deal with grief yet. The war had barely touched their lives, for all that Bannister's Textiles were now providing cloth for uniforms instead of fine top quality wool for ladies' and gentlemen's garments.

The war was insidiously touching them now, Fred thought. His eldest daughter's husband had enlisted; his second daughter was comforting a war widow; and his youngest had apparently had some secret liaison that was still holding her entranced as she buried her nose in the sweet-smelling flowers accompanied by the cryptic note.

'Thank-you, Frederick.' Clemence assumed the haughty tone for which she was famous. 'The very last thing I wanted was to encourage Ellen, and you've just undermined everything I've tried to do with one stroke.'

'Because I've offered hospitality to some poor woman whose husband was blown to bits in the trenches?' He didn't try to soften the words, and he saw her flinch. 'Have you so little humanity in you, my dear? I thought your knitting parties and tea and soup wagons on the railway stations were in the same good cause, or am I mistaken?'

'I do those things because I choose to do them. I don't have them rammed down my throat,' she said stiffly. 'And Angel – take those flowers and put them in water in your room. Their scent is making my head ache!'

Angel escaped gladly, knowing that everything was going to make her mother's head ache now. Out of the corner of her eye, she saw Louise – dear Louise – go to her mother and place gentle fingers on her mother's brow to soothe the pain away. Angel went to the kitchen and asked Cook for a large vase of water, and took it and the precious bouquet upstairs.

Their perfume filled the room. Angel arranged them with

as much care as if they were priceless gems. To her, they meant as much. Jacques de Ville had not seen her as a flighty piece of fluff to take to an hotel room for a night and then forget her. He had cared after all. She had known it in her heart.

She fingered the silken petals of one of the pink tea roses and hugged the secret of her love to herself. There was no way of knowing when they would meet again, but it was certain that they would. Not even Kaiser Bill could destroy what last night had begun. She felt buoyant for the first time since waking up alone in the bedroom of the Hotel Portland.

There was a tap on her door, and she turned away from the artistically-arranged flowers and turned to see Louise.

'I say, Angel, who are the flowers from? Is it someone Stanley and I know? Do tell. I won't let on, honestly.'

Angel gave a half-smile. Louise meant it sincerely, but Clemence would worm the secret out of her in no time. And Angel would be in deeper disgrace than she was already.

'I can't tell you, Lou,' she said lightly. 'It must be a secret admirer. A mystery man!'

Louise stared at her.

'I'm not sure that I believe you –'

Angel opened her eyes wide, knowing how it always gave her an air of artless innocence.

'Do you think a well-brought-up young lady would tell such a fib, sissie dear?' She gave an elaborate shrug. 'Anyway, whoever he is, he'll have to wait to show me the lights of London, if we're all to move down to Somerset.'

Her heart seemed to churn as she spoke. Jacques knew this address, but he wouldn't know where to find her in Somerset. It hadn't been necessary to give him the country address. Her parents would naturally arrange for mail to be sent down, but then her mother would know if a letter arrived for Angel with masculine handwriting on the envelope. And knowing Clemence, she would connect it immediately with the writing on the florist's card.

Perhaps he wouldn't write to her anyway. He might just turn up at Hampstead one day, expecting her to be here . . . her thoughts raced on haphazardly, just thinking of this complication, but knowing better than to suggest that she should be allowed to stay on alone in the town house with a handful of servants. What an outcry that would cause!

'I'm not sure that I want to go, but I suppose it's for the best,' Louise said slowly, her attention already wandering from Angel's mystery man. 'At least Stanley can come down from time to time. He loves the country, of course. I do worry so over where he'll be posted. It would be too much to expect that it will be somewhere near us, of course.'

She rambled on, already back in her own closed world, selfish enough to dismiss Angel's wan face, and hardly giving a second thought to Ellen and her friend's problems. Was that how marriage affected people? Angel wondered. Certainly it had done so with Louise and Stanley.

It created a barrier between the two of them and the rest of life. They had become one entity instead of two, which was why Louise was so disorientated all of a sudden because she would have to think for herself once more.

Angel suddenly thought of Rose Morton, whom she didn't know, but who was going to become part of their lives from tomorrow. She too must learn to think for herself all over again. And there would be thousands of women like her before this war was over. The thought had never occurred to Angel until now.

Afternoon tea the next day was a fairly awkward affair. Clemence had ordered Cook to prepare tiny sandwiches and little cream cakes and ginger nut biscuits, but Rose Morton only toyed with the food and looked very ill at ease. Ellen constantly glanced at her, as though she were a child in need of mothering.

Angel was shocked to see how young Rose Morton was. She looked little older than Angel herself, yet she had been married and widowed in the space of a year, and she was independent enough to have joined the suffragette movement and to find support in women like Ellen now when she needed it most. She was quite obviously of a different class, but to Ellen that made absolutely no difference. Angel grudgingly admired her sister for the ability to accept people for themselves.

Angel tried to find topics of conversation with Rose, but Louise clearly found her a great embarrassment, because of Stanley's recent commission. She had heard that very morning that he would hold the rank of Major, and he had told her jovially on the telephone that he was to get a desk job somewhere near the south coast of England, and it was unlikely that he would ever leave British shores.

Louise was thrilled and relieved when she heard, but seeing Rose Morton's pretty, pale face and sad eyes, she felt a strange sense of shame, and a fierce wish after all, that Stanley could come home a hero.

Clemence had risen to the occasion as Fred had known she would. By the end of the day, one would have thought that Lady Bannister herself had graciously issued the invitation to Rose to accompany them all to Somerset.

'We hope to move down to Meadowcroft at the end of next week, Rose dear,' she said kindly. 'Can you be ready by then?'

'Of course.' Rose gave the quick tight little smile that vanished as soon as it came. 'There's nothing to keep me in London. The movement will go on whether I'm here or not. I do appreciate your generosity, Lady Bannister.'

Clemence smiled back uneasily, thinking it a pity that young women should be so passionate about politics and the like these days. And all those girls they called canaries, having their skin dyed yellow by the dreadful TNT that Fred had spoken about, and content to wear those terrible mob caps over their hair, and the uncomfortable oilskins or overalls when they worked. So unladylike. So undignified.

War did that to people, of course. It stripped one of one's dignity. Knitting diligently and pouring tea at railway stations was quite quite different, but just as vital . . .

At least Angel seemed more docile today, Clemence thought with some relief. She resolved to keep a stricter eye on Angel in the future. One never knew who one's daughter might be meeting in these dreadfully modern days of going without a chaperon.

A letter arrived for Angel on the day before they left for Somerset. Thankfully, her mother was ensconced with her knitting circle when Sophie handed it to Angel on a silver salver. Her heart leapt as she saw the same forceful square handwriting that she would know anywhere now. Some of Jacques' flowers had already started to fade, no matter how hard Angel had tried to keep them alive. But one of the pink tea roses was already pressed between the pages of her heavy Bible.

The letter was dated on the morning they had parted. Incredibly, it had taken five days to cross London, its envelope crumpled and dirty. She threw the envelope onto the fire, and concentrated on the words, hearing his voice as she did so.

'My dearest Angel,' she read, feeling her pulses race at the endearment. She read it several times before going on to the letter itself.

'Perhaps it is improper for me to address you so. Perhaps you hate me for leaving you as I did. I pray that it is not so, *chérie*. I could not bear to say good-bye, and there was so little time that morning. It is my greatest wish that one day we shall be together. We knew each other for such a brief while, yet I feel that I have known you always, loved you always. I cherish the hours that we shared, for they meant all the world to me. You gave me something to come back to, Angel. Something to fight for. I shall take your memory into the sky with me. I believe that I also take your love as a talisman. I leave you mine.

Ever Yours, Jacques.'

Angel's breath was tight in her throat when she finished reading. There was so much more that he hadn't said. She knew that it was unwise to give military details away, even in a personal letter. But she had already guessed that he was flying to France the day after they had met. One day out of their lives was all they had had. She sent up a silent prayer that it was not all they would have.

She pushed the letter into the pocket of her skirt as she heard the knitting ladies preparing to leave the house. This was their last meeting at Bannister House, and Clemence had particularly asked that Angel should bid them good-bye with her mother. It was the done thing, and Clemence was a stickler for doing things right.

Angel tried to compose herself, hoping that her cheeks weren't as pink as they felt, nor her eyes as bright. Despite the poignancy of the letter, her blood sang in her veins, for Jacques was as much in love with her as she was with him. She no longer tried to deny it, nor to pretend that it couldn't happen in a moment. And one day, they would be together for always . . .

'Angel, dear, please try to pay attention when Mrs Moncrieff is speaking to you,' she heard her mother's cool voice when she had seemed dazed for several minutes.

'I'm sorry, Mrs Moncrieff!' Angel's face went scarlet then, knowing she would be reprimanded later, and wanting nothing to spoil this joyous day.

The lady laughed indulgently, her eyes twinkling. 'Angel probably has a young man on her mind, which is far more interesting than a group of virtuous elderly ladies! I know that look in a young gel's eyes, and good luck to you, my dear.'

'Nonsense, Violet, Angel's far too young to think of anything like that,' Clemence said crisply.

Mrs Moncrieff touched her lips to Clemence's cool cheek. 'My dear, it's a healthier occupation than throwing oneself beneath the King's horse, wouldn't you say? The sooner you get dear Ellen out of the clutches of those awful women, the better. Find her a husband to keep her in order.'

Clemence kept the smile firmly fixed on her face. Violet Moncrieff was an old friend, and therefore entitled to be freer with her advice and opinions than most. All the same, some things were private family matters, not to be bandied about publicly.

One of those matters was Ellen's involvement with the suffragette movement. Another was the undoubted glow on Angel's face at this moment, which she too began to recognise with alarm. In fact, it had hardly left the girl since the arrival of that extravagant bouquet of flowers from an unknown admirer. Clemence resolved there and then to investigate further.

Violet finally left the house, and Clemence gave a sigh of relief. Good Works were all very well, but nothing could compare with the peace and quiet of one's own home. She turned resolutely to Angel, just as the girl gave a great sneeze, fumbling in her skirt pocket for a handkerchief.

As she dragged it out, a piece of paper went flying to the floor, and Clemence bent to pick it up. Seeing the handwriting, she too knew it at once. She heard Angel give a little cry, but it was too late.

Clemence held the letter out of Angel's reach, scanning it in mingled horror and misbelief.

'Please give it to me, Mother. It's mine, and it's private,' she said in a high, tortured voice.

'I have no doubt of that,' Clemence said shrilly. 'It seems I can no longer trust my own daughter. I'm appalled by the contents of this letter! Am I believe that you have been so – so wicked as to be – *intimate* – with this man?'

Despite herself, Angel felt a wild desire to laugh. How absurd to defile that glorious night in Jacques' arms by calling it wicked! But then that other word – that delicious, awesome, and scary word – sent her thoughts scattering to a direction she had never even considered until now.

She knew very well that to be intimate with a man meant taking the risk of becoming pregnant. To be disgraced in society, and to shame one's entire family. The thought of it dried the saliva in her mouth, and made her heart thump sickeningly.

'Mummy, you have no right –' Angel whispered.

'I have every right!' Clemence was outraged at her daughter's apparent admission. 'Please go to your room until your father has seen this disgusting piece of literature, and we decide what's to be done about it.'

Angel looked at her wordlessly. Jacques' letter had given her hope, support and love, and without it she was lost. But her mother's face was implacable. Angel turned and rushed out of the room, knowing that the fatuous phrase of feeling as though one's world was falling apart, was a truism after all.

Chapter 5

Black clouds scudded across the dawn sky, and there was a smell of rain in the air. It made no difference. Jacques de Ville's flight was scheduled to leave for France that morning, to report to Brighton Belle, the code-named headquarters of his squadron. The base was very near to the Belgian border, and previously Jacques had only flown as crewman on the recce trips over enemy lines.

Now, he was a pilot in his own right. The all-too-brief training over the skies of Salisbury Plain was over, and he was at the controls of his own two-seater aircraft. His observer and gunner, Phil Brakes, was seated in front of him. The brief fear that shivered through Jacques was quickly smothered, giving way to exhilaration. The aircraft was his responsibility, and two lives depended on his skill.

He prodded Phil, who gave him the thumbs-up sign as the propeller was swung by the ground mechanic, and the shuddering engine notes nearly deafened him. The machine shook and throbbed as if threatening to tear apart at any moment, but as it did so, Jacques felt excitement overtake all other emotions.

In his eyes, to fly was the nearest thing to heaven, literally and metaphorically. To soar into the clouds was a sensation unknown to most. To experience the dense sea of cotton wool below, and then to emerge into brilliant blue skies and stunning sunlight was to be humbled by eternity and the vastness of space.

His artistic eye could appreciate the spectacular scenario; the temperament of his race could tighten his throat and make him wish he had a poet's words to express his feelings as the aircraft trundled over the uneven grass, preparing to take off, the others in his flight gathering behind him like attendant worker bees . . .

Not everyone saw things the way he did, of course. He knew better than to enthuse too lyrically about the changing skies as he flew into the sun or back to base through a vaporous indigo evening.

But most of his squadron pals were eager for his sketches of themselves lounging nonchalantly against their craft, to keep as souvenirs or to send back home to wife or sweetheart. They were only just discovering that they were the elite new breed of heroes . . . Jacques smiled thinly as the six craft in his flight moved forward along the flattened grass in ragged formation, preparing for the long slow invasion of the sky.

'Bloody olive oil!' Phil's voice yelled back at him as the spurt of oil from the engine drifted back into their faces as usual, ingraining their skins almost before they were airborne. 'No wonder most of us have the daily shits! They say the poor bloody infantry are suffering with dysentery in the trenches. They should try swallowing this muck.'

'Keep your mouth shut, then you won't swallow so much of it,' Jacques shouted forward, his voice almost lost in the roar of the other aircraft beginning to bounce skywards towards the grey sheen of the English Channel.

'Is that an order, Cap'n?' Phil said in his cracked Norfolk accent.

'No! Just common sense!'

Jacques swore loudly as the aircraft dipped and shuddered alarmingly in a pocket of turbulence. The first few minutes were always hazardous, hard on the nerves as the heart palpated and hands grew sweaty as the pilot tried to keep the joystick steady and the wings level.

And then, as though drifting into another world, the turbulence ended; you were above the clouds; you were floating; and seemingly the only living thing in the universe.

'Bloody well done, Cap'n Jax,' Phil's faintly sarcastic voice bellowed. 'We'll be over Jerry's tail before we know it.'

'I hope not. We only have to report to base, not get caught up in a fight.'

'Not much point in being fitted out with a machine gun then, is it?' Phil was in a belligerent mood, his fingers happy on the trigger, his keen eyes already scanning the skies for a hint of silver against the sun that might indicate an enemy aircraft ahead. Jacques gave a short laugh.

'There'll be plenty of time for that. Let's get this little war horse safely to France first.'

Phil snorted in reluctant agreement. Despite the deceptively easy flying now, all Jacques' concentration was needed in controlling the dangerously flimsy machine that often seemed to have a will of its own. It only took a second's relaxation for the wings to dip and the horrors of a dive begin. Even in training, in the safe skies over Wiltshire, Jacques had seen pilots go into a spin and crash to their deaths before ever seeing enemy action. He knew the risks.

All the same, his thoughts wandered a little. Ever since meeting Angel Bannister and that one emotional night they had spent together, he hadn't been able to get her out of his mind. He had dearly wanted to call on her, but official orders had put that right out of the question.

As it happened, bad weather had stopped the squadron departing that same morning, but they were all confined to base until they were given orders to fly out. It was an entire day and night of frustration and waiting, closeted with other officers and men in steamy, dank-smelling mess rooms, and he had whiled away the time in sketching and writing to Angel.

He had despatched one of the bored mechanics into the city to order the flowers to be delivered to Angel's house, later entrusting the letter to the same young mechanic. Once the squadron had left for France, God knew how long it had been before the boy thought of posting it.

But in his breast pocket now, Jacques had the perfect likeness of Angel next to his heart, and thanked God for the talent that meant he could at least keep her image near to him, if not her sweet warm self.

He had known many women, and there were plenty who had wanted to marry the handsome young de Ville, whose family home was a gaunt gothic chateau south of Bordeaux, and who had excellent social connections. No doubt it had been a bitter disappointment to many a French *maman* when his father had agreed to Jacques being educated in England in deference to his mother's death-bed wishes.

Comte de Ville had made no protest at his son's own request to remain in England and serve with the Royal Flying Corps when it was first formed, knowing of Jacques' obsession with all things that flew. For him, there could have been no better choice.

Strange how a war could be the catalyst to fulfil a man's ambitions, Jacques thought briefly. To meet the one girl with whom he wanted to share his life . . . and to be flying an aircraft over his own country in a way he had never imagined in his wildest dreams . . .

A week or so later, Jacques wondered grimly if this was really his vocation after all. The pleasure of flying for its own sake was unchanged, but the dark side of war was revealed to him hourly. Each flight in the squadron flew in shifts, on recce work at first, and ever-increasingly in fighting combat with the fast little German planes that seemed to fill the sky like irritating insects, but with far deadlier effects.

Already, several of his pals had been shot down. He had seen one of the planes of his own flight, engulfed in orange flames as the short fuel lead from the tank to the engine exploded. He had seen the observer's hands tear at his face and been near enough to hear him scream in agony, the pilot losing control as the burning oil spattered over him and the aircraft plunged to earth, producing a great dazzling fireball beneath Jacques' own plane.

'Christ almighty, let's get out of here,' Phil had croaked, his usual cheerfulness swept away.

'Not yet!' Jacques had sworn profusely, which was the only way to vent his feelings at that moment. 'We'll get the bastard who killed Browning first.'

They had wheeled around, the sunlight dazzling them, the German plane heading towards them like a dart. But somehow they had avoided the impact, and Phil had swung the machine gun like a mad thing, blasting furiously, until they had seen the enemy go down with a whine of black smoke, to crash near Browning's wreckage. The German pilot scrambled out of his cockpit seconds before it exploded, and they had seen scattered fuselage and burning fabric set his clothing alight so fast that he quickly resembled a demented fried skeleton.

Only then did they fly away from the scene, with Phil cheering wildly that that had got their first Jerry, and Jacques so sick inside that he could hardly see the sky for the memory of that inhuman thing that had changed so frighteningly from a man.

'Get her up, Cap'n!' Phil was still drunk with success. 'Let's get up among the angels and head for home and put a cross on the side of our cockpit for one enemy less to worry about!'

Up among the angels . . . it was ironic that his gunner should have used those very words. It reminded Jacques of Angel . . . and right then he hadn't wanted to be reminded of her. She was everything that was gentle and good . . . and what they had just done to another human being was beyond all dignity, and should fill them with shame.

On that same day, the Bannister family was preparing to move en masse down to Meadowcroft. Angel was still in disgrace, but Clemence had decided that things being what they were with this dreadful war, the girl would obviously be far better off well away from temptation, and that the serenity of the country would work its own healing for whatever ailed her.

Obviously, Clemence could see that Angel was far from her usual self, but any thought of this – man – having despoiled her was put bluntly to rest by Angel herself telling her mother in a brittle manner that the monthly visitor had arrived, and so she need have no fears of becoming an early grandmother.

Clemence was scandalised at Angel's very turn of phrase. The girl seemed to have lost control of her speech and all sense of decency, let alone her morals, and Clemence completely failed to see or hear the hurt in her youngest daughter.

The cramps in her belly had awoken her during the night before they were to leave for Somerset. Angel knew she should be overcome with relief, for the alternative was unthinkable. But in her heart, she felt more than just relief. She had lost all that she had had. For a little while, she had still had a part of Jacques with her. Now she had nothing. That beautiful night might never have happened. She was as she had been before. It was over.

And now she had to face the long bumpy ride down to Somerset with her stomach tied in knots, and the misery of not knowing what had happened to Jacques, or if she would ever see him again. The flowers had wilted and died, save for the one she had pressed. The letter had been confiscated, and no amount of tears and pleas would make Clemence agree to give it back to her.

Fred and Clemence set off early for Meadowcroft in the stately splendour of the Daimler. Louise was to follow later in her own car. In the smaller Sunbeam, the chauffeur, Hobbs, eyed his three pretty charges with a ready cockney smile. Miss Ellen and her friend, the pale Rose Morton, and the beauty of the family, Miss Angel.

He didn't mind in the least that the stuffier one of the Bannister girls, Miss Louise – Mrs Crabb now, he reminded himself – wasn't in his company. At least he could have the occasional laugh with the other girls, providing he was careful not to upset the young widow, of course. He must remember that.

Hobbs was bursting with news of his own, and he couldn't wait a minute longer to tell somebody. They had been on the road for a couple of hours and stopped for a cup of tea at a small café, and Miss Angel was rubbing the small of her back as if he had bumped her to hell and back.

'I'll slow down if you like, Miss,' he offered obligingly. 'But it ain't going to alter the state of the roads, and we'll get there all the slower if I do –'

'No, it's all right, Hobbs. I just slept awkwardly, that's all.' Angel sat upright immediately. 'You get us there as fast as you like, and don't bother about me.'

'That's all right then, because this'll be the last time I drive any of you lovely ladies about.' He beamed at the two sisters as their mouths dropped open.

'What do you mean?' Ellen demanded. 'You're not leaving us, are you, Hobbs? You can't! We need you!'

The chauffeur laughed.

'So does King George, Miss Ellen. Ain't you heard that there's a war on? I'm enlisting. Signing on the dotted line to glory. Goin' off to France to see all them places that the rich folk see, only I'm doin' it at the country's expense.'

'Hobbs, for heaven's sake –' Angel breathed, wondering just what effect all this patriotic claptrap was having on Rose. But to her surprise, the girl spoke up, her cheeks pink.

'No, please don't stop him, Angel. It doesn't upset me to hear him speak so. It's an honour to know that there are still fine young men willing to go and do what my husband did. Willing to fight for their country, and to die, if need be.'

'Yeah well, I ain't akchully given much thought to dyin','

Hobbs said, suddenly hot under the collar. 'But all the rest of it – yeah, King and country and all that. 'Course I'll go. Any red-blooded young man wants to do his bit, especially for all them young French mamselles if you get my meanin'.'

He caught the tight-lipped look on Ellen's face and grinned sheepishly. Cocky he might be, but it was a daring thing to say to the three young ladies, and if he wasn't about to leave the Bannister employment, he would never have risked his job.

'Sorry for speakin' so bold, Miss. Truth to tell, I don't much fancy telling your Mama I'm leaving. I had a drop of rum this morning to give me Dutch courage, and it's gone to my head.'

'So that's why we've been rattling around the countryside like idiots,' Angel muttered feelingly.

'But what about us, Hobbs?' Ellen quickly veered him away from the subject of the French mamselles. 'We need a chauffeur, for heaven's sake! How will we get about when Father takes the Daimler off to his wretched Yorkshire all the time?'

Hobbs stretched himself out in the wooden chair, his jaunty grey cap tilted on the back of his head in a way that would infuriate Clemence if she could see it.

'I s'pose you'll just have to learn to drive, or rely on Shanks' pony,' he drawled without concern. 'And you've all got them bicycles at Meadowcroft, ain't you? You're always pedalling about the place when you're down there.'

'I think you're being totally unfair,' Ellen said indignantly. 'Leaving all of us in the lurch like this –'

'Oh, don't be such a stinker, Ellen,' Angel put in. 'Hobbs is perfectly right to enlist. We wouldn't want him hauled up in court like one of those awful conchies, would we? Everyone has to do their bit, and if ours is – well, to ride bicycles around the country, we shall just have to do it.'

Even as she said it, Angel knew how appallingly pathetic it sounded, and she was ashamed that the hovering waitress with an eye for Hobbs' smartly-turned-out uniform might have overheard. Was that all they could do for the war effort? Ride bicycles, for heaven's sake?

'I'm sure it will be all right, Angel,' Rose murmured as Ellen's eyes glinted in annoyance at her sister.

Rose was tired. The last thing she wanted was to be caught in the middle of a family squabble, and with Ellen hinting nonstop about some dark secret of Angel's, she was beginning to wonder if she had made a mistake in joining the Bannisters after all. They were all so strong in their different ways, and Rose still felt so weak and lost after Ronnie's death . . .

'Of course it will be all right, Rose.' She heard the sudden note of triumph in Angel's voice. 'I shall learn to drive the Sunbeam myself. If Louise can do it, I'm sure I can master it, even though Daddy's so against it. Louise only had to get around Stanley, but why don't you start teaching me now, Hobbs? Then I shall drive Mummy wherever she wants to go, and anyone else will have to ask me nicely!'

Ellen looked aghast. 'I'm not sitting beside you while you drive us into a ditch, thank-you very much. If the parents agree to it, you can take proper lessons on your own, not with Rose and me in the car!'

'She's right, Miss Angel.' Hobbs looked at her with undisguised admiration all the same. 'Tain't fair on you to have any distractions when you're learning. You'll pick it up easy enough, and I'm sure you'll find someone to teach you.'

'All right. I'll ask Daddy, and insist on it. If that's settled, let's pay the bill and get on our way.'

She spoke airily, but in reality she was suddenly glad no one had taken up her reckless suggestion to start her driving lessons right now, as the cramps tightened her stomach again, and she felt momentarily giddy.

It wasn't just because of the monthly visitor though. It was the thought of what being able to drive might mean. It meant an independence she hadn't considered before. It could even mean driving an ambulance, and really helping the war in a more positive and involved way than by joining her mother's knitting circles. Perhaps she could be a nursing auxiliary.

She might even go to France . . . to the Front . . . her mother would faint with shock if she had any notion of Angel's careering thoughts, but that was the very best thing about a person's thoughts – they were private.

'Angel's put on her dreaming face again,' Ellen broke in, still irritated with her sister, as they got back into the car and it lurched off towards the west. 'A penny for them, Angel.'

'Sorry, sissie dear. You couldn't begin to afford them,' Angel said sweetly.

And they certainly weren't for sharing, especially when her thoughts had been inevitably winging towards Jacques de Ville. Angel sometimes despised herself for allowing him into her mind so often, but it was impossible to keep him out. He was like a sweet and deadly drug, once tasted never forgotten; once possessed, craved for all the more . . .

'Are you quite well, Angel?' Rose leaned forward in the car to peer into Angel's face.

Her pretty face was filled with concern at the sudden stillness of the youngest Bannister girl. Angel unnerved her a little. She was so self-possessed, outwardly so young and innocent, and yet with an air of sophistication that Rose admired tremendously.

She was different from Ellen, who was of the straightforward, no-nonsense brigade, and a wonderfully loyal friend. Not that Rose sensed Angel would be any less loyal. But Angel had hidden depths to her character that made her an intriguingly sensual young woman, as well as a beautiful one.

'I'm quite well, thank-you, Rose,' Angel answered warmly. 'Just wondering how to get round Daddy to let me learn to drive the car, that's all.'

Ellen gave a snort. 'You can always get round him, and you know it. He always gives in to you in the end.'

'Does he?' Angel said in genuine surprise. 'It doesn't always seem that way to me!'

Hobbs gave a chuckle as he negotiated the car round some deep ruts in the road, unable to resist putting his oar in.

'All rich daddies have their favourites,' he said cheerfully. 'It's easy to see why Miss Angel is Sir Fred's.'

'Thank-you, Hobbs. When we want your comments, we'll ask for them,' Ellen's voice was freezing.

Hobbs glanced sideways at Angel and winked broadly. She giggled, and lapsed into silence as the motion of the car lulled her into dozing. They had a long way to go yet, but they would stop somewhere for lunch. Cook had packed them a picnic basket, since the weather was not so cold as a few weeks ago. As the towns gave way to lush green countryside, signs of spring were everywhere. London, and even the terrible war seemed very far away.

How strange, Angel thought suddenly. It was Britain that was at war with Germany, and yet the fields of France and Flanders were being desecrated.

She must have slept, for she awoke with a start as she realised the car had stopped moving. Hobbs was in the process of hauling back the canopy of the Sunbeam tourer to make it an open-top while they ate their picnic, and all around them were flat green fields. The late March winds had dropped, and thin sunlight warmed the day.

'I thought you were never going to wake up,' Rose said. 'You must have been really tired, Angel.'

'I suppose I was. I didn't sleep very well last night.'

She stifled a yawn, knowing that it was impolite to do so in public. Ellen had leapt out of the car, and was helping Hobbs to spread out the picnic feast on a checked cloth on the grass verge. Ellen believed in keeping the hired help in their proper place when they threatened to become too familiar, but when it came to mucking in, she was always ready to lend a hand.

In the middle of the preparations, a noise like the buzzing

of a hundred bees droned overhead. Angel looked up, startled, craning her neck, her hand shielding her eyes against the brightness of the sky.

'It's them flying machines!' Hobbs said excitedly. 'I was told that there's a training area around here, over Salisbury Plain. Dandy little machines, ain't they? I wouldn't go up in one if you paid me a thousand pounds, though.'

Angel stood up in her seat, twisting round to watch the three flimsy aircraft flying low above the tree tops. As they approached, the noise was deafening, and Rose put her fingers in her ears as she stood up too, to watch the three planes, silhouetted against the sunlight.

Angel felt oddly exhilarated, watching them. Jacques would have done exactly this. Maybe he would have trained here too, and flown over these very fields. Before she could stop herself, she had dragged off her blue silk scarf and was waving it furiously at the pilots. Their goggled faces grinned down at them, and their free hands waved back with enthusiasm.

'Angel, how can you be so common!' Ellen snapped, when the roar of the machines had passed overhead and she could make herself heard. 'And you too, Rose, I'm surprised at you!'

Until that moment, Angel hadn't realised that Rose had been waving too. She saw the young widow blush crimson.

'Well, don't be, Ellen. If my Ronnie had been alive now, I don't think he'd have begrudged me a few waves to a pilot who may be killed over the skies of France tomorrow.'

She spoke with an edge to her voice that stopped Ellen at once, and made her shamefaced.

'I'm sorry. I didn't think,' she began clumsily. 'Oh God, Rose, take a sandwich, for heaven's sake, before I start to smarm all over you for my being such an idiot.'

Rose took one and bit into it delicately.

'Was Ronnie your husband?' Angel said unnecessarily in the small embarrassed silence.

‘Yes. Awful, isn’t it?’

‘What?’ Angel said, puzzled by the remark. The girl gave a short laugh.

‘Ronnie and Rose. The terrible twins, they used to call us. We knew one another right from when we were at school. Nobody took us seriously when we wanted to get married. They all said we were far too young, but if we hadn’t, I’d never have felt so close to Ronnie, even though he’s not here any more –’

Her face suddenly crumpled, her hands trembled and the sandwich dropped onto the grass as she fumbled for a handkerchief. It was Hobbs who held one out to her, and it was Hobbs against whose grey-uniformed shoulder Rose was suddenly held tight, sobbing her heart out.

‘Just you cry it out, love. Tears were never meant for keeping shut up inside,’ the chauffeur said gruffly, while the two Bannister girls stood helplessly by at this outburst of grief. It was almost as if they weren’t there, as Hobbs comforted the distraught young widow.

‘I miss him so,’ Rose wept against Hobbs’ chest. ‘I feel as if I’m only half alive without him.’

‘ ’Course you do, love. It’s natural to feel that way. It will pass, but don’t you try to rush it. Tears are for washing pain away gradually. It can’t happen all at once.’

It was such a painful scene to watch that Angel walked quickly away from the two of them, locked together in so unlikely a fashion. She felt that it was an intrusion to witness such emotion, and the fact that it was the chirpy Hobbs who had the means to console Rose Morton was the most extraordinary thing of all. She brushed a shaking hand across her face, surprised to find that her own eyes were damp. Seeing Rose give way like that brought home the full extent of her loss far more deeply than anything so far.

Before, it had been just words. Ellen’s words, begging their father to let her bring Rose to Meadowcroft. The polite platitudes of her mother’s words, with Rose answering in the same polite, chillingly brave manner. But this was simple raw grief, and even Ellen was keeping very busy sorting out the picnic and not allowing herself to intrude on something very private.

Angel walked along the verge to where a wicket gate led into the field beyond, the thick blackthorn hedges on its perimeter just beginning to show tender buds. She leaned on the gate, her eyes gazing blindly into the distance, to where the little flying machines were now no more than a shimmering blur in the distance.

What she had seen in Rose today was the way she would react should anything happen to Jacques. This same desolation, this anguish . . . was Rose's pain any deeper for having known her Ronnie a lifetime instead of for just one magical night?

Angel knew in her heart that the two couldn't compare, but how could one measure one person's pain against another's? She had rarely bothered to think so deeply about anything before, and that thought was followed swiftly by the sweeping panic that if anything did happen to Jacques, she would probably never know.

'Angel, let's eat this bloody food and get on our way,' she heard Ellen's tetchy voice right behind her, and the fact that her sister was swearing, in the modern way she did at times of stress, told its own story.

They went back to the car, where Rose looked more composed now, and Hobbs lounged against the side of the car to eat his lunch. He was a curious mixture, Angel thought. She supposed he was what they called the salt of the earth, which was why Rose found him comfortable to be with.

'What service are you going to enlist in, Hobbs?' Angel asked, for want of something to say.

'Army, Miss. They need men in the trenches, and I'm not afraid to stick a bayonet up Jerry's backside,' he reverted quickly to his usual form, but seeing the little smile at the sides of Rose's mouth, the Bannister girls didn't attempt to reprimand him.

'I'll pray for you, Hobbs,' Rose said quietly. 'I'll add you to my list, next to Ronnie.'

'Thanks, Ma'am,' he said gravely. Neither of them noticed the incongruity of the words. The other two looked at each other and glanced away again, as if each had just discovered the meaning of mortality. And Angel felt as though the ground beneath her feet had suddenly turned to shifting sand.

Chapter 6

By the time they had been at Meadowcroft for two months and resigned themselves to Fred's ultimatum that they must stay there for the duration, they began to feel as though they had never lived anywhere else. The news from the Front was so bad that none of the girls even wanted to be in London now, where the thick of the air raids was concentrated, and posters and newspaper cartoons depicting the police parading with placards telling everyone to take cover when danger threatened, only added to the feeling of alarm. Anyway, Clemence too was adamant in not going back until it was all over, and just hoped that their dear Hampstead house would be spared.

Meadowcroft was like another world, and Clemence busied herself at once in gathering up a new knitting circle among the countrywomen, and enlisting poor Rose to help, even if Ellen and Angel grumbled about it so annoyingly.

During April, the newspapers had reported the dreadful new German secret weapon, poison gas. As it had drifted towards the French and British lines at Ypres in a bluish white mist, the area became horrifyingly thick with dead and dying soldiers.

There were no gas masks available, and once the gas had been dispersed, even the Germans were unable to advance and attack for risk of being caught in their own trap. If they, like the Allies, slipped into a shell hole where the gas had accumulated, they could as easily be killed by their own poisonous fumes.

'Bloody madmen!' Fred blasphemed loudly, uncaring for his wife's disapproving face. 'The Boche are creating nothing but a stupid stalemate that neither side can win!'

As if to confirm his words, weeks of fruitless fighting followed, with only the casualty lists growing longer, and then the French and British resorted to using gas themselves.

'I simply fail to credit this.' Fred scanned the latest reports in disbelief. 'Since there wasn't enough wind to blow it into the German lines, many of our men were killed by their own gas, to add to the appalling number of fatalities.'

Those who continued to exist in the daily mire could hardly be better off than those who died, according to the more hard-hitting news reports. The conditions of the trenches were said to be filthy and lice-ridden, the trenches awash with mud and effluent. The winter had been especially cold and wet, the spring a long time coming in the Allied lines.

'It grows more terrifying every day.' Clemence threw down the newspaper she was reading, as if the very touch of it tainted her. 'Why doesn't the government do something? What are the other friendly nations doing about it?'

The answer came in May, when Italy entered the war, to set up their own meagre line of defence on the French/Italian border against the Germans. In England at the same time, Lloyd George organised a Ministry of Munitions.

Munitions workers were to be better paid and exempt from call-up if conscription became necessary, as seemed increasingly likely, and a little daylight was thought to be seen in the haphazard running of the country's affairs.

'At the rate soldiers are being killed at the Front, they'll be sending old men soon,' Ellen muttered. 'I wish I was a man. I'd follow in Hobbs' footsteps!'

'I'm very thankful that you're not,' Clemence said sharply. 'You'd go and get yourself killed at the very first opportunity, thinking you could win the war single-handed!'

'Thank-you, Mother! I shall take that as a compliment, however you meant it.' Ellen grinned. 'Hide that newspaper before Rose and Angel come back from the village. Rose takes a morbid interest in reading the casualty columns since Hobbs enlisted. She prays for him every night. Did you know?'

'Gracious me!' Clemence stared at her daughter. 'You mean that your friend Rose prays for the chauffeur?'

Her affrontery was almost comical. Ellen would dearly have loved to encourage it, but then her mother would probably take Rose gently aside, and tell her that such an association just wasn't suitable, and Ellen couldn't risk the thought of her friend being so embarrassed.

'There's nothing of *l'amour* about it, Mama,' she said airily. 'Rose has merely added Hobbs to her list of prayers for dead and prospectively dead heroes. Ronnie first, Hobbs second, that's all. Quaint, isn't it?'

'Really, Ellen, you can be very objectionable at times,' Clemence went hot at such outrageous talk.

'Why? Because I'm not afraid to talk of death? Isn't it time it stopped being such a forbidden subject, Mother, when all about us are dropping like flies?'

Clemence rose stiffly to her feet.

'I won't stay in the same room with you while you're behaving like this, Ellen. You shame me with your so-called clever talk. Accompany me and my ladies to the railway station at Temple Meads one afternoon to give the poor wounded boys tea and comfort, and see some of them who come home from the Front with limbs missing and eyes blinded, and then see how glibly you dare to talk of death.'

She swept out of the room, and Ellen bit her lip. God knew why she had to take things out on her mother, who was definitely doing her bit, despite her own refined upbringing, but Ellen felt so abominably frustrated down here. She and Rose were out of sorts with one another, and even their interest in women's rights had inevitably waned, since Mrs Pankhurst had patriotically stopped her rigid campaigning while the war lasted. But without the shared interest, both Ellen and Rose realised uneasily that they had absolutely nothing in common.

Buried in the country and with all such activities curtailed, there were no great rallies, no heroic speeches to listen to, no sacrifices to be made. It was all so deadly dull. The others didn't seem to find it so stifling as Ellen did, she thought irritably.

Louise had become involved in some sort of charity work in nearby Bristol, and drove herself in and out of the city with a determined nearer-to-God expression every afternoon.

Angel had wheedled their father into teaching her to drive, and was crashing about in the Sunbeam all over the place. Either with their mother, who held on to the seat as if it was going to be her last excursion on earth, or taking the willing Rose to explore the country which she had never seen before. Ellen felt very much adrift.

The only way she could rid herself of the annoyance she constantly felt was to bait her mother, which was a frustration in itself, because she always felt so God-damned awful about it afterwards.

She heard the screech of tyres outside. Angel was far from being a proficient driver, but according to their father she would get there in the end. Ellen hadn't even sat beside her sister in the car yet to find out. Seconds later Rose and Angel came rushing into the room, obviously brimful of news. Ellen lifted a bored eyebrow.

'All right, what's going on now? Let me guess. We're to be billetted with soldiers. I said it would happen. Why would they allow us to get away with it, when smaller houses than ours have to have their quota – ?'

She stopped her laconic surmising as she saw the excited look on Rose's face. It was a while since she had seen her look so animated, even if it probably wouldn't last very long. Ellen sat upright from her sprawling position on the sofa.

'What's happened? Tell me at once!'

Angel's voice shook as she answered. 'Oh, Ellen, do you remember that nice Mr Strube with the greengrocer's shop in the village? We always called him Mr Roly-Poly German Sausage when we were small, and Mother said we weren't to be so rude –'

'What about him?'

'Well, you know all the fuss there's been lately about Germans living in Britain when we're at war with them. Last night Mr Strube's shop was broken into, and everything was smashed up, and the vegetables were thrown into the street. It wasn't discovered until morning, though I can't think how people could have missed hearing the noise. Early this morning, when the postman was doing his rounds, he saw the mess and sent for the police, and they found poor Mr Strube.'

'What do you mean, they *found* him?' Ellen was struck by the little break in Angel's voice, and by the curious fact that Rose seemed to be enjoying herself hugely.

'He's dead, Ellen!' Angel said in a hushed voice. 'He was beaten to death by the thugs who broke into his shop. Who would want to do that to such a nice harmless old man?'

Rose stopped smiling as Ellen opened her mouth in astonishment at this news. And before Ellen could reply, Rose was suddenly screeching.

'I'll tell you who could do it! All those who believe in justice, and want to be rid of every rotten German who's lived off our country for years. One of them killed my Ronnie, and I'm *glad* that your Mr Roly-Poly Sausage-man is dead, do you hear? I wish I'd been there to help them finish him off —'

She stopped abruptly, her voice ending in a strangled scream as Ellen leapt up and struck her hard across the side of her cheek. The blow was so spontaneous that Rose lost her balance and fell to the ground, while Angel looked on in horror.

Rose had given no sign of this reaction in the car, but Angel should have known. She should have guessed . . . apart from that one outburst on the way here, Rose had been too calm for too long. She had to crack sometime . . .

Clemence walked quickly into the room, shocked to see what appeared to be an undignified scuffle between two women as Ellen dragged a sobbing Rose to her feet.

'Leave me alone,' Rose blazed at her. 'You don't understand. You can't possibly understand. You're turning into a shrivelled up old maid, Ellen, and if you'd ever been capable of loving a man as I loved my Ronnie, you'd hate all Germans, however sweet and bouncy a shopkeeper might be. They're our *enemies*. Can't you see that?'

'Rose is quite right,' Clemence said crisply. 'It's all over the newspapers. Any one of them could be a spy, and none of us will feel safe in our beds while there are Germans living and working among us. For their own safety as well as ours, the government will have to detain them until the end of the war. They should have used their own common sense and got out as soon as war was declared. The Germans lost no time in ridding their own country of undesirable aliens!'

Angel stared at her mother, and for once, she and Ellen were totally of the same mind.

'Mother, you can't be serious! *Prison*? There are dozens of Germans, waiters and barbers and shopkeepers who have lived here for years and years. This is their home. Why *should* they run away like cowards?'

'Because it's not their country, and while Germany is at war with Britain, the government will have no choice but to put them away for the duration, Angel.'

'I never heard of anything so idiotic,' Ellen raged. 'You obviously don't know that Mr Roly-Poly Strube was beaten to a pulp last night until he was dead. What justification is there in that, *Mother*?'

Clemence went white with shock, but she was too angry with Ellen to comment on the cruel murder at that moment.

'Perhaps it will help to prove to you that all this independent women's movement nonsense will get you nowhere. The government decides what's best in the end, and it's as perfectly clear that these foreigners must be put safely away,' Clemence said coldly, using the moment to chip away at Ellen's beliefs.

As Ellen threw up her hands in despair, she turned to Rose, putting a kindly arm around her shoulders.

'Let's go and find some witch-hazel for your poor face, dear, to prevent it bruising too badly.'

'Thank-you, Mrs Bannister,' Rose sniffled. 'But in the circumstances, I don't think I can stay here any longer. I shall go back to London, or into lodgings –'

'We'll think about all that tomorrow when you're rested,' Clemence said soothingly. 'London's not the safest place for you, but I know someone who's looking for a companion housekeeper, and the position might just suit you, Rose dear, with your experience in housewifery.'

Their voices faded away as the two of them went out of the room, and while Angel wanted to die with embarrassment at her mother's implication that Rose's future status could be little more than a servant, Ellen exploded with anger.

'If that doesn't beat all! Rose is more of a ninny than I took her for, if she can't see how Mother is patronising her. Experience in housewifery indeed! She was married for such a short time, Ronnie could hardly have got the knickers off her!'

'Ellen!' Angel felt the ghost of a grin tug at her mouth despite herself.

She felt so damned responsible for Rose's outburst. She should never have let her get so interested in the goings-on at Mr Strube's shop, and she should have recognised that burning light in Rose's eyes when she heard what had happened. To her surprise, she felt Ellen's hand on her shoulder, holding her tight for a moment.

'Sorry, old thing. My tongue runs away with me at times. Don't go blaming yourself on Rose's account. Most of the women in the movement found her odd at times. Highly-strung, not to say teetering on the edge! You couldn't have foreseen what was coming. I mean, look at the way she carried on with old Hobbs. Probably scared him to death, if the truth was known.'

Angel let that pass.

'Still. I suppose it was stupid of me to go on so about poor Mr Strube –'

'Why? We'd known him for years. Why shouldn't we be sorry he'd been killed? It's not every day a murder occurs in the village, is it?'

Angel shuddered. It *was* murder, and someone would have to pay the price. Unless it was all hushed up, of course, and no criminal ever discovered. With her new-found wisdom, Angel wondered if it would be exactly like that.

'What will they do?' she asked Ellen.

Ellen shrugged. 'The police will make enquiries. No one will admit to anything. No one will have seen or heard anything. There will be no witnesses. Case unsolved. End of case.'

'How wise you are about such things!'

Ellen half-smiled. 'I haven't lived on the wrong side of London with some very dubious characters without learning more of life than I ever learned in the schoolroom, darling,' she said.

Her face suddenly drooped.

'I shall miss Rose. We've been friends a long time. But when something's over, it's over.'

Angel looked at her sister, seeing the strength and the sorrow in her face. Impulsively, she hugged her.

'I don't really know you at all, do I?'

The brittle mask came over Ellen's face again.

'Did Rose know me? Am I really like she said? An

embittered old maid?' She pulled a crazy, cross-eyed face, which made Angel laugh against her will.

'Of course not. The right partner just hasn't come along for you yet, that's all. When he does, you'll know it.'

'Has he come along for you?' Ellen's voice was so quick and soft that Angel answered before she had time to think.

'Oh yes. And if I never see him again, I'll always know how beautiful it was –'

She blushed furiously, knowing she had betrayed herself with her breathless words, but instead of Ellen's usual scoffing, her sister suddenly leaned over and kissed her, and her eyes were tender.

'If it makes you look so starry-eyed, maybe the same sort of miracle should happen for me too,' she said. 'Shall I risk taking a spin in the car with you, since Mother's taken Rose under her wing? Then you can tell me more.'

Angel laughed, her eyes dangerously close to tears.

'We'll go for a spin, but I shan't tell you any more. This is *my* bit of independence, darling!'

As if to exasperate them further, they found that the car was out of petrol and the can was empty, and they would have to send down to the village hardware shop for someone to deliver it. Since the day was fine and warm and mellow, it was back to the bicycles, rather than spend the afternoon indoors with all its difficult undercurrents.

Better to be outside in the clean fresh air, with the country breezes wafting away the tension. The lanes were winding and empty, and they could almost forget that somewhere a war was raging, and men who were known to them were being blown to bits, or drowning in mud in the Flanders trenches.

They dismounted after a while, and stretched out in the corner of a field, squinting up at the sun through the leafy network of young green trees. The branches sighed as the wind whispered through them, and Angel remembered another tree outside the window of a small hotel, and the memory was enough to make her give a small involuntary sigh.

Ellen leaned up on one elbow, looking down at her sister, lovely in her lemon-coloured dress, tied low at the waist in a frivolous bow. Angel's green eyes were closed, the crescents of her lashes caressing her cheeks. Her soft fair hair, unrestricted by the smart Mayfair salon's torturing now, was feathered against her forehead. Angel could seem so distant at times, as if she was somewhere else, and not with the rest of them at all, but here and now, Ellen felt extraordinarily close to her.

'When do you think it will all end?' Ellen said slowly.

'What? The war, you mean?'

'The war. The killing. The way people are tearing one another apart.'

'It can't last long,' Angel spoke with a desperate hope.

'They said that last year. It was all going to be over by Christmas. The opposing soldiers in the trenches had that ridiculous truce. Waving at each other and wishing each other a merry Christmas, and sharing cigarettes across land that had been hastily cleared of bodies. And the next day, shooting all hell out of one another again. Can you make any sense out of that?' Her voice was bitter and bewildered.

'I can't make any sense out of war at all.'

Ellen looked thoughtful, a grass blade held tightly between her teeth. She lay back on the grass again, wanting to know something, having to ask the question that had been burning inside her ever since Angel's indiscretion had been discovered, the subject since becoming a taboo one within the family. Now seemed as good a moment as any.

'Angel, what's it like to lie with a man? You don't have to tell me if you don't want to, but I'm dying with curiosity, and it was never something I could ask Rose. Not before Ronnie died, and certainly not after. Louise would never discuss such things, even if I cared to bring up the subject. Besides, I can't imagine that Stanley's the most scintillating lover. I know that you know all about it, and I really wish you'd tell me.'

Her voice stopped abruptly, and Angel's first feeling of acute embarrassment gave way to surprise as she caught the uncertainty in Ellen's voice. Why, her sister really was curious, and a little afraid. It was the way Angel herself had been before she was thrust into the situation with Jacques almost before she had time to think.

Until now, she hadn't ever considered that she had a knowledge of which her superior and clever sister was totally ignorant, and the flippant retort to Ellen to mind her own business died on her lips. They lay side by side, not looking at one another, and Angel's voice was soft and dreamy.

'It's like being led to the edge of a precipice and finding that the fall is a delight and not terrifying after all. It's like floating somewhere in space. It's like touching the stars. It's exciting, and humbling, and being a part of someone else, and wanting him so badly that you ache for him every minute of the day. And it's a feeling that can only happen when two people are right for one another. When you're so much in love that the thought of sin never enters your head. It's – it's like being in heaven for every second that you're together, and once you've found that heaven, it's sheer misery to be apart.'

Neither of them said anything when she finished speaking, and the words seemed to hang in the air between them. Then Angel felt Ellen's hand give hers a squeeze.

'Thank-you,' she whispered. 'That was the most moving thing I ever heard. I'll respect your confidence, Angel.'

The sound of an engine broke in on their closeness. For a moment, Angel thought it was an aircraft, and sat up quickly, gazing into the sky, her heart pounding. Jacques had seemed so near while she was talking. It was almost as though she had conjured him up . . . instead, it was a car on its way to the village, its occupant giving no more than a glance at the two bicycles thrown down on the grass beside the field. But Ellen's instincts were alerted by her sister's movement.

'Is he an aviator, your man?' she guessed.

Angel gave a short laugh.

'Yes. My man is an aviator. And that's all I'm going to tell you. What you don't know, the parents can't get out of you, and Mother would still dearly like to know all about the scandalous affair! She thinks I'm quite a scarlet woman now.'

'Instead of which, you're just a woman in love,' Ellen concluded with more perception than usual.

'That's right.' She gave a little shiver. 'I'm cold. Let's go down to the village and see if we can find out any more about Mr Strube.'

Ellen jumped up at once, all remorse.

'How awful! I'd forgotten about him already.'

Clearly, the villagers hadn't forgotten, and weren't likely to for some time. As the Bannister girls pedalled through the long winding street of the sleepy village, with the public house at one end and the church at the other, and the hotch-potch of cottages and shops in between, there seemed more activity than usual in the place.

Folk stood on doorsteps chattering and nodding together. The village bobby leaned on his cycle, taking notes from anyone willing to make a comment. As they rode along slowly, the sight of Mr Strube's hastily boarded-up shop was a sober reminder of how people could take matters into their own hands, and to Angel it was suddenly frightening.

'I don't think we should stay,' she muttered. 'We're outsiders as much as Mr Strube was –'

'Of course we aren't. We've been coming down here since we were children.'

But Ellen realised that what Angel said was true. A small community could close its doors on those who didn't belong, and they had enough to contend with without the daughters of the smart London folk from the big house poking their noses in.

'We could call at the tea room for a drink of lemonade. It's a hot day, and what could be more natural?' Ellen went on, still reluctant to be forced out.

Angel agreed, but it became clear that neither the plump tea room owner nor her few other customers were going to talk about the unfortunate incident at the greengrocer's shop. Not to the two of them, anyway. They were kept politely but firmly in their place.

'I wouldn't have believed it,' Angel said in amazement as they pedalled back through the lanes. 'Even Miss Norton seemed to want us out of there, and we've known her for years!'

'They want to keep their stories correct without any awkward questions cropping up,' Ellen said shrewdly. 'The whole village could be involved in poor old roly-poly's death, and the truth of it will probably never come out.'

'I don't want to think about it any more.' Angel leaned over her handlebars, upset at the very thought of such injustice.

'You can't close your eyes and ears to every nasty thing that comes your way, Angel. That's being chicken-livered.'

'I don't care.' Angel's voice floated back to her as she rode ahead furiously. 'There's no law that says I have to keep imagining Mr Strube's head being bashed in, is there?'

Ellen guessed instantly that it was Angel's way of saying that she did keep imagining it. That because she was so sensitive and finely-tuned, there was no way she could keep the atrocity out of her mind, any more than she could forget what had obviously been a very deep and emotional experience for her with the unknown aviator.

Ellen didn't have much room in her make-up for envy, but in those shared moments when Angel had bared her innermost thoughts to her sister, Ellen had envied Angel with a fervour that had stunned her.

They didn't talk much for the rest of the journey back to Meadowcroft. Each was concerned with her own thoughts, each wishing vaguely that the earlier closeness wasn't evaporating, and not really knowing how to recapture it.

The house was beautiful in the late afternoon sun. Angel wondered with a catch in her throat just how many lovely buildings across the English Channel were at this moment being blown into fragments, to be left as smoking ruins. The war was definitely worming its way into her. She hated it, but without any conscious effort, she couldn't escape it. It was as though she was becoming a part of it, and it was part of her. It was as potent a factor in her life as love.

They left their bicycles in the out-house and walked towards the house together, linking arms. It was the nearest either of them could come to putting into words how they felt. They were met in the hallway by their mother, who was looking sorely put out.

'Your friend has gone,' she announced accusingly to Ellen, as though it was her fault. 'After all we've done for her, and my efforts this afternoon to find her a place of work, she's packed her things and left. Cook said she telephoned for a taxi, and went as soon as our backs were turned. I knew it was a mistake to bring her here. Didn't I say so from the beginning?'

'Yes, Mother, you did.' Ellen breathed a long sigh of relief, allowing Clemence to have her say. What did it matter? The fact was, Rose could only have been an embarrassment from now on, and she had saved them all the problem of what they were going to do with her.

She caught sight of Angel, who was trying hard not to smile, and blatantly grinned back at her. And then the two of them were suddenly holding on to one another and doubling up with laughter, while Clemence stared at them in disbelief.

Such a display! It was good riddance to Rose Morton if she could have this kind of influence on her girls, and the sooner they were all back to normal, the better. Mercifully, they seemed to have forgotten for the moment the upsetting incident of the little German shopkeeper's death, and as she went out of the room with her head held high, Clemence completely failed to discern the desperation in her daughters' laughter.

Chapter 7

'Angel, *darling*, whatever's been happening to you?'

Margot Lacey's voice screamed through the telephone wires, so that Angel had to hold the instrument a few inches away from her ears to avoid being deafened.

'Margot, how wonderful to hear your voice!'

'I tried telephoning you *heaps* of times, but there was never any reply, and so I decided you must have gone up north with your father, or something equally *ghastly*. Then I gave you one last chance, and your old retainer fellow answered, and said you'd all gone down to the country for Lord knows how long. Darling, is it simply *awful*?'

She paused for breath, and Angel laughed at the metallic sound of Margot's voice. Right now, it was like a breath of fresh air blowing through the house. And the assumption that anywhere outside London was *ghastly* was so typically Margot.

'Not awful, just pretty boring! Oh, except that we had a murder in the village a couple of weeks ago –'

'A *murder*?' Margot squealed. 'But how frightful! And they say nothing ever happens in sleepy old Somerset. Weren't you all simply terrified?'

Angel considered this.

'Not really. More sad than anything else, because the man who was killed was a perfectly nice old German shop-keeper –'

'*Ah!*' Margot's tone said everything. 'And he was quietly

disposed of afterwards, I'll bet, and no witnesses ever found. Does that sound about right?'

'Exactly,' Angel said bitterly. 'Isn't it all beastly?'

'Absolute hell,' Margot said with the frankness that had made her tutors despair of her. 'But when am I going to see you, Angel? Can you get up to town, or do you insist that I come down there? You know that I go faint at the thought of cow muck and gumboots, but I'm dying to know what you've been doing since the night I caught that rotten chill and your visit had to be cut short. I was so sorry about all that, darling, and I did mean to contact you long before this, honestly.'

Angel listened to her prattling, hardly registering the words. Swift nostalgia for that night that had begun so badly, and ended so stunningly, surrounded her like a soft blanket. She could almost taste Jacques' mouth on hers. She could feel the strength of his arms around her. She knew at last the mysteries of love. She was warm and safe and alive . . . she started as she heard Margot's insistent voice.

'Are you still there, Angel? Have we been cut off?'

'No. I'm sorry. I was just thinking.' Angel tried to drag her thoughts back to the present from the hazy warmth of remembering. 'Tell me what it's like in London now.'

She could almost see Margot shrugging her slim shoulders, and running her hand through her mass of dark hair in unconcern.

'Not so bad. The Jerries send their beastly Zeppelins to frighten us most nights, and we have to keep our doors and windows closed to stop their pilots seeing any lights. A waste of time if you ask me. The skies are criss-crossed with so many searchlights, they light up London far more than any gaslights would. Still, you can't argue with the government.'

Her tone said that she would certainly do so if she got the chance. Angel found herself laughing again.

'Oh, Margot, it is good to hear you. I've missed you!'

'Well then? Come up to town if the parents will let you,

and stay for a night or two. It will help relieve the dreary arguments Mother and I keep having.'

'I didn't think you and your mother ever argued.' Angel was somehow cheered to think that other families had their problems too.

'We do now. Edward came home from his boarding school absolutely keyed up with this enlisting nonsense, and as you can imagine, Mother went berserk.'

'*What*? But he's only fifteen, isn't he?' She remembered Margot's pimply brother as being red-faced and stammering whenever she came into the room.

'Sixteeen now, and grown so huge in the last six months that he'd easily pass for older, and Mother thinks he'll lie about his age and be in France before we know it. Edward's really grown up, Angel. He has a mind of his own now, and I have more than a sneaking admiration for him, but I can see Mother's point of view too – well, just about,' she added obstinately. 'Anyway, what do you say to coming for a visit?'

Angel spoke positively. 'It would be better if you came here. We're all getting on each other's nerves, as a matter of fact. Mother wants to get me involved in her Good Works, and Louise is a pompous ass, and Ellen's miserable because her friend who was staying here has gone back to London and she doesn't know what to do with herself.'

'Good Lord. It does sound as if you need someone to cheer you up! All right. I'll try and get down in a week or so if my mother hasn't thrown a fit over Edward by then. She always thinks of you as a calming influence on me, anyway. I'll find out the times of the trains, and perhaps someone can meet me at Bristol.'

Angel smiled into the receiver.

'I'll arrange that as soon as you confirm the date and time. It will be marvellous to see you. We've got such a lot to talk about.'

She hung up the receiver. Margot didn't know that Angel

could now drive a car. She would surprise her by turning up at Temple Meads station herself. In fact, she thought guiltily, she was quite capable now of driving her mother there for her returning heroes rotas. The tea and biscuits once provided were now tea and a cigarette, which the soldiers appreciated far more, Clemence said a mite primly.

Angel sought out her mother at once to make the suggestion, and also to ask if Margot could come for a visit. She had already put the cart before the horse, but she didn't anticipate any objections.

'I'm not sure that I approve,' Clemence said, to Angel's intense surprise. 'I haven't forgotten the furore after the last time you and Margot were supposed to be together, though to be fair, I presume none of your indiscretion was planned, and that Margot knew nothing of it.'

'She still doesn't,' Angel said quickly, her face fiery.

'Then she may come, of course,' Clemence said graciously. 'I shall look forward to seeing her again, and some fresh company may revive Ellen a bit.'

Angel hesitated, and then spoke her mind.

'I think she's lonely, Mother. You and Louise are so self-contained, somehow, and I have my driving practice, but now that Rose has gone, Ellen seems to have no purpose in her life.'

Clemence was decisive. 'Nonsense. A young woman with no purpose in her life? She has everything to look forward to, not like some of the poor boys coming home crippled from the Front. Perhaps you would drive me to the railway station today, and see for yourself, Angel. Ellen could come too. Where is she, by the way? I haven't seen her for hours.'

'Neither have I,' Angel said noncommittally. But from the few hints Ellen had dropped recently, she had a strong suspicion as to her sister's whereabouts, and if her mother even guessed, she would be scandalised.

*

The small group of people on the Downs overlooking the Clifton Suspension Bridge in Bristol crowded together a little more closely, as if to present a solid front to the angry hecklers and spectators in their audience. Two of the group held placards on which were painted the words, Justice For All.

One of these two was Ellen Bannister. Her nearest companion was a man in his late twenties, with a shock of unruly dark hair above the collar of his jacket, and a noticeable limp when he walked.

'It's time we got out of here,' he muttered to Ellen, as the crowd that had gathered around them looked more and more menacing. It was their third different venue in a week, and they had met with the same hostile response each time.

'Not yet, Peter,' Ellen pleaded. 'Let's have one more try to make them see reason.'

'All right. But only a few more minutes.'

He conceded as he usually did, because he thought she was the most beautiful thing he had ever seen. Strong and fearless and beautiful. Not in a simpering, silly way like some of the harshly made-up film stars at the bioscope show, but in a way that made him feel he could walk shoulder to shoulder with Ellen Bannister in any emergency, and she would never let him down. She was a woman who could be a true partner to a man with none of the love nonsense intruding. Unless he wanted it to, of course.

'You all know why we're here,' he shouted to the angry onlookers, and suddenly ducked as a rotten egg was aimed his way. It missed his jacket, but smeared over the placard.

'We know, all right, Jerry lover!' One and another in the crowd began to scream and jeer. 'Tain't only them who should be put in prison. 'Tis all Jerry lovers as well. You're as disgraceful to your country as they conchie bastards!'

'Just listen to us, *please*!' Peter and the others tried to shout above the roar of approval. 'All we're saying is that the Germans who have lived here most of their lives should be allowed to remain peaceably, in separate communities, perhaps –'

'So that they can start up a private war right here in England, I s'pose –'

'There's no reason to kill a man just because he's of a different race to our own!' Ellen shouted back, tears of frustration very near. Why wouldn't they understand?

'Have any of you seen how an ordinary shopkeeper can be victimised in a small village where he was always loved and respected? Have any of you seen how he can be killed in cold blood, and then realise there's not *one witness*? No *killers*? We're all killers, while we allow these things to happen. These are *people*, the same as us –'

'They ain't the same as us. They're Jerries, and they're killing our men in the trenches, so we've every right to kill them in return! They know the risks they take. They should go back where they belong. We don't want them here!'

Other missiles were hurled towards the group of pacifists. Stones, rotten fruit, sticks . . . one of them struck Ellen on the side of the face, causing the blood to spurt. She gave a little cry, and rubbed furiously at the graze.

The ultimate insult came when a woman onlooker dragged a handful of white feathers from her shopping bag and threw them into the faces of the men. Sensing even more trouble if they stayed, the group began edging away from the Downs to where an old van stood by the side of the road.

'Come on, Ellen. We're doing no good here,' they yelled back at her as she lingered. Peter grabbed her hand and bundled her into the van in front of him.

But not before a woman in a small car on her way through the city from her charity organisation headquarters had taken in the scene with horrified and disbelieving eyes.

Once the group was safely inside the van, the driver moved

away quickly, and Ellen leaned back, her small breasts heaving with fury.

'Are we so wrong?' She almost wept with the stinging pain in her cheek now that she was out of the cooler air. 'We're acting in the name of common humanity, for God's sake!'

The others muttered and whispered uneasily among themselves. In the beginning, it had seemed a noble enough effort to campaign for the rights of the German immigrants, and the smart city girl had encouraged them with an inspired fervour. But it was clearly time to come to a decision.

At Meadowcroft late that afternoon, Clemence and Angel sat exhaustedly together over a very welcome pot of tea. Angel was more unnerved than at any time in her life before. She had gone to Temple Meads station with her mother, not really knowing what to expect, but vaguely assuming that everything would be clean and tidy and clinical; sweet-faced nurses helping the wounded into the waiting ambulances; calming doctors on hand to give relief to those in any real pain.

The reality was a nightmare. The casualty train had been packed. One end of it was for the slightly wounded and the walking cases; the middle was for the more serious; the rear carriages for the hopeless, for whom there was no hurry. It was neither the railway's nor the army's fault that the men were herded inside like cattle. They simply couldn't cope with the sheer numbers of returning wounded, and this was only one station among many.

Temple Meads railway station was the setting-down point for the southwest, for the city and country hospitals and the outlying convalescent homes, and for those fortunate ones returning to their own homes on compassionate leave, those who were still able to walk and talk and see . . .

With her mother and the other helpers with their trolleys and tea urns and vast quantities of cigarettes, Angel waited quietly, but with nerves suddenly on edge as the train slowly approached the platform, hissing steam and enveloping all those who waited in its damp hazy cloud.

One moment the platform was half empty save for the stalwart ladies and the ambulance people. The next, it surged with noise and swarmed with nurses and pathetic figures clad in blood-stained khaki. Some of them seemed barely human. Some had their entire faces covered in bandages, with not even slits in the cloth for the eyes to see as they were led gently away from the train like children.

Others were pushed along the platform in wheelchairs, with nothing beneath the seat of the chair where their legs had been torn or shot away in battle. Some had armless jacket sleeves hanging pathetically by their sides, and the gaunt, haunted eyes of shell-shock. Others had weeping sores on their faces or showing through their torn uniforms, the result of being too long without proper medical attention.

There was an endless trail of stretchers being carried along the platform from the rear carriages. The sweet sickly smell of gangrene quickly permeated the air and the overall stench was enough to make Angel want to gag. She suppressed the feeling with a huge effort.

Angel lost count of the grasping hands that reached out for hers for a moment of comfort. She thought that her head must surely throb for days with the sounds of groaning, the muted sobs and the occasional scream that was all the more terrible because it was wrenched from a man's throat.

A man . . . but these were mostly *boys*, she realised in shocked horror. A year ago they were probably still at school . . . a swift vision of Margot's little brother, Edward, surged into her mind. Oh God, let him see sense, she prayed. He was still a baby, and too young for sights like these . . . she suddenly felt much older than her own eighteen years.

She caught sight of her mother gently holding a tin cup of tea to a soldier's lips, and then put a lighted cigarette into his mouth, and knew a sudden fierce admiration for Clemence, who had risen above all the distaste she must feel, to give succour and comfort where she could. How vapid Angel must have seemed in the past, by dismissing the so-called Good Works. And how ashamed she was now, as she too bent to hear a soldier's weak words from his cracked lips.

'You're a sight for sore eyes, girl. Best thing I've seen since I left the trenches. God bless you, angel.'

Her eyes smarted. He didn't know her name, but those words were to be repeated time after time.

'God bless you.' 'God bless you.' 'You're a bloody angel, begging your pardon, Miss.' 'God bless.'

And yet she did so little. She gave them a cup of tea and a cigarette and a comforting word. But she *cared.* Right now that was all that mattered. If Jacques was ever wounded, she prayed that somewhere, some caring woman would offer him a word of comfort too . . . Jacques . . . until this moment, she had never really thought about him being wounded too, and it was enough to make her heart beat painfully fast.

Angel bent her head to the next soldier eager for a squeeze of her hand, knowing that her eyes were blurred, and hoped that her silent prayer for Jacques' safety wasn't totally selfish. Like Rose Morton, she embraced everybody in the prayer, and no longer found the idea faintly amusing. And then she heard a thin quavering voice that she didn't recognise.

'Miss Angel, is that you?'

She blinked, startled by the poor wretch on the stretcher. The blanket had been pushed away from his body by his restless clawing in the air. He had no legs below the thighs, and his head rolled from side to side as if eternally trying to see or hear something beyond his reach. His eyes were swollen and bloodshot and glazed in his parchment face, and the orderly with him shook his head slightly at Angel, who reeled back with absolute shock.

'Oh – Hobbs! Oh my God – oh Hobbs, it's you!'

Her voice was high and choking and filled with anguish as

her mind almost refused to believe what she was seeing. Such a little while ago Hobbs had left their employ, to go chirpily to war, bragging about all the French mamselles he was going to charm. Now he was no more than a broken shell of a man, and clearly with so little time left on earth. And Angel just couldn't bear it . . . she just couldn't . . .

'Hobbs, how simply wonderful to have you home again,' Clemence pushed past her. 'You'll drink a cup of tea, won't you?'

Her mother knelt down in the dust so that her face was level with Hobbs' beside the stretcher. She gently held up the chauffeur's head with one hand while touching the cup to Hobbs' lips with the other. She did it all with as much finesse as though she dispensed tea from their own silver teapot, ignoring the fact that most of the tea dribbled instantly down Hobbs' chin as tremors shuddered through him.

'Where will he be taken?' Clemence asked. The orderly lifted his shoulders as if to say it really didn't matter, and the Bannister women watched their chauffeur being carried away, knowing it would be the last they ever saw of him. Angel felt her mother's hand grip her shoulder.

'There are others who need help, Angel,' Clemence said quietly, and turned immediately to the next man. Angel saw the strength in her mother's elegant shoulders, and somehow smothered her own terror to carry on.

The afternoon had been a revelation to Angel. Had she once imagined blithely that she could be a nurse? She had never given a single thought to what it really entailed. She had perhaps romantically visualised for a few moments the glory of tending a patient, of receiving adoring glances and smiling thanks from those she had helped to heal.

She had never once considered the open suppurating wounds or the recurring nightmares after the terror of being gassed, the cauterising and disposal of amputated limbs. She hadn't known before the appalling sweet heavy smell of blood . . . There was so much she didn't know, and never before had she felt so ignorant nor so helpless.

Louise stormed into Meadowcroft while Angel and her mother were still recovering after the afternoon's ordeal. She burst into her tirade before she had even removed her hat and gloves, and stood like an indignant schoolmistress having caught a small boy up to mischief.

'You'll never guess what I've just seen, Mother!'

'Then you'll just have to tell me, won't you, dear?' Clemence was in no mood for guessing games. The whole world was turning upside down, and sometimes dear Louise came out with the most fatuous and inconsequential statements.

'I've just seen Ellen with a group of the most impossible people up on Durdham Downs. They were holding some kind of demonstration, and from the look of it the crowd was just going to see them off. She was holding a placard, and so was the man with her –'

Clemence gave a heavy sigh. 'Oh dear. I thought she had forgotten all that suffragette nonsense –'

Louise sat down abruptly, careful to unbutton her coat as the daughter of a good textile man should.

'It's more serious than that, Mother. It's *dangerous*. The placards were calling for Justice For All, and from the shouting that I could hear, it was quite obvious that Ellen's got herself involved in some of this pro-German campaigning. It's perfectly disgraceful, and she must be stopped at once. My Stanley's fighting for King and Country, and Ellen's parading about the city wanting the Germans to have fair treatment –'

She was stopped by the sudden sound of hysterical laughter coming from her youngest sister. Angel couldn't stop herself. If she was acting in the same shocked way that Rose Morton had done on the day that Mr Strube was killed, then she just didn't care. Tears streamed down her face, and she could hardly speak at the sight of Louise's astonished expression.

'Oh, Louise, you're unbelievable!' she managed to choke out. 'Stanley has done nothing more than drive about in official cars in the South of England for the last three months. He's no more than a factory inspector in uniform! If you have any real complaints about the Germans, you should have seen our poor Hobbs coming home on a stretcher with no legs and probably no more than hours to live. That would have really turned your stomach and might even have made you as human as the rest of us.'

The hysteria dissolved in a bout of weeping that racked her body. Clemence held her tightly to control the paroxysm and told a white-faced Louise to fetch Angel some brandy from the decanter, and that they would discuss the question of Ellen when her father came home from Yorkshire that evening.

Why was it that Fred was never there when a family crisis arose, Clemence thought angrily? But this time Ellen had gone too far. This new craze must be stopped at once, before Ellen put herself and their entire family in danger.

At that moment, had she known it, the Justice For All group was reluctantly coming to the same conclusion. Most of their members had already departed on their bicycles from Peter Chard's farmhouse where the impromptu meetings had been held after the atrocity to Mr Strube. The driver of the van was the last to go, moving awkwardly towards the door.

'I'm sorry, you two, but I've got my family to think of, and I need my van for my living. If it gets spotted too often –'

'It's all right, Ralph,' Peter said calmly. 'I think we're all agreed that as from this moment, we're officially disbanded. We tried and we failed. Plenty of folk can't even say that much.'

He and Ellen sat gloomily together in the old farmhouse kitchen when the man had left. It was very quiet in the countryside two miles south of Meadowcroft. No one would ever guess that a war was going on elsewhere. Outside, birds sang in the afternoon air, and hens clucked noisily. In the distance, a church clock chimed the hour.

'Shall I make us a cup of tea, Peter?' Ellen glanced at her watch. She would have to be getting back soon, to change before dinner. Countries might fall, but Clemence still observed the niceties of life, and her father would be home from Yorkshire in a little while.

Peter nodded, his thoughts far away. As she passed him, Ellen tweaked a white feather from his shoulder, finding her eyes smart with indignation as she did so. It was all so unfair. Peter was the most fearless man she knew, and only she guessed how much he resented the fact that he too couldn't join the brave soldiers in France.

An accident with some farm machinery several years ago had left his leg weakened and permanently scarred, but it hadn't affected his brain nor his ability to know that there were those who wondered why a young virile man like himself couldn't put his farm in an older person's hands for the duration and go off to fight like all the other courageous boys.

He felt the touch of Ellen's hand on his shoulder, and his fingers reached up to capture hers in his own. Her hands were square, like her strong handsome face, the compassion in it quickly hidden, because she knew how much he despised pity.

'What will you do now, my Ellen?' he said roughly, knowing that she must have a cause in her life.

She answered airily, because if she didn't, she would probably break down. 'Oh, I don't know. I'll have to do something. I can't just stay here and stagnate. I did a commercial course at college. I dealt with the accounts and administration in my branch of the movement in London, although my parents never knew quite how deeply I was involved! I could always take up secretarial work with some boring solicitor or something, I suppose.'

'You could always come and work for me.'

Ellen began to laugh. 'Doing what? Mucking out pigsties and milking cows?'

Actually, it didn't sound so bad. Not the filthy parts, of course, but tossing hay about in the summer into those dear little ricks and things, might be quite fun . . . She wasn't as prissy as her sister Louise, but one had to remember one's background, Ellen thought with a glimmer of humour as she imagined her sister's voice saying the words.

'This is a working farm, Ellen. I employ people. At harvest time, it seems as though half the village lends a hand. I have to keep accounts. If food rationing comes, as it must if the war goes on much longer, it will be even more important to keep things in order, and I'm hopeless at paperwork.'

She looked at him suspiciously. She didn't think he'd be hopeless at anything. Was he creating this job just to stop her from being bored? Or even just to keep her around . . .?

Quickly, she took her hand from beneath his, suddenly aware that it had been there too long. Her fingers felt cold without Peter's clasping hers, but she felt an odd nervousness, and moved away from him to fill the kettle with cold water at the stone sink.

'I'll have to think about this, if you're really serious, Peter.' She didn't look at him.

'Of course I'm serious. Did you ever know me say anything I didn't mean?'

It was true, but he realised that he didn't always say everything that he was thinking. What would she say, his straight-backed Ellen, if she had been able to read his mind seconds ago? It had been on the tip of his tongue to say to blazes with looking for a job for which she might be totally unsuited. That there was a perfectly good job for her here. She should marry him and become a farmer's wife.

Thankfully, the words had remained inside his head. He admired her tremendously. They got on well, and the sparks that sometimes flew between them only added a piquancy to their relationship. But they were worlds apart. She was a city girl, born into a rich family, and he was a Somerset farmer, with all the uncertainties which that kind of living brought.

If he once tried to bring romance into their relationship, he had the feeling that she would panic and fly, like a moth about to be caught in a flame, and he couldn't bear to lose her. He knew the limitations between them. They were better as they were. And he could go on adoring her from afar.

Chapter 8

Dinner that night was fraught with tension. Fred knew something was up the minute he stepped inside the house, but he forestalled Clemence by insisting they had dinner first, and talk later. He was tired after the long drive from Yorkshire. It would be so sweet never to have to come all this way to be met with the usual build-up of family problems . . . but that would be shirking his responsibilities, and Fred had never been one to do that.

So it was not until they were in the drawing room drinking coffee out of the ridiculously tiny cups that Fred hated, and through whose handles he couldn't get even his smallest finger, that he allowed Clemence to come out with it. And once she began, he felt as though he was being hit by a torrent of words. He was bruised by the battering, but knew he could do nothing to stop it until she had had her indignant say.

Startled, he stared in disbelief at Ellen. The village murder had been a bloody affair, of course, but he thought his middle girl would have more sense than to condone the presence of Germans in England so brazenly. She had a great compassion, but this was going too far.

Louise said nothing, sitting almost smugly beside her mother, while Angel looked distressed on Ellen's account. Fred reacted at once.

'Your mother is quite right, Ellen. I will not allow you to endanger the rest of your family in this way –'

'I'm not endangering anyone!'

'Yes you are, my dear.' Fred tried to be patient, whilst longing for his bed. 'Once the national fanatics get their claws into you, do you think they'll believe your family thinks any differently from you? Before we know it, our house will be daubed during the night, windows will be broken, and we'll suffer the same fate as the poor wretches being hounded out of their homes and businesses through no fault of their own.'

'You do agree with me in principle, then?' Ellen ignored the rest for the moment.

'What I think has nothing to do with the wider implications. But since I know you'll never be satisfied with such an evasive answer, then yes, I agree with you. I think it's appalling that the poor devils have to be shipped off to a neutral country or sent to prison or risk being murdered in their own beds, but it's a risk they take. If we lived in a country at war, we'd make damn sure we got out of there pretty quickly, wouldn't we? Wouldn't *you*?'

Ellen was sullen. 'I suppose so.'

Clemence was tired of all this discussion in which Fred seemed to be more in sympathy with Ellen than dictating to her.

'The point is, Frederick, what's going to be done about it?' She spoke smartly.

Ellen gave her a glimmer of a smile. 'I'm to be smacked on the hand like a naughty little girl, Mother, and made to promise never to do such a thing again. Is that it?'

'No, it is not.' Fred's voice hardened. 'You will find some sort of gainful employment, Ellen, to keep you out of mischief. I paid good money to educate you girls, and I expect you to do something useful with your lives. I shall see about finding you a position in some worthy organisation –'

Clemence hated this sordid mention of money. Education was their right, not their father's sacrifice.

'Why not take her to Yorkshire with you, and set her up in

an office up there?' she said shortly, failing to notice how Fred blanched beneath his robust colouring. Having any of his girls in Yorkshire was the very last thing he wanted.

Ellen suddenly jumped to her feet, her own face blazing. She hadn't really considered her future at all, but now it was perfectly clear-cut.

'None of you need worry in the least about finding me a position, not that I shall embarrass you again. Since you're so determined that I shall work for my living, you may as well know that I've already found employment.'

For a moment she almost enjoyed the little cries of consternation. Clemence's face was comical, clearly wondering what Ellen was getting into now. Louise's glance said much the same. Angel was merely anxious that Ellen shouldn't rush from one disaster to another, while Fred's eyes glinted.

'Without my approval? What kind of employment, may I ask? If it's not respectable, I shall forbid it completely, Ellen.'

He felt a stab of guilt at his own pomposity. What right did he have to censure his strong-willed daughter, when he indulged in the most delightful clandestine relationship on every trip he made to Yorkshire? But he smothered the guilt and waited for Ellen's reply.

'I assure you it's highly respectable, Daddy dear. I'm to take on the accounting and book-keeping for Mr Peter Chard.'

'Who is this man, Ellen? I've never heard of him,' Clemence said at once, alarm and annoyance all over her face. 'Where did you meet him?'

'He's a farmer, Mother, and he lives quite near Meadowcroft. He's very nice – and before you ask, he's fairly young, but he can't go to war because he has a wounded leg.' Her voice grew mocking. 'Oh – and I do believe he has all his own teeth and his own hair –'

'That's enough, Ellen,' Fred said coldly. 'I would like to

meet this Mr Chard before I give my approval. I can't allow my daughter to work unchaperoned without being assured that the man's not a rogue.'

'Especially on a farm with all those uncouth animals,' Angel breathed the words to Ellen before she could stop herself, and saw her sister's mouth twitch.

'Shall I ask him to tea on Sunday?' Ellen said. 'I'm sure he'll wash his hands and wipe the farmyard muck off his boots if I ask him nicely.'

'A very good idea. Yes, ask him to tea,' Fred said steadily. 'And before then, try to prevent all that acid cutting your tongue, darling. It will rot if you don't.'

Ellen and Angel made their escape, knowing that Clemence would surely begin making objections to Peter Chard coming to tea. But if Fred had ordered it, then it would happen, and Angel wanted to know more about this farmer friend of Ellen's. In her room, she sprawled across the bed on her stomach, while Ellen flopped in the easy chair, exhausted by the unexpected scene, and still furious with Louise for splitting on her to Clemence. That was something she would have out with her older sister later.

'*Well?*'

'Well what?' Ellen said airily.

'You know what! Who is this Peter Chard that you've never mentioned before? Is he one of your campaigners? Or is he your secret lover? Have you been having me on all this time, pretending you know nothing about anything?'

She was teasing, and then, when her sister didn't answer immediately, she saw to her surprise that Ellen's eyes were filling up.

'No, he's not my secret lover. He's so nice I cringe at the very thought of Mother walking all over him at Sunday tea. I like him enormously, and I know he likes me. We're – the very best of platonic friends, and that's all.'

Angel realised that all the family fuss had undermined Ellen's usual brash self-confidence. She knew that feeling only too well. She sat up and smiled encouragingly at her sister.

'Well, I shall like him, anyway. If he's a friend of yours, I like him already.'

Ellen suddenly snapped at her.

'That's the daftest thing I ever heard. How the hell do you know you'll like him when you've never met him?'

'I was only trying to help. And you know you're not supposed to say hell.'

Ellen's mouth was mutinous. 'Hell and damnation. Hell-fire and buckets of blood. Oh – rats and bats and creepy-crawlies –'

'Ellen, stop it!' Angel burst out laughing. 'Calm down a minute and tell me about Peter.'

'Do you realise that's the first time anybody's used his Christian name?' Ellen said, still resentful. 'Thank-you for that. At least it makes him sound like a real person instead of somebody who's out to seduce me. As a matter of fact, I don't think he even thinks of me as a woman. I'm just a good sort. It makes me sound as exciting as an old washcloth. I don't have your luck to meet a mysterious and dashing aviator and get swept off my feet in the secrecy of some little hotel!'

Angel knew that Ellen didn't mean to cheapen it all, but that was how it sounded. And it hadn't been cheap. It had been beautiful. It was just that after all this time it was becoming more dreamlike every day.

'Are you sure you're not in love with him?' she said matter-of-factly to Ellen. She went to her dressing table to take the pins out of her luxuriant fair hair and brush it out over her shoulders, watching Ellen's reflected face. She couldn't tell if the flush the words produced was from anger or something else.

'I'm perfectly sure that I'm not going in for all that stuff, especially in wartime. People get killed in wars, and the people left behind are those who suffer all the pain. I'm not risking all that wasted emotion.'

Shocked, Angel twisted round on the dressing table stool, her eyes huge and dark.

'Oh Ellen, that's a terrible thing to say!'

'Well, it's the way I feel, and I don't want to talk about it any more. I'm going to bed.'

She departed in a huff, and Angel was left to ponder on the fact that Peter Chard wasn't going off to war anyway, so Ellen's peculiar reasoning didn't apply.

Or was it all just some strange kind of self-defence mechanism against the very idea of falling in love with someone who merely thought of her as a 'good sort'? Whatever the reason, Angel couldn't wait to meet him on Sunday.

Before the great day, a packet of mail arrived at Meadowcroft from London. Jones, the retainer who stayed on with his wife to air and take care of the Hampstead house, had instructions to send any mail in one packet every week. Clemence always opened it ceremonially after breakfast, and she studied two items very carefully before deciding what do with them.

Fred was still at home for the weekend, but had already gone off early shooting rabbits, and she and the girls were now having breakfast together.

Clemence thought very deeply, weighing up several things in her mind. Angel had been remarkably quiet lately. She had caused no disruption in the house, her nice friend Margot was coming down shortly to brighten the household, and Angel had also shown remarkable fortitude in the several trips to Temple Meads station with her mother recently. She deserved a little treat.

'These two are for you, Angel,' Clemence said quietly, handing over the two items.

Angel took them curiously, and then felt as though her heart would leap right out of her chest. One of them was a letter in a very creased envelope. She recognised the handwriting on it immediately. The other was a postcard in sepia tint, showing a wan-faced young lady holding a single rose, with elaborately printed words alongside. 'All My thoughts of Home Begin and End with You.' She turned it over quickly. Both communications had French stamps on them.

'Will you excuse me please, Mother?' She choked out the words, hardly able to believe that Clemence had handed them over so uncomplainingly. Clemence nodded, sensing for the first time the depth of her youngest daughter's emotions.

Angel went into the garden, where the sun shone warmly in the late May morning. She walked away from the house to the small gazebo, where she could be alone with Jacques' words. She could hear his voice so clearly in her head as she read what he had written. The brief postcard first of all. Not many sentiments on it, where all could read them – and her mother had undoubtedly done so – but the words were still infinitely dear.

'Just to tell you I am well, and that I think of you constantly. Jacques.'

No more than that, but she hugged it to her chest, remembering the richness of his voice, and the brush of his cheek against hers. She kept the letter a moment longer, savouring it, before tearing it open. It was dated a month ago.

'My dearest love,' she read.

'The war goes on, keeping us apart, and I have to keep reminding myself that we really met and loved, and shared our hearts. Perhaps only in wartime can a man express himself so emotionally, when all around me shells are bursting, and eternity seems never more than a heartbeat away. The countryside that was once so beautiful is desecrated and bereft, and I weep for it.

'I do not mean to sadden you, my Angel. I write also with

hope and expectation, because I am to have a few days' leave in the last week of June, and I shall be in England.'

Angel realised anew that her heart was pounding.

'I am desperate to see you. I have to report to my base near Calne in Wiltshire, where my aircraft is in need of repairs. Is it possible for you to get away and meet me without causing too much trouble? I know I ask too much, and yet I must ask it, for I cannot bear to think that we will never meet again.

'Angel, my *chérie*, I shall stay at the Swan Inn on the outskirts of Calne from June 27th. Please come there if you can. My arms ache to hold you.'

Her hands were trembling as she held the thin pages of the letter and read the final sentences. Jacques didn't know that she was already away from London, near enough to Wiltshire to get there easily. And independent enough now to drive herself, which suddenly made all things possible. Her thoughts fizzed in her head, as though she were intoxicated with champagne.

From the direction of the house, she heard a voice calling her, and sobered immediately. By the time Ellen reached her, it was only her flushed face that gave her away, but Ellen knew her too well . . .

'What's happened? Is it bad news? Is it your aviator?' She always said the word with regal importance.

Angel hesitated, then held out the hastily folded letter.

'Yes, it's from Jacques. And no, it's not bad news, just the opposite. Read it, Ellen.'

'But it's private!' She was well indoctrinated in the rules of etiquette, despite her controversial opinions.

'I know, but I want you to read it. The way Jacques feels is the way I feel. His letter says everything – and I want you to understand. Please, Ellen.'

She looked away as her sister quickly read Jacques' words, then handed the letter back without comment. Her voice was thicker than usual when she finally spoke.

'You'll go, of course.'

Angel looked at her with bright, luminous eyes. She gave her a quick embarrassed hug.

'You *do* understand. I knew you would –'

Ellen spoke dryly now. 'I'm not such a horse-box that I can't comprehend true love when I see it!'

'Oh Ellen, I do love you!'

The other girl pulled a face.

'I know you do, old thing, but save your emotions for your aviator, and for deciding how you're going to get to the Swan Inn without Mother's eagle eyes on you.'

It was enough to make both girls silent for a few minutes. And then . . .

'*Margot!*' Angel said joyfully.

Ellen looked round, as though expecting Margot Lacey to materialise through the lattice work of the gazebo at any second.

'Where?' she asked.

Angel began to laugh, as the hazy plan took shape.

'Margot's coming to stay in a week or so. She doesn't know anything about Jacques yet, but she will soon. I know she has an aunt who lives in Wiltshire. She must tell Mother that she wants to visit her, and I shall naturally offer to drive her there and stay for a couple of nights.'

The blood seemed to flow faster in her veins, knowing that those few nights would be spent with Jacques. Shivers of delight, of apprehension, of joy, mingled together in her mind as she saw the doubt on Ellen's face.

'It sounds terribly risky. You haven't thought it all out. Mother will expect a letter from this aunt of Margot's, and even then, she may well forbid you to go.'

Angel frowned and then nodded.

'Margot will receive a telephone call while Mother's out,' she said swiftly. 'Auntie will be ill, and since Margot's mother wrote to tell her Margot was staying at Meadowcroft, Auntie said she would be so cheered up to see her niece, and her friend would be welcome to stay a few nights at her home as well. How does that sound?'

'It sounds as though you should be in the acting profession, darling. Are you sure you haven't done this kind of thing before?' Ellen queried admiringly. Angel went a fiery red.

'Does it sound too awful to you? No matter how badly I want to see Jacques, all these lies are wicked, aren't they? Will St Peter bar me from entering the pearly gates, do you think, Ellen?'

She spoke facetiously, but there was an underlying worry in her words. Religious instruction was too deeply ingrained in her upbringing for her to practise deceit with any degree of comfort. Ellen squeezed her hand.

'I think even St Peter would understand, darling. What's the old saying? Love makes the world go round. Without it, none of us would be here at all, would we?' She stopped, suddenly round-eyed, as a thought struck her. 'Oh, Angel, you will be careful, won't you?'

'Of course.' Angel's voice was muffled, her face more scarlet than before as she thrust the letter into its envelope. There were some things she was definitely not prepared to discuss yet, not even with Ellen, with whom she seemed to have found an unexpected rapport lately.

'Then you can count on my help,' Ellen said more cheerfully. 'When the time comes, I'll support the fact that Margot had this telephone call from Auntie in Wiltshire – providing Margot agrees, of course. What will you do with her while you and Jacques are canoodling?'

'I haven't got that far! But she'll agree, I know she will. Margot will see this as a tremendous lark.' She could be sure of that. 'And talking of Peters – which we weren't, strictly speaking, how does yours feel at being invited to the royal tea party on Sunday?'

To Angel's surprise, it was Ellen's turn to go pink.

'He's not exactly *my* Peter. He's an independent spirit, like me – like *you*. I enjoy his company enormously. He thinks for himself, and I admire that. He believed in what we were doing with the group, and he knew when it was time to stop.'

'Well. He's obviously got quite a champion in you.'

Ellen laughed. 'And he's quite capable of coping with anything Mother deals out to him. He won't be demoralised by the Chinese silk afternoon gown and the flawless pearls and the wafer-thin sandwiches served up on the best china!'

Sunday afternoon followed the pattern of Ellen's words so exactly that she and Angel found it hard not to keep looking at one another and exploding into undignified laughter. And it would all have been such a shame, Angel thought generously. Clemence really was being the gracious hostess to perfection.

The cream Chinese silk afternoon gown gave her an added elegance, as did the flawless strands of pearls around her neck. Peter Chard was offered the plate of wafer-thin sandwiches time and again, and did his best to hook his finger into the tiny handle of the bone china teacups . . . he and Sir Fred had the same difficulty and exchanged the same sympathetic glances.

'You realise, of course, that one doesn't really care for one's daughters going into commerce, Mr Chard,' Clemence spoke with the cool self-confidence of breeding that somehow completely exonerated the snobbery in her words.

'I do realise it, Lady Bannister,' Peter replied gravely. 'I think this war has much to answer for, when we must call on our young women to perform work normally done by men. Ladies such as yourself are to be greatly admired, for being unafraid to move forward with the times.'

Clemence looked at him thoughtfully. If she detected a snuffle into Sir Fred's teacup, she chose to ignore it.

'In what way, Mr Chard?' Clemence said pleasantly.

Peter put down his cup and saucer with relief. Out of the corner of his eye, he could see Ellen and Angel, both in their pretty afternoon tea dresses, and nearer to the window was the other sister, Louise. They were like beautiful butterflies, he thought suddenly, and yet there was more strength of character in the one dear to him, than would be imagined by onlookers to this little cameo scene.

Of the others, he wasn't so sure, though Ellen had already hinted that her sister Angel was less of a flippity schoolgirl than a few months ago. He halted his wandering thoughts and looked their mother directly in the eyes.

'Ellen has told me much about you, Lady Bannister. Of your knitting circles and your care for the returning wounded. That a lady in your position should be so concerned is a tribute to British womanhood, and for what it's worth I salute you.'

Fred cleared his throat noisily. 'I think it's worth a great deal, my boy. And what of you? Did you not feel the urge to go to war, or does your farming interest prevent it?'

Peter smiled slightly.

'My farming interest, as you put it, Sir Frederick, is my life's work. I am no gentleman farmer, but one who must work hard for every penny. The country needs farmers to provide food. Even so, I would have enlisted but for personal reasons.'

Louise's cup clattered into her saucer.

'You're not one of those dreadful Conchies, are you, Mr Chard?' Her voice was sharp and accusing.

'Don't be so objectionable, Louise,' Angel said shortly. 'Do you think Ellen would be friendly with someone like that?'

'I really don't know. After the exhibition I witnessed last week, and all her other activities, nothing would surprise me. Ellen makes friends with the most impossible people –'

Clemence gave her daughter a freezing look.

'I think you had better apologise for that remark, Louise. It's most unlike you, and I trust that Mr Chard will overlook it.' She turned to Peter. 'We're all tense these days, Mr Chard, and the only excuse I can offer is that Louise is feeling so disappointed because her husband was expected home this weekend, and has had his leave cancelled.'

She looked pointedly at her eldest daughter.

'All right, I'm sorry,' Louise muttered. 'But I would still like my question answered.'

Peter looked at her with more interest. This one wasn't as spineless as she looked after all. Given the right company and the right circumstances, Louise would probably be as forthright as her sisters.

'The answer to your question is that I'm not a conscientious objector, Miss Bannister. A farming accident makes me less than perfect in the eyes of the military, I'm afraid.'

Despite himself, Peter couldn't stop the small edge creeping into his voice. No one knew that he had tried to enlist, only to be told brusquely that because of the weakness in his leg he could not be considered a whole man. It had been a bitter blow to his pride.

'Does that satisfy you, Louise, or would you like Peter to explain further? I'm sure we could produce his doctor to confirm it, if you insist,' Ellen said sarcastically.

Louise was hot with embarrassment. 'Don't be ridiculous. I do apologise, Mr Chard. One is in such confusion these days.'

'Think no more about it.' Peter smiled easily as she retreated behind the safety of her mother's affectations.

Clemence came to a decision about the self-assured young farmer, and her middle daughter's association with him.

'Then if that's all settled, perhaps you would tell us more about the work that Ellen would be expected to do for you, Mr Chard.'

'Certainly.' He managed not to look at Ellen at that moment, but they both knew they had won. 'And I would be honoured if you would call me Peter.'

Clemence nodded graciously. She listened intently as he outlined the need for proper farm accounting books to be kept, and in the process found a growing respect for her daughter who apparently was capable of dealing with such things.

While Ellen could hardly keep from laughing out loud. She was actually going to work for Peter Chard, with her mother's approval! She hadn't anticipated much argument from her father. As long as Clemence was satisfied that all was well, then Fred would go along with her decision.

She would work in the little room Peter used as an office, and sort out the enormous muddle of his books and papers. She would be a part of something solid and continuing, and it gave her such an astonishing feeling of well-being that she wondered why on earth she hadn't got what was termed 'a proper job' before!

It would hardly take up all of her time, and she knew that. She might get bored with it. It wouldn't be as exciting as campaigning or rallying, but it was a step towards her own independence, and as such she treasured it.

Chapter 9

The expertise with which Jacques de Ville landed his aircraft was second nature to him now. For a few seconds he sat with his gloved hands gripping the joystick, as if he was still somewhere above the clouds, and not safely on terra firma after all. It was only when he heard Phil Brakes yelling at him that if he was ever going to turn off the bloody engine they could get started on their few days' leave, that Jacques let out a long-held breath without even realising he had been sitting so motionless.

They were on British soil. They were in the pleasant green of an English airfield, with the scented summer grass of Wiltshire beneath them. He switched off the engine, and the quiet was like balm to his senses.

There were no blasts from enemy guns. No shells bursting all around him. No skimming the Front lines and the trenches in his flimsy and battle-scarred machine to report back to Brighton Belle on the air raids he and his wing had performed. No need for pride in assessing the number of Jerries he had slaughtered, or the enemy aircraft he had sent down in a whine of smoke and flame, trying not to imagine the German pilot's frenzy to get out, nor to hear his screams as his skin shrivelled like blackening paper scorched to a cinder in the fireplace. No sightings of the British Tommies and his own countrymen being torn to shreds beneath him in the midst of a brilliant red-orange glow that lit the sky and silhouetted remnants of bodies being flung into the air like rag dolls. No scenes of tattered corpses spread-eagled on barbed wire in No Man's Land between the lines, hanging like pathetic bits of discarded washing. No more fear . . .

'Are you going to sit there all day, Cap, or are you coming in to report? I've got me a nice little popsy tucked up and waiting for me, even if you don't!'

Phil's voice penetrated through the temporary deafness that always came after flying. Phil's oil-blackened face peered at him from the outside of the plane, and Jacques forced a grin to his lips, chapped from exposure to the air. They had three days' leave, and with the kind of desperation that every serviceman recognised, they were determined to forget the war for that brief while. If it were possible . . .

He scrambled stiffly out of the cockpit, slapping Phil on the shoulder in the strange wartime camaraderie that knit them together closer than Siamese twins. They knew more about one another than their own relatives.

Each loved and hated the knowledge. It was a responsibility that neither could shirk. If one of them met with disaster, the other would go through fire and hell to see that their nearest and dearest were informed. But that day was far away from the here and now, and Jacques spoke with forced heartiness.

'I hope she's worth it, Phil. And don't do anything I wouldn't do,' he said as they headed for the operations room.

'That gives me plenty of leeway then,' Phil said cheekily. He eyed his leader enviously. 'If I had your luck with that little beauty you told me about, I might never report back. Seeing her, are you, Cap?'

'Perhaps.' Jacques held up two crossed fingers. Phil chuckled, his round face mischievously owl-like now with the white circles around his eyes where he had removed his goggles.

'Garn. A bloody good-looking Frenchy like you! 'Course you're seeing her, and good luck to you. Still, I reckon I'll be having just as good a time with mine. They're all the same beneath the blankets, when all's said and done.'

He whistled jubilantly as they reached the door of the operations room, and Jacques gave a sigh of relief. Phil was a good pal, one of the best, but he was in no mood to listen to his coarseness right now. And he was trying hard not to admit privately that he was suddenly nervous at the thought of seeing Angel Bannister again.

Apprehensive might be a more accurate way to describe how he felt. What if he had glorified in his mind their one magical night? What if they looked at one another and each saw a stranger? What if she didn't come to the Swan Inn? He could hardly blame her. He presumed too much. He should never have written to her in the way he had, baring his soul, his heart.

She had never written to him – that was his fault, for not giving her his field address, but how did he know if she had wanted to write to him? He knew nothing about her, except that she had felt so gloriously right in his arms. And Jacques de Ville, who rarely felt uncertain about anything, was filled with anxiety and self-doubt for the first time in his life.

Well, he wouldn't have to wait much longer to find out if she was coming or not. A few more hours, and he would know . . . a few more hours to find heaven or hell . . .

Margot had been installed at Meadowcroft for two weeks, and was pondering on whether or not she was really enjoying life with Angel's family. It wasn't that she minded the country all that much. It was just that time seemed to slow down so drearily, and she and Angel had always had such fun at college, where everything had moved at a fast pace.

And in London, of course – dear old London – everyone was so much busier and keener and – well, less *countrified.* There was no other way of putting it. Not that she would upset darling Angel for the world by telling her so.

If she was strictly honest, it wasn't half as bad down here

as Margot had expected. There had even been a bit of excitement on the day she arrived, when Angel had wanted to show her around the village, and she had borrowed Ellen's bicycle and wobbled her way along the lanes with Angel on her own machine, amid shrieks of laughter.

It wasn't the hideous excitement of the village murder, if one could apply the term to it, but *real* excitement. The sort that could get a girl's pulse racing and put some extra colour into her cheeks.

A battalion of soldiers had arrived for billetting in the area, marching through the village and whistling those dear little army tunes that were becoming all the rage. 'Pack up your troubles in your old kit bag and smile, smile, smile . . .'

And all the village girls were smiling and giggling as the soldiers winked and waved, and the children marched along beside the soldiers, waving their Union flags, and trilling along with them. Such fun!

She and Angel had been in the village when the leading trucks came through, rattling on the cobblestones and stopping every now and then while the sergeants consulted sheafs of papers and detailed the lower ranks where they were to be billetted for the next couple of weeks.

'There's a new training area this side of Bristol,' Angel told Margot. 'Daddy said that Bristol is bursting at the seams with soldiers, so they're having to find accommodation farther afield for them all. I suppose we'll get our share.'

Margot looked at her with shining eyes. She was as dark as Angel was fair. They made a startling and attractive contrast as they leaned on their bicycles and waved the soldiers through.

'I hope we'll get some nice ones. Won't your mother object frightfully, Angel?'

Angel laughed. 'I daresay. Though Mother's becoming *frightfully* resigned to everything the war is doing to us all. Haven't you noticed that already?'

'Yes, I have. She's quite a lady, isn't she? I can see where you girls get your independence.'

'Except for Louise. She still hangs on to Mummy's apron strings, in spite of being married.'

Margot gave a little snort.

'Oh well, you can hardly count Stanley as a real man, can you? I mean, he's not like any of *these*, is he?'

She waved furiously at the line of soldiers turning to whistle at them.

'We've all changed, haven't we?' Angel said, waving dutifully. 'Can you imagine this kind of behaviour being condoned a year ago? It would be scandalous – and even now, we're getting some very funny looks from some of the village folk. We'd better go home before I disgrace myself by forgetting that I'm Miss Bannister from the big house!'

They turned reluctantly away from all the noise and excitement.

'How's Ellen getting on with her farmer?' Margot said as they wheeled their bicycles through the unusually crowded village and into the open lanes. 'I haven't seen her yet.'

'I think it's all fairly blissful,' Angel commented. 'Though if you're looking for a romance there, don't bother. Ellen's just not interested.'

'What a funny girl!' Margot smiled broadly. 'She's not much like her sister then, is she?'

'As a matter of fact, Margot,' Angel said in a studied voice. 'I rather wanted to talk to you about that.'

Margot slid off the bicycle in an ungainly heap.

'I *knew* there was something going on! I could tell by your voice on the telephone – and it's not just the fact that you kept your driving prowess a secret from me! We've shared too many secrets, darling, and you've had that about-to-burst look all over you ever since I arrived! So do *tell* me, before I begin imagining all sorts of things!'

They walked slowly, leaning on the bicycles. Angel didn't look at Margot as she told her everything in a rush. About the night she and Jacques had met, when she had spent the night in an hotel in London instead of going straight home; about the awful fuss when her mother had discovered her *faux pas*; about the roses, and the letter that had arrived recently.

Only then did she glance at Margot, to see her friend's eyes round and shining and admiring.

'I say, old thing, what a simply marvellous adventure. And have you fallen madly in love with your Frenchman? Is it the Real Thing, as they say?'

'Of course it is! Do you think I'm in the habit of spending the night with every stranger I meet?' She bit her lip as the angry words tumbled out.

'Oh Margot, I'm sorry. I didn't mean to snap. It's just – it's just –'

Margot's voice was gentle.

'It doesn't matter. I'm a thoughtless idiot for being flippant as usual. I'm the one who should be sorry, Angel darling.'

Angel turned away again, her face fiery.

'I haven't told you everything yet. I feel so guilty for involving you in deception without your knowledge, Margot, and I ask your forgiveness for that –'

'Don't be silly. When did you need to ask?'

'I'm asking now,' Angel said carefully.

Margot stopped walking again, and Angel was obliged to stop too, turning to face her. A long way behind them, the slow march of footsteps and a distant singing told of the soldiers' progress through the village.

'Is there a chance for you to see him again? Is he on leave? Tell me what you want me to do,' Margot said instantly.

Weak tears filled Angel's eyes.

'Oh, I can't think why I was getting such cold feet about asking you. You're the tops, Margot –'

Margot was brisk and businesslike. 'Well, I might be if you tell me of your plan. You do have a plan, I suppose?'

They moved hastily onto the grass verge as the trucks came slowly through the lane, followed by a depleted line of soldiers. The truck driver learned his head out of the window.

'Can you tell me the way to a place called Meadowcroft, ladies? Sounds like a few of these lads are going to have it cushy for a few weeks,' he added cheekily. 'Real lady of the manor in residence, so I'm told.'

Angel kept a straight face as she pointed out the direction of the house. So they were to get their quota of soldiers after all. She didn't know whether to be pleased or irritated, since civilians clearly had little say in the matter.

They waited until the little convoy had gone, but Margot's interest in the soldiers was less than her excitement over Angel's plan, which she quickly outlined.

'It'll be no trouble at all, darling. Auntie doesn't have a telephone, but she could easily be contacting me from a friend's house, but we'll make it clear that it'll be no use your mother calling her to check up on you. You must call your mother from your hotel to say that you've arrived safely, and while you're in the arms of your beloved, I shall make the supreme sacrifice and visit dear old Auntie, who will be absolutely delighted to see me. When Jacques' leave is up, you can drive to Auntie's cottage and collect me. How does that sound?'

'Wonderful! I knew I could rely on you, Margot. I shall never be able to repay you.'

'You probably will, one of these days. I haven't given up hope of finding myself a lover yet!' she teased. 'I shall call on you for assistance then, Angel.'

'You'll have it,' Angel said at once.

It all worked incredibly easily. The presence of the four soldiers billetted in the big house deflected some of Clemence's attention from the girls. She found it frequently necessary to pacify Cook's irritation at having to prepare meals for four extra heartily-eating men, when food was beginning to be in short supply. She greeted Margot's request a few days later with nothing short of undisguised relief.

'I'm sorry I was out when your dear Auntie telephoned, Margot dear, but I see no reason why you shouldn't visit her for a few days. And it was charming of her to invite Angel too.'

'She didn't invite me. I did ask Margot while she was speaking on the telephone, but no luck,' Ellen pretended to pull a face, adding her weight to the authenticity of the tale. To her horror, Clemence took her seriously.

'Perhaps Margot would write to ask her Aunt if you could go too, Ellen –'

'Oh no, I was only teasing! I'm far too busy at the farm,' Ellen said hastily. 'Besides, Margot is really Angel's friend. I wouldn't want to chime in.'

'You know you wouldn't do that,' Margot said. 'But unfortunately, Auntie's cottage is very small, and there's not much room for visitors. We shall have to squeeze up as it is.'

'That's settled, then,' Ellen said with relief. 'At least we'll have a bit more room around here with you two out of the way. Perhaps Louise will be a bit less rattled with more space in the house too.'

'That's not very gracious of you, Ellen dear.'

'Oh, Margot knows what I mean. She's not the sort to take offence, Mother!'

'Of course not,' Margot said brightly. 'Then is it all right for Angel and me to go at the end of the month, Lady Bannister? That was the time Auntie mentioned.'

Clemence smiled, pleased at the girl's consideration in visiting an elderly aunt. 'I'll have to confirm it with Angel's father, but I'm sure he'll make no objection.'

They drove away from Meadowcroft in bright sunshine. The two small suitcases were stowed securely, and Angel promised Clemence that she would telephone as soon as possible to report on their safe arrival. Only when they had got well away from the house and were spinning along the road in a north easterly direction, did she let out a gleeful whoop of relief.

'I never thought we'd actually do it! Oh, Margot, are we very wicked?'

Margot laughed, pulling off her straw hat and letting the warm breeze lift her dark hair as she leaned back against the seat. Angel discarded her own hat with a little gesture of bravado, uncaring as the pins tumbled out of her fair hair to let it cascade around her shoulders, and Margot openly admired her friend's confidence in handling the motor.

'Well, if you're not going to be, darling, this whole escapade is a waste of time!'

A thrill as sweet and sharp as a flame ran through Angel's body. This day had seemed as though it would never arrive. But she was really on her way to meet Jacques. She was going to stay with him at the Swan Inn, and it would be as ecstatic as the first time . . . her heart jolted, and she spoke without thinking, her voice abrupt with sudden nerves.

'I'm scared.' She ran her tongue around lips that were suddenly dry.

'Of Jacques?'

She shook her head vigorously. Her hair swung over her shoulders like a shining cloud.

'Not of Jacques. Of me. Perhaps I've just been imagining how wonderful it all was. Our feelings might have changed. Could I have been in love with love, and not with the man?'

Margot spoke frankly. 'You're such a goose, Angel. If you could see the way your eyes sparkle when you speak of him, and the way they soften when you're thinking of him, you wouldn't question it. It's perfectly obvious that you love the man!'

'But does he love me? Truly love me, I mean.' She mumbled the words that tormented her.

‘Didn’t he ask you to stay with him? Didn’t his letters tell you so? Why this sudden doubt?’

Angel looked straight ahead as the reliable little Sunbeam took her nearer and nearer to Jacques.

‘I keep thinking of those wounded boys coming home in the trains, Margot. You’ve never seen them as I have. Did you know our chauffeur, Hobbs, is dead? He was on one of the trains Mother and I met. It was terrible. He had no legs, and he was shell-shocked and gassed, and I began to think I could never face another wounded man. Well, I’ve seen plenty more since then, and it’s made me realise how vulnerable we all are.’

‘Vulnerable?’

Angel glanced at her. ‘Men on leave have a kind of desperate desire for security about them, Margot. They never know if they’ll see another tomorrow. Perhaps that’s the way Jacques felt when we met. Perhaps he’ll see me differently now.’

‘Of course he won’t. He’s coming back to you, isn’t he?’

Angel ignored the question.

‘Margot, have you ever thought how many lonely women there are going to be after this war? Fifty years from now, there will be an entire generation of elderly spinsters. Young widows, or those who chose to stay unmarried after their sweethearts died at the Front. I sometimes think about them –’

‘For goodness’ sake, stop being so morbid. It’s not like you, Angel. You’ve changed, darling. But you’re Jacques de Ville’s sweetheart now, so cheer up! If you’re going to be miserable for the next three days, he’ll wish he’d stayed in France.’

‘You’re right. And if I didn’t have butterflies in my stomach, it would mean that all this wasn’t so terribly important, wouldn’t it? Remember how Miss Phipps always used to say that at college? It’s still ridiculous though. I’m the happiest girl in the world, so why should I be thinking such dismal thoughts?'

'Because you're too nice, that's why. Much nicer than me. I'd only be thinking of myself, not all the unknown women who aren't lucky enough to be meeting a delicious Frenchman!' Margot spoke candidly, and Angel laughed at her nonsense. Yes, she was lucky, so lucky. She must cling on to that thought.

By late afternoon they had reached the cottage where Margot's Auntie lived. Angel saw the affection with which the two Lacey women greeted one another. As soon as she could, she said good-bye to them both and continued alone. Not for anything could she have endured sitting through a formal afternoon tea, knowing that Jacques was waiting for her. The brief uncertainty was passing, and in its place was a soaring excitement.

She arrived at the Swan Inn and sat in the car for a few moments, wondering what to do. Should she enquire if Jacques had arrived? Was she supposed to announce herself as Madame de Ville . . .?

And then, as though she watched the scene in slow motion, she saw a tall figure emerge from the open door of the lovely old Inn. A uniformed figure that she recognised at once, and her heart began to beat so fast she thought it would burst.

She was only a short distance from the building, yet it seemed an agonising wait until Jacques was at her side. Her breath was tight in her throat. He looked just as she remembered. Dashingly continental, with the breeze ruffling his dark hair, and his eyes deep and fathomless, and infinitely dear . . .

The car door was open, his fingers were touching hers, and in seconds she was outside and in his arms.

'So you came! I prayed that you would. I've waited so long for this, my Angel,' he spoke the thickened words against her mouth. She tasted his breath, sweet and fresh.

'I too! Oh Jacques, it's so wonderful to see you.'

But she was suddenly conscious of how they must look to any curious eyes behind the windows of the Inn. 'Jacques – can we go inside?'

'Of course, *chérie*.' He released her at once, and reached for her suitcase. For a moment he hesitated, then looked straight into her eyes. What she saw there made her hold her breath for an instant. 'Angel, I've booked a room for us as husband and wife. Forgive me if I did wrong –'

'No,' she said quickly, feeling the warmth in her face as she lowered her eyes in a burst of shyness. 'No – it's all right, Jacques. It's – what I expected.'

Yet the moment put an odd little constraint between them. It had been necessary for him to ask, and for her to affirm, but it made the assignation no more than it was – a lovers' meeting in an anonymous hotel. While Angel realised with a fierce urgency that more than all the world she wished it was true. Mr and Mrs Jacques de Ville . . .

The Swan Inn was a more discreet and elegant old inn than the Hotel Portland. The receptionist welcomed Mrs de Ville, pleased that the officer hadn't had too long a wait for his wife to join him. She eyed Angel enviously, from her fine clothes and lovely face, to the handsome flying officer who so clearly adored her.

Clearing her throat a little, she informed them that dinner would be at seven-thirty, but that they could order afternoon tea in the lounge if they wished.

They declined the tea. There was no lift, and they walked up the two short flights of stairs to room 32. Jacques' belongings were already scattered about, making it instantly less formal. He closed the door behind them, threw Angel's case on the bed and swung her off her feet in a crazy, ecstatic spiral.

'You'll make me dizzy!' She gasped and laughed as the room spun, her arms tight around his neck. He looked down into her shining, luminous eyes, her hair tumbling and dishevelled, her mouth soft and parted.

He slowed his spinning, circling her slowly in his arms, his body so close to hers she could feel every warm part of it like a second skin, his hard and masculine, hers soft and melting against him, and his eyes never left her face.

'God, how I've missed you. Was it really just one night we shared, my Angel? The memory of it has been etched on my mind, yet at times it's been like a beautiful, shadowy dream –'

'The same for me,' she whispered, recognising that sexual awareness between them was quickly replacing the childlike excitement.

'Angel, I want you so much.' His voice was deep and almost tortured. 'God knows I never intended to drag you up here and behave like an animal. I'd planned a sunlit stroll, perhaps, and later a lingering dinner with candlelight and wine, but I'm not sure that I can wait that long –'

'Oh, Jacques –' she breathed his name, unsure how to reply. Her needs were as urgent as his own, her waiting no less painful.

She was too innocent to know how to take the initiative, nor to guess whether women ever did such a thing. The subject of sexual relations between men and women was never mentioned in families such as Angel's. It was just assumed that somehow one got to know about it. Perhaps on the night before a wedding, some sketchy information would be given, and the young bride would learn that on the wedding night, the husband would initiate her into the art of lovemaking, whether gently or brutally. From then on, it would be a duty between them.

Because of natural embarrassment in a parent, there would be no mention of this sweet flowering of emotions, of love so tangible it seemed to flow like heady wine between them, of a passion that made duty a word with no meaning. They were as truly married in spirit as if a preacher had intoned over them, and Angel swayed against Jacques' body with a clear and loving invitation in her eyes.

He lifted her bodily as easily as if she was weightless. He carried her to the bed, interspersing each step with tiny kisses on her neck that sent exquisite little shivers running through her. He lay her on the coverlet, and his fingers moved to unfasten the buttons on her blouse. She saw how they shook, and knew that Jacques was as affected by her nearness as she was by his. It endeared him to her all the more.

He didn't tear at her clothes, nor act with the wild impatience to possess her that she sensed in him. His desire was controlled, but she felt its power, strong and vital. When at last he wrapped the coverlet around their naked bodies so that they were nestled like two lovebirds inside it, her loveliness opened up to him like a flower in the sun, and Angel knew with certainty that tonight he would not leave her.

For the next three days, they were like children, not recognising tomorrow, living only for today. They walked the lanes, explored the green meadows and sat by gentle streams, climbed wooden stiles and ran laughing when a curious cow thrust her wet nose too near to where they lay on the grass. At night they were lovers, enraptured with each other, oblivious to the world outside, deliberately pushing aside the fact that it must all end very soon. That this was only an interlude . . .

On the last night, Angel slept peacefully, still wrapped in Jacques' arms, his body still warming her. Suddenly she was awake, aware that it was difficult to breathe, and that the comfort she had derived from him had changed.

His arms held her as if in a vice. The warmth of his body was unpleasantly damp against her skin, and he was muttering in his sleep. Unintelligible, broken words at first that frightened her. And then his voice was filled with terror.

Angel, horrified, translated the words from Jacques' native French.

'. . . *No* . . . dear God, Phil, keep him in your sights . . . we've got him . . . don't let him burn . . . *Christ*, why doesn't he die! . . . I'm climbing, climbing . . . can't get above the clouds in time . . . they'll see us, they'll be on us . . . the noise nearly splits my head in two . . . burning, burning . . . kill the bastard before he kills us . . . must do it, *must* . . . don't let me see his face . . . empty sockets of his eyes . . . nothing left . . . just fear and burning . . .'

Jacques jerked violently in his sleep, his arms squeezing Angel so much that she cried out. He awoke immediately, breathing heavily, and Angel could see the sweat glistening on him in the light from the window. His eyes were open wide, but as yet he was still somewhere else, in the private hell of his own imagination, and the nightmare went on . . .

'Jacques.' Angel whispered his name, trembling. She didn't know if she should break the spell or not. You didn't waken people from sleep-walking, but this was something very different, something she only half understood.

He turned to her with a shuddering sigh, his hands relinquishing their grip on her. From her ashen face, he knew at once that she had witnessed his shame. He had seen it too often in others, not to know the ugliness of the nightmares.

'Forgive me,' he said harshly. 'It's something you shouldn't ever have to see –'

She put her arms around him, as if to shield him, as if he was her child.

'Do I seem so fragile that I can't share your pain? Don't shut me out, Jacques. Don't make me less of a woman than I am.'

He spoke with a mixture of emotions in his voice.

'No one could ever be more of a woman to me than you, my darling one.'

Her eyes pricked as he said the endearment in English instead of his usual French. Somehow to Angel it bound them closer, and still holding each other, they finally slept.

Chapter 10

Jacques gave Angel an address where she could write to him. On their last morning, they clung together for a final moment before parting, and then she had to go and collect Margot, her eyes stinging so much she could hardly see the road she was driving along, already bereft.

She refused to talk to Margot or Ellen about the time she had spent with Jacques. It was too precious, too private. It was all she had.

After another week at Meadowcroft, Margot went back to London, and the house was as before, except for the breezy billetted soldiers who brightened the days with their nonsense. None of them looked old enough to shave their whiskers.

Angel found herself watching them, making private wagers with herself as to which of them would come back from the Front. When she realised what she was doing, she was horrified. It was the war. The phrase was on everyone's lips. The war took the blame for everything.

There was a succession of billetted soldiers. Then Clemence and Fred offered the use of their house as a convalescent home for any soldiers far from home, and there were usually half a dozen of them there as well.

The Bannister girls were polite and friendly, but careful not to overstep the mark. It wasn't done to be too free. Clemence gave them their lead, and they stuck by it rigidly. Even though many of the old conventions were gone, some things were still adhered to, and would always be so.

Surprisingly, Louise struck up an odd friendship with a Scotsman, Dougal Mackie. He'd been one of their first guests, as Clemence called them, came back wounded in December, and asked particularly to convalesce at Meadowcroft until returning to France. His arm had been very badly gashed, and he was partly deaf from shell-shock, but none of his spirit had been deflated. He wasn't coarse like some of the others, and he intrigued Louise especially with tales of Scotland. He had bright red hair, and his eager blue eyes flashed with pleasure whenever he talked about his beloved Highlands.

The Bannister girls, who had travelled extensively in Europe before the war, had never been to Scotland, and Louise decided it was an omission she must put right someday.

'Old Stanley had better watch himself, don't you think?' Angel said teasingly, when Ellen came home from the farm one evening. 'Louise may be quite unaware of it, but Dougal's eyes follow her wherever she goes!'

Ellen snorted. The Ministry men had been swarming over the farm, and she and Peter were sorely put out by their silent insinuations that the books weren't in order, and that more food could be produced for the war effort.

'I'm not in the least interested in Louise's affairs –'

'It's not an affair!' Angel said quickly. 'I'm just glad that Louise isn't so bored any more.'

Ellen looked mildly surprised. 'Was she ever bored? I thought she was too busy being a do-gooder like Mother to waste her energies in being bored.'

'That's unfair. They both work tremendously hard. And it can't be pleasant for her, hardly ever seeing Stanley. He might just as well be in France for all the leaves he gets.' Angel was indignant and Ellen had the grace to look shamefaced.

'All right, it was rotten of me. If you'd had a day like I've had, you'd feel bitchy too. What have you been doing for the war effort today, sister dear?'

'I've pushed Private Wilkins down to the village and back in his wheelchair, and I've delivered some of Mother's knitted socks to the posting station in Bristol. Any more questions?'

Ellen gave her a quick hug.

'Sorry, old thing. It's just that you seem to be handling your war much better than I am. Odd, isn't it?'

She strode away from Angel in some embarrassment, saying she was going to find something to eat in the kitchen.

Angel overlooked the inference that Ellen considered her own character stronger than either of her sisters'. She was too busy hiding her own feelings, and the sudden lump that filled her throat. She wasn't handling her war at all. Every day, she scanned the newpapers, fearful at the growing casualty lists, terrified that one day the name of Jacques de Ville would leap out at her, sending the sunshine out of her life.

June seemed an eternity ago. Jacques hadn't been back to England since. And why was it that the minute he was out of her sight, the memories faded so fast? Why didn't they linger, giving her something to cling to, to remember . . .? Wasn't that what memories were supposed to do? It wasn't that they weren't beautiful. They were the dearest and the best.

She had written to him, of course, but his replies had been sketchy and brief, and in the last month, there had been nothing at all. She was so afraid. Her letters hadn't been returned, and it was the one hope that she had that he was still all right. And the war to end all wars dragged on . . .

In September there had been a frantic letter from Margot to say that her young brother Edward had lied about his age and enlisted and was already in France. Her mother was distraught, and was insisting on their leaving London and going to Norfolk to her family home. Margot would simply hate it, and she longed to see Angel again, and what did

Angel think about them getting some V.A.D. training and going over there themselves?

Angel's heart leapt when she read the words. Her parents would never allow it. Margot's mother had reluctantly said that she would agree, if only so that Margot could keep an eye on dear naughty Edward, as if she would find him waiting for her on the quayside at Calais.

'At least *think* about it, Angel darling,' Margot's letter beseeched. 'Who knows – you may find a way to see Someone Else!'

The thought had screamed into Angel's head long before she reached that part of the letter. A chance to find Jacques. To be with him in France. To be part of that bloody war . . .

The saliva dried in her mouth as the remembered babblings of some of the convalescent soldiers at Meadowcroft surged through her mind. The terrible gas that seeped insidiously into eyes and lungs. The shattered bodies of comrades who had been talking to them seconds before. The horrific trench songs . . .

'If you want to find your sweetheart,
I know where he is,
Hanging on the Front Line wire . . .'

The unforgettable sights she had seen with Clemence of all those coming home at Temple Meads station . . . poor Hobbs . . . the despair and the humiliation of those young boys who had gone away so eagerly, and come back as broken heroes, every one . . .

She was still thinking about Margot's suggestion, and the months had gone on. Margot's mother had had a slight stroke and all thoughts of Margot leaving her had vanished for a while, but she was now quite well in her old family home near King's Lynn.

In October, King George V had paid a second visit to the Western Front and been involved in an accident when his chestnut mare reared up in fright at the cheers of the men of the Royal Flying Corps. The King had fractured his pelvis and suffered severe bruising.

'The poor man!' Clemence had exclaimed, reading out the news from the newspaper. 'But doesn't it just prove that he's human like the rest of us?'

'Did you suppose that royalty didn't have pelvises and flesh that could bruise, Mother?' Ellen said in amusement, winking at Angel.

Angel didn't hear her. The imagery of the scene was too vivid in her mind. She was sorry for the King, of course, and it must be horribly painful . . . but the group of RFC men may well have included Jacques among those who were cheering and smiling . . . and he was suddenly close to her in spirit, as it seemed he hadn't been for months.

'Mother, I think I'd like to learn First Aid.'

Angel said the words in a tremendous rush before she could stop to think.

Clemence lowered her newspaper a fraction. A year ago she would have been horrified. Now, after looking doubtfully at Angel's determined face for a moment, she gave a small resigned sigh.

'I suppose it's not a bad thing to do. There's an establishment in Bristol where you could learn to roll bandages and things like that. It would be a useful occupation. Yes, I think it's an admirable suggestion, my dear.'

Angel tried not to look at Ellen. Ellen had a knack of reading her mind. Ellen would know immediately that learning First Aid was not going to be confined to rolling bits of cotton into bandages in a First Aid Depot in Bristol. Ellen would *know* . . .

Christmas came and went. The soldiers still in the house helped to make it a jolly affair. Dougal's arm had got infected now, and he was receiving daily medical attention in Bristol, and so still remaining at Meadowcroft.

'My God, I think you may be right,' Ellen whispered to Angel.

'His eyes do follow Louise around. He's like an adoring sheepdog.'

'I'd say he's more the handsome wolfhound, if you get my meaning,' Angel said. 'Stanley definitely comes out second-best in the vitality stakes!'

Stanley was home on leave for Christmas, and oh-so-correct in his dealings with the billetted soldiers. He couldn't relax. He was an officer, and would always be aware of his status. Let the girls play their party games, and his parents-in-law sit back and smile indulgently. Stanley knew his place, and would have a word or two with Louise later. It was hardly seemly to cavort about like this. Christmas or no Christmas, it really wasn't cricket.

Sir Fred Bannister sat dreamily, his mind many miles away from the homely little scene. Big house or small, the traditions were the same. The great Christmas lunch, somewhat depleted by necessity this year, the holly and the ivy, the huge tree in the window adorned with painted fir cones and decorations, the paper chains the girls made every year to drape across the room, the bowls of Christmas roses and greenery from the hedgerows that Clemence arranged so artistically. Christmas was Christmas . . . and in a snug little cottage in Yorkshire, his Harriet would be spending a lonely day with only an elderly neighbour or two for company. He raised his glass of port wine in silent tribute to his love, and wished with all his heart that he could be there with her now.

Soon, he had promised her. As soon as he could get away from the jollifications at home, they would have a late Christmas of their own. He would take her to the coast, to Scarborough, perhaps, and they'd spend a few nights in a posh hotel as plain Mr and Mrs Anybody. Harriet had kissed him with her soft lips, her arms holding him close, the warm musky scent of her pervading his nostrils and intoxicating his soul.

Ah, Harriet, Harriet . . . the music of her name drifted

through his mind, an echoing refrain that had been repeated a thousand times. Why didn't I meet you a lifetime ago . . .?

'Daddy, you're going to spill port wine all over the carpet if you drop off to sleep!'

It was Angel's amused, melodious voice that penetrated his dreaming, and his eyes opened quickly. She knelt down in front of him, his precious girl, and gently took the glass from his hand. He bent swiftly to kiss her. She was the best reason for having married Clemence. To his shame, Fred acknowledged it yet again.

Angel straightened, strangely moved by the tender, faraway look she had momentarily glimpsed in her father's eyes. How odd. How extremely odd. It had reminded her so much of the yearning in her mirrored face when she was thinking of Jacques.

They were shrieking at her to join in the game of charades with the rest of the young company, and she forgot all about her father's dreaming look. Or rather, it was filed away in her mind, the way interesting bits of unrelated information were.

In January, 1916, conscription came in. Single men were called upon first. There was much confusion. Those of the Quaker faith refused to join, being adamant against killing. Many conscientious objectors were brought before local tribunals, and if the objections were genuine, they were given other important work to do, such as First Aid assistance at the Front, or working on the land. If they totally refused to help the war effort, they were simply sent to prison.

'Poor things,' Angel said sympathetically. 'Why should they be penalised for their faith?'

'People always have been. Religion has caused more trouble in the world than any other factor. Don't you know your history, darling?' Fred said, preparing to leave for Yorkshire, and thankfully so. A whole three weeks at home, and he was straining at the leash, stifled by Clemence's very presence.

'We've got one at the farm,' Ellen said suddenly. 'At least, we're being sent one. I'm not at all keen to meet him.'

Angel was offended on the unknown man's behalf. 'Why not? He's no different from any other man. If he does a good job for your Mr Chard, that's all that matters, isn't it?'

'He's not *my* Mr Chard,' Ellen replied automatically. 'Anyway, he's probably very dreary, one of those pompous young men we used to see in London all the time. Thank God Mother can't fill the house with those any more!'

Angel agreed wholeheartedly, watching Ellen as she pedalled away on her bicycle towards Peter Chard's farm, well wrapped up in a heavy coat and boots, for the winter months were not the best farming weather. The new man was arriving that day. He was called Andrew Pender, and he was neither dreary nor pompous. He was a Cornishman, very tall and dashing, with crinkly brown hair and a wide wide smile. Ellen took one look at him and fell head over heels in love.

'I shall be leaving here soon.' Dougal Mackie made the statement one morning, the day after Fred had gone to Yorkshire, intending to stay for several weeks, ostensibly to supervise the adapting of the old machinery for the new intake of cloth for army uniforms.

'Surely not!' It was Louise who answered Dougal, her face slightly flushed, her eyes lowered quickly. 'Your arm still pains you badly, Dougal. I've seen how you wince at times –'

He gave a short laugh. 'I doubt the army will think it a fitting reason to keep me away from the Front, lassie!'

Clemence had taken offence at the soldier's free use of the term, until informed scathingly by Ellen that it was a perfectly natural Scottish way of speaking.

Clemence added her own thoughts.

'Dougal, don't be in too much of a hurry. We shall miss you. You've become almost a – a fixture here.' It was going too far for Clemence to say he'd almost become one of the family.

'I thought the doctors weren't too happy about the torn ligaments,' Angel put in. 'What use is a soldier whose arm collapses in the midst of firing a rifle?'

Dougal smiled at her. 'You've become so canny, Miss Angel, with your First Aid training! Aye, mebbe 'twould be a mistake to return too soon. But I've been here too long, taking advantage of your hospitality. I'm thinking of asking for leave to visit my mother. She's unwell, and she's no young any more.'

Angel could see that Louise was dying to say that Dougal hadn't been here too long at all, but such sentiments would clearly be indiscreet from a young married woman. They had become remarkably attached, but she was quite sure that Louise would never betray her husband. Nor go away to an hotel with a man the way Angel had done with Jacques . . .

She felt a catch in her throat. There had been a long letter from him at last. A letter that terrified Angel. They were now bombing German factories. Flying right over Germany and dropping bombs that destroyed munitions and armaments, and although Jacques' words were restrained, Angel didn't need telling how dangerous these missions were.

She prayed for him every night. There were times when she wondered if anybody was listening to her prayers. Her faith was no longer as intense and all-believing as it had been at school. She was questioning the very basis of her upbringing. But what kind of God could allow these terrible things to happen, such needless slaughter and agony? Her own shaky belief was one more thing to appal her.

Before Dougal Mackie could make any enquiries as to his future, the infection in his arm worsened dramatically and he was admitted to hospital in Bristol with a raging fever. Gangrene was suspected, and for several weeks a very real fear of amputation. They all visited him at various times, and Angel guessed that Louise made many more visits than she told the rest of them. Several times Angel thought she could hear her weeping in her bedroom. She wanted to go to her, but knew that Louise's pride would forestall any such comfort.

At long last the danger of amputation was past, but Dougal was to be discharged from the army. His right arm was not entirely useless, but would never stand up to the rigours of warfare. He came back to Meadowcroft far more subdued than when he left, with a bitterness in his heart that matured his young face considerably. And as soon as he was fit to travel, he was going home to Scotland.

In February, in Europe, there was news of a terrifying new German bombardment of the historic fortress of Verdun in northeast France. The Bannister girls had visited the city once long ago, and could identify with the horrors more readily than in any other newspaper report. The snow was thick on the ground in France now, and the reporters made much of the 'mincing machine' of Verdun, where French and Allied men were being cut down by the minute. The once green fields were now a barren wasteland, with only the stumps of trees where lush vegetation had flourished. It was said that the noise of the battles could be heard across the Channel in the southern coastal towns of England as a low rumble resembling an earthquake.

In February, in England, The Honourable Stanley Crabb was blown to bits while inspecting the site for a larger munitions factory on the remnants of an old one, converted from a small cramped button factory. The explanation given for the explosion was that spilled dregs of gunpowder had collected in small pockets when the old building had been pulled down, and some careless newspaper reporter accompanying the military men had inadvertently lit a cigarette and thrown down the match. There were six casualties and one fatality.

Louise wondered what time Clemence and Angel were going to get back for dinner that evening, having gone to meet the ambulance train at Temple Meads. She sat aimlessly at the pianoforte, trying very hard to sort out her muddled feelings on certain matters, when the housekeeper announced the arrival of two gentlemen in uniform.

She turned almost gladly. More billetted men would be a relief, whatever they were like. Their presence may stop her from thinking what a terrible mistake she had made in marrying Stanley to please her mother, and may help to squash these other wicked longings creeping into her mind every single day – the minute she saw the officers, she knew this was a different visitation.

Louise wasn't normally a hysterical woman. Nevertheless, the village women who came in to help Cook with the kitchen work reported afterwards that it was pitiful to hear that poor Mrs Crabb wailing and carrying on when the officers told her that her husband was dead. Must have thought a lot of him, for all his stuck-up ways. There was no accounting for folk . . .

Louise wept into her lace-edged handkerchief, sick to her stomach at realising that the feeling she felt most was the most acute, yet appalling sense of relief. The officers cleared their throats and murmured comforting platitudes, one of them daring to put an arm around the grieving young widow and sensing the tautness of her supple body.

Poor young woman, he thought sympathetically. But a handsome one too. Perhaps in time she would find someone to take the place of that pompous Crabb fellow. An officer and a gentleman, Stanley certainly was, but the general opinion of him was that he was the most boring bore in the British army.

Snuffling into her lace handkerchief, Louise couldn't shake off the image of Stanley being blown to bits. But it was not in the least as the embarrassed officers imagined.

She was seeing Stanley's arms and legs flying off in four directions. His head shooting upwards, the eyes still slightly surprised and affronted at what was happening, the fleshy mouth hanging open in that stupid vacant way of his. And then there was that other bit in the middle. That ridiculous, flaccid appendage that rarely stood up straight like a little soldier the way it was supposed to, and was probably filling up with pee as it wobbled about, showering everybody around him . . . Louise, who hardly ever let such coarseness enter her mind, let alone pass her lips, was suddenly giggling wildly at the thought of dear departed Stanley's penis suddenly having a life of its own and peeing over everything in sight.

'Whatever's happening?' At that moment, Clemence came in from her evening at the railway station, followed by an open-mouthed Angel. The sight of Louise, dear, correct Louise, in the throes of high-pitched laughter and apparently being embraced by a stranger while another looked on, was nothing short of – of scandalous!

'I'm so sorry, Lady Bannister,' one of the officers began, when Louise suddenly shrieked at her, tearing herself from the other's arms.

'It's Stanley, Mother. He's got himself blown up. He'll be a hero after all, even if it's only a dead one! Doesn't that please you, *Mother*?'

She sounded so much like Ellen as she hurled out the news. Clemence's face lost all its colour. Louise rushed out of the room, and Angel rushed out after her. The officers looked gravely at Clemence.

'It's shock, I'm afraid. It affects people in different ways. It may take a few hours for her to calm down and accept the truth. If I may suggest it, I would send for a doctor right way, Lady Bannister.'

'Yes. Yes, of course. But please tell me quickly if what my daughter says is true. Is poor dear Stanley really dead?'

The officers managed not to look at one another while they related the facts. Clemence was still listening in horror while her hand reached for the telephone to call the doctor for Louise. In the midst of her shock and sincere grief, she was already planning a splendid funeral. It would be the last thing they could do for Stanley.

No one knew of Sir Fred Bannister's involvement with the widow of one of his millworkers. While he was in Yorkshire he spent some nights in his hotel and the rest at Harriet's cottage. Only the hotel manager had Harriet's telephone number in case of emergencies, and all he knew was that it was a contact number. Better to be safe than sorry, even though he would dearly love to spend all his time with Harriet. All his days and all his nights. To sink himself in her soft warmth and never come out . . . he said as much to her one cold night in February, when they were snuggled up together in her creaking old bed, and had just spent a glorious hour in the pursuit of happiness.

'I'm always amazed how good it is with you,' Fred marvelled. 'Clemence was always such a cold fish. She used to gaze at the ceiling so much, I swear she could tell you how many flakes of paint there were on it.'

Harriet giggled, nestling more comfortably into his rotund stomach, her hand flat against his buttocks.

'You're a wicked old man, Fred, and I love you for it!'

'I love you too, my Harriet. You keep me sane. But not so much of the old! There's plenty of life in me yet.'

'Don't I know it.' She smiled in the darkness as he pushed against her, reminding her of his virility. Women such as Clemence Bannister were fools if they didn't appreciate a man like Fred. She felt no compunction, no guilt, in sharing him. If Clemence didn't want this lovely man and she did, then so be it. Harriet's cheerful, simple philosophy ended right there.

The thin sound of a bell ringing somewhere in the house made Fred swear lustily with words Clemence wasn't remotely aware that he knew, and wouldn't recognise if she heard them.

'Hell and damnation. Just as I was beginning to feel

broody again. Who can be calling you on the telephone at this time of night?'

'I'd better answer, love.' Harriet slid out of bed, her ample curves rolling slightly. Fred didn't mind her plumpness. It was fantastic to dig his hands into so much flesh and feel it wrap around you. He had never felt so welcome anywhere in the world as he felt with Harriet. She slipped the warm dressing gown over her nakedness, pushed her feet into her old slippers and padded down the stairs. Fred stretched luxuriously, grinning as the bedsprings creaked again. He liked their creaking. When he and Harriet began cavorting, they sang a joyous song of reunion every bloody time . . .

He heard her run back up the stairs. She was surprisingly light for a heavy woman. She'd be cold now. He threw back the bedclothes for her to come back to him . . .

'Fred, it's the hotel for you. There's been an accident. Somebody's been hurt. You'd best speak to him, love –'

He was already out of bed.

'Not Angel. Please God, not Angel –'

He hardly knew he'd muttered the words as he ran downstairs, heedless of the cold Yorkshire night and his lack of clothes. He had the bedspread held tightly around him like a Roman toga. Harriet smiled slightly in spite of the anxiety she felt. Naturally, Fred's first thoughts would be for his Angel, his best-loved daughter. If Harriet had been the jealous sort, she would be jealous of Angel.

It was a while before he came back upstairs. Silently, she handed him his clothes, knowing he must leave her, because this was the price they had to pay.

'It's my son-in-law. My stupid, pea-brained son-in-law. Blown to bits inspecting a site for a munitions factory. No one but Stanley could come to such an incongruous end. I've telephoned Clemence, and I have to get home. Louise is acting very strangely. They need me, Harriet. I'll leave some money for the phone call –'

'Don't you dare. Just come back as soon as you can. I'll be

here, Freddie,' she said, her voice threatening to break, because what troubled him, troubled her. She hugged him swiftly, not allowing the sentiment to show.

'You know I'll always be here.'

Chapter 11

Black didn't suit the older Bannister girls. It drained Louise, and made Ellen look harder and squarer. By contrast, Angel looked stunning, her long fair hair swathed into a discreet knot beneath the veiled black hat for the solemn occasion of Stanley's funeral. Clemence too, her smart black costume softened with pearls, looked elegant and queenly. Sir Fred fidgeted awkwardly in the front pew of the village church where Louise had insisted Stanley be buried rather than anonymously in London.

Fred wished himself miles away. He wished he didn't have this bloody guilt feeling over where he'd been when the telephone message had come through to him. He wished he didn't have to tramp over the frosty, slippery Somerset earth behind the coffin draped with the Union flag, flanked by the small group of military dignitaries who had arrived that morning.

Fred was feeling more of a hypocrite than ever before, because he had always despised Stanley, and now he felt obliged to grip his daughter's trembling arm and mutter platitudes at her snuffling tears.

'It's sensible to plant him here,' Ellen had breathed to Angel when the coffin had been lowered, and they had all walked dutifully around the hole to peer down into it. 'He's just as likely to be blown up all over again in a London churchyard, and there'd be hardly anything left of him next time. It's only bits and pieces now –'

'Ellen, for heaven's sake!' Angel said, scandalised at the brittleness in her sister's voice. 'Have some compassion for Louise! I don't know what's got into you lately.'

'Louise doesn't need compassion from us. She's getting all she needs from Haggis Dougal,' Ellen muttered.

Angel refused to speak to her after that. Ellen was becoming impossible. Everyone was in a heightened state of nerves, but Ellen was just about the end.

What neither Angel nor anyone else knew, was that Ellen was being bombarded by attentions from Andrew Pender, the Cornishman, who knew a good thing when he saw one, and sized up Ellen Bannister immediately. A fine beauty, just ripe for the plucking, and untouched by human hand, if he was any judge. And he considered himself an expert when it came to women.

It was fortuitous after all, that his Conchie protestations had brought him away from his home county, where things had been getting a little sticky with all this patriotism nonsense, and even more so in his personal life. Being sent off to do his duty on this sleepy little Somerset farm had sounded a bore, but Ellen Bannister was going to change all that. Andrew had every confidence in it.

There was now the question of what to do with Louise after Stanley had been disposed of, as Fred put it to himself baldly. Of course, she would stay at Meadowcroft as long as she wished, but once they all went back to London after the war . . .

Louise and Stanley had had their own home, and presumably she would want to live there on her own. Or she may not. She may well prefer to come back to the fold, and remain a war widow for the rest of her natural. A prospect that made Fred go cold, picturing the future with Louise and Clemence constantly together . . .

Stanley had been dead for two weeks when Louise startled them all by announcing that she had to get right away for a while. By then, Fred had returned to Yorkshire, and Clemence put down the socks she was packing in tissue paper for the troops, and looked at her eldest daughter in amazement. Louise's cheeks were quite pink, as though she had been steeling herself for this moment, as indeed she had.

'Mother, I know you may think it odd, but I can't bear everyone looking at me with such sympathy. You're all being very kind, but I simply can't cope with it all. And when I go to the village, it's ten times worse. People either stare or look away in embarrassment, but I know they're talking about me all the same. I don't want to feel an object of pity, Mother. Please understand.'

'Of course I do, darling.' Clemence's heart went out to her, standing tall and slender in her unflattering black, and sensing how her pride would be affected by village folks' stares. One had one's dignity to consider, after all. 'But in a few weeks from now, people will have other things to think about. They're naturally sad for you, Louise –'

'I don't want them feeling sad for me!' Louise's hands were clenched tight at her sides, her well-shaped nails digging into her palms. 'You know that Dougal is leaving here next week, don't you? He's asked if I would care to visit his family in Scotland for a few weeks as a sort of recuperation. It's all perfectly proper, Mother –'

'Are you out of your mind, Louise?' The socks and tissue paper slid to the floor with a little rustling noise as Clemence rose from her chair to face her daughter. 'Of course you can't go off to Scotland in the company of a young man! Whatever are you thinking of?'

'I'm thinking of recovering from the shock of losing my husband,' Louise said deliberately and with great solemnity. 'I'm thinking of accepting a friend's kind offer to stay with his family, not to set myself up as his paramour, and you insult me by suggesting otherwise. I was not asking for your permission, Mother. I was informing you of my intentions.'

Clemence's mouth dropped open at the sudden edge in Louise's voice. This was not the rather colourless daughter who had complied so dutifully when Clemence had found a suitable husband for her. This was a defiant young woman, more in the mould of her strong-willed sisters than the Louise who had been such a perfect echo of herself.

Before she could speak, Louise had rushed over to her and put her arms around her. Her voice was muffled against Clemence's shoulder.

'I'm sorry, Mummy. But I'm not your little girl any longer. I'm a married woman who has to learn to be alone from now on, and to make her own decisions. Dougal will telephone his parents in Edinburgh and ask them to speak to you. But that is as much as I will compromise.'

'Compromise! It seems a very apt choice of word, Louise.' Clemence twisted it bitterly to suit the waves of shock running through her. 'Can you not see how it will look to be running off with this – this man, so soon after dear Stanley's death?'

Louise moved away from her mother. Her eyes were sorrowful but filled with a determination Clemence couldn't miss.

'Sometimes I think you don't know me at all, Mother. You're just not listening to me. I've done nothing to be ashamed of, and nor do I intend to. I have to get away, and this is my salvation.'

Angel had come into the room at the tail end of the conversation, and quickly got the gist of it. Clemence immediately appealed to her, futilely hoping for some support from Angel as to the wickedness of it all.

'I could drive you and Dougal, if you like,' Angel offered instead. 'It will give me some long-distance driving practice. I can be your chaperon, if Mummy thinks you need one.'

Clemence threw up her hands.

'I might have expected something like this. Has my entire family taken leave of their senses?'

Angel felt briefly sorry for her. The world was changing so fast, and despite her good intentions, in some respects Clemence was totally unable to keep up with it.

'Wouldn't you rather I drove them to Scotland than let Louise travel alone with Dougal, Mother?' She hoped the Sunbeam would be up to such a journey, they would obviously need to do it in easy stages, if Louise were to accept the offer.

'Thank-you, darling.' Louise hugged Angel in a rare rush of affection. 'I accept your offer unreservedly. I'll ask Dougal to put through the call to his parents this evening. You'll be here, won't you, Mother?'

Wild horses wouldn't have dragged Clemence out of doors in the circumstances, but she merely pursed her lips and nodded silently. It must be some kind of post-bereavement shock, she decided. Dear Louise would never normally act so irresponsibly. And perhaps it wasn't so awful, after all. Perhaps when she saw the fellow in his own home, with his family, she would realise just how marked was the difference between them, and be more than thankful to come home. There couldn't be any real attachment between Louise and Dougal Mackie. Clemence simply closed her mind to such an absurd possibility.

Ellen half-heartedly pushed away the strong arms holding her, feeling the rich low laughter vibrating in the male chest so close to her own body, and sending the oddest sensations through every vein, every pore.

It was dark and pungent in the hayloft, and she had come in here at Peter Chard's request, climbing the rickety ladder carefully, her skirts held above her ankles, to take stock of the bales of straw for winter feeding for the animals.

And there, waiting for her, was the handsome Cornishman, and now here they were, tumbling in the musty hay like two wanton village lovers, and she didn't know whether to laugh or cry, or scream or shout . . .

He saved her the trouble of deciding by covering her mouth with his own, in a long open-mouthed kiss that was nothing like Ellen had ever been kissed before. His body was a weight she found heavy and sensual on her own, the sound of his breathing suddenly rasping and hoarse, and hot on her cheek. He raked his hands through her hair that had somehow come unpinned and fell about her shoulders.

'God, but you're the most devilishly handsome woman I've ever met, little Ellen,' Andrew muttered into her neck, where the pressure of his lips made her shudder delightfully.

'Handsome? Is that good?' She felt so strange and elated at this unexpected encounter with him, and the fact that no one in their right minds could call her little passed completely unnoticed. Nor did she think of it as a bit of patronising male seduction patter – then.

Andrew's low laugh throbbed against her breasts again. She felt the deep rumble of it against her, and then the caress of the small firm breasts that had never known the feel of a man's hand before. Shivers ran deep and strong inside her. She should protest. She should thrust him away from her. God knew she was probably strong enough to cope with this. But somehow she didn't feel strong and capable any longer. She wasn't the Ellen who had marched with the Women's Movement in London, carrying banners, shouting slogans, receiving insults as to her suspect gender, and hurling them back in language no lady should even know, let alone use . . .

She felt . . . as Andrew wanted her to feel. Little and protected and wanted . . . and a woman . . .

'Handsome is very good, sweetheart,' he whispered against the skin at her throat that had somehow become exposed as his experienced fingers undid the fabric of her high-necked blouse. The fingers stroked gently, knowing that if he went too fast she would fly like a frightened bird, yet the ache for her was becoming unbearable. He had to know more of her. He had to possess her . . .

Ellen felt the hand slide down the length of her body while his mouth still covered hers with kisses, interspersed with sweet whispering against her lips. And oh, it was so tempting to just let it happen, this thing that was reputedly more stupendous than a flight to the stars. This was love, and she yearned to know its mysteries . . .

The dimness of the hayloft was split by a wide shaft of light as the barn door below was unceremoniously thrown open. Motes of dust danced in the thin February sunlight. The two people above had been too absorbed in their own pleasures to be aware of the rumpus outside, but now both sat up with a shock as the screaming began.

Andrew cursed loudly, while Ellen re-arranged her clothes quickly, and simply wanted to die as she looked down into the good-looking, disbelieving face of Peter Chard, glimpsing the agony in his eyes.

She didn't register it for more than a second, because her attention and that of Andrew Pender's was totally taken up by the young woman yelling furiously at him in an accent similar to his own.

'So I've tracked you down at last, you bastard! I'll have the law on you for tricking me, though mebbe I'm in time to save your latest floosie from the mess you've got me into! Married me, so-say, and left me with a babby, Miss, saying he was going off to enlist, only I had me doubts about that, knowing him for the snivelling coward that he is. All his guts are in his trousers, and that fizzles out soon enough. There ain't nothing of the real Conchie about this one. The truth is he's too yellow to fight for King and country! And he's already got a proper wife and kids down Penzance way, and I'll have him up before the Magistrate on a charge of bigamy if 'tis the last thing I do!'

She began to wail in a fury, while Ellen sat rigid with shock. It couldn't be true! But one look at Andrew's grey face, and she knew that it was. All his vitality had died, and he looked hunted and pathetic, and she felt sick at the sight of him. And even worse at the name the Cornish girl had called her.

His latest floosie . . . she was swallowed up by shame. What an idiotic, gullible fool she was to have fallen for his line. In a rage, she suddenly leaned over and wrenched at his long dark hair, nearly pulling it out by the roots, dimly aware of the girl below screeching at her to grab him where it hurt most, and put the bastard in queer street for a while.

Peter was up the ladder in seconds, pulling her away from the cowering man. Ellen knew she acted like a street-woman, and she didn't care . . . she didn't care . . . she felt the stinging slap on the side of her face, and it was Peter's way of showing that he did care.

'Remember who you are,' he snapped at her. 'There are better ways of dealing with this. Tidy yourself up before you go into the house and telephone for the constables. We'll get this fellow taken in custody and arrange for the young woman to be sent home on the train. There are legal matters here that others can sort out. It's nothing to do with us.'

He spoke with harsh authority, and Ellen nodded dumbly. He would despise her now, and she didn't blame him. He had always thought her so strong, and now he knew how weak she was. She couldn't look at him, nor at the other swine who had so nearly seduced her. Love died as quickly as it had flamed, and beneath all the humiliation she suffered, it was a thought that could still astound her. What use was love, after all, if it was so fleeting an emotion? She should be thankful to the Cornish girl, but she couldn't look at her either. She pinned her hair as best she could with shaking hands, climbed down the ladder with legs that felt as though they didn't belong to her, and ran towards the farmhouse.

She made two telephone calls. One was to the constables to come to Chard Farm at once. The other was to Rose Morton in London, begging her to let her come and stay at the old shared house for a while, since she needed to sort herself out. Ellen had never begged for anything, but if she ever needed sanctuary, it was now, and Rose gladly forgave her everything and welcomed her back to the fold.

She was gone before the constables arrived, and before she had to face any of the three people in the barn again.

'I suppose life is a little easier now,' Clemence admitted to her only chosen confidante among her knitting circle ladies. Mrs Fitzwarren was 'county', and therefore a suitable companion and helpmeet on the circle afternoons at Meadowcroft. Mrs Fitzwarren usually arrived long before the lesser ladies, to take up their clacking needles and chatter in their country accents in the fine drawing room with its chintz furnishings and deep carpets, waited on by the Bannister maids with afternoon tea and buttered scones.

'But for all your girls to have left at the same time must have been a wrench for you, Lady Bannister,' commented Mrs Fitzwarren. Not for them the easy first-name terms of village folk. Etiquette was still to be observed in the best houses, and was all the more precious because so many people seemed to be throwing aside the old values.

'Well, of course, Ellen was always very self-willed, and her roots are very much in London and her business affairs. I doubted that a farming life would suit her for long.'

Mrs Fitzwarren nodded sympathetically at the controlled voice of her hostess, learning nothing from the careful words. Clemence had seethed to the point of apoplexy at Ellen's sudden departure with only a note to say she was desperate for her old life, and not to think too badly of her for going back to London. But no one would ever guess it.

'And the others –'

'Dear Louise simply had to get away, of course. It was understandable, and Angel is such a dear to accompany her. The Highlands of Scotland will be very beneficial to Louise after the shock of poor Stanley's death. Such a blessing that dear Mr Mackie could accompany them for protection.' She neatly twisted the truth of it to her own satisfaction. She had repeated the phrase so many times, she began to believe it herself.

'Will you have some more tea before the ladies arrive, Mrs Fitzwarren? Cook has made some splendid seed cake, and we might indulge in a slice, if you wish.'

Knowing the lady's sweet tooth, Clemence deftly moved the conversation away from her girls. They had all behaved so badly that she didn't even want to think of them any more, let alone discuss them. She smiled blandly, and Mrs Fitzwarren privately assumed that the few tales going around about the upsets at Meadowcroft must be wrong after all. Either that, or dear Lady Bannister should have been on the stage for the fine performance she was giving!

Already, the raging battles at Verdun were becoming no more than fading newspaper reports in the minds of folk who weren't actively involved or who had loved ones at the Front. It was frightening, Angel ruminated, but it was even possible to get used to reading of enormous casualties, of mud and still more mud, of privations and barbed wire and yet more mud, where the soldiers trampled over one another to go 'over the top' of the trenches, and slither back down with bullets shattering their faces. How easy it was to become complacent when every day reported the same thing, the same horrors, the same mounting lists of the dead, with only the names differing.

She shivered to think of Margot's young brother Edward caught up in such horrors. He was such a boy, always ready for a lark. Little more than a year ago, she remembered his birthday party at Margot's elegant home, and the way the so-correct public schoolboys had been allowed to let their hair down in games of charades and find-the-thimble and other harmless pursuits. And now he was a soldier, hard and tough as soldiers must become, and how could he possibly change so overnight?

A year ago . . . her heart jolted as she drove steadily through the changing countryside, with Louise and Dougal in the rear seats of the Sunbeam. They conversed quietly, and she was left with her own thoughts. This time last year she had been caught in a miserable downpour of rain, and looked into the eyes of a handsome Frenchman who was to change her life.

Jacques . . . the longing for him swept over her in a surge of pain. How long before she saw him again? Would she ever see him again? Or was the Kaiser's lust for power going to destroy something more beautiful than she had ever imagined?

To her wild relief there had been a short note from Jacques before they left for Scotland.

'My heart aches for the lovely memories of Verdun,' he had written. 'My family spent some time there when I was a boy, and to think of it so desecrated now is to feel they are tearing at the very soul of France. Forgive my eloquence, *chérie*. Only to you can I say the words that are in my heart. Remember that I think of you always.'

Such a short, poignant letter. She had wept over it, sensing all the things he didn't say. So many other women must receive such letters, hiding the fear from their loved ones, the hopelessness of a war that seemed to be going nowhere. She had squared her shoulders, and got on with the business of packing her clothes for the journey north. This much she could do for Louise, and whatever Clemence's thoughts on it, she intended driving the couple to Edinburgh.

As it happened there was no need for her to go so far. Dougal's father had business in Newcastle-on-Tyne, and would meet them there and take Dougal and Louise the rest of the way. It was a long enough journey for Angel, despite stopping at a wayside inn overnight, and she was thankful when they arrived at the plush hotel in Newcastle.

Dougal's father was clearly a prosperous man. Angel hid her slight surprise, feeling guiltily that like Clemence, she had assumed that everyone who spoke without proper King's English diction, must be less well-connected. She couldn't have been more wrong. The older Mr Mackie was a director of a Scottish newspaper, and it was clear that he and his wife welcomed the bereaved friend of their son, and would make her comfortable in their estate just outside the city of Edinburgh for as long as she cared to stay.

It was all said in the natural way that moneyed people spoke, and Angel knew that Louise would be in good hands. It was too soon to think beyond the friendship between her and Dougal, but privately Angel thought they were well-matched.

She hugged her sister when they parted after a night spent at the Newcastle hotel, waving her off in the smart Bentley motor with Mr Mackie at the wheel. Angel's eyes were misty. Dougal's war was over. However embittered he might feel, his family would be thankful to have him back safely with only a stiffened arm to remind them. And together, he and Louise might well find solace as well as love.

Her restless thoughts roamed on as she began the long drive home again. There was no hurry, and the crisp panorama of the northern countryside in its mantle of frost and lingering snow was enchanting. Where the snow melted in the thin sunlight, evidence of an early spring made itself felt in the lacy network of tiny buds on trees and hedgerows. It was so hard to think of the war raging in France, yet so impossible not to think of it, and to compare it with the lovely peacefulness here.

They had all made an early start, and it was mid-morning when Angel reached the Yorkshire town with the familiar name. Bannister Textile Works was situated here. She had never seen the place. On an impulse, she asked directions and drove towards the imposing red brick building.

What fun it would be to call unexpectedly on her father. How delighted and surprised he would be! Clemence had declared that she had no intention of telling him of Angel's decision to drive her sister north, washing her hands of the whole foolhardy scheme.

She parked the Sunbeam, and walked up to the entrance, her boots scrunching on the hard-packed ground. There was a small office inside the building, and a bored typist looked up curiously at the beautifully dressed young woman standing in front of her.

'Is Sir Frederick Bannister available, please?' Angel asked the girl.

'No, Miss. He's not coming in today. Were you seeking employment?'

Even as she asked, the girl looked doubtful. This one was not the usual kind who sought work on the looms or machines or in the packing sheds. After her brief disappointment, Angel hid a smile. This visit was to be a surprise, and she had no intention of giving away her identity.

'No, but I did want to see him especially. It's a purely private matter.'

'Oh, I see,' the girl said in her flat nasal accent, glancing Angel up and down. She shrugged. It was no concern of hers. 'I can give you the name of the hotel where he stays, if you like. He'll no doubt be doing some paperwork there.'

Five minutes later, Angel was following the girl's directions. The hotel was some miles away from the factory, and the manager looked at her blankly when she enquired after Sir Fred Bannister. He recognised the educated accent, and came to a decision.

'Sorry, Miss. I can give you a telephone number where you can reach him, if it's urgent.'

It was all very odd. Angel began to feel as if it was some

kind of detective work, tracking down her father. She looked at the number the manager scribbled down for her, and he suddenly took pity on her.

'I can't give you the address, Miss, but young Georgie over there might be able to help.'

The young boy sweeping the hotel lobby glanced up. Angel went across to him and asked her question. He glanced at the hotel manager, who nodded slightly.

'Oh aye, Miss. I know of it, because me auntie lives nobbut a spit away from the cottage, and I memorise numbers. It's me hobby, see?'

'Can you tell me the address?'

'Oh aye, 'tis Beckside Cottage, about three mile from here as the crow flies. Turn left at the bridge and follow the road. You can't miss it.'

Angel thanked him and went out into the sunlight. It was getting even odder. What was her father doing at Beckside Cottage, whatever it was? Perhaps it belonged to one of the outworkers he employed, and he needed to check up on orders or something.

She found the old stone cottage easily, sitting square and solid beside the small running beck. Around the back of it, she could glimpse the nose of her father's Daimler jutting out from its parking place. Angel's heart began to beat unevenly. She left her car in the lane, and began to pick her way carefully towards the front door, tapping the well-polished knocker.

A woman opened the door, well-rounded, still pretty in late middle-age, her bright eyes smiling in polite enquiry at the visitor. Behind her, Angel could feel the warmth of the snug interior, the whole place emitting an air of comfortable friendliness.

'I'm sorry to disturb you, but I'm looking for my – for Sir Frederick Bannister. I was told he might be here.'

Caution made her refrain from giving her name immediately. But then several things happened at once. She saw recognition surge into the woman's eyes. They hadn't met before, but Harriet realised she should have known Fred's youngest daughter at once from his loving descriptions of her.

And behind her, dressed as casually as ever in his second home, and giving everything away in an instant, Fred suddenly appeared, to gape in mingled pleasure and horror at Angel's shocked and disbelieving face.

Chapter 12

Margot Lacey exclaimed in amazement when she opened the door of the Norfolk family home and saw Angel standing on the doorstep. At her feet was a small travelling bag. Outside in the road was the Sunbeam car, dusty from long spells of driving.

'Darling! What on earth –'

'Can I come in, Margot? I've got to talk to you.'

The instant Margot heard her speak, she knew something was badly wrong. Angel normally spoke in a lilting voice that was unconsciously sensual and appealing, but now the voice was husky and near to breaking. Margot drew her inside at once, and led her to a small drawing room.

'Mother's taking a nap, so we shan't be disturbed. Now tell me what's happened. Has Louise gone berserk or something?'

Angel looked at her blankly for a moment. Almost guiltily, she remembered the recent bereavement, about which she had naturally informed her friend. Already, the sadness of Louise's new status of widowhood seemed years ago. Her shocked thoughts made no proper sense, and she had to force them to be sequential, like a child memorising facts.

Because of Stanley's death, Louise had decided to go to Scotland to Dougal Mackie's family. Because of that, Angel had offered to drive them north, and had decided to pay a surprise visit to her father. Because of that . . .

Suddenly she was weeping uncontrollably, and Margot's protective arms were around her.

'Hush now, darling, it can't be as bad as all that, surely. Whatever it is, old Margot will share it with you. All for one and one for all, and all that rot, remember?'

Angel gave a deep sob and searched for a handkerchief. She had never intended to let go like that. It wasn't done. Clemence would hate to see her like this . . . thoughts of her mother almost made her howl afresh, but instead, she took several long shuddering breaths, and faced Margot with huge drowned eyes.

'Margot, do you still want to go to France? I mean, *now*, *this week*, *today*!'

Margot stared at her. Whatever had happened was obviously too traumatic for Angel even to talk about it. Oh God, it wasn't her flyer, was it?

'Of course!'

'Good. In case you're wondering how I got here, I've taken Louise to Scotland and come here via Yorkshire, so I'm feeling all in. I'll have to let Mother know what we're planning to do, of course. It's rather a sudden decision.' She stopped abruptly, and Margot could hear the strain in her voice.

But she had to ask. 'Darling, is Jacques all right? Nothing's happened to him, has it?'

Angel still had the strange huskiness in her voice, only now it was tinged with a strange bitterness. It wasn't directed solely at Jacques. It encompassed the entire male species, but Margot wasn't to know that.

'He's written a few times, and he says he loves me, so I presume he's all right – as far as any woman can tell when a man goes away. He might be in the throes of a wild affair by now, for all I know. He might even be dead!'

She ended on a strangled note, and after the initial shock, Margot decided it was best not to pursue this line of questioning.

'And you're really prepared to go to France? What about your mother? She's not going to like the idea –'

'Father will persuade her,' Angel said, more cynically than usual. 'I promise you, Margot, Father won't refuse me anything just now, I'm sure of that.'

It was odd how a small thing like Angel referring to Sir Fred as 'Father' instead of the old loving 'Daddy' told Margot instantly that it wasn't Jacques who was having some wild affair. But surely not *Sir Frederick Bannister*?

Margot remembered his twinkling eyes, and the way he liked to catch a pretty girl's eye at a party, so that she was obliged to smile back at him. He could often be seen twirling his moustache in the presence of ladies in the manner of a wickedly attractive Victorian roué. Margot had never thought of the similarity before.

The sly old devil, she thought, with half-grudging admiration. No one could blame him really. He and Clemence were so mismatched. She with her airs and graces, and he with his earthy appeal. But Angel had clearly had one hell of a shock, and wasn't prepared to tell any more at the moment.

And knowing Angel as she did, Margot guessed that presumably finding her father in some cosy affaire d'amour, had sharpened her own guilt over her meetings with Jacques. She gave her friend a hug and spoke cheerfully.

'You've picked a good day to arrive. Everyone's gone out to a country fair, except for Mother and me, so we can slum it in the kitchen and make tea for ourselves. Do you want to stay a few days while we decide what to do, or do you want to go back to Meadowcroft immediately? You'll need some fresh clothes, presumably.'

She prattled on, ignoring the bleakness in Angel's lovely eyes, and gradually, over steaming cups of tea, Angel's nerves relaxed a little. Margot left her alone for a few minutes while she took some tea upstairs to her mother. And alone, Angel took stock of herself.

What an immature fool I'm being, unable to handle this

situation, she thought in a rush of self-censure.

Rushing down here in a blue funk, after confronting her father with that woman. Harriet Garth. Hardly the name for a mistress. Her nerves flinched as she thought the word. Mistress. Her father had a mistress, and was clearly so well ensconced in the little cottage that it had probably been going on for years. Angel had felt as betrayed at the knowledge as if it was her own husband, instead of her father.

As yet, she refused to let herself wonder how her mother would react if she ever knew. Telling her never entered Angel's head. It would be too painful and embarrassing for her, and too humiliating for Clemence. In a way, it only emphasised the superficial relationship Clemence had with her daughters. It was so hard for her to show love, which was where she and Fred differed so much . . .

The scene at the cottage was etched sharply in her mind. The shock on Fred's face, the dawning realisation on the woman's. And Angel herself, suddenly staggering as her legs seemed to turn to jelly beneath her, so that the woman held her arm and helped her inside to a chair. The woman smelled of health and fresh air, and the sight of her father's portly stomach and unbrushed hair, in an open-necked shirt with its rolled-up sleeves, reminded her of a farmhand.

How appalled Clemence would be to see him so inelegant. The incongruous thought had swept through her mind, even through all the other, more disgusting thoughts.

'Fetch her some brandy, Harriet,' Fred had said quietly. 'God knows what she's doing here, but she obviously needs it.'

His heart ached at the sight of his daughter. Her beautiful skin was the colour of porcelain now, the deep-hued eyes even darker with pain and shock, the soft mouth trembling as she felt the cool glass touch her lips and swallowed the bitter spirit. She choked on it, brushing the woman's hand away.

'Feeling better, my dearest girl?' Fred spoke to her as he always had. His feelings for her hadn't changed, nor ever would. While Angel . . . he couldn't bear the look in her eyes as the faint tinge of colour came back to her cheeks.

'How *could* you?' Her voice was a thick throb of sound. 'I've taken Louise to Edinburgh and thought I'd give you a surprise. I never expected – I can't *believe* – and don't call me your dearest girl ever again! Somebody else has obviously taken that title from me!'

'Angel, no one will ever take your place in my heart.'

Fred spoke quietly, refusing to be angry. He felt more sorrow than anger. All these years he and Harriet had harmed no one, and now, through no fault of theirs, the one he loved best in the world was filled with hurt and pain. She looked so young, so vulnerable and untouched. She didn't understand about loving and needing. How could she know of the void in his heart that Harriet filled?

'And what about Mother's place?'

Angel hardly understood just why she wanted to hit out so bitterly. She felt shock, yes. She felt a fierce loyalty to her mother, and the family as a unit. She felt almost hatred that these two could be cosily enjoying themselves while others lost everything, husbands, sweethearts, fathers . . . and shamedly, Angel knew there was also a burning feeling of resentment that her father should be free to indulge himself, while young men such as Jacques de Ville was God knows where, being blown to bits perhaps, as Stanley had been blown to bits.

The woman suddenly spoke up. Angel hadn't looked at her again, and Harriet's voice was steady and calm.

'Your mother's place is the same as it has always been, Angel. Your father and I have never disputed that, nor ever will. I give him a refuge when he comes to Yorkshire, and an ear to listen when he wants to talk. I know so much about you, lass, and I grieve for your finer feelings now. I feel that I've shared so much of your young life, from your catching the measles on holiday when you nearly died, to every graze on your knees when you were such a tomboy and wouldn't stay out of the treehouse at Meadowcroft. Is it asking too much for your father to have someone to share such times, to laugh and cry over the memories with him?'

Angel had glanced at her then, seeing the warm compassionate woman that she was. Homely and yet sensual, a loving companion for a man whose wife could rarely be bothered to give an ear to listen when he talked. She felt a brief flicker of sympathy, but she wasn't ready to understand, and she didn't want to forgive. As yet the grief was too raw for her to let go of it. She got to her feet, swaying a little, ignoring Harriet.

'You have a wife to share your memories, Father. The memories you made together, which you seem to have conveniently forgotten. I'm leaving now –'

'You can't! Not like this. I won't allow you to drive when you're so distressed, Angel –'

She looked at him, her expression totally blank. It tore at his heart to see it.

'You can't stop me from doing whatever I want to do, ever again, Father. You've lost that right.'

She turned and rushed out of the door, seeing the woman put a restraining hand on Fred's arm as he would have gone after her. She went blindly to the car, and grated the gears before driving off so fast that the wheels spun and skidded on the gravel road. She didn't care. All she wanted was to get away.

She headed south, not knowing where she was going. She hadn't meant her last words as a threat, or a hint of blackmail, but while the Sunbeam hurtled along the roads, the solution gradually came to her. She couldn't go home yet. She couldn't face her mother, knowing what she knew. Nor could she go to Hampstead. Their London house would be cold and bleak.

She would go to Margot. Perhaps the time was right now

for them to go to France. There would never be a better time. The V.A.D.s were always screaming for volunteers. She would do anything that was required of her. Her thoughts careered ahead in little staccato bursts of decision.

If she got caught up in the Front Line, and ended up drowning in mud, she didn't care about that either. At least she had some purpose. As yet, she couldn't think about finding Jacques. Today's discovery was too close to her own experience to want to think of him. It was one more painful thing to add to the anguish her father had brought her. It made her love for Jacques no more than a shameful affair.

She could hear Margot's heels clattering back down the stairs, and dragged her thoughts back to the present. She had to be practical. Yes, she would have to go to Meadowcroft to fetch some clothes. Those she had with her were soiled and dusty. And she owed it to Clemence to inform her of what was happening. She couldn't just send a note as Ellen had done, nor did she have the status of new widowhood like Louise to add dignity to her cause.

Clemence would try to dissuade her, but Fred would make her see that Angel had a right to do what she felt was her duty. Angel swallowed the lump that kept rising to her throat every time she thought of him. It was hard to keep her thoughts steady. Her head ached so much. Margot had obviously been thinking too.

'I've told Mother of our plans, Angel, and she's resigned to it. She's known for ages that I wanted to go, though I don't know what I shall do, since I'm not exactly trained for anything. I don't even have your driving skills, nor Ellen's secretarial efficiency. I'm a complete idiot when you boil it all down.' She said it quite cheerfully, and Angel managed a watery smile.

'You're my dearest and best friend, and if you only sat and held a wounded soldier's hand, he'd be your devoted slave, and well you know it.'

'Oh well,' Margot laughed. 'I can always do that, of course. It could be fun to be doing things together, anyway. What say we find an information office tomorrow and see what's what? Then we could go down to Meadowcroft the following day and face your mother with a *fait accompli.* It's too late for doing anything today, and you really do look all in, darling.'

'Yes. Tomorrow.'

It couldn't come quickly enough. The evening was an ordeal, sitting through dinner with Margot and her mother, answering questions about her family, and trying to talk naturally about them. If Mrs Lacey's eyebrows were raised slightly on hearing about Ellen's unexpected departure from Meadowcroft, and Louise's trip to Scotland, the lady showed remarkable forbearance in not commenting too much.

What would she say if she knew of the other two . . . Sir Frederick Bannister with his mistress, and Angel with her French lover . . .? The Bannisters were turning into quite an unconventional lot after all, Angel thought, with a glimmer of grim humour, the very opposite from what Clemence had schooled them for so diligently.

She spent a sleepless night, tossing and turning, and trying to make her mind a complete blank, until the pale pink dawn finally appeared. And then there was no more time to think, to back out, to change her mind.

After breakfast the girls drove through the narrow streets of the town to where the posters at the information office assured them that Kitchener Wanted Them. That women could be of immense service to their country as well as men, that nurses were valued above all, but every female hand was needed . . .

'Ellen must love all this,' Angel muttered. 'She was right all along. The war is doing as much to change attitudes to women as anything Mrs Pankhurst and her suffragettes did. It's tragic to think it takes so much killing to prove a point.'

'Stop being so morbid and let's find out what we can do to help.' Margot linked her arm in Angel's, and together they went into the cramped office, where the efficient little clerk handed them some forms to fill in.

By the time they came into the sunlight, they were officially V.A.D.s. With a stern warning that if they intended working in factories they would do well to have their hair cut off. More than one girl had been scalped when her waist-length hair got caught in machinery.

'You can always donate it for the war effort,' the man added helpfully. 'Payment isn't much, and I daresay the pittance won't mean a lot to you two young ladies. But there's a reputable salon in Lynn that pays a fair rate if you're interested.'

Outside, Angel and Margot looked at each other. Cut off their beautiful long hair? Margot used to be able to sit on hers, though it was shorter now for convenience. Angel's had been trimmed to shoulder-blade length because of the heavy weight of it when piled into a bun.

'Let's do it,' Angel said recklessly. Anything new appealed to her at present. Anything to change her from the old susceptible Angel to someone more worldly, more modern. The image of a girl wearing cheap scent and bright Tango lipstick swept through her mind.

She hadn't thought of Dolly Dilkes since the night she had gone to Beezer's Club in the taxi with her three new companions. She didn't particularly want to think of her now.

'Hold on a minute. I'm not so sure about this haircutting business,' Margot sounded uneasy. 'I don't want to look like a boy. It's all right for you. No one would ever mistake your shape, but there's not much of me where it matters.'

'No one would mistake you either! Put a bit more rouge on your lips. Your mother will really think you're fast then. I'm going to do it anyway. I shall emerge as an entirely new personality.'

She still couldn't quite keep the harshness out of her voice. Everything she thought about at present, everything she said, or did, seemed in relation with her father having a mistress. She couldn't seem to escape the knowledge. Coming to terms with it was a different matter. It was done, and she knew that nothing could undo it. She couldn't change it. But she could change herself, and assert her new independence from *them*.

Them meaning the old regime; the frothy, heady days before the war; the family who still saw her as a child instead of the woman she had become, through Jacques' loving tenderness, through her father's sleazy affair . . .

'All right. Why not? It will be a lark!' Margot agreed, eyes sparkling with admiration at Angel's words. 'All the same, I'm glad I'll have you to back me up when Mother sees me. And I'll do the same for you, darling!'

An hour or so later they entered the house nervously, and Margot's mother looked at them speechlessly for a moment. But not for long . . .

'What on earth have you done to yourselves! You look positively alien! I'm more distressed than I can say –'

Margot ran to her side as she burst into noisy tears at the sight of the two cropped girls.

'Please don't be angry, Mother. It's for the war effort.' She looked at Angel in desperation, not expecting quite such a reaction as this.

'We all have to do what we can, Mrs Lacey,' Angel was firm but kind. 'Lord knows what they do with the hair – use it for stuffing mattresses or making wigs or something, but it was a small sacrifice to make. Our boys are giving so much more –'

That was a mistake. She bit her lip as Mrs Lacey sobbed even louder. Why did she have to refer to 'our boys', when young Edward Lacey might well be in the thick of the fighting right now, even hanging in tatters on the 'Front Line wire', in the words of that dreadful song.

'Angel and I have joined the V.A.D.s, Mother,' Margot went on in a rush. 'We're going down to Meadowcroft tomorrow to fetch Angel's things, then we'll go to Dover on the train. We have to report to a leave ship in a week's time.'

'So I'm losing you as well as Edward?' she wailed.

'Yes, Mother, I'm afraid you are.' It was time to be strong. 'We'll both come back safe and sound, like bad pennies, you'll see.'

Behind her back, Angel could see Margot's slim fingers crossed for luck as she spoke.

Once they had broken the news, they decided not to prolong the parting. It was too unnerving. Margot quickly packed the essentials, and Angel put her few things together, catching sight of herself in the dressing table mirror now and then. Her heart lurched every time she did so. The hair cutting had changed her appearance dramatically. She had been acknowledged beautiful before, with her long abundance of silky hair a truly crowning glory, as glowing as sunlight.

Now, her face had a gamin look, a mixture of childlike innocence and the new 'fast' style, with the hair softly curling around her chin and ears, and slightly raised on top to lessen the stark effect. Her mother would have a purple fit. Her father would mourn the loss of her lovely hair . . . but she no longer cared what he thought, and hardened her feelings towards him.

She tried not to think of Jacques twining her hair around his seductive fingers, burying his face in its springlike freshness, loving the wantonness of it spread across the pillow like a soft golden cloud . . . she tried not to think of anything to make her heart ache even more . . .

'Ready?' Margot came into Angel's room, her own dark hair a similar stylish crop. She patted it defiantly, seeing herself beside Angel in the mirror. 'I say. We really look rather good, don't we? Poor Mother. She never could keep up with the times. Everyone will be wearing their hair like this soon, you'll see. It will be far less trouble.'

They arrived at Meadowcroft late in the afternoon. Angel had telephoned to say that she and Margot were coming, but giving away nothing of their plans. Clemence was cross at not knowing Angel's whereabouts, and Angel was very sensitive to the petulance in her mother's voice.

Clemence was quite undemonstrative towards her family, but was still possessive of them in a strangely distant way. An unloving wife for a husband who needed a show of love. The thought edged annoyingly into Angel's head.

As the girls entered the serenity of the drawing room at Meadowcroft, Clemence took one look at the two cropped heads and put her hand to her throat in horror.

'You look like street women,' she gasped, her composure deserting her. 'What on earth possessed you to do it?'

Angel felt suddenly bored and weary.

'There's a war on, Mother. We donated our hair to the war effort. We even donated the money we got for it to the Red Cross box at the salon. Aren't you proud of us?'

How bizarre it all was. Boys little older than herself were being shot to pieces in a foreign country. Her lover's plane might have been burnt to a crisp for all she knew. And still the domestic details of everyday life produced pain and indignation. A father's infidelity; a daughter's independence in having her hair cut. One might think the large-scale disasters would far outweigh the others, but they never did . . .

'Hello, Lady Bannister,' Margot said awkwardly, in the small brittle silence.

Clemence gave her a brief nod, her reply distracted. 'So you're paying us another visit, Margot –'

'We're not staying, Mother. We've joined the V.A.D.s. We leave for France next week.'

Clemence's face changed colour. Angel sounded so – so decisive. If Clemence had ever thought she would be a pliant youngest daughter, she was revising her opinions very quickly.

'Frederick!'

At a small noise in the passageway, she suddenly shouted her husband's name, as if totally unable to deal with any more of this. Angel felt a shock. She hadn't expected her father to be home. Before she had time to think any further, he came into the drawing room.

He was dressed impeccably, stiff collar and neat tie, hair sleeked down, shoes gleaming. For the life of her, Angel couldn't help comparing him with the last time she had seen him, so comfortable, so much at home. Here, he looked more like a visitor than master of his own home.

She tried not to consider the implications of it, her heart beating unevenly as Fred looked at her with an unfathomable look in his eyes.

He's wondering if I'm going to give him away, she realised with a huge shock. He's nervous. Of me! Oh God, how can this be happening! Normally, she would have run to him, to be hugged to his chest, to be kissed with great enthusiasm. His best girl, his dearest girl . . . after Harriet . . .

The continuing shock of seeing the girls with their hair shorn effectively stopped Clemence from noticing that neither her husband nor her daughter made any move towards one another.

Margot noticed it, and was certain now that her suspicions were correct. Poor, poor Angel, to have her illusions about her beloved father shattered. Whatever had happened, it had gone very deep.

'Margot and I have joined the V.A.D.s.' Angel's voice was strained as she repeated the words yet again. 'We sail for France in less than a week. Unless you have any objections – *Father*?'

His eyes never left her face. He was unsmiling, and to Angel he seemed to have aged. She smothered any pity on his account. Let Harriet revive him . . .

'I think it's an admirable thing to do. May God go with you both and bring you back safely.' He ignored Clemence's outraged gasp of fury.

'What about their hair? Their lovely hair?' Clemence could almost have wept in her frustration, if it hadn't been so unladylike.

Fred shrugged. He spoke distantly. 'There's one thing about hair, my dear. It grows. Now, if you didn't want me for anything else, I have more important things to do than to stand here gossiping.'

He went stiffly out of the room, and Angel bit her lip. If she was suffering, then so was her father. How he must hate the knowledge that his beloved daughter knew of his indiscretion. Even more, he must hate the accusation in her eyes, the dumb misery she couldn't hide.

She had never believed herself to be so unforgiving. But that was the way she felt, and for the present it was the one thing she was unable to change.

Chapter 13

The leave ship was crowded with khaki-clad veterans who were all of nineteen or twenty years old, and eager new recruits, full of show and aggression, all ready to put a bayonet up Jerry's backside. There was a sprinkling of Queen Alexandra's nurses, some officers, and the V.A.D.s, each group keeping strictly to themselves.

'It's like belonging to separate clubs,' Angel commented, when they had found a space to put down their belongings. They wore their uniforms now, and eyed each other in the dreary dark cloth, trying to give false encouragement.

Why couldn't they have joined something more dashing, and worn those jolly little swishing nursing hats? Bravado made them flippant as they were crushed together on the none-too-sweet-smelling ship.

'The damn thing will sink before it gets to mid-Channel at this rate,' Margot grumbled.

'There can't be any English people in England any more,' Angel agreed in the same spirit. 'They're all on board ships travelling between the Channel coasts.'

'Or filling the trenches at the Front Line,' Margot muttered. Despite their jocularity, the enormity of what they were doing struck them forcibly. Listening to the varied catcalls from the soldiers testified to that.

The old hands . . . some bawdy, some subdued, having seen so much of the war . . . the new ones, arrogantly swaggering, having as yet seen nothing . . .

'They say the trenches stretch for five hundred miles,' Angel tried to make interesting conversation as they were shoved along to make room for others. 'How many do you think it takes to fill them if you have one man to every three feet of space?'

Margot's voice had an edge to it. 'How the hell do I know? I was never any good at arithmetic –'

'It takes a bloody lot, I can tell you!' A group of Tommies clustered together on the deck as the ship got under way, and grinned down at the two girls. 'You'd better change your ideas if you think we each get three feet of space, sweetheart.'

A second soldier added his piece. 'More like three inches when the going's rough, and if you count the dead 'uns buried in the mud beneath your feet, it's less than that.'

Margot felt decidedly queasy. The ship was lurching broadside as it moved out into the Channel, and she had to swallow deeply to keep down the bitter rush of bile in her mouth. Angel too, was gripping on to the rail and trying not to let the soldiers' words conjure up a ghastly picture in her mind.

'Where're you two lovelies going?' one of the Tommies said cheerily. 'You can warm up my bit of trench any day –'

'Are you going to the trenches?' Angel looked directly into his eyes, instantly feeling a fool for asking such an inane question. Presumably that was where they were all going. Going to die, many of them . . .

' 'Course we are, sweetheart. It's our home from home. Can't you see our webbed feet?'

'We don't know where we're being sent yet. My friend can drive, so she expects to be doing ambulance duty. I'm going to ask to go to a factory to pack food kits,' Margot said.

She and Angel looked at each other. If they did as they intended, they would be separated. In this unreal world, it was a worse thought than working in one of the field hospitals.

'I might change my mind, though,' Margot added.

'That's right, darling,' one of the older soldiers said lazily. 'You stick to rolling bandages. Maybe I'll see you again. When I'm crying out for somebody to hold my hand in the night, I'd give a week's ration to see your pretty face looking down at me. I'll ask for you, if you tell me your name.'

'Don't wish yourself into a hospital bed,' Angel said quickly. 'It's bad luck to talk like that.'

The man laughed, a slightly chilling sound. 'P'raps it was bad luck to be born at all. When you've been at the Front for a year or more, you get a gut feeling when your number's coming up, and this was the leave for me to put my affairs in order . . .'

'Stuff it, Jimmy. You'll be frightening the poor lassies before they've even set foot in France. They're nobbut babbies, either of 'em.'

Angel's face burned. The man who spoke had an accent similar to Harriet Garth's. She turned her back on the group.

'Let's walk around a bit,' she hissed to Margot. 'If we keep moving, we may not feel so peculiar.'

She didn't need telling that the ship's motion was doing odd things to Margot. The whiteness of her face told her so. Angel was a reasonably good sailor, but it gave her an excuse to get away from these disturbing revelations. There was no use anticipating what they would find when they arrived in France. They were to be allocated their jobs then.

They managed to find a corner near the nurses, and leaned on the rail. Dover was a hazy mist behind them. Ahead of them was the narrow stretch of choppy grey sea, busily populated with craft plying back and forth between the two Allied countries. Taking the well and whole; bringing back the dead and maimed . . .

'Did you mean what you said?' Angel asked. 'About changing your mind about working in a factory?'

Margot nodded weakly. 'Please don't talk about packing food right now. The thought of food at all makes me –' she paused while she breathed deeply, trying not to retch as she fought down the nausea. There was nothing Angel could do but wait until the paroxysm subsided.

'I don't want us to be separated,' Margot managed eventually. 'We should stick together. I'll ask if I can be a hospital helper, then at least I'll see you between your ambulance journeys.'

'We may have no choice,' Angel said worriedly. 'But it won't do any harm to ask, and of course I want that too.'

'Have you written to tell Jacques you're coming?'

The Channel breeze cooled the sudden heat in Angel's cheeks. It had been her first instinct . . .

'No.' Her voice was flat.

'Why on earth not? He'd get leave, try to see you! I thought you'd have written to him immediately.'

Angel didn't answer. Of course she'd wanted to let Jacques know, but the confusion in her mind still raged. The longing to see him again was tempered by a bittersweet fear that he may have changed in the months they had been apart. People did change, feelings altered, love died. It was almost better not to know than to risk seeing that in Jacques' eyes. Her own father had proved to her that love didn't last for ever. How could he still love her mother when he was consorting with that Yorkshirewoman? How long had the pretence gone on? Living a lie . . .

'Angel, when are you going to tell me what's hurt you so badly?' Margot said quietly. 'It's something to do with your father, isn't it?'

Angel drew in a painful breath. They were jostled on all sides by anonymous uniforms and unknown faces. She had meant to keep the hurt to herself, but somehow, as she stared out to sea and saw the growing line of the French coast turn into green and gold, she felt as though she and her closest friend were alone. And she was finally able to say the words that lay like gall in her heart.

'He has a mistress. Doesn't that shock you? My so-respectable father!'

Margot knew what it must have cost Angel to confess to something that wasn't her fault, but which nonetheless touched every one of her family. And it wasn't so staggering, since Margot had already guessed the truth.

'No, it doesn't shock me,' she said evenly. 'Your father's human, like all of us. The Royals have had mistresses and lovers for centuries. Why should we lesser ones be so different?'

'I don't care about Royals! I only care about *us*!'

'Isn't that being a little selfish?'

Angel turned to look at her now, her face flushed with anger. To her friend, it was a healthier emotion than the blank bewilderment that had masked her face for much of the time since arriving on Margot's doorstep.

'*Selfish*? It's my father who's being selfish –'

'Who's he hurting? Not your mother, who's always been so self-sufficient she probably only ever needed him for procreation, and once all that sordid business was done with, I'll bet she never allowed him into her bedroom again. Can you deny it? Remember how wicked we used to feel at college, taking bets on it?'

'I know, but –'

'He's certainly not hurting Louise, who by all accounts is well rid of that chinless wonder, Stanley, and good luck to her with her haggis man. Ellen couldn't care less what your father does, as long as she goes her own sweet way. So that leaves you – Daddy's darling. Face it, Angel, you're jealous.'

Angel glared at her.

'Don't be ridiculous –'

'You're just plain, old-fashioned jealous. You can't bear to think that some other woman has claimed your father's affections. All these years when your dear Mama has been frigid and unloving, he's lavished all that generous love on little Angel, and now he's found a real warm flesh-and-blood woman. At least, I presume that's what she is. Do you care so little for him that you begrudge him that?'

'I thought *you* cared about my feelings.'

Margot put a sympathetic arm around her.

'I do, darling. That's why I can't bear to see you so unhappy, but don't blame your father for being a normal healthy man, and don't punish Jacques for just being a man.'

The V.A.D.s were being called together, and given brief instructions where to go when the ship landed at Calais. There was a depot there to deal with the fresh intake, and they would receive their orders. There was no more time for soul-searching or confidences, to Angel's relief. Margot's words had been too near to the truth she wouldn't admit and hadn't realised, to want to dwell on them.

Three hours later, after endless delays and arguments, they were given space in the same truck leaving for northeast France the following morning. Angel's First Aid training and ability to drive had given her slightly more status than Margot, but their insistence that they must stay together had finally worn down the Section Leader, who dismissed them as being of little use anyway.

They'd learn, she thought grimly, stamping their cards with a flourish. If they were out here for a lark, the way some of these upper class girls were, they'd soon be cut down to size. The hospitals receiving casualties from the Front Line soon decided which of the women volunteers were made of steel and which of cotton wool.

They had to sleep in makeshift quarters that night, on hard fold-up beds with little bedding. It was cold and miserable, and the other girls who had travelled with them eyed them suspiciously, in the same way that factory girls treated them with inverted snobbery. Resenting the air of breeding and money that no rough clothing could disguise; refusing to show friendship for fear of being taken down a peg or two.

'Little snots,' Margot muttered to Angel. 'What do

we care, anyway? We've got each other.'

They were on the road early next morning, herded into an army truck with two other V.A.D.s going to the same clearing hospital and a group of men returning to their unit. The other girls giggled and flirted with the soldiers, and completely ignored Angel and Margot. It didn't bother them. By the time they got out of the bone-shaking truck that jolted every bone in their bodies, they felt ready to crawl into hospital beds themselves.

The 'hospital' caring for British wounded was part of the Town Hall in a small town called Piersville. The regular cottage hospital could never have dealt with all the casualties arriving almost hourly. Piersville was a typical French town, such as Angel and Margot had often visited with their families.

In its centre was the town square, surrounded with trees and little shops, *patisseries* and *pharmacies* and *boulangeries*, all the lovely names that tripped so delightfully off the tongue.

Nostalgia for times past swept over Angel. As children, she and Ellen and Louise had always loved the quaint French patois of the shopkeepers, charmed in their turn to find the little English girls practising their French with solemn attention to vowel sounds and accents. She had never been to Piersville, but the essence of the place was that of every small French town and village . . .

Except . . . the minute they alighted from the truck, stiff and aching in every muscle, she knew it was vastly different. In time of war, the very character of a country changed. The normally sleepy square throbbed with the sound of trucks and ambulances. The trees in the square, usually alive with chirping, gaily twittering birds, merely rustled their leaves as the traffic rolled by. There were no birds to be seen in the grey unseasonal sky over Piersville.

In the distance, Angel suddenly became aware of the dull

sound of gunfire to the east. It had probably been there all the time, but until the engine of their truck was silenced, she only just registered it. It wasn't so far away, she thought, her heart jumping, as a blast that was louder than the rest split the afternoon air.

There was something else. A sickly, unpleasant smell that drifted all around them as the doors of the hospital were opened wide. It was a weird mixture of the dank sweat of hopelessness, disease, excreta and vomit. It filled the very air, tainting it. Glancing at Margot, she could see by her pinched nostrils that she was aware of it too. But come what may, they were in it now. They were part of this bloody war.

A hospital official came out to the truck, a sheaf of papers in his hand.

'There should be four for us today,' he said shortly to the truck driver. 'Bannister, Lacey, Green and Martin.'

They sounded like a music hall act, Angel thought with a feeling of rising hysteria. The four of them side-stepping out onto some brilliantly lit stage, spangles glittering in the spotlight, Tango-orange smiles flashing at the audience as eight feet tapped their way across the stage to the sounds of wild applause . . . Bannister, Lacey, Green and Martin . . .

Within weeks they had become seasoned V.A.D.s, and thoughts of anything so light and frothy, anything so normal, as a stage show, was farthest from any of their minds. Green and Martin had been put straight into the surgical section of the hospital, having done some nursing in England. The Sister in charge told Angel and Margot to report to the recovery wards, where Doctor Lancing was expecting them.

'What a bloody name for a doctor,' Margot stuttered. 'God, I'm scared, Angel. And what about you? Why aren't they giving you an ambulance?'

'I don't know! Why do you expect me to know everything?'

'I was only trying to be helpful,' Margot said resentfully. 'I thought that was why you came, to drive ambulances.'

They learned very quickly that they did as they were told. If there were weeping wounds to be dressed that didn't need expert attention, they dressed them. If there were sheets to be changed from the disgusting mess some of the poor devils made on them, they changed them. If there were heads to be held while wounded soldiers spewed blood and vomit into metal containers, they held them. If there were nightmares to share in the dead of night, they shared them.

They learned of more horrors of the Front from the babblings of delirious men than were ever reported in English newspapers. They heard young boys boast of the effectiveness of pissing on rags and pressing them to their noses to combat the awful gas attacks. They learned of the lice that crawled into a man's skin until he felt he was being eaten alive. They came to recognise the pungent smell of creosote as the endless stretcher cases were brought in from the trenches.

'Kills the bloody lice all right, darling,' one of the remnants of Kitchener's army could still joke in the midst of appalling wounds. 'They tell us it makes the trenches more hygenic, see? What a bloody laugh that is, when you're slipping and sliding in somebody else's shit. 'Course, they forget to tell you the creosote brings you out in blisters if it gets on your skin or your clothes. Seen some of the blisters, big as ass-holes, have you?'

Angel nodded without expression, feeling the depth of the men's degradation that they could speak so freely and not notice.

'You should do as I did, mate,' the man in the next bed guffawed. Angel found it hard to look at him because of the gaping hole in his face that was raw and livid. 'The little bastards lay their eggs in the seams of your clothes, so you run a lighted candle up the seams. That soon gets the little turds hopping. You learn plenty of new tricks in a war.'

Angel and Margot were learning them too. They learned to close their ears to the interesting discussions between patients on the merits and demerits of ridding themselves of lice. They tried to ignore the scathing insults that passed between the genuinely wounded, and the despised S.I.W.s who had worked their passage home – their 'Blighty one'. Cowards who were brought in with knowingly self-inflicted wounds were the lowest of the low.

They had to harden themselves to the terrible cries and screams that permeated the hospital walls, because if they didn't, they would never have been able to carry on. They shared the hazards of nursing to the best of their capabilities, and tried to hide their pity at the sight of the men in their torn and ragged blood-stained uniforms, and the disagreeable shock of finding some of the clothing alive with maggots and lice. They tried not to notice the nausea that came with the reek of ether and the appalling sickly-sweet smell of gangrene. They held the hands of the dying. They wrote letters home for men who had no hands to hold a pencil, or eyes to see the writing paper.

They were constantly ordered to take their time off and not waste it by doing extra duties. It was little enough, and the Ward Sister snapped at them that they would be less than useless to her if they dropped from sheer fatigue. They had borrowed bicycles several times and ridden in the direction away from the Front Line, where fields still grew green, and the wild poppies and daisies and waving cornflowers, still flourished despite a war.

In the cramped quarters they shared, they stretched out wearily every night on their narrow beds, generally too numb to move a muscle. As if to underline her resentment towards the Sister, Angel swore in the colourful phrases they heard daily on the wards. Margot grinned, leaning up on one elbow.

'Sister's right, Angel. We should get away from here more than we do, if only for an hour or so. Where shall we go? Is there a dance in town, do you think?'

Angel's eyes suddenly filled. A dance in town! It seemed years since she had even thought of such a light-hearted, frivolous thing. So long since she had been held in a young man's arms and teased in the meaningless way she had flirted with the young bucks in London, ardently professing true love if she would but spare them a kiss.

She looked at Margot. Both of them changed, older, having seen sights those other two girls could never have imagined. Young men's bodies had been exposed to them, all their dignity stripped, and neither they nor the men had felt shame or embarrassment. There was nothing but deep sorrowing pity for their plight, a reaching out of the senses towards all humanity. They were two different young women from the butterflies of pre-war days. Angel felt a brief sadness for those other two, and scrambled to her feet before it overwhelmed her.

'All right, let's find something to do. There are cafés in this town. There must be music, if not dancing. Do you remember the accordions in the evenings at Montmartre?'

'Piersville isn't Paris,' Margot said drily, but Angel's desperately gay mood was catching, and they changed out of their uniforms in a trice, wearing their own clothes and feeling the comparative softness against their skins.

They washed away the grime of the day and touched their mouths with lipstick, running combs and powder through their sweat-stained hair until it felt reasonably clean and fragrant. Feeling human again, and pushing away the guilt that they left behind them the broken bodies of the wounded still lying in agony on hospital beds. And holding on to Sister's stern words. What good would they be if they collapsed from sheer fatigue?

The evening was still warm as it should be in mid-June. It was a shock to realise they had been here so long. Days had merged into weeks, into months. There had been mutters of leaves due to them, but so far nothing had transpired.

Tonight, they didn't think about it. They had a little time to themselves before they tumbled exhausted into bed as usual.

They had gone out very little since arriving, but if there were any dangers of roaming around in a small French town near enough to the Front Line, they didn't consider them. Tonight, they could pretend they were tourists. The war didn't exist. Just for a few hours . . .

In the intimacy of a small crowded café where they drank cheap red wine and listened to the plaintive singing of a husky-voiced French singer, accompanied by an old accordion player, Angel felt her throat constrict. She spoke excellent French, and the words of the song told of lost love, of empty partings and sweet reunions, and shrieked to her of Jacques. She had deliberately kept him out of her mind of late, filling her days with her self-imposed tasks, letting the exhaustion of the nights take her into oblivion.

'When are you going to try to find him, Angel? Isn't it what you came here for?'

Margot's soft voice broke through her dreaming. She had forgotten that Margot's French was as good as her own. Margot could read every expression on Angel's face, and know how brittle was the mask she constantly wore. There was no use denying where her thoughts lay, and she spread her hands as if in supplication.

'I don't know. It's all so confusing –'

'What's confusing? You love him and he loves you, and he doesn't even know you're in France. I think you're touched in the head. Have you read those letters your mother sent you?'

Angel shook her head. She and Margot had been diligent in writing home, and Clemence had posted a small packet of letters written in Jacques' familiar handwriting, and the temptation to rip open the envelopes had eluded Angel so far. There was so much Margot didn't understand. She didn't know that Angel began every letter home with the words 'Dear Parents', unable to make any reference to her father more personal than that. She mourned the loss of the old relationship with Fred, but she couldn't seem to break past the knowledge that Harriet was somewhere in the background, taking the love that belonged by right to Clemence and his daughters.

She was a prude, after all, Angel discovered bitterly. And with the knowledge came a closing of her mind to all that she and Jacques had been to one another. Even the sudden realisation that several Tommies in the crowded smoky café were eyeing her and Margot up and down appreciatively was sending cold shivers up and down her spine. God, I'm going to end up as frigid as Mother, she thought in a fright.

'Read Jacques' letters, Angel,' Margot said calmly. 'At least have some consideration for his feelings, wondering what the hell's happened to you. You owe him that.'

'When I'm ready, all right? I'll know when. Let's get out of here, shall we?'

She scrambled to her feet, suddenly stifled by the atmosphere, the determination by everyone in the café to be bright and cheerful, when such a little distance away men were dying at this moment. The Tommies bragged of some big offensive to come. They hinted at July, only weeks away, and they spoke as if this was the last big push to finish it all.

And if it really was to be the final battle, then the Royal Flying Corps would certainly be very much involved in it. Jacques might be killed. The torment wouldn't let her be. She might never see him again, and she would only have a packet of unread letters as souvenirs . . .

Margot followed her out of the café into the cool dusk of the evening. They made their way back to the splendid portals of the Town Hall, magnificent as all French official buildings were, the little shops with their closed and shuttered windows more insignificant now by contrast. Piersville would once have been a sleepy little town in the middle of nowhere. It had assumed an importance now that it had never sought, and the erudite Town Hall stank with the suppurating wounds of foreigners.

The town and its citizens bore it all with quiet dignity. British and French were inextricably bound together in the desire for peace, to live normal lives again. She and Jacques were bound together by love.

'Are you taking your usual walk tonight, Margot?' she said huskily. Her friend had become a fanatic for exercise, wailing that she was getting fat, when they both knew that their meagre rations wouldn't put weight on a flea.

'Of course. Green and Martin actually spoke to me today, and I offered to lend them an English magazine, since neither of them can speak the lingo. I'll take it along to their room.'

If she guessed that Angel had decided the time was right for reading Jacques' letters at last, to laugh and cry over them a little, she kept her voice steady and didn't betray it.

Chapter 14

Green and Martin had become slightly less resentful of the two girls with the posh accents, since discovering that they worked as hard as the rest, and didn't flinch from doing the disagreeable jobs. Green sought out Angel and Margot while they were snatching a break for a cup of tea. It was the morning after Angel had finally wept healing tears over Jacques' letters. The girl waved a handful of papers at them.

'We've got a week's leave. Replacements are taking over until we get back, before being transferred to their regular jobs. We've got passages booked on the hospital ship going home tomorrow.'

Angel had other plans for her next available day off. Green looked at her in disbelief as she said she wanted to stay.

'Are you crackers? Who'd want to stay in this hell-hole when we can go home for a bit? Anyway, you've got no choice. We're to escort six stretcher cases to the ship and be responsible for them until we get to Blighty. Sister wants to see you, Bannister, and she's not looking too pleased.'

Angel marched off in a fury. She had just decided to pay Jacques a surprise visit, and now it seemed that she was thwarted . . .

She went to the office. Sister Yard was a stern, mannish woman, and her aggressive manner told Angel that she wouldn't relent over the enforced leave.

'I understand that you can drive, Bannister?'

At Angel's nod, she spoke decisively. 'Good. Two of our ambulance drivers have influenza, so you'll be responsible for getting the stretcher cases to Calais tomorrow. The other V.A.D.s will care for them en route. You'll be met at Dover by another driver, and be free to carry on with your week's leave. Think you can handle it?'

Angel gulped. She had no choice. But driving the familiar little Sunbeam, even to Scotland and back, didn't compare with driving a notoriously unreliable ambulance with six wounded men and three other women over unknown terrain . . .

Sister looked at her keenly. 'I'm relying on you, Bannister. You've proved to be solid. Don't let me down. I may be able to recommend you for more ambulance duty when you return.'

Angel resisted the temptation to click her heels and salute. She mumbled her thanks and backed out of the office, leaning weakly against the outer wall for a second. She had proved to be solid. Coming from Sister, that was praise indeed, even if it did make her feel as unfeminine as a lump of lead.

Margot added her own praise. Margot's usual exuberance was returning in leaps and bounds at the thought of going home.

'You'll be fine, darling!' she said boisterously. 'Just remember to apply the brake when we get to the coast. I don't fancy swimming back to Blighty! I'm going to spend the entire week in a hot bath, and restoring my fingernails to their former perfection.'

'Is that all?' It sounded comical after the way they had been spending their days and nights these past few months. How quickly the abnormal had become the normal, she realised poignantly.

Margot laughed. 'Well, I might manage the odd social event or two. What will you do, darling? Home to Meadowcroft? Unless you'd prefer to stay in Norfolk with us. Not so much travelling and all that,' she added delicately.

'No, I shall go home,' Angel said evenly. 'Mother would be hurt if I didn't.'

'So would your father. Don't shut him out, Angel.'

Just recently, she had been able to shut him out most effectively. Life had been too busy to spend time on sentiment. Days were filled to capacity, nights spent in exhausted sleep. It was what she had needed. It delayed thinking and making decisions. Now the thinking had been done for her, and she was going home.

And despite the embarrassment she would feel at facing her father again, England and Meadowcroft and all the lovely memories of home tugged at her heart.

There was no point now in writing a hurried note to tell Jacques she was in France, when she was about to depart. It must all wait until she returned in a week's time.

There was another thought to cling to. If there was to be a splendid battle in July as was surmised, and victory followed, then she and Jacques and countless others could pick up the threads of their lives again.

She must think positively, buoyantly. She must see this new task of safeguarding the stretcher cases back to England as a challenge and an omen. If they all got home safely, then it boded well for the future.

The journey was a nightmare. The ambulance jolted over the rough roads, and time and again the girls asked her to stop while the stretcher cases leaned out of the vehicle and vomited on the roadside, or emptied their bowels into containers that had to be disposed of unless they wanted it spilling over everything. The stench was indescribable, but they had to grit their teeth and bear it.

Time and again, Angel dashed the tears from her eyes, knowing she mustn't weaken at the moans and retchings, because she must get them to the coast on time. They couldn't afford long delays, not even for the men's comfort, or to let the air in the ambulance freshen.

She mustn't even think of them as men – or boys, which most of them were. They were the stretcher cases. Only by continuing to think of them so impersonally could she cope with the human degradation, guiltily thanking God that at least she was driving and not constantly tending them, like the others.

When they finally arrived at the port, she got out of the ambulance with shaking legs, feeling worse than she had ever felt in her life when her charges thanked her cheerfully for getting them safely to the ship. Poor devils . . . one with only one leg, one with chest wounds that kept him coughing up blood, two with shell shock and internal bleeding, and the other two looking so near to death that Angel wondered at the sense of bringing them all this way to suffer more.

She was instantly ashamed. If they were to die, how much better to die at home in England with a loving family all around, than in some anonymous foreign military hospital.

Other hands took care of the soldiers on board ship, but they were still officially responsible for them until they reached British soil. Angel handed them over with a great wave of thankfulness, knowing uneasily that this might well be only the first of many such sojourns. How blithely she had once said that she could drive ambulances in France, with no idea of what it entailed. How values changed . . .

At Dover, she and Margot parted from Green and Martin and took the train to London. They spent the night at the station hotel, and in the morning they hugged and parted, Margot to go on to Norfolk, Angel to wait impatiently on the crowded station for a train on the Great Western line to Bristol, and then a taxi to Meadowcroft.

Not until then did the strain of the previous day begin to recede. Everything had happened so fast, she couldn't let anyone know she was coming, and it was better so. She wanted no fuss, no talk of heroics. She just wanted to be home.

Weak tears filled her eyes. She was no heroine, home from the Front. Those wounded boys were the heroes, every one. A sudden overpowering dread of going back overcame her. She wanted to crawl away into hiding, and never have to face those wards again, the smells, the terrors, the screams . . .

But she knew in her heart that of course she would go back. What right did she have to refuse help to those who needed her? They too would want to see these patchwork English fields in their soft green summer mantle. With faint surprise, Angel saw how the seasons had moved on.

'Angel, my dear girl! Why on earth didn't you let us know you were coming? Just look at you! So thin and dishevelled. You need fattening up before you tell us all about it. Your things are still in your room, and you do look so stained after travelling, darling. I'm sure you'll feel better after a bath.'

Clemence's stunned surprise in seeing her daughter gave way to practicalities.

Angel stood perfectly still for a moment, drinking in the warmth and the luxury of the lovely old house. In effect, it reached out its arms to welcome her home, which was more than Clemence had done. There had been a brief hug and a peck on the cheek, but maternal concern for Angel to resume her role as young lady of the house quickly took precedence over everything else.

She wondered how this woman, so attentive at the hospital trains, could be so incapable of showing love to her own family. But of course, the dear boys at the railway station didn't have to be shown real touching and holding affection, did they? Their outward needs were attended to, and in that, Clemence admirably played the part of their ministering angel. It was a minor revelation in those first bittersweet moments of coming home.

She heard the bang of a door, and then her father came into the room, crossing the space between them and holding her tight to his chest, all else forgotten.

'Thank God you're safe, my dearest girl. I thought I was imagining things when I heard your voice. Sit down and let me look at you!'

Fred drew her onto the sofa, still holding tightly to her hands, his eyes searching her weary face. He could only guess at all she had experienced. He wanted to protect her from all ills, his darling child, hardly aware that she sat momentarily stiff, distant from him.

Angel couldn't help registering the difference in him and Clemence. The one so warm and loving, the other so aloof. Without analysing them further, she suddenly leaned her weight against her father's chest, and let his arms hold her as they had done so many times in the past. It may not be total forgiveness, but it was a beginning.

But Clemence was right. When she had had a hot bath and washed her hair, and changed into a light summer frock, dallying in her old room with her own belongings, she began to feel human again. She was almost loath to go downstairs to have to talk about the war. Here she felt safe. Home and all the things she had so ached to get away from were now the things she most needed.

Sister Yard had been right too, insisting that the girls take their leave. Angel acknowledged that there was a limit to a person's endurance. The independence she had coveted so much was forgotten for the moment. It was good to feel pampered and part of something deep and abiding once more. Meadowcroft was truly the haven Fred had always called it.

Downstairs, the soldiers billetted at the house were impatient for news of the Front. The convalescents had varying reactions to her guarded reports. She didn't want to talk of it, or think of it. Fred was sensitive to her feelings, and decided when enough was enough. He suggested that the two of them should stroll down to the village after dinner.

'Get your land legs back to normal again, old thing. What do you say?'

Angel agreed slowly. They had to talk. She knew that. Might as well get it over with, as let it fester. She had heard those same cheerful words from so many lips of brave boys preparing to have limbs amputated . . . it was as if the ghost of them would be forever in her head and heart.

'Have you heard from Ellen lately?' she said quickly.

Clemence's eyes were steely. 'I've washed my hands of her. She and that dreadful Rose Morton now work in a munitions factory of all things! You'd think that dear Stanley's accident would have put Ellen off such an idea for life.'

'I thought Rose had become your favourite, Mother,' Angel said mildly.

'Never!' Clemence could dismiss facts from her mind like other people changed their stockings. 'I blame her for much of Ellen's waywardness.'

'Ellen's not afraid to exercise her own mind, Mother. What of Louise? I thought she might have been home by now.' Or sent word that she and the dashing Dougal Mackie had eloped to Gretna Green in romantic fashion . . .

'Louise is spending the summer fruit picking in Scotland.' Clemence's voice implied that it was only slightly better than soliciting on street corners. 'She'll ruin her hands and her skin, but since she's an independent woman, as she frequently tells me in her letters, she does as she pleases.'

'Good for her,' Angel said softly. She felt a brief pity for her mother, all three of her ewe-lambs turning out to be such a disappointment to her.

'Naturally, I didn't expect you to agree with me!' Clemence went on. 'From the look of you, I guarantee that you forget to put protective cream on your skin at night.'

Angel laughed helplessly, a hint of tears in her eyes.

'Oh Mother, you really are the giddy limit!'

Later, she and Fred walked in uneasy silence until well away from the house. In the old days, she would have tucked her hand in his arm. Now, she felt the awkwardness that prevented her from doing so. The night was soft and mellow, the sun a great glowing crimson ball in the sky where it met the horizon. Cows chewed contentedly in English fields. Birds sang, darting in and out of the rustling trees, lush with summer fragrance. A meandering stream gurgled over stones as a kingfisher skimmed its surface, and the evening bees went busily about their work seeking nectar from wild blossoms.

All Angel's senses were tinglingly alive, thinking she had never known anything so beautiful, so serene, as pastoral England, so far removed from the hell of Piersville British hospital. She shivered at the memory, and it was as though she had briefly held happiness in her hand and felt it splinter like broken glass. Fred glanced at her, troubled.

'How do you and Margot really fare, darling?'

She shrugged. She'd expected him to bring his own affair into the open at once. He made her nervous. Her voice was tight and strained.

'We live from day to day. We're like a human factory. New intakes of casualties every morning, old ones packed off every evening. Those who are well enough to fight go back again to the trenches. The others get sent home in an ambulance or a box. We're frustrated by the sheer waste of it all. We can't afford pity. If we did, we'd produce an ocean of tears.'

She stopped abruptly as her father's big hand covered hers. She snatched her own away. Fred looked at her steadily, forcing her eyes to turn to him. She saw the pain in his face, the saddened laughter lines about his eyes.

'Have you made contact with the friend who writes to you?' he said quietly.

She stared at him for a moment. He saw the bitter twist to her lovely mouth and ached to kiss it away as he had kissed her bruises away when she was a child. But this was no child's eyes that looked back at him.

'No. And what about *your* – friend?'

Fred took a sighing breath. 'Harriet is my love, as you very well surmised. She is well, although I suspect you weren't merely enquiring about her health.'

'I was not! I couldn't care less about her –'

'But I care very much about her, Angel. I'm sorry if it pains you to know that a father can have a life beyond the four walls of the family home, but please understand that this is far more than a casual affair between me and Harriet.'

She wished he hadn't spoken her name. It made her real, when Angel was trying so hard not to think of her that way. It brought her image between them.

'I really don't want to hear it, Father,' she spoke defiantly, the brief tender feelings towards him gone.

All the hurt was back, all the smouldering anger. And she welcomed it, because it helped her to replace in her mind some of the horrific memories of Piersville.

'Do you still want to walk to the village, or shall we go back?' she asked pointedly.

'We came out to walk to the village, and that's what we'll do,' he replied just as doggedly.

He spoke of other topics, forcing Angel to answer, insisting that she remembered that he was still her father, and as such commanded her respect. It meant something more than pride to Fred that she respected him. He made just one more attempt to clarify his own feelings on the subject of Harriet Garth.

'Your mother has been ignorant of my relationship with Harriet for a good many years now.' He confirmed her suspicions. 'The last thing I want to do is to hurt either of them, Angel. Do you understand?'

'You want my silence,' she answered baldly. 'Don't worry. I've already decided to save Mother the humiliation.'

He didn't notice her trembling lips, suddenly realising that never in a thousand years could she have foreseen this conversation. It was Angel then, who deliberately talked about Ellen, about Louise, about anything but the subjects dearest to both their hearts. By the time they returned to Meadowcroft, they were both exhausted from the pretence of trying to act normally in what was a far from normal situation.

She was almost thankful when the week's leave was over and she could meet up with Margot in London. One look at Margot's face told her that her friend's week hadn't been greatly successful either.

'Mother seems to think I can call at a reception desk and ask for Edward, as though we're staying at some luxurious hotel,' she complained as they were crushed together in the corridor of the train taking them to Dover. 'She's expecting me to wet-nurse him, just because we're both in France. She's conveniently forgotten the size of the country, and she spent the entire bloody week making me feel guilty because I haven't tracked him down yet.'

From Margot's tone, Angel knew that she did feel annoyingly guilty because there simply hadn't been an opportunity to find Edward Lacey, apart from the barest enquiries.

'I know she's damnably worried about Eddie,' Margot suddenly capitulated. 'He was her little pet after Daddy died, and she simply can't come to terms with him being old enough to go to war.'

'He's not old enough. None of them are. He's a schoolboy. He's not ready to fight or –'

'Go on,' Margot said relentlessly, as Angel's jerky words stopped. 'Not old enough to fight or to die. That's what you were going to say, isn't it?'

'All right! He's too young to die. So is Jacques. So are we. So is every other poor devil who comes into the hospital at Piersville. Try telling that to the power-crazy men who juggle with ordinary people's lives.'

Other people in the corridor glanced their way as their voices rose, half-amused to hear two educated young ladies arguing so vehemently. Angel looked shamefaced.

'I'm sorry. We shouldn't be quarrelling like this.'

'I'm sorry too.' Margot's voice was oddly muffled. 'If you want the truth, I'm frantically worried about Eddie too, and I've had the devil's job not to let Mother see it all this week.'

'Hasn't the little stinker even written home yet?'

Margot gave the semblance of a smile. 'No, the little stinker hasn't. I shall give him a piece of my mind about that when I catch up with him.'

She cheered up, having something positive to think about. It was a good thing that she couldn't read Angel's mind, as the fervent hope ran through her head that young Edward Lacey was still around to be caught.

Angel had her own enquiries to make. The code name of Jacques' squadron headquarters, Brighton Belle, was used more as a flamboyant gesture of allegiance to England than to any hope of fooling the Germans of its presence. It wasn't difficult for Angel to find its whereabouts.

How to get there was another matter. The base was about thirty miles to the south of Piersville. To Angel's surprise it was the hard-faced Sister Yard who came to her rescue. Nothing was kept private for long at Piersville.

'I understand you want to visit the British air base, Bannister. I know you haven't been given an ambulance yet, but if you want to do replacement duty tomorrow, you can take four convalescent cases to an overflow hospital, and bring back any medical supplies that they can spare. Take the afternoon to visit the air base, but get those supplies back as soon as possible.'

'Thank-you, Sister!' Angel was overcome with gratitude, despite the trauma of driving more unknown roads. At least the convalescents wouldn't be terminal cases, and for that she must be thankful. She sped through the wards to find Margot.

'Best news I've heard all day.'

All Margot's attention was on the man she half-supported in the bed, ignoring his filthy rags in deference to his apologetic vomiting splashing all over her uniform. His body convulsed, and a strong, distinctive smell rose from the middle of the bed as the man retched and spewed.

'Both ends at once, old thing,' Margot said cheerily. 'Fetch me some clean sheets, will you, Angel?'

Angel fled, tears blinding her eyes. Dysentery afflicted many of the men from the trenches as well as everything else. If the bullets didn't get you, then the shells would. Or the gas or the pneumonia, or the piercing hell of a bayonet wound. When would it ever end? She rummaged for clean sheets in the linen cupboard, and then heard Margot's cracked voice behind her.

'No rush, Angel. The orderlies will clear the bed.' It was her way of saying that in that short space of time, the man had died.

She was gone before Angel could answer. Angel secretly worried about her. She was often too bright, too effervescent, a little ray of sunshine, according to the patients. But Angel suspected that someday that sunshine would go out, and when it did, Margot would never be the same again.

She pushed such thoughts away. Tomorrow she was going to find Jacques. The joy that had been absent in her life for so long suddenly soared at the thought.

And tomorrow didn't start off too badly. The convalescents were cheerful, none of them stretcher cases, able to sit in the back of the ambulance and enjoy their smokes, and crack a few jokes with the unexpectedly beautiful young driver.

Each of them looked at Angel's straight back, the gloss of her golden hair framing her head, and thought wistfully of a sweetheart or wife at home. They teased her, making outrageous suggestions that would have appalled her a year or so ago, but which now had her laughing back, recognising the need in them for feminine responses, to make them feel less emasculated than the endless useless fighting did.

They reached the overflow hospital in a state of camaraderie, and Angel was given the boxes of medical supplies Piersville so badly needed. On enquiry she discovered that a mere five miles separated her from Jacques' air base.

She drove more erratically than usual, without the usual cargo of wounded in the ambulance. At the base, she was uncertain what to do. She was dusty from travelling, and feeling far from fresh. A young airman asked her business, and she saw him redden with embarrassment that filled her with unease.

'Captain de Ville, Miss? I don't know. You'd best enquire in the Officers' Mess – that way.'

He pointed to a large hut, and Angel walked across the churned-up field to the Officers' Mess. From inside, she could hear sounds of merriment. She remembered instantly something that Jacques had told her.

'Commander Trenchard has a policy of "no empty chairs" in the messes.'

Angel had looked mystified until he had gone on to explain with grim humour.

'An empty chair means a pilot is missing, shot down in flames or blown to pieces. Trenchard is ruthless in getting replacements to fill the empty chairs. It keeps up morale, despite the fact that raw recruits are more likely to get shot down than old hands. But no empty chairs is the rule, and Trenchard abides by it.'

Angel's heart beat uncomfortably fast. There were officers inside the hut, other ranks filling the other messes. No empty chairs. But how many deleted names in Brighton Belle's personnel records? She knocked on the door quickly, before she lost her nerve. An officer answered it.

'De Ville?' He glanced round as the talking hushed. 'Are you a relative, Miss?'

'No. I'm – I'm – a friend.' She felt an acute sense of dread as one and another officer looked away. The words tumbled out. 'Has something happened to Captain de Ville?'

The officer took her arm. 'Let's go outside, Miss –'

'Bannister. Angel Bannister,' she replied automatically, as though they were new acquaintances at a garden party.

Outside in the warm afternoon air, he told her quickly.

'Captain de Ville didn't come back after his last bombing raid. We're pretty sure he got back over Allied lines, though. His plane was seen –' he stopped.

'Seen?'

'I'm sorry. It was seen going down in flames by one of our chaps. It wasn't clear if Captain de Ville got out or not. But it's very probable that he did.'

The voice droned on, hating having to prevaricate to this pretty girl. A stunner, the officer observed. And what rotten luck to receive such negative news. Privately, none of them thought de Ville had made it alive after seeing the inferno of his plane. But he couldn't tell the girl that. She needed some hope. He saw her sway and put out an arm to hold her.

'I'm all right,' she muttered between gritted teeth. 'Can I talk to the person who saw the plane go down?'

The man hesitated. What good would it do? He saw the pleading in her lovely eyes and nodded briefly. She had guts, for all her apparent gentle femininity.

'Stay here. I'll fetch him for you.'

He strode off, and Angel's legs wouldn't hold her up any longer. She sank to the ground, refusing to believe it, yet having to believe it. Jacques was missing . . . missing, and obviously, the rest of them believed him killed.

Missing, believed killed . . . wasn't that the official phrase? She heard the whine and roar of aircraft winging into the sky, and in their drumming the words kept going over and over in her head.

Tears blinded her eyes, realising she had come too late. Jacques was missing, believed killed . . . believed killed . . .

Chapter 15

'You really are an idiot, Rose!'

Ellen spoke in exasperation as she leaned over the girl in the bed. She bathed Rose's burning forehead, trying not to flinch at the sight of the yellow, broken skin, fluid seeping from it.

It was a good thing that Rose couldn't see the effects of the TNT poisoning for herself. The doctor had said she would be unable to see for about three days. She wasn't aware of how her face and neck and legs had swelled, making a caricature of her normally pretty appearance. She was home from her job at the munitions factory now for ten days on half pay, and Ellen did all she could to ease her discomfort when she wasn't away working at her own machine.

She didn't let on to Rose how tired she was. The munitions girls worked a six-day week from eight o'clock in the morning until eight o'clock at night, with an hour for lunch. The factory wasn't far from the house the two girls shared with several others, and Ellen nipped home in her lunch hour, to bathe Rose's irritated skin, and to give her a sandwich and some of the two pints of milk a day that she was allocated to combat the TNT poisoning. Despite its help, it would be months before the affected skin returned to anything like normal.

'You're a comfort, I must say!' Rose croaked. 'Why am I an idiot?'

'Letting yourself breathe in so much of the damned stuff! I

told you to keep your mouth shut and stop being the life and soul of the party, didn't I? We're supposed to keep silent in working hours.'

'I get bored with being a dummy,' Rose sulked. 'Anyway, it was better than being stuck-up.'

'Like me! That's what you mean, isn't it? Well, *isn't* it?' Ellen goaded her.

'Yes, it is. They call you Miss High-and-Mighty Bannister behind your back, if you must know. They wonder what you're doing here, instead of queening it over society functions.'

Ellen snorted. 'And I hope you put them right on that! When did I ever queen it over anything or anybody? I'm an out and out socialist, and well you know it.'

Rose spoke less forcibly, the irritation subsiding a little as Ellen's ministrations took effect.

'I do know it, old duck, but you have to admit that you're different from the rest of us! If you came out with a bit of good old Cockney sometimes, it might make you more acceptable to the other girls –'

'Why the hell should I? They don't put on airs and graces for me?' Ellen said belligerently, her eyes sparkling.

'You see?' Rose sighed. 'Isn't that what I've been trying to point out? Your airs and graces come naturally. That's what makes you different. You don't belong here, Ellen.'

Ellen stood up and brushed the crumbs off her skirt, still resentful of this criticism. Normally, it was a relief to come home for a while and be able to remove the fireproof overall and rubber boots that were so unbelievably hot in the summer months. To say nothing of the miserable cap that made her feel scalped, whether she was or not. Too many girls had accidents with their hair. She and Rose had witnessed one of them get her hair caught in a machine, and took no chances. She glowered down at Rose's swollen, pathetic eyes.

'I'm not going to listen to you,' she said shortly. 'They can take me as I am, or move to another factory. I'll see you tonight, Rose. Do you need anything else before I go?'

'No, thank-you. Mrs Gresham from next door is coming to sit with me this afternoon.'

'That's all right then.'

And hopefully, the old witch would be gone long before she got back, Ellen thought grimly.

She left the jug of milk where Rose could reach it, instructing her sternly to drink it herself and not give the old harridan from next door as much as one sip for her motley collection of stray cats. Ellen knew that tonight she would be opening doors and windows to rid the place of the cat stink that always wafted around the old woman.

She gave an involuntary sigh as she walked back to the factory, her back as straight as usual. Was she such a snob as Rose intimated? She had never thought herself to be so. Did she think herself superior to the other girls? She had always been ready to 'muck in', but she had to admit she wasn't given the easy friendship that existed between Rose and the rest of them.

Did she care? She brushed back a stray wisp of hair from her cheek. If she had anywhere else to go, she probably wouldn't stay on. Never one to balk at the truth, she admitted as much to herself. But where else could she go?

Not back to Meadowcroft yet, with the memories of the farm still painful. She couldn't forget the shame of meeting Peter Chard's eyes when she had scrambled down from the hayloft, obviously still warm from Andrew Pender's embraces.

She shivered, wondering how she could have been such a fool. Andrew Pender was a leech, preying on women. She was well rid of him, and love had died as quickly as it had grown. Peter was worth ten of him, but she doubted that he would even look at her now, and if she was the crying kind, she would weep for the loss of his friendship.

She straightened her shoulders as she approached the

dreary factory gates, merging in with the chattering girls, freed from their imposed silence until they donned their anonymous garb again and let the machines take over. It was like something out of a horror dream, Ellen thought. The humans were silent, while the machines clattered and roared, producing their shells to feed the weapons of war.

Silently, as she worked, inside herself she sang the song that said it all.

'Good-bye-ee . . . Don't Cry-ee . . . Wipe the tear from your eye . . . Good-bye-ee . . .'

The Battle of the Somme began on July 1st. News of the long-awaited onslaught was greeted in England with cheers and optimism. Soon it would all be over. The noise of the artillery bombardment prior to the day was so tremendous that it could clearly be heard across the Channel in England.

Since most of the Allied losses at Verdun had been French, their numbers were depleted, and the majority of the army at the Somme were British. In the battlefields and trenches of the once-lovely valley of the Somme, the two opposing armies were separated by a fifty-yard stretch of barbed wire and desolation, each wanting desperately to win a war that refused to end.

It was a perfect summer day, the sky a cloudless blue, the larks singing their hearts out. The Germans were deep in their superior dug-outs, but already alerted to the approaching attack by the heavy bombardment of days before, intended to blow up the worst of the wire. Because of the expected certainty of the Allied cause, the British leaders gave the complacent orders to the soldiers to march at a steady pace towards the tangled barbed wire, where the enemy would undoubtedly surrender.

It was the worst possible command. As the soldiers went over the top of the trenches, they were slaughtered, wave upon wave of them, by the waiting German machine guns.

When the numbers of dead and wounded were reckoned up, on that day alone, British casualties numbered sixty thousand, a number too staggering to comprehend unless you were personally involved: unless it was your leg that was sheared off, or your guts that were spewing out into the mud, unless you were one of the exhausted doctors or nurses or ambulance drivers, or the hapless V.A.D. workers, even now totally unprepared for the effect of an endless succession of human debris.

There was no time to think of personal matters. No time to worry over a loved one, or to leave the confines of the hospital or unit where you were assigned. The thought of Jacques de Ville's fate was pushed from Angel's mind. It was one of the penalties of war that there was no time to weep or to mourn. There was always another soldier's hand to be held to ease his suffering, another drink to be given gently to a mouth that couldn't hold any liquid because only half of it remained, another bone-shattered boy to be guided along the road to death.

Every hospital in the vicinity of the Front was strained to desperation point with the sheer numbers of wounded. It was a lasting nightmare, week after week after week . . . By September everyone's job had become a dual or a triple role. Doctors became aides, nurses were stretcher-bearers, anyone who could drive took turns with the sorely-pressed ambulance drivers to go to the Front and bring back the wounded . . .

'You'll go out tonight, Bannister,' Sister Yard ordered, her voice wooden with strain. 'Doctor Lancing wants every ambulance we've got sent out on the road. Follow the others, and keep your head down. And good luck.'

Angel's mouth was as dry as dust, her stomach a hollow emptiness as she was given her instructions. So far she had no real knowledge of the Front. Only what she had heard from the men and boys reliving their own nightmares, and she and Margot had both thanked God that their hospital wasn't in sight of the Front Line fighting. And now she had to drive right into it.

'Oh God, Angel, don't go!' Margot said in a fright when she heard. She gripped Angel's arms, her once-elegant fingernails chipped and digging into Angel's flesh. 'Say you've got the runs, say anything, but for God's sake, don't go! You'll be killed –'

Angel slapped her hard, thankful they were in their own room where no one else could hear. Lately Margot had been going rapidly downhill, succumbing to the trench nerve that affected men and nurses alike. Strong-willed or weak, trench nerve took no account of personality. When it struck, it reduced a person to a shivering wreck, until they could finally shake it off. But strangely, Margot's snivelling strengthened Angel's own reserves.

'Don't be ridiculous,' Angel snapped. 'Of course I shall go. I didn't come to France to whimper like a baby. And of course I shan't be killed. I have to bring the wounded back here, so a fat lot of good I shall be, stopping a Jerry's bullet. Besides – I've promised myself that I shall survive – at least until I know for certain what's happened to Jacques. No bloody Kaiser's going to wipe the two of us off the earth without giving us the chance to find each other again.'

Margot hugged her without speaking, her tears damp against Angel's face, her voice husky with emotion.

'You're so damn brave, Angel. You look as though a strong wind would blow you away, but although you may bend a little, you'll never break. I envy you so much. And I'll pray for you, every minute until you get back.'

'All right. But save most of your prayers for the poor devils I'll be carting back here. It won't be much fun for them to have me jolting them about.'

She tried to make light of it, because she wasn't feeling brave at all. She was more scared than she had ever been in her life before, but so was everyone. It didn't need putting into words. She got ready as calmly as possible, reporting to the ambulance shed at dusk and being allocated her vehicle. From then on, it was a case of following the one in front, a long snaking convoy of rescue trucks winding through the French countryside, the only lifeline for an army of wounded soldiers . . .

Afterwards, Angel could only think of that night in a series of vivid, nightmarish impressions, like some garish modernist painting. Brilliant orange glows in the blue-black night that burned the eyes; explosions that rocked the eardrums with a pain more intense than anything she had known; gunfire, incessant and deafening; screams and shouting, hoarse and desperate; no longer merely classed 'the wounded', but young men, mere boys, crying for their mothers, entreating God to let them die.

She lost count of the number of times she drove the ambulance to and from the Front Line. Stretchers were bundled into the rear and she was given the shout to go. She tried not to listen to the moaning, tried to block out every sound but the drone of the engine, praying that it wouldn't let her down, that there wouldn't be a puncture, or some other horror to stop her being relieved of each new cargo . . .

'Angel. Is that you, Angel?'

She heard the croaking voice as if from another world. It reminded her instantly of poor Hobbs, returning to Temple Meads station, coming home to die. But this wasn't their chauffeur. She leaned over the stretcher case being put none too gently into her ambulance, his legs and feet wrapped in some evil-smelling bandages, his anguished mouth coughing blood, still more seeping from a gaping wound in his chest.

'My God!'

She couldn't say the words out loud. It was as though they were snatched from her throat as she recognised the cheery young face. It wasn't cheery now as she had last seen it. It was drawn with agony, old before its time, the smell of death emanating from it. She caught at his hand, still so young, with all of life ahead . . . tears almost blinded her for a moment.

'Edward! Oh, God, Edward!' She was a shivering mass of

nerves as she recognised Margot's young brother. He was here, at the Somme, and being sent to Piersville hospital to die. She knew it as surely as she breathed. She looked up desperately as the orderly told her curtly to make room for a few more, and was forced to move out of Edward's hearing.

'I know that one,' she stuttered. 'He's my friend's brother. What are his chances?'

The orderly looked briefly sympathetic.

'I'm no doctor, Miss, but I know the smell of death when I sniff it. He'll be a gonner before the night's out if I'm any judge. Best get on the road quickly if you don't want a stiff on your hands.'

He spoke as he did, knowing there was no point in dressing up what was so obvious to them both. In an odd way, the clumsy words helped stem the appalling reality of what was happening. She climbed past the other casualties to cling to Edward's hand a moment longer before driving back to Piersville.

'Just hold on tight, Eddie. Margot's working with me at the hospital, and she'll be so thrilled to see you.'

'Margot? Didn't think she'd know how to tie a bandage!' He tried to be pleased, but the pain made the smile a grimace, and Angel knew there was no time to spare. She started the engine, spun the wheels in a fury at the bloody outrage of war, the sheer waste of so many young lives, and drove as if possessed on the road back to Piersville hospital.

Other hands took over as soon as she arrived. It was her last run of the night. She was near to dropping with sleep, but there was no way she could sleep. She wanted to prepare Margot . . .

The moment Margot heard the news, she rushed past Angel and into the ward where Doctor Lancing was bending over Edward Lacey's bedside. The girls heard him speak sharply to a nurse to give him some morphine, and then he moved on to the next patient. As Margot knelt down beside her brother, tears blinding her eyes, Angel caught at the doctor's arm.

'Can anything be done for him, Doctor?' she stuttered. 'He's her brother –'

'They're all somebody's brother, Miss,' the doctor said tersely. 'The boy's got trench foot. His feet are rotting. There'd be no point taking them off, gangrene would have galloped up his legs before I began. Besides, the hole in his chest is going to kill him in a matter of minutes or hours. His lungs are full of blood. He's breathing it. We don't have the staff or the ether or the time. I'm sorry.'

He moved along the line of beds, while Angel stared after him, tears stinging her own eyes. Damn him! He didn't mean to be callous, just practical. What was the use in trying to keep one boy alive for a few hours longer, when there were others more likely to live, who needed all his skill and attention? She turned back to Margot and Edward, fighting back the emotion.

'We'll soon have you well, Eddie. Just be brave, old thing,' Margot was saying shakily. 'The nurse will give you something for the pain –'

A swish of starched skirts, and a nurse leaned over with a hypodermic, injecting the precious morphine into Edward's vein.

'That hurt more than the bloody bullet,' the boy muttered, a shine of tears on his lashes as she moved away.

'Language, Eddie!' Margot reproved him, in the same way her mother and Angel's mother used to speak, a lifetime ago.

Edward began a paroxysm of coughing, and when it was over, he lay back, his face ashen and waxy.

'Do – something for me – old girl,' his breathing was harsh and laboured, the words a mere whisper.

'Of course.' Margot leaned forward to catch them.

'My train set – for Stinky Hughes – always wanted it – see to it, Margot –'

'You'll see to it yourself, you ninny –'

'Promise me –'

Angel pressed Margot's arm. Humour him, for God's sake, she entreated her silently. Margot nodded, her throat nearly too full to speak.

'I promise, Eddie, darling. Get some sleep now.'

His eyes closed obediently, and she kissed the cold cheek and smoothed back the unruly dark hair from his forehead. She gave a sudden gasp, and Angel reached for the boy's hand, feeling frantically for a pulse in his wrist. There was nothing.

Margot's nerve went completely after Edward's death. She spent the rest of the night weeping torrential tears, unable to be comforted, blaspheming at war, at God, at creation. Angel was so afraid for her, but in the morning, after neither of them had got more than the occasional cat nap, Margot emerged, strangely calm, insisting that she see Sister Yard at once.

'I want to take my brother home for burial,' she said imperiously. 'There's no question of him being buried in France. The Laceys have a family plot in Norfolk, where generations of Laceys have been buried. My mother would insist on it, and I shall take full responsibility for escorting my brother back to England. Money is not a problem, naturally, for the very best coffin to be found. You'll see that his body is released as soon as possible, I trust?'

But for the circumstances, Sister Yard would have put this young miss severely in her place. But the other girl, Bannister, had already alerted her of Lacey's wishes, and was hovering in the corridor outside the cramped office. She was beckoned inside and Sister spoke briskly.

'Bannister, you will escort Lacey and her brother to England. There will be five other deceased to go, and you'll leave the ambulance at the depot at Calais. You'll merely need to sign over the coffins on arrival, making your own arrangements for Private Lacey as you wish. Lacey will take compassionate leave. You will take whatever time is necessary before reporting back here, considering Lacey's emotional state. I know I can rely on you. You'll cope, of course.'

Angel gulped. Driving an ambulance, even with badly wounded men was one thing. Nobody liked driving the 'dead wagon', but one look at Margot's agonised face, and she nodded at once. She would cope.

They left in the early afternoon. Coffins were always taken out of the back door of the hospital in consideration of other patients, and loaded into the 'dead wagon'. Margot sat in the passenger seat, so grim and silent, she might well have been a corpse herself. She refused to speak one word for the entire journey to the ship.

The silence unnerved Angel more than anything. Despite herself, she couldn't help remembering conversations among the less sensitive V.A.D.s, regarding similar journeys.

'They douse the stiffs with preservative, o' course, otherwise they'd stink out the whole ship when they putrify. They have to plug 'em too – every orifice, to put it politely – so that nothing starts to leak out when rigor mortis ends and they go limp again.'

'Poor devils. Limp when they're born and limp when they die,' another one sniggered. 'I don't fancy the thought of being plugged, do you, Mabel?'

'Thank God they are! Imagine what would happen if you were driving the "dead wagon" and you heard an involuntary fart from one of the coffins. It 'ould scare the living daylights out of you, wouldn't it?'

'If it was an arse-tearer, it 'ould blow the plug out anyway!' The two of them had doubled up with laughter, imagining it, and Angel had felt sick to her stomach, not knowing how they could joke over something that so diminished human dignity. She had been green on the wards then. Now she knew that sometimes you only got through the days and nights by making a joke out of something terrible.

She began to breathe a little easier once they had crossed the English Channel and reached Dover. Army personnel had been there to receive the coffins, and Margot suddenly rallied, found a telephone and ordered a large car to take her and Angel and Edward to Norfolk. The cost never entered her head. Edward was to have the best transport available for his last journey. Margot was acting very strangely in Angel's opinion, but she was in no mood to listen to suggestions.

Margot's next phone call was to her mother, where she broke the news about Edward's death with gentle efficiency. She put her hand over the receiver while she murmured to Angel, 'Mother's being very stoical. She has just gone to find a handkerchief, then I must talk to her about arrangements.'

It was all like a bad dream. Margot organising and planning, almost as though she were taking charge of a garden party. Margot suddenly remembering something, and speaking rapidly to her mother, as though someone had wound her up.

'Oh, and you must get in touch with Stinky Hughes, Mother. Edward was most insistent about that. He'll want to see Stinky especially. And you're to wrap his train set in some nice paper, and we'll have a sort of presentation of it to the boy, once the preliminaries are over. We must feed everyone afterwards, of course. What will you get in? Is there still cold ham and tongue to be found in the shops? Something nice, for Edward. He'll want everyone to have a good time. You must see the Vicar at once, and the undertaker, and arrange it all for the day after tomorrow, Mother. We shall be there as soon as we can. Oh – and you'd better get someone to dust Edward's room. It's always such a tip, and it will do him good to see how spick and span it can be. Good-bye, Mother.'

She hung up and turned to Angel with an elated look in her eyes.

'Isn't that splendid? It's amazing what you can accomplish when you put your mind to it. Now, let's see if Edward's all right, and then find somewhere where we can all have a nice cup of tea.'

'*Margot!*' Angel gripped her arm.

'What is it?' She looked at her friend in surprise.

'Edward's dead. He doesn't want tea, or a tidy room, or care whether everyone has a good time or not –'

'Well, I know *that*! Good gracious me, do you think I'm going out of my mind or something?'

She smiled pleasantly, as though she hadn't really understood a word that Angel was saying. It was only when they were in the car on the long drive to Norfolk, that she suddenly looked pinched and afraid, and hugged Angel's arm.

'You will stay, won't you? I hate funerals. All those long faces and everyone trying not to cry, and having to be brave. I'm not brave, Angel –'

Angel leaned sideways and kissed her. 'Yes you are, darling. You're very brave. Eddie would be proud of you.'

'Would he?' Margot said in a pleased voice. 'Oh well, that's all right then.'

Angel found her own nerves jumping. The entire time in Norfolk was like a continuation of the bad dream. Margot still acting so oddly; her mother alternately weeping and being so conventionally polite it was almost ludicrous; the schoolboys, scared at witnessing the trappings of death for the first time; the guilty delight with which Stinky Hughes, in reality John Henry Hughes, received his posthumous gift from his old dorm-mate. It was a weird occasion, more tragic than Stanley's funeral, because of Edward's youth; less traumatic than might have been expected, because of Margot's determination to see that everyone enjoyed themselves and had a jolly good time, just as if darling Eddie was still here . . .

Angel had hugged her close when she decided she must leave, and said she looked forward to seeing her again as soon as she felt able to leave her mother and return to Piersville. Margot smiled vaguely and said good-bye, the gracious hostess.

Since she could do nothing about the situation, Angel decided it was best to try and stop worrying over Margot, and hope that time would heal whatever ailed her. The five days away from Piersville had exhausted Angel. She didn't realise what a strain it had all been until it was behind her. It was almost a relief to be boarding the first available leave ship, and hear the cheery baiting of the soldiers.

They were healthy and normal and *alive*. No matter what tomorrow might bring, here on this ship there was still time to indulge in a little harmless flirtation; to enjoy the wink of a man whose eyes told her he found her attractive; to feel like a woman, instead of a nameless driver with a tragic cargo in a silent ambulance; there was still hope.

If she didn't believe that, Angel thought desperately, she might as well lay down at the Front and wait for the next German bullet to claim her.

And there was still Jacques. Through all the harrowing days with Margot, Angel had been conscious of a growing feeling inside her, stronger than hope, as certain as a premonition. If people felt such things when a loved one died, then why wasn't it possible to feel it in reverse? To will someone to live? She had seen enough of death. Had seen it too closely, too many times in her young life.

Jacques wasn't dead. If he was, she would feel it, know it instinctively. Love didn't die, and hers for him would act like a talisman to keep him safe. She had to believe that too. And however much she might dread the horrors of the battlefield, she had to go back, because somewhere out there, was Jacques.

Chapter 16

The coifed nuns moved quietly between the long rows of beds in the old Abbey of St Helene, leaning towards one wounded man and then another, giving comfort and sanctuary to those who would survive, and to the dying the assurance of a better life in the hereafter, promised and reaffirmed in the glint of sunlight on the heavy crosses dangling from their necks.

Sister Therese paused at the foot of the mystery patient they had named Papillon, because of the way he had flapped his arms in his delirium, and because of the crude, grotesque sketches he made, some like gigantic butterflies, some resembling great winged birds with blackened faces and blank eye sockets, or drawings of hideously grotesque bats.

Always flying creatures . . . they wondered if perhaps he had been attacked by something. That the man was tortured, the nuns had no doubt. That his memory had been lost to him, through whatever suffering he had endured, was also a certainty. That he would one day recover, they could only hope and pray, and had bestowed the gentle name of Papillon on him, meaning butterfly, to aid that eventual return to health, because for all his ravings, they sensed that here there had once been a gentle man.

'How are you today, Papillon?' Sister Therese spoke softly. The nuns spoke only French in the converted Abbey, and since the man understood them perfectly and responded when he felt so inclined in a natural accent, they had no reason to believe he was anything but a Frenchman.

Where he had come from, they did not know, and so far he could not tell them. He had been almost naked when he had been brought in, what clothes he had worn were burnt off him save for a few tatters, and it was a miracle he had survived. Had it not been that he had been found half-drowned in a pool at the edge of a wood, he would undoubtedly be dead long before now.

Jacques looked vacantly into the sweet face of the nun. Along one of his cheeks were livid scars, but in time they would fade. He had been assured of it. He hardly cared. He cared about nothing. He was consumed with an anger as bitter as gall, and he did not fully know why. If only he could remember.

He wasn't stupid. He was fully aware that he had lost his memory. During the months he had been in the Abbey of St Helene, tended so caringly by the nursing nuns, he had recovered enough to know that he was in some kind of a hospital, that there were many other men here suffering far more than he, that he was one of the lucky ones who would eventually get well. And in time, the nuns hoped confidently that his memory would return . . .

In time! The phrase was uttered constantly, confidently, meant to give him sustenance, courage, endurance. Instead, it left him raging and boiling inside himself. Didn't anyone understand that time was no more than an empty vacuum, stretching into infinity, when there was no past, no more than a hazy uncertain future, a searingly painful, red-rimmed present?

He refused to speak to the nun who had taken his pulse, and was now swishing away from him. He could almost taste the smell of her, gagging him with its cleanliness, its godliness. She was all starch and cheap soap and clinical perfection. Too perfect to be womanly. Sterile. Unsullied. The words swam through his mind, but remained without voice, as Jacques did. Only occasionally did the words he produced make sense, but mostly they did not. They were the bleatings of animals in pain. Bleatings or roarings, depending on the pain. Everything depended on the pain.

'Poor sod.'

He had heard the chirpy Englishman's voice many times, and struggled to get him into focus. No clinical smell now. Sweat and stale blood, the whiff of excreta still lingering on the air. Going back soon, the Englishman kept saying cheerfully. Back to the war, the war, the bloody war . . .

He heard the man discussing him with someone called Jock in the next bed. They thought that because he couldn't concentrate, had difficulty in speaking, probably had only half a face for all he knew – that he couldn't hear, couldn't feel . . .

'Christ knows what they'll do wiv 'im,' the Englishman went on. 'Set 'im up as the Abbey artist, p'raps, and sell off his drawings. They ain't bad, if you like being scared to death. Not the kind of thing my old woman 'ould want, or I might take one 'ome to her.'

The other man grunted as usual before he spoke in his gravelly voice. What was he? Scots, presumably. Jacques was too tired to think, and too uncaring to bother.

'Nice wee lassie he's drawn. Have ye seen it? Keeps staring at it, poor devil. His wife, mebbe.'

Jacques turned his head a fraction, away from the two men. The face of a pretty girl was crudely drawn on a piece of paper. The nuns had propped it up beside his bed, so that when he turned he had no choice but to see it. It wasn't that he kept staring at it. If he needed to holler for help, he had to turn his head that way. The girl's face was a meaningless series of black lines and curves on the paper.

If he screwed up his eyes, he could make better sense of the bad drawing. He had enough sense to know that he was capable of better, which must be something in his favour. The face had large, expressive eyes, pale hair framing her cheeks, soft wide mouth. Part of another life, when such things had the power to stir his loins, to make him a man with a man's needs for such a woman. He didn't recall drawing her. She was a stranger to him, like everyone else in this bloodied world right now . . .

He closed his eyes tightly, before the black fear dragged him down once more. Better to shut it all out than to go on seeing a frightening place in which he was an alien thing, a man with no memory, therefore no soul.

The Englishman studied the drawing on the other side of Jacques' bed, and gave a sudden lewd chuckle.

'She's a nice bit o' crackling, whoever she is, Jock. I could give her a bit o' the old heave-ho, given 'alf a chance –'

'And given a guid right arm to hold her down,' the Scot sniggered. 'A lassie like that wouldn't give ye a second look, Harry! She'd go for the aristos, like yon laddie.'

Harry looked thoughtfully at Jacques' apparently sleeping face, too used to the Scot's sharpness to take offence. It was true enough anyway. He was rough-hewn stone, compared with the classic elegance of the Frenchman. Despite the injuries, breeding showed through. But an aristo?

'Is that what you reckon him to be, Jock?'

'I dunno, and I couldna care less.' Jock was tired of all this speculation. His own wound burned and throbbed, and he wanted attention for himself, not for this mystery man whose physical injuries were mending, but whose mental wounds never seemed to improve, and was taking up a bed.

Harry was the lucky one. Getting out of here in less than a week with any luck, and back to the Front. Back to being blown up all over again, and sent back to some hospital for repairs. Doctors and nurses were no more than bloody mechanics these days, Jock thought humourlessly, repairing those that still had enough parts to mend, sending the rest to the scrap heap in the sky. Boxed if they were lucky, heaped into a communal spit of earth if they were not. And hopefully, God would know where to find them and sort out the tangle of bodies and legs and make them whole again for eternity.

He shivered, as if he could feel the damp cloying earth already suffocating him, mouldering his bones. He bellowed for a nun to bring him a piss bottle before it was too late. Shocking the nuns was the tiniest diversion in the boredom of waiting to get well. They all did it.

Angel felt as though she had lived a lifetime at Piersville. Since returning from taking Margot and Edward home to England, there had been little time to think. If an army of men had been sent into battle, then an army of men was being sent back into the hospitals, daily, hourly, incessantly. All those wasted, wasted lives.

All the wasted days that could have been spent so differently. Lovely, summer hours that had once drifted by in a haze of heat, the hum of insects on the air, the scent of blossom heavy and sweet, the raw tangy grasses soft underfoot, the caress of the ocean on bare feet, the nights warm and balmy. Summer, summer, all gone in a bloody stench of choking dust and burning sorrow, of pain and grime and tears, and stinking wounds that violated God's earth and sky.

Why did He allow it? Angel wept for the poor wretches who could no longer see or taste or hear or feel . . . those were the fortunate ones, those who couldn't feel. The rest of them limped painfully towards death, inch by harrowing inch, and all that women like Angel could do was watch and comfort, and hold hands until there was no pressure left in those dead fingers to hold.

There had been several letters from Margot, beseeching Angel not to think too badly of her because she simply could not return. The way she wrote the words told Angel that already the old Margot was reasserting herself, but she couldn't blame her for relinquishing her job at Piersville.

Margot had always been more vulnerable, despite her outward froth.

Angel was constantly surprised at her own resilience. Sister Yard was pleased with her, informing her so in that odd, mannish way of hers. Bannister had proved to be solid. Angel no longer flinched at the unfeminine analogy. She was deeply moved to be thought an essential part of the team at Piersville, of whom Sister Yard was a tireless and humane worker. There was no room for lightweights here. Margot had been right to retire gracefully, and besides, her mother needed her . . .

Since the horror of Edward Lacey's death and subsequent loss of Margot's friendship, Angel had made no real friends. Acquaintances she had in plenty, but the work was what kept her going. The months slipped by, and although she kept the memory of Jacques alive in her heart, she admitted that it was harder and harder to believe in his survival.

All the same, she clung to the fact that his whereabouts were as much a mystery to his unit. Twice she had been to Brighton Belle, to be met with the same embarrassed looks and evasions. No one knew what had happened to Jacques de Ville. Clearly the officers and men there believed him dead. But without actual proof, no one came out and declared it. Not to this girl, whose love for the man shone out of her . . .

Angel had to keep the hope alive. If she didn't, no one else would. Only his father, somewhere in Bordeaux. He probably knew nothing more than she did. He would have been the one to receive the message that his son was missing. Missing, believed killed . . . at that point, Angel always clamped her imagination. If she didn't, pain rushed in, heartache began, the numbness that was her salvation wore off.

In late December, one of the day's intake of badly wounded moaned and cussed with all the ripeness of his Cockney background. Angel hid a smile, despite her sympathy. She didn't think much of his chances. His chest had caved in, and he would need constant care if he was ever to recover from the mangled mess the bullets had made of him. She forced him back on his bed, her arms stronger than anyone would believe in so slender a girl, and uttered soothing words to him.

'The doctor will be along very soon, and he'll see that you get something for the pain. Try to lie still, please –'

The soldier looked up at her in dumb amazement. Angel was perplexed by his look. She thought she had seen it all. Lechery, adoration, hatred, rage, slobbering tears, de-humanised weeping . . .

'Gawd almighty, where've I seen yer before?' Harry gurgled through the heaving jelly of his chest.

Angel shook her head gently. The poor devil was probably having hallucinations. It happened all the time. A face, a look, reminded some poor devil of a girl at home, a wife or a sweetheart. She put a cool hand on his forehead. It burned with fever, despite the bitter cold outside.

'I ain't bleedin' crazy, ducks. Not yet. I've seen yer, I tell yer.'

'I've been here a long time. Perhaps you've been to Piersville before. Is this your first time in hospital?' Angel asked gently.

At least the irritation over where he had seen her was taking his mind off the evil-looking wounds in his chest. He must have been ripped right open, and only a hastily stuffed piece of darkly reddening padding was holding him together.

'Nah!' Harry said with scornful pride. 'I bin at the Front off 'n on for two bleedin' years, though I've seen the inside of more bleedin' 'ospitals than you've had hot dinners!'

His whole body heaved with the effort of talking now. He squinted his eyes at Angel's face, until she became more of a blur, an image, a sketchy image of black lines on white paper . . .

'Good Gawd almighty, I know where I seen yer!' he croaked. 'It was that bleedin' loony chap at the Abbey – St Helene! 'E had a drawing of yer by his bed.'

'What chap?' Angel's stomach retched with shock. Her heart raced so fast she could hardly hear the Cockney's words. She felt like dragging him out of the bed and shaking him to tell her . . . tell her . . . but if she did that, he'd probably die right in front of her, and she'd know nothing . . .

The voice was dwindling, fumbling for sounds, losing its control. She leaned forward desperately.

' 'E never said proper words. Only bleedin' rubbish. Posh chap. One o' them Froggies –'

The sounds were rasping and gurgling now, as if they came from under water, as if they were drowning. Angel knew that was precisely what the man was doing. Drowning in his own blood. So many of them did it. Edward Lacey had done it. She wept for them all. She wept over the man, listening desperately for one more word, for him to mention Jacques' name . . .

'Bannister, there's nothing more to be done here.'

Sister Yard's voice, sharp as a whiplash, was beside her ear. Sister Yard's hands were hauling her away from the dead body of the soldier who had given her flaring hope. The front of her uniform was stained with the blood that had erupted from the useless padding. The wounds disgorged blood, poured out blood like a fountain. An orderly was scuttling to the bed, removing the body, making way for yet more bodies, either fit for repair or to be made ready for disposal. It was an endless nightmare. But for Angel, out of the nightmare had come a sliver of light. A hope. Angel turned to scream at Sister Yard to tell her so, but before she could say anything, it seemed as if the floor came up to hit her between the eyes.

She heard nothing of the panic among the hard-pressed staff in the next hours. She was put to bed under sedation, ordered complete bed rest for a week. She was no use to anyone if she collapsed, and she had worked as hard as anybody. Sister Yard herself gave the orders, finding an odd attachment for the golden-haired girl who gave so much of herself so tirelessly. And those poor lady's hands that cared nothing for the rough work they were given, were laid carefully over the bedcovers while the girl was restored to health and strength.

The doctor insisted that Angel be kept sedated. She had been under a terrific strain lately, and the mind and body could cope with only so much. The drugs dulled Angel's senses. She hated them, while knowing that they healed. But at last she was allowed to wake with her head clear, to see the girl called Jones beside her bed.

'You're awake! I just looked in to see if you were all right. How d'you feel, Bannister?'

'Better,' Angel said cautiously. Everything was winging back to her. The soldier who had died. The certainty that he had seen a drawing of her. The only person who could have made it was Jacques. And the name of the hospital. Oh God, she couldn't remember it. Some Abbey. Some saint's name. There were probably hundreds in Catholic France.

'The Abbey of St Helene!' she said in sudden, joyous triumph. Jones backed away uneasily, as though Angel was experiencing a holy vision. As Angel made to leap out of bed and then clutched quickly at the side table, Jones disappeared through the door, calling quickly that she'd fetch Sister.

There were more urgent things to attend to than visiting a recovered nurse. By the time Sister was free, Angel was washed and dressed, and wishing that her legs didn't feel so much like wool. She was ready to return to the wards, and ready to beg with a request of her own.

'You'll do no such thing. You'll be in the same state as before if you start work immediately,' Sister said in annoyance. She thought the girl had more sense. 'One more day taking it easy, and tomorrow you may return to the wards.'

'All right.' She would give in on this, and then Sister would grant her request. The next minute she felt as if she had been slapped in the face.

'There's no question of a transfer at the moment, Bannister! I hardly need tell you how hard-pressed we are for every nurse and helper. Perhaps in the new year. We're promised some new V.A.D.s then. I'll see if I can release you then.'

Angel could have wept. 'But Sister, don't you see how useful I would be? The man who died was British, and the nuns would be French. I speak excellent French. Oh please, Sister, won't you think again?'

'In the New Year, Bannister. I can say no more than that. As soon as we get some replacements, you may go. But I'll be damn sorry to lose you, all the same. You're a good egg. Solid.'

Left alone, the incongruity of the words failed to amuse Angel. A good solid egg, hard-boiled . . . but she was none of that. She was soft-centred, ready to spill over right now. For a moment she had almost breathed Jacques in her lungs, held him in her arms, as real and surely as she lived. And now she had to wait until the new year to find out if it was really him. If he was well, or injured beyond help, mentally or physically. He needed her, but she couldn't go to him because she was needed here.

The frustration of it all overwhelmed her, and she threw herself down on her narrow bed and wept until she felt as though there were no tears left inside her.

Early in January, Ellen snuggled into the collar of her coat, wishing she had somewhere to go. She felt decidedly unsettled, shocked, everything jarring and worrying inside her. It wouldn't be so bad if Rose had stayed with her after they had come out of the cinema into the pale cold daylight. But Rose had gone scurrying off to meet the young man of whom she was now enamoured, unfit for war service, but apparently fit for everything else, according to Rose's irritatingly coy descriptions.

Ellen would have liked to go to a tea shop with Rose, mulling over the disturbing film together, instead of standing here like a left-over scone at Sunday tea. The film was appalling. I mean, one heard of the dreadful things that were happening in France and at the Somme, but to sit through such a terrible film about it, seeing the men, laughing into the cameras, but nevertheless with that awful mud and the trenches, and the tanks, and all the things one never really thought about in too much detail . . .

Ellen groaned to herself, listening to her own thoughts. God, she sounded just like her mother, distancing herself from the real world so that she didn't have to be too deeply involved in it . . . she wasn't 'one', she was herself, she was Ellen Bannister, munitions worker, lost in a world where she didn't belong, living with a friend who indulged too freely in sex with strangers, conveniently forgetting her avowal to remember her dear departed Ronnie for always and always . . .

'Ellen, is that you? Good Lord, it is! Ellen, how splendid to see you!'

The cut-glass voice shattered the silence of the winter afternoon. Ellen realised that the crowds outside the picture palace had dispersed, and she had been standing there as if she was waiting for a bus. She stared in disbelief for a moment, and then seized the other girl's hand as if it was a lifeline.

'Margot! Why aren't you in France? Oh God, I'm sorry. Didn't something happen to your brother? You look awful if you don't mind me saying so. Have you been ill?'

She blundered on, embarrassment putting words into her mouth she didn't intend. Margot had gone to France with Angel, and nostalgia for her sister rushed at Ellen with a speed she didn't expect, making her blink the stupid tears away. It was the sight of that damn propaganda film, terrifying and terrible, and the loss of the friendship she and Rose had once had, and now seeing Margot so unexpectedly . . .

'You've seen the film, I suppose?' Margot said matter-of-factly. 'You and thousands of others. Some people fainted when they saw the men going over the barbed wire into No Man's Land. They don't show it all though. They don't show the numbers of the wounded.' Her voice was bitter. 'Nor the reality of the hospitals and the things we had to see. They prefer to glorify the Somme to make money from gullible people at home –'

'You can't believe that, Margot!'

'Why shouldn't I? Oh, for heaven's sake, let's get some tea. Do you have the time? There's a little place near here that's not too bad.'

Margot was Angel's friend, not Ellen's. They had little in common. But Margot was a link with Angel, and Ellen badly needed something, someone of her own to cling to. She followed this brittle girl almost obediently, in a very uncharacteristic way, until they reached the warmth of the tea shop and ordered tea and buns, and Ellen began to feel very uneasy at the burning light in the other girl's eyes.

'D'you know what ended the fighting?' Margot went on as if she was an authority, as indeed she was, keeping up avidly with every communiqué she could, as a kind of penance for opting out of the war. Ellen noticed for the first time how thin she was, how nervous and jumpy.

'What ended it?' she queried, sipping the hot tea gratefully.

'Mud. Bloody filthy mud. They fought until November, until they couldn't see for mud. They drowned in it. Except Eddie, of course. He was already dead by then.'

'Margot, I'm so sorry.' Ellen clattered the cup in the saucer, in a way that would make her mother frown.

'It's all right.' Margot waved away the apology. 'I'm used

to it now. Sometimes, it still takes me by surprise and I remember with a start that he won't be coming back, and then it hurts like fury.'

'The film showed plenty of German prisoners being taken,' Ellen tried to steer away from the uncomfortable subject of her brother.

'They didn't show the real slaughter, did they? The Red Cross people being blown up while they were taking the wounded away to hospital, the men caught on the wire, hanging there until they disintegrated.'

People around them were beginning to whisper and to glance their way. Ellen finished her tea and bun, and picked up her gloves, sliding them onto her square fingers.

'Margot, darling, I shall have to go. Will you be all right?'

Margot gave her a sunny smile, her mood changing like quicksilver.

'Oh, of course! Why shouldn't I be? I have to go, anyway. Mother and I are seeing Eddie tomorrow, and we like to look our best and not be flustered.'

Ellen's mouth felt as if it was opening and shutting like a fish. She had to get away from this strange girl who didn't seem to know if her brother was dead or alive, and who seemed to epitomise all the terrible things that could happen to people in a war. Yet Ellen felt a swift shame as they parted company outside with a tiny peck on the cheek. All these others were so much braver and worldlier than she. They had seen it all, knew it all, while she knew nothing, *was* nothing.

She walked for hours until finally returning to Rose's house. The lover, unfit for war service, was upstairs with Rose. She could hear Rose's high-pitched giggling interspersed with the lover's deeper rumblings. She could hear the whine of bedsprings, and she felt an unjust, fierce dislike for the two of them. Rose, with her pious widowhood, and the lover, fornicating on Ronnie's bed with Ronnie's wife, clearly fit for something . . .

Quietly, Ellen went to her own room and packed her

things. The old days were gone for ever, and she didn't like the new ones. She should never have tried to resurrect a friendship that had died when Rose had screamed abuse at the poor dead image of Mr Roly-Poly Strube. She scrawled a note for Rose while the bedsprings reached a more feverish urgency, and slipped out of the house before consummation was complete.

She would make for Paddington railway station. There would be trains going to Bristol, and she didn't care how long she had to wait. She never stopped to consider going anywhere else. There would be refuge at Meadowcroft. Almost to her own surprise, Ellen realised that like the rest of her family, she sought its comfort when she needed it. Even when she hadn't been aware of her need, Meadowcroft was there, waiting to enclose her in its arms like a mother welcoming home an errant child.

Chapter 17

Clemence gave her daughter a perfunctory kiss. She did not approve of anything Ellen did, though she was forced to admit it was good to see at least one of her daughters, since in her opinion they had all abandoned her.

'Why on earth couldn't you have let me know you were coming, Ellen?' Clemence said with mild irritation. 'The bed would have been properly aired, and arrangements made –'

'What arrangements, Mother? I've come home, and you could at least look pleased to see me!'

Ellen was exhausted. There had been no train to Bristol last night, and she had had to wait until the early hours of the morning, huddled up in a most undignified way on the station platform with an assortment of dubious characters and soldiers. She was cold and tired, and she didn't want to be questioned until she had had at least a week's sleep . . .

'Of course I'm pleased.' Clemence's huffed voice made a mockery of the words. 'It's good to see anyone these days. Your father hardly ever comes home, and I rarely get a letter from Angel. Louise does write, and I suppose you might as well know that she and that Dougal fellow have been married. With indecent haste, without even a complete year's mourning for poor dear Stanley –'

'Oh Mother, don't be so prissy. What do such things matter nowadays? Good for Louise!' She reversed her feelings over Rose's similar situation without a qualm. Louise hadn't loved Stanley. *Nobody* could have loved

Stanley, so why shouldn't she begin a new life? Lucky Louise, to have found happiness at last.

'Oh well, I might have known you'd approve of such an outrage. Louise wrote a long letter, saying she's perfectly happy living in Scotland, though it must be appallingly cold and miserable there right now –'

But surely not for Louise, warmed by her husband's love, Ellen thought enviously . . .

' – and she's asked your father to organise the renting out of her London house, which keeps him away even more. If he's not in London, he's in Yorkshire. Really, one needs to be a saint these days, to deal with everything.'

'Poor Mother.' Impulsively, Ellen put her arms around her and hugged her. She felt genuinely sorry for Clemence, unable to cope with this brave new world, where daughters left home and conducted their own lives, and husbands simply had too much to do to spend time with their wives.

Clemence moved away from Ellen. Showing so much affection without good reason was bad form, and Clemence did so hate to be patronised by anyone thinking she needed sympathy. Clemence breathed deeply and resolutely, regaining her usual fortitude.

'It's the war, of course. One does have to make sacrifices.'

'Yes, Mother, one does,' Ellen said, poker-faced, trying not to remember the propaganda film of the Battle of the Somme, and Edward Lacey in particular.

It was strange to be back at Meadowcroft. Life in the country had its own soothing pattern, regardless of any ruffles within the house itself, and Ellen found herself responding to the tranquillity and comparative isolation, compared with the hectic pace of wartime London.

The war had touched everyone here too, she reminded herself. She was striding out one morning through the bare wintry lanes, needing time to herself as ever. The poor old German shopkeeper had been brutally killed. Many of the young men of the village who had gone to war wouldn't be coming back. Their own country house knew a succession of billetted soldiers. Stanley had been blown up. And the lives of Ellen and her sisters had taken vastly different courses from those their mother had mapped out for them.

She was pensive, her head down as she walked, coat collar turned up against the crisp January morning, when she became aware of a shadow across her path. She had been so deep in thought that it startled her. Her head jerked up so fast it cricked her neck, and the blood rushed to her face when she realised Peter Chard was blocking her path in the narrow lane.

She hadn't seen him since that terrible day when he'd caught her in the barn with the Cornishman. The memory of it all was sharp and painful and acutely embarrassing, and the fleeting thought ran through Ellen's mind that the old standards were not so very far removed from her after all.

She took in Peter's appearance in that glance. He looked just the same. Dark and forceful, hunched into his country overcoat, breeches tucked into workmanlike boots. His hands were dug deep into his pockets, and he didn't take them out to shake Ellen's hand. For some reason, the omission made her swallow.

'How are you, Peter?' Her voice was huskier than she would have wished. She seemed to have lost much of her aplomb, and the knowledge of it made her almost nervous. She could have laughed at herself for the feeling, if it wasn't so important to her that Peter Chard should respect her . . .

'I'm well. And you?' He was polite, but his mouth was unsmiling. She ached to see it smile. She longed for the old camaraderie they had had when they were campaigning together. Like the easy elegance of pre-war life, the spark between them seemed to be quenched.

'Oh, well enough.' She was brittle now, not wanting him to see how much his attitude was hurting her. 'I thought I'd come down and rusticate a bit. London's so tedious nowadays.'

'Really?'

She could hear the sarcasm in his voice and couldn't blame him. Even to herself, she sounded appallingly snobbish and middle class. She sounded more like her mother, more like Louise while she had been married to Stanley.

She went to step sideways to get out of Peter's way, since there seemed no point in standing there not knowing what to say. He stepped to the same side at the same moment. Ellen gave a small nervous laugh.

'I'm sorry. I do seem to be a nuisance to you, don't I? How's the farm?' It was an inane thing to say. *How was the farm?* Things grew. Cows grazed. Hens lay eggs for the Ministry Men to count and take away . . .

'The farm's fine, Ellen. Rusticating nicely. Now, if you'll excuse me, I'm sure you have plenty of we humble country folk to visit before you go back to London, so don't let me stop you. Remember me to your family.'

He moved past her, and tears stung her eyes at the snub. He was so stupid, she thought furiously! Couldn't he see how much she wanted to be friends with him? Didn't he know that she didn't look down on him, or anyone else, for that matter? Didn't he know that she loved him?

Ellen bit her trembling lower lip hard as the thought swept into her mind. She loved him. All that stuff about never letting herself get caught up in all that hearts and flowers nonsense was as meaningless as will-o'-the-wisp. She knew exactly how Angel had felt over Jacques. How Louise had been swept off her feet by Dougal.

She never thought it would happen to her, but it had, slowly and insidiously, and it was only when she came face to face with Peter again that she knew how badly she had been missing him. But Angel was wrong in one respect. It wasn't glorious at all. It was bloody painful.

She stuck her head in the air and trudged on down to the

village, making small talk with one and another of folk that she knew, and trying all the time not to notice that her heart was breaking. And gradually her own feelings receded into the background as she encountered one and another family who had lost someone at the Somme. The whole village was a sadder place than it had been when she left it.

Ellen wanted to weep to see how crushed many of the women appeared. Women without men . . . and she felt bitterly ashamed of the little glad feeling that at least Peter would never have to go to war. A feeling that was at the same time completely hollow, because he had made it plain that he cared nothing for her.

It was a relief to turn back towards Meadowcroft again. The lovely old house seemed to Ellen to be a symbol of other days, when their lives were frothy and untroubled. How little any of them had appreciated it then. England itself was so lovely, in all its moods, all its seasons, from the biggest mansion to the lowliest dwelling.

The scent of woodsmoke drifted across the bare fields from the directions of the outlying farms. Peter's farm was out there. The big old kitchen with its flagstone floor, the homely furnishings and brass ornaments, the leaping flames of a log fire in the parlour . . . her nostalgia was so great that for a moment, Ellen was tempted to go marching there to see him, to demand that he stop treating her as a wanton hussy, and try to regain some of their old friendship again. But she was bedevilled by too much pride. And her mother would be scandalised if she even guessed at Ellen's thoughts.

Clemence scolded her as soon as she went indoors.

'You'll catch your death of cold, walking about in this weather, Ellen. What can you have been doing all this time?'

Wishing that my would-be lover would sweep me in his arms and ask me to stay, Mother . . .

For a second, Ellen wondered if she had said the words out loud, but one glance at Clemence's face assured her that she had not. If she had spoken aloud, Clemence would surely have fainted right off by now. She gave a tight smile.

'I've been paying my respects to the village women, Mother. Poor things. So many of them on their own now. I suppose there'll be a stone erected to the fallen once the war's over. That's the correct phrase, isn't it? As if the poor devils were all propped up like a pack of cards and somebody pushed the one at the end –'

'Ellen, will you ever learn respect? I do despair of you,' Clemence snapped. 'I blame it partly on your choice of companions –'

'Do you, Mother? Can't you even give me credit for being bloody-minded? I do have a mind of my own. Anyway, I thought you'd be pleased I was offering sympathy to the bereaved.' At her mother's dubious look, Ellen gave her a quick embarrassed hug.

'I was, truly! Don't look so doubting. I'm not as beastly as you sometimes seem to think. I can be quite nice when I want to be!'

Clemence commented that they had better have some tea, feeling somehow inadequate as always in her daughter's presence. Ellen gave a shrug, knowing that any closeness between the two of them was as remote as ever. They did care for one another, she thought defiantly. The tragedy of it was, they could never seem to show it with any sincerity.

'By the way, your father's coming home this weekend,' Clemence said as she rang the bell for afternoon tea. 'He's decided he can spare the time away from his wretched factory to spend a week with his wife, so please try not to upset him, Ellen.'

Ellen opened her mouth to protest, and closed it again, deciding that it wasn't worth it. It would be good to see her father again. It seemed ages. And she ignored her mother's irritating little dig at Fred's frequent absences. If it wasn't for the war, the factory wouldn't be working at full stretch, producing uniforms and blankets, so as usual, everything could be blamed on the war. It was becoming extraordinarily useful, Ellen thought without humour.

Fred didn't really want to come south, but it was hardly fair on poor old Clemence to spend so much time without any of her family around, and he could hardly expect her to suffer the billetted soldiers' company on her own without ever being at Meadowcroft himself. It was perfectly true that business had never been so brisk at Bannister Textiles, although it certainly wasn't the kind of business he wanted. Producing uniforms that would be in tatters within days or hours after they reached the Front, according to all the grim reports, and blankets that would be blown to smithereens almost as soon as they were packed, was a sorry end to the toil of his industrious workers.

He needed to be on hand constantly, and Clemence must realise this. Even more, he needed to be with Harriet. Not only for the comfort and pleasure they drew from each other, but because of the worrying way she seemed less robust of late. Fred constantly worried about her.

She was losing weight for no apparent reason. She had an irritating little cough that woke her in the night and hacked at her during the day. But she didn't hold with doctors, saying airily that such minor complaints were of no importance. To Fred, they were of monumental importance. It was almost as though he could see her slipping away from him, day by day. And because of his fussing, it was Harriet who had urged him to go down to Meadowcroft for a week.

'You owe it to Clemence, Fred, and besides, you're getting on my nerves,' she said in her comfortable Yorkshire voice. 'I'll still be here when you come back.'

'That's a promise, is it?' Fred tried to joke, knowing it was the way she liked him to be. 'You're not going to do anything foolish, like dying on me, are you, while I'm gone?'

Harriet gave a chuckle, suppressing the nagging cough with an effort. The shine in her eyes could have been suspiciously like tears, Fred thought.

'Go on wi' you! You and me have got a lot of years together yet, Freddie. Unless you're getting tired of my little cottage, of course, and hanker after those big London parties you used to tell me about that you had before the war –'

His arms went round her. They met behind her back now, where he had once had difficulty in clasping his fingers together. He nuzzled his moustache against the softness of her cheek, breathing in the warm homely scent of her.

''Twill be a long day before I get tired of you, my bonnie Harriet,' he slipped into the Yorkshire idiom with the ease of long practise. 'Start eating properly and put some more meat on those bones before I come back, that's all I ask.'

'Aye. Providing Kaiser Bill allows us enough rations to make do,' she said cheerfully.

Fred snorted. 'Rations! You need nourishment, and you know damn well that you'll get all that you need. I've seen to that. Promise me you'll eat, and stop picking at your food like a bird. It's not like you, Harriet, and I don't like to see it.'

'Are you ordering me about now, Sir Freddie?' she teased him, touching her lips to his mouth. 'Since when did you know me take orders from anybody?'

He gave a low rumbling laugh, despite the worry. It was one of the things he liked about her. She professed not to take orders, but he knew that for him, she would move mountains and do it cheerfully. He let her go with reluctance, knowing he must make a move on the long journey to Somerset. His factory was in order, and he must become the dutiful husband once more. If only his girls were going to be there, he thought with swift regret. It was so long since they had all been together . . .

Fred could hardly believe his eyes when Ellen came running out of the house when he arrived at Meadowcroft. He was stiff and tired after the long drive, but the unexpected warmth of his daughter's greeting made up for it all. Ellen didn't normally show such affection, and he guessed rightly that she and her mother had been prickly with one another.

'Well, this is a lovely surprise, my dear girl! Your mother didn't tell me you were going to be here.'

'That's because she didn't know, Dad.' Ellen tucked her arm in his, a comforting feeling of things being the way they used to be creeping over her with his familiar manner. 'You know me. Always unpredictable, and wanting to surprise everybody!'

Although Fred laughed, he was acutely aware of the tension in his daughter's arm, and a false brittleness in her voice. Why, she's not so tough as she likes to pretend, he thought with some surprise, and felt a sudden tenderness towards her because of it. It was as if he had a sudden insight into Ellen's mind at that instant, and saw how tortured it was.

'It'll be a third like old times then,' Fred grinned. 'At least I'll have one of my girls to banter with when your mother puts on her stuffy expression.'

Ellen grinned back, the faint shine in her eyes reminding Fred of Harriet, and endearing her still more to him. Ellen felt protected and relieved. It was Angel who had the easiest repartee with their father, but his sympathetic reaction to her presence, with no questions asked yet, was like balm to her senses.

They walked into the house together. There would be time later for someone to bring in Fred's baggage, and Fred released his daughter to give Clemence the usual peck on the cheek that was all she expected.

How different, he thought fleetingly, from the way Harriet greeted him, even after only a day, as if she was thrilled to see him, as if she truly loved and wanted him. He gave a small sigh, and prepared to play the part of Sir Frederick Bannister, husband and father.

He and Ellen depended on each other's presence that

week, without either of them admitting the fact to each other or themselves. They went for drives in the country when Clemence was too busy with her knitting circles or visiting the sick. They played chess in the evenings in front of a roaring fire while Clemence protested that such heat was terribly bad for the complexion and that Ellen was a foolish girl to risk it by sitting so close.

They exchanged news about Angel and Louise and the factory and Rose Morton and seeing Margot Lacey and how awful it was about poor Edward, and neither could touch the subjects dearest to both their hearts, Fred's anxiety over Harriet, and Ellen's heartbreak over Peter Chard. Superficially, they were as close as father and daughter could be, and if Clemence resented their closeness, she didn't show it until Fred had left for Yorkshire once more, and she and Ellen began to find each other's company intolerable.

'I think it's time I left, Mother,' Ellen declared one evening in early February. 'Rose will be wondering what's become of me.'

'Well, if you think it's best, dear.' Clemence's elegant fingers didn't falter in the packing of the new batch of thick knitted socks as she spoke. Had those fingers ever caressed a man? Ellen wondered disbelievingly. Had her mother and father really enjoyed those pleasurable moments Angel had recounted so vividly? They must have done, at least three times . . . Ellen felt a wild desire to laugh. It could hardly be only three times in a lifetime together that her parents had been as intimate as two people could be, yet they were as coldly polite as strangers now. It was pathetic and terrible . . .

'I said, which day were you thinking of leaving, Ellen?' her mother repeated. 'You must telephone for a taxi in good time. Everything is so disorganised these days.'

Ellen forced herself to concentrate, and to get her thoughts away from the unlikely picture of her parents being ecstatic together . . .

'Oh. In a few days, I should think,' she said, in confusion, thankful that Clemence was not a mind reader. 'That will be all right, won't it?'

'My dear girl, of course it will. Don't think I'm pushing you out, for heaven's sake!' Clemence smiled, and they both knew that the smile held relief that this awkward situation was coming to an end.

Of all the Bannister girls, she and her mother were the least likely companions, Ellen thought sadly. It had often been said in jest at her college that one didn't have to like one's parents or relatives, did one? What was always neglected to add was that one's parents didn't have to like one, either! Though she knew that Clemence would be genuinely astonished and hurt if Ellen ever suggested such a thing.

She toyed with the idea of calling on Peter, just once, and rejected it almost as quickly. What would be the point? He would be glad to be rid of such a troublesome young woman, whom he undoubtedly saw as merely dabbling in campaigning and book-keeping, and could be as flighty as any village girl in the pursuit of pleasure.

He probably thought Ellen worse, chasing every excitement and new experience that life offered, in the way that bored young middle class girls did. She could have wept with the frustration of it all, but she couldn't risk that cold censorious look from him again.

Nor could she go back to Rose Morton's house. She had left it for good this time. And if she had hated the presence of the new lover in the house, then how much more would she hate it now, with all the misery of her own thwarted feelings held so tightly in check?

She simply didn't know where she would go, as she boarded the train at Temple Meads station for London. She was jostled on all sides by women saying good-bye to the men they were sending away. Older women with heads held high as they fought back the tears and sent their sons to France; openly weeping young wives who clung to pink-faced youths in brand new uniforms who looked more fit for the schoolroom than for a war.

There was hardly a seat to be found on the train, but Ellen preferred to stand in the corridor where there was more air than in the staleness of the compartment. She was stifled by her own inadequacy, when she had once thought herself so strong and so capable; by the appalling waste of these boys all around her singing the war-provoked songs of hope; by suddenly realising she was not a part of it all. She had worked doggedly beside Rose in the munitions factory, but it was still not enough, not enough . . .

The thunder of the wheels on the track as the train rocked and hurtled through the night seemed to drum the words into her brain. Ellen had not given enough . . .

Louise . . . well, surely Louise had given enough to the war. Whether she loved him or not, Stanley had been her husband, and he had been her sacrifice.

Angel . . . Angel was the brave one, the unexpectedly brave one, doing things that no young girl could be expected to do, seeing sights that would make brave men flinch. Ellen was fiercely proud of Angel, and had never realised it until that moment.

She dismounted from the train at Paddington station, still unsure where she was going. A small hotel for the night, perhaps, and then she would decide whether to go up to their old Hampstead house and stay there for a while. What did it matter if her parents had decamped? They needn't know of her plans.

Or she could take the long journey to Scotland and stay with Louise for a while. She was sure her sister would be pleased to see someone from home. She felt as disorientated as when she had left Rose's house to go to Meadowcroft, weary with the sheer effort of trying to think.

She left the station and walked into the nearest hotel. Once in her room, she undressed and almost crawled into bed, pushing aside everything but the immediate need for sleep, and trying not to mind that everyone else seemed to have a purpose in life except herself.

Angel's request to be sent to the hospital at the Abbey of St Helene was still not granted. It was blisteringly unfair. She could be of such help in translating . . . no matter how much she badgered Sister Yard, she was always met with the same crisp response.

'You're too useful here, Bannister. I've promised that you'll be released just as soon as it's possible, but I don't need to tell you we need every hand we've got, and I know you're not the type to desert a sinking ship.'

It was emotional blackmail, Angel raged, but there wasn't a thing she could do about it. She was given more and more ambulance duties now, and short of absconding in a hospital vehicle, she was as tied to Sister Yard's commands as if the two of them were Siamese twins. She had tried getting a message to the Abbey hospital, but there had been no reply, and the anxiety over Jacques' safety was as gnawing as ever.

Sister Yard was right, of course. She would never desert. Not when so many needed her and all the other willing helpers at Piersville. But she longed for news of Jacques, and the hope that had flared when the dying soldier told her of the unknown artist, was beginning to dwindle. She tried to keep the hope alive, but it was so very hard when she was surrounded by death and despair . . .

'Somebody's asking for you, Bannister,' one of the other V.A.D.s called out to her when she was snatching a quick cup of tea. 'Sister says you can just take a minute. It's a woman, by the way.'

Angel put her cup down with shaking hands. It took so little for the hope to surge again, only to crumble . . . she went into the hospital corridor, brushing her hand across her eyes. She was solid, she reminded herself. Sister Yard had told her so repeatedly. She wouldn't break . . .

'Ellen!' she croaked, staring in disbelief at the strangely uncertain figure of her sister, standing so incongruously in her smart coat and hat, her expensive travelling bag at her feet, when everyone else around them was dishevelled and unkempt from too many hours doing too many unpleasant tasks.

'Hello, darling,' Ellen's voice was high-pitched, as if she too were seeing all these things in an instant. 'Sorry to burst in on you, old thing, but I couldn't think what else to do. Do you suppose your person in charge could give me a job, typing up reports or that sort of thing? I wouldn't be any trouble –'

Her voice suddenly broke, and the strain of making the decision, and travelling nonstop from London very early that morning, was making her mouth lose control of itself. It hardly mattered, though, because the next minute she was being hugged and kissed, and it was so good, so bloody marvellously good, to know that somebody was glad to see her, anyway.

Chapter 18

Tears of joy overcame both girls as they hugged each other. Old aggressions were forgotten as the sweet familiarity of family ties drew them together. Angel mopped her eyes and gave a shaky laugh.

'I still can't believe that you're here, Ellen! I thought you'd be firmly settled on Peter Chard's farm by now, and have hayseeds growing out of your ears!'

Ellen's smile was tight.

'They always called me unpredictable, didn't they, darling?' she said with forced gaiety.

Out of the corner of her eye, Angel saw Sister Yard coming towards them.

'Oh, I'm dying to talk! But I'm due back on the ward, and Sister doesn't spare us the time for social chit-chat. Did you really mean it about working here, Ellen?'

'Of course I did! I didn't come all this way to stand about in a draughty corridor and envy the way you can even look beautiful when you're dressed for business, sister dear.'

Angel laughed at the artless compliment, and turned to face Sister Yard's enquiring eyes. She spoke quickly, before she could be reprimanded for wasting time.

'This is my sister, Sister.' She stopped, unable to resist a short laugh at hearing Ellen's stifled giggle.

Angel tried again. 'Sorry, Sister Yard. This is Ellen Bannister, and she very much wants to do any office work that's available. She's an excellent book-keeper and kept records for a branch of the suffragette movement in London –'

'There's no place here for young women on soapboxes,' Sister Yard said sharply, at which Ellen's face sobered.

'I've no intention of doing any such thing!' she said indignantly. 'I want to help in the hospital in any way I can, and I thought I would be most useful at some paperwork, since I have experience in it.'

Sister Yard looked her up and down. 'I see. Fresh from college, are you?'

'Certainly not. I'm Angel's older sister,' Ellen was even more indignant at being thought the younger of the two, although she had to admit that Angel's whole mien showed more maturity than when she had last seen her.

Sister Yard allowed herself to smile.

'And I think you'll do,' she said thoughtfully. 'You're not attached to any organisation, I presume? You're not a V.A.D.?'

Ellen shook her head, her heart sinking.

'No. I didn't know it was necessary. It was all decided in rather a hurry. I took the first available train to Dover and waited for hours until I could get a passage on a boat, and then cadged a lift in an army truck to get here.'

It sounded awful, as though she was too impetuous to have given any thought to the consequences. As though she were still playing the butterfly, and had thought the whim of going to France and penning a few documents would be such fun . . .

'Right,' Sister Yard said. 'You're obviously a girl with spirit, like your sister. I'll speak to the doctor in charge about you, Bannister. I daresay you'll be a useful addition in the office. Lord knows it's difficult enough to keep proper records of all the patients here.'

'Oh, that's topping –' Ellen began, eyes shining, when Sister Yard cut her short.

'You'll be useful because two of the office girls are away with 'flu. When they return, I shall ask for you on the wards. I can guess that you're not a nurse,' she said, as Ellen's mouth dropped open. 'But you're big and strong, and I need girls of your stature to help lift the patients. You'll be more use to me as a ward helper.'

She turned to Angel.

'Take half an hour off, Bannister, to show your sister around. She can share your room, and you can make up the time at the end of your shift.'

She swished away down the corridor, and both girls let out a long sigh of relief.

'Phew. Is she always such a dragon?' Ellen muttered.

Angel laughed, too thrilled at seeing Ellen again to let anything spoil the moment.

'She's better when you get to know her, and she's wonderful with the patients, which is all that matters. Come on. Let's go to the room, and you can tell me everything.'

'In half an hour? Oh well, I'll try!'

They linked arms in the old familiar way. Angel had never imagined how good it would feel to have someone of her own at Piersville. Until this moment, she never realised how much she missed Margot. And it was Margot's name that cropped up almost at once, as she sprawled on her own narrow bed, and Ellen grimaced at the hardness of the other one.

'You'll get used to it. So what happened in London? Mother said in one of her letters that you'd gone back to live with Rose and were doing munitions work.'

'It was a disaster,' Ellen said flatly. 'Rose and I have got different ideas now, and this time we've parted for good. But I saw a friend of yours while I was in London –'

Jacques . . . his name leapt to Angel's mind, and just as quickly left it. Of course it wasn't Jacques. Ellen didn't even know him . . .

'I met Margot outside the picture palace, and we had tea together. Dear God, Angel, what's wrong with her? Is she losing her mind? She spoke about going to see Eddie as if they were going to the theatre or something.'

'Still? I thought she'd be over all that by now,' Angel said, aghast. 'I wonder if she's seen a doctor.'

'A head doctor is what she needs,' Ellen said, blunt as ever. 'I tell you, it unnerved me, and my stomach's pretty strong.'

She hoped it was. The smells that had assaulted her ever since arriving at Piersville had begun to make her queasy. She hadn't eaten for hours, she realised in some surprise. But right now, food was the last thing she wanted.

'How's Mother? Is she well? And what about Louise? Still happy with her Dougal?'

'Blissful, apparently. Mother's washed her hands of her, of course, but good luck to her, I say. I can't think that Stanley ever did very much for her. Mother's all right. Grumbling as usual, and complaining that Father hardly ever comes home nowadays. He's terribly involved with the factory, of course, but you can't get Mother to understand such things. She doesn't really want to. It's all too too commercial. He came down for a week while I was there though, and it was good to see him again. I thought he looked harassed. Overworked, I daresay.'

She prattled on, hardly noticing the strained look on Angel's face at the mention of her father. She hadn't asked about him, but Ellen hadn't noticed. And Angel was perfectly sure that it wasn't just overwork that kept Sir Fred up in Yorkshire. The bitter feeling of betrayal swept over her again, and she forced herself to look at Ellen as her sister paused for breath.

'And what about you, darling? You haven't said anything about yourself. Did you see Peter while you were in Somerset?'

Ellen felt her tongue stick to the roof of her mouth. Angel

didn't know of her humiliation. Nobody knew. Angel thought that she and Peter still had a fondness for one another . . . she blinked quickly, before the wretched tears made a fool of her.

'I'm all right. Still looking for something to do to be useful, which is why I'm here. The munitions factory was a dreary place, with nobody allowed to talk for fear of inhaling the fumes, and then Rose got TNT poisoning, which made her look so ghastly, Angel. I thought she'd never get over it, but she did, and has a new beau hanging around.'

She looked at the small clock on Angel's bedside table.

'I say, hadn't you better get back to the ward? The old dragon will be looking for you, and I shall get the blame for keeping you, which won't start me off too well. I'm dropping with sleep, so I'll just have a nap until you get back. She won't expect me to report for duty just yet, will she?'

'Of course not,' Angel laughed. Ellen lay flat out on the bed, fully dressed, and Angel pulled the coverlet over her, leaning down to kiss her square cheek with real affection.

'Oh, Ellen, I'm so glad you're here. I can't tell you how good it is to see you.'

'Me too,' Ellen mumbled, already drifting into sleep. 'Just as long as I don't get all the dogsbody jobs because I'm big and strong. That's some recommendation! Is this how a railway navvy feels?'

Angel tiptoed out as the voice dwindled away. She felt better than she had in weeks, she realised, even hummed a little tune as she sped down the stairs to the wards. It was only later that she realised that Ellen had avoided any mention of Peter Chard, as neatly as Angel had avoided asking about their father.

By the time she came off duty exhaustedly that night, Ellen was sound asleep. At some time she must have roused herself enough to undress, and her clothes were scattered at the foot of the bed. Angel hung them up mechanically, knowing they would be a mass of creases otherwise, and there was always a race for the flat iron among the girls.

She awoke to a clear, crisp morning, the kind of morning that somehow filled you with anticipation with no definite reason for it. It was the joy of having Ellen here, Angel decided. She looked across the tiny room to smile at her sister's sleeping face, so cherubic in sleep, so often waspish when she had every intention of getting her own way.

It was a good thing that Sister Yard was genuinely in need of office help, Angel mused. If Ellen had got up on her high horse last night when she had travelled all this way, then things might have got off to a very different start. As it was, Sister had told Angel to pass on the message that Ellen could report to the office for duty that morning.

'I'm not doing you a favour, Bannister,' Sister had added keenly. 'If I didn't think your sister could be useful, then she'd be sent back. There's no room for young women who think that playing at being a heroine is fun.'

'Ellen would never think that –'

'If she's half the girl her sister is, then that should prove to be so,' Sister paid her the obscure compliment, and left Angel wondering how anyone could call her a heroine. Florence Nightingale and her nurses were heroines. What Angel and the others did was sheer bloody hard work . . . but perhaps that was the stuff of which heroines were made. It was something you never had time to think about.

'Good morning,' she said now, as Ellen opened her eyes and groaned at the daylight.

'Is it good?' Ellen said cautiously. 'I was dreaming I was in France. Tell me I'm still dreaming. Stick a pin in me or something. I didn't actually volunteer, did I?'

'You did and you are,' Angel said cheerfully. 'Get up and wash and dress, and we'll go and get some breakfast, then I'll show you where to report. You'll meet Doctor Lancing –'

'Doctor *who* – ?' Ellen spluttered.

'You'll get used to it,' Angel said briefly. 'Come on. We're late. You know what Mother used to say. Never be late anywhere on your first day. It's bad form.'

She grinned as she spoke. Clemence had always tried so hard to instil good form into her girls. Had they really turned out so badly? But this was no time for introspection. There was a small washbasin in their room and they washed quickly in the cold water, brushing their teeth in the minimum of time, and walked sedately down the corridors until Ellen was shown into the office. A beefy man rose to greet her. Doctor Lancing, she presumed, resisting the urge to smile at such an impossible name for an army surgeon . . .

They saw little of one another that day, except for the briefest of meal times. But the mere knowledge of Ellen's presence had the power to lift Angel's spirits. Or perhaps it also had something to do with the strange feeling of elation she had felt early that day.

'Goin' out wiv yer bloke or summat, are yer, Miss?' one of the patients winked knowingly at her as the day's shift neared its end. Angel laughed, tucking the bedding around him more securely. It was hard for men with no arms to keep their balance in the beds. It constantly amazed and humbled her to see how cheerful they kept.

'What bloke?' She teased him back. 'I'm too tired from dealing with all my blokes here to be going out at night.'

'Garn! A good-looker like you! I bet there's a bloke somewhere who can't wait for yer to go on to 'is special night shift!'

'Stop trying to shock me, Les Higgins,' she said in mock severity. 'Don't you know that nurses are unshockable?'

The man chuckled. They had to be, poor little devils, he thought sympathetically, with all the rotten jobs they had to do. Even to holding a man's privates for him to have a pee. When there were no hands to do it, it became a job for somebody else. Some blokes thought it a bonus to have a pretty little nurse doing the necessary, but for Les, the prospect of the future became too mucky to contemplate.

'Come on, Nursie,' he coaxed. 'Tell us yer bloke's name.'

Angel bent down to remove the man's glasses before he settled down for a sleep. He squinted at her short-sightedly.

'Well, just between you and me, it's Jacques,' she said.

'A Froggie, is he? Might have known you'd have summat a bit special, a girl like you –'

'Bannister, please come to my office when you've finished there,' Sister Yard's voice cut through the conspiratorial chat, to Angel's relief. Even though it gave her sweet comfort to speak Jacques' name, she didn't intend getting into conversation about him with Private Higgins or anybody else.

She went into Sister's cubbyhole of an office. Beyond it was the larger room where Ellen was working now with another girl, both heads bent busily over some ledgers. Recording names and addresses of the dead and wounded to be sent to commanding officers must be a grim and mountainous task, Angel thought.

And then she dismissed it from her mind as Sister told her to sit down and made the statement that proved to Angel that her feelings of optimism in the day were not unfounded after all.

'Bannister, we're to get a new intake of V.A.D.s in two weeks' time. You have the option of staying here, or of being transferred to the Abbey of St Helene as you requested. I realise that you may wish to change your mind now that your sister's here –'

'No! Oh no, Sister! I still want the transfer!'

She clasped her slim hands together, her eyes glowing like jewels, and even Sister Yard could see the delicate luminous beauty of the girl. She cleared her throat.

'I hope you find what you're looking for, Bannister.'

'I know that I will, Sister. And thank-you!'

Sister Yard shrugged. 'Don't thank me. I think I must be a fool to lose one of my best nurses, but I know that this means a lot to you. You do realise that the young man may not be who you think he is? The enquiries we made for you were all far from satisfactory, and the nuns could tell us nothing.'

'And they refused to allow him visitors, while the balance of his mind was so disturbed.'

Angel repeated the words somewhat bitterly. She had desperately wanted to go to the Abbey to see for herself, but the nuns had been adamant. The mystery patient was their responsibility, and until he had recovered some of his memory, they had ordered no visitors. Nothing to disturb that fragile hold on sanity . . .

'Your sister will be sorry to see you go, so soon after her arrival, Bannister. I'll leave it to you to explain to her, and at least you'll have two weeks together.'

Angel was dismissed. She stood outside the tiny office, her heart thudding. She could hardly believe it. At last her request for a transfer was granted . . . but she felt a swift compunction now that she had to tell Ellen. But surely Ellen would understand. She must, if she had any soul at all. And after all, she hadn't known Ellen was coming here out of the blue!

Ellen's face was filled with consternation when they both fell onto their beds that evening for a short rest before the evening meal. She leaned up on one elbow, looking at the flushed face of her sister, and knew that she couldn't begrudge her this chance, once Angel had explained her reasons to her. Until then, Ellen had had no idea of the torment Angel must have gone through, not knowing whether Jacques was alive or dead.

She *still* didn't know, Ellen thought uneasily. And even if the mystery man *were* Jacques, what kind of state was Angel going to find him in? Ellen was more troubled than she admitted, and tried to warn Angel that it might not all be plain sailing. Jacques might be no more than a shell of the man Angel remembered . . .

'Do you think I haven't told myself that a hundred times?' Angel said painfully. 'But it makes no difference. I have to go, to see for myself. And if it is Jacques, and if he's badly disfigured, that won't make any difference to me either. I love him and I shall always love him. Looks don't matter, Ellen. It's the heart and soul of a person that matters.'

'You make me feel ashamed –'

'Why? Wouldn't it be the same for you if it was Peter? Don't pretend that you don't feel something for him! You can pretend to the others, but not to me. I know something happened between you, so you must understand something of what I feel.'

Ellen suddenly sat up with a jerk, her arms hugging her knees, her head bent over them. Appalled, Angel realised that the unlikely sounds her sister was making were great racking sobs.

'Ellen, darling, what is it? What have I said?'

Ellen couldn't speak for some minutes. She hated herself for being so weak, and letting go like that. Clemence would think it terribly bad form . . . at the thought of her mother's censuring look, Ellen howled afresh.

'Are you ill, Ellen? Please tell me. Can I get you something?'

At last the paroxysm stopped. Ellen's shoulders were tense, her mouth still trembling, vulnerable as a child's as she looked up and spoke in a husky voice.

'I did something awful, Angel. I nearly let myself be seduced by a despicable man – oh, he was charm itself, and I was so besotted by him –'

'Well, that's not the end of the world,' Angel was gentle with her. 'You had a bad experience, that's all –'

'No, it's not all.' Her voice was low and intense, and Angel had to lean forward to catch the shamed words. 'The man was a bigamist, but of course I didn't know that at the time. He was just an exciting, handsome Cornishman who came to work on Peter's farm. We got on famously, and I really thought he loved me.'

She caught her breath on a sob as the painful memories swept through her mind. Reliving them was almost as terrible as when they actually happened.

'Go on, darling,' Angel said quietly, sensing there was more to come.

'We were in Peter's hayloft – Andrew and me. That was his name, Andrew. We were almost – almost – well, you *know*, Angel! And I was doing nothing to stop it. I was letting it happen – and then there was a terrible shouting outside, and the door flew open, and there was Peter and a strange girl who stood there accusing Andrew of being the father of her child when he already had a wife, and there we were – in the hayloft – oh God, I never want to live through something like that again. I was so ashamed – so humiliated –'

Angel rocked her in her arms, hardly knowing what to say. Her strong, capable sister had obviously been badly shocked, and had still not recovered from it.

'What was the worst thing, Ellen?'

Ellen's eyes were drowned in tears.

'All of it, of course! The entire, terrible day –'

'But the very worst thing,' Angel persisted. 'Was it the fact that you made a mistake in trusting this Andrew? Or being caught by the other girl, and being made to feel foolish for falling for this unworthy man? Or losing Peter Chard's respect?'

Ellen didn't speak for a moment. Then she took a deep shuddering breath.

'Losing Peter's respect! I could cope with all the rest. It's the thought of facing Peter again, and knowing what he must think of me. I did meet him briefly, when I was down at Meadowcroft a few weeks ago, and it was so awful. He looked at me as though I were an insect. I couldn't bear it, Angel.'

'And that's why you came here.'

Ellen shifted out of her arms. She spoke defensively.

'You think I came for the wrong reasons, don't you? I'm not patriotic like you, or brave, or dedicated –'

'Yes, you are, love. You're all of those things, but you're also very foolish in letting this situation go on. Why on earth haven't you told Peter all that you've told me? He'd understand. It's obvious that you were made for each other.'

'Perhaps we were,' Ellen said bitterly. 'Until he saw me for the idiot that I am. How can I possibly explain to him? I've got too much pride.'

'Then write to him. It's sometimes easier to write things down than to say them.'

Ellen shook her head decisively.

'No. If he can't believe that I made a mistake without my grovelling to him, then so be it.'

Angel sighed. There were times when pointless pride got in the way of happiness, but she knew better than to argue with her sister any longer. When she got that mutinous look in her eyes, all her family was aware that any discussion was at an end.

At least, telling it all to Angel seemed to be something of a release to Ellen. The guilt had been festering in her mind, and Angel had put it all into perspective. There was nothing she could do about Peter for the time being, since she refused to consider writing to him, so she set about becoming an asset to Sister Yard and Piersville hospital.

Angel was very relieved at the way Ellen took to her new regime so readily. The days were passing, and soon she would be leaving with an ambulance full of convalescents on their way home, driven by one of the other girls, and making a special detour to the Abbey of St Helene.

The anticipation of seeing Jacques again was almost making her ill, and she and Ellen hugged one another when the day arrived for Angel to leave.

'Promise to write and let me know what happens,' Ellen begged.

'If you promise to keep writing to Mother, and think about writing to Peter.'

'I'll think about it.' Truth to tell, Ellen had been thinking about it quite a lot in the last two weeks of working in the hospital office. Making so many sad entries into the ledgers had reminded her forcibly of her own mortality. Was she being so very silly not to give herself and Peter one last chance? But she couldn't promise Angel that she would write. Not yet.

They hugged each other, each wondering when they would meet again.

'Chin up, darling,' Angel whispered, in Clemence's tones. She turned blindly, and climbed into the passenger seat of the waiting ambulance, blowing kisses back to the dwindling figure of her sister as the vehicle trundled over the cobbled streets of Piersville and away from the vicinity of the Front Line fighting.

As they drove for seemingly endless miles, Angel couldn't help giving a shiver, listening to the soldiers talking in the back of the ambulance, each trying to outdo the other in superior knowledge of the war strategies.

'Thank the stars you ain't back in Blighty, mate. Hear about the Suffolk coast bein' badly hit end of last month –'

'I'm just thankful I'm not at sea. Did you know the Jerry bastards have begun submarine warfare now? They'll be sinking hospital ships before we know it. If you don't get blown up at the Front, you'll end up as fishes' bait.'

'Put a sock in it back there,' Jones, the V.A.D. girl trying to steer the ambulance over the bumpy roads, shouted back. 'I swear they take delight in spreading as many grisly details as they can,' she muttered to Angel.

'It's all they can think about, the war and home,' Angel said. It was all anybody thought about. Getting through the war, and going home, and taking up the old life where it left off . . .

But that wasn't what Angel wanted. Whenever she thought of the future, it was with total confusion. All the old ideas of a coming-out season in London, of balls and social afternoons and being seen at Ascot and at Wimbledon and all the fashionable places, seemed of so little importance compared with the enormity of surviving the war to end all wars.

What was dearer to her heart than any of those things, was being with Jacques. Living and loving together, for the rest of their lives . . .

'I say, Bannister, you're not being much help,' she heard Jones say crossly. 'You're supposed to be navigating to this Abbey place, and I've asked you twice which way we go at the crossroads ahead!'

'Sorry!' Angel bent her head, feeling embarrassment heat her cold cheeks. At least it was better than feeling frozen. The day was bitter. February was living up to its reputation, and even the soldiers had gone silent in the back now, huddling together to keep warm.

She gave directions quickly and efficiently after that. It was to her benefit, after all. The sooner they reached the Abbey of St Helene, the sooner she would know the truth . . .

'That must be it,' Jones pointed ahead in the late afternoon, after what seemed an interminable ride through flurries of snow, and increasing areas of choking fog making the journey hazardous. Looming ahead of them was the gaunt outline of an old abbey, typically French, and the most welcome sight Angel had yet seen. Jones and the convalescents were to stop here for refreshments before driving on to Boulogne for the night ship.

Angel's heart beat sickeningly fast as she climbed down stiffly, obliged to help Jones with the men, though most were able to walk unaided and were going home on compassionate leave. Once they had reported to an orderly by way of Jones' hesitant French, Angel left them and found the Mother Superior's office. Hands trembling, she knocked on the door.

'*Entrez,*' came the brisk response, and Angel entered a sparsely furnished room with thick stone walls, made even more atmospheric by the coifed and black-robed figure seated magnificently behind an ancient desk. The ambience of historic France seemed strangely personified in this quiet room, and for no particular reason, Angel felt a sudden terror, as though she were about to be guillotined.

Chapter 19

The Mother Superior gave the young woman a polite smile, and looked at her enquiringly. Angel explained who she was in fluent French, and her reason for being here.

'Ah yes!' The nun was clearly relieved at being addressed in her own tongue, but her expression changed slightly, her smile a little uneasy. 'You have been highly recommended to us, Mademoiselle Bannister, and I'm sure you will be an asset in the Abbey, my dear, since we speak very little English.'

'Thank-you,' Angel said. 'But Mother, please tell me – the Frenchman you have here – you know how anxious I am to see him, since I think he may be my fiancé –'

The nun rose. Angel was surprised to see how tall she was. She towered over the low furniture like some great eagle, Angel thought.

'My dear, I am sorry to have to give you bad news –'

Waves of nausea swept over Angel. Dear God, surely nothing had happened to Jacques after all this time, when she had not even been permitted to visit him . . .?

'I am afraid that the man you came to see discharged himself from the hospital two days ago. I'm so sorry. You should have been informed, but we have been so terribly busy this past week that I'm afraid it was overlooked.'

Angel stared at her in disbelief. Jacques was well enough to have discharged himself? Why hadn't she been informed of such an improvement? Her thoughts were so muddled she couldn't take it all in.

'So his memory has returned?' The words seemed to be dragged from her. She saw the nun shake her head.

'No. He was certainly much more lucid of late, but we still have no idea who he is, nor how he arrived here.'

Angel sprang to her feet, tears of frustration and disappointment making her forget her manners. 'Then why could I not have come to see him? I could have told you –'

She felt the cool hand of the nun on her arm, and subsided onto the chair again, trembling with this new shock. She was certain she had been so near to being with Jacques again, and now all her hopes were in ruins.

'Mademoiselle, it was Papillon's insistence that he should see no one, as well as our wish. He was badly burned, and although the scars have faded, his mind was tortured. In his more sensible moments, he begged for no prying eyes until he was whole in mind and body. We could only respect those wishes –'

'Even when you knew that there was someone who might have identified him?' Angel cried bitterly. 'Someone who was in anguish, believing him dead? What kind of a God is yours, Mother, if you think He would have been proud of such actions?'

The nun didn't answer, and incredibly, Angel could see that her words had hardly touched her. Such people were beyond human feelings, she wept, but why should they believe themselves nearer to God than boys who were torn apart by war, and young women hardly out of school who tended them so tirelessly? What did this person know of the love that flowed between a man and a woman? How could she have any knowledge of how badly Jacques would have wanted her, needed her?

'Please compose yourself, my dear, and I will show you the note that Papillon left behind.'

Angel raised streaming eyes to the calm face of the nun. It

was all the more incomprehensible to her that the woman didn't take offence, that Angel could rage and scream, and it would all be accepted passively. It *wasn't* human . . .

'There was a note?' she said raggedly. 'If it was Jacques' handwriting, then I'll know it –'

'You may not. His hands often shook abominably, presumably when he relived what had happened to him, the truth of which is sadly still locked away in his memory. I fear he was in an agitated state when he left the Abbey, and the writing is barely legible. The Sisters and I fear for his safety, and I assure you we pray for him constantly.'

Angel wanted to hear nothing of prayers at that moment. She took the piece of paper offered to her, burning to find some clue in the note that this was truly Jacques' writing, but there was nothing. It consisted of shaky scratchings of a child, or worse, of a senile old man. It merely thanked the Sisters, and beneath the words was a crude drawing. A bird soaring into the sky above some low hills, seeming to have arched doors fashioned into their bases.

Angel stared at the drawing, willing some message to come to her through it. She frowned, deep in concentration, and at last, as if out of a mist she seemed to hear Jacques' voice, speaking softly and nostalgically . . .

'One day we'll go to my home in Bordeaux together, *chérie*. I'll show you the vineyards, and the deep, dark cellars beneath the hills where the wine is stored at a constant temperature. If the Germans ever reached so far into France, we would always have a refuge beneath the hills.'

'I know where he's gone,' Angel said tremblingly. 'And I know that he was Jacques de Ville.'

The Mother Superior looked at her sorrowfully.

'We suggested that name to him after the doctor at Piersville passed on your message to us, Mademoiselle. There was no flicker of response at all. I beg you not to build up your hopes. The man is gone –'

'Then I will go too!' Angel said passionately.

we shall all be together again, and what tales we shall have to tell.

'Take care of yourself, and of Meadowcroft. How I miss it when I talk to the soldiers of home. My best love as always.

'Your loving daughter,

Angel.'

She re-read the letter quickly, knowing she had made no reference to her father, and hoping that Clemence would assume that she had written to him separately as she had often done in her schooldays.

'Dearest, Darling Daddy, your best girl is waiting impatiently for a letter from you . . .'

She bit her lip, folded Clemence's letter quickly, and put it in an envelope. She didn't want to think of those other days. Instead, she would think about Easter, when she had been promised some leave, and rather more than she had intimated to her mother. Ten whole days! Ample time to beg a lift to Paris in one of the Red Cross lorries that were always going back and forth. And then to take the train for Bordeaux, and to find Jacques.

Her heart skipped a beat. She *must* find him. She must know for certain what had happened to him. If he had been well enough to travel, then some of his faculties must be returning to him. And his rough sketch the Mother Superior had given her, of the hills and the arched doors that Angel was sure led to the cool dark wine cellars, had given her the first real clue that instinctively, Jacques had known he was going home.

She waited for her Easter leave with a gnawing impatience, knowing she must not neglect her duties here, and knowing too that the time would pass quicker if her hands were kept busy. And they were *always* busy at the Abbey. Casualties arrived constantly. Sometimes they would come in an ambulance from Piersville, and it would be driven by someone she knew, bringing a note from Ellen.

'How are you, old thing?' Angel could almost hear her sister's breezy voice as she read the words. 'Our war here is much the same as when you left it. What stinking weather. We have to cut the boots off some of the poor devils, so caked in mud it's a wonder they could ever lift their feet. I'm on the wards now. Sister Yard praises my strong muscles, which makes me feel like a prize bull on market day. Still, it keeps me fit. How goes it, darling? Any news of J? You know I'm longing to hear.

'Fondest regards, Ellen.'

She made no mention of Peter Chard, and Angel wondered if she'd written to him yet. She wrote back to Ellen whenever she could, needing to feel close to someone, because then she wouldn't feel quite so much in limbo.

And at last the longed-for leave arrived. She climbed into the Red Cross lorry that was going back to Paris after bringing much-needed supplies to the Abbey, and gave a great sigh of anticipation. At last she was on her way!

The driver gave her a typically French smile, the appraisal in his eyes taking in everything at once about this elegant young Englishwoman with as much chic as a Parisienne. It still shone through, despite the rigours of hospital life, and the driver appreciated the fact that she was sitting beside him.

'I am Henri, Mademoiselle Bannister,' he spoke in French, since it seemed to be her second language. 'We have some hours to be together, so forgive the informality.'

'Of course. And I am Angel.'

She smiled back, thinking briefly that this war had done much to sweep away the sort of stuffy conventions when lack of introductions restricted friendships. Such etiquette would undoubtedly return after the war, but it all seemed so petty when the hand a nurse held might be lifeless within minutes, and all a soldier needed was to hear a caring voice speaking his name . . .

'Staying in Paris, are you, Angel?' Henri was prepared to

chatter to this pretty young travelling companion, and she shook her head as they drove through sheeting rain, their wheels throwing up showers of mud on all sides.

'I'm taking a train to Bordeaux as soon as I can –'

'Won't be one today.' Henri shook his head decisively, and Angel stared at him in dismay. 'It'll be too late when we arrive, *chérie*. First thing in the morning will be a different matter.'

'But I hadn't planned to spend a night in Paris!'

He gave a low chuckle. 'It's unusual to hear a pretty young Mademoiselle say so! Everyone loves a night in Paris!'

'But I have to get to Bordeaux as quickly as possible,' Angel spoke desperately.

He shrugged. 'Tomorrow morning, the train will get you there quicker than any other means, unless you have your own private car and are prepared to travel through the night!'

Angel blinked back the tears of frustration, knowing that what the man said was probably true. And she didn't have her own private car. Memories of the reliable little Sunbeam came longingly to her mind.

But she had to be sensible. If tomorrow morning's train was the only means of reaching Bordeaux, then she must make other arrangements for tonight. The thought daunted her for a minute. She glanced at the profile of the man sitting beside her. A family man, she hoped, who would not take her words amiss.

'Do you know of a small hotel where I can get a room for the night, Henri?'

'Better than that. I know the owner of a safe café who rents out rooms to students. It's very near the railway station you'll need for the train to Bordeaux, which makes it useful for the students going home from the universities and the Sorbonne. I can take you there, if you wish.'

'It's very kind of you, thank-you.' There was so much

kindness in the midst of a war. You had to endure it to realise it, Angel reflected.

It was almost dark when they arrived in Paris. Ghostly outlines of the monuments she remembered from another part of her life, the Eiffel Tower, the brave Arc de Triomphe, the wide, beautiful river Seine with its bridges, the gothic structure of Notre Dame . . . everything seemed to conspire to thicken her throat and fill her with nostalgia for times past . . . and even more than that – the sheen of rain on the streets reminded her vividly of a night in London, when she had first met Jacques de Ville and lost her heart.

'Are you all right, Angel?' Henri glanced at her, suddenly silent, and she nodded.

'Just remembering Paris as it was,' she spoke with an effort, realising how gloomy it all looked now. Where was the sparkle of Paris, the gaiety and vitality, the brilliant lights? All dimmed for the duration . . .

'We all remember,' Henri said quietly. 'But she'll live again, I promise you. Now then, I'll take you to the café and see you settled, and then be on my way.'

She looked at him, solidly respectable, and probably wanting to get back to his family, like everyone did.

'I'm very grateful.'

'We're Allies, aren't we?' He was cheerful now, and she gave a small laugh.

'We're friends,' she corrected him.

They called at the station first to check on the train times for Bordeaux. It was all very haphazard, but there was one due at six-thirty in the morning, which would hopefully reach Bordeaux by early evening. The clerk said dourly that there was no certainty in anything these days.

Angel thanked Henri for all his help and entered the café on his recommendation. It was a small place, run by a Monsieur and Madame Dupont. The room Angel was given was spotless, with several pictures of saints above the bed and wash basin. She wasn't a Catholic, but they gave her comfort.

When she went for her evening meal, there were red checked cloths on the tables, wine bottles as candle holders with the stalactites of melted wax adorning them, and an old man playing plaintive tunes on an accordion.

Students laughed and chatted, lovers in corners looked into one another's eyes in the candleglow, oblivious to everything around them. The essence of Paris survived among all its privations.

But it was wiser not to go out at night. Angel stayed in the café, drinking in the sounds of the music and the quick city accents of those around her. If she half-closed her eyes, she could almost imagine it was another era, when she came here with her parents and sisters, and everything was new and wonderful to a young English girl.

She slept fitfully. Street noises woke her several times; the rumble of lorry wheels as soldiers were taken through the night towards the Front Line; the hurtling of a train as it went through the railway station.

And then it was morning. Almost before it was light, Angel was awake, dressing quickly, and eating the early breakfast provided for her. She crossed the street to the grand edifice of the station. The clerk was still grumbling, resigned to expecting delays, commenting that if an ambulance train arrived, then ordinary passenger trains must wait. It was the war, he said expressively, rolling his eyes and spreading his hands as his shoulders hunched up into his chin.

The train wasn't late, but it was late in the day when it finally arrived at Bordeaux, after many stops and starts, shuntings into sidings while other trains went by, and the inevitable gesticulating by angry French passengers and the important dramatics of railway officials.

But at last she was in Bordeaux, an ancient town that she

didn't know. Wine country, she remembered from her geography lessons, never dreaming that that small fact might have such significance on her future life. At least it wasn't raining, and she took the pathetic little thought as an omen, finding a likely-looking *boulangerie* to enquire if anyone knew the whereabouts of a family called de Ville.

She was enveloped in the delicious, yeasty smell of fresh-baked bread and buns. There was not such a parade of wonderfully exotic concoctions now as in days gone by, no luscious cream-filled gateaux or petit fours arranged daintily on tiny fluted doilies, but the aura of the *boulangerie* was still teasing to the senses, tempting to the eye.

Angel ignored it all, and made her enquiry.

'De Ville?' The old man behind the counter looked at her blankly as he echoed the name, and her heart sank. Either this was a town filled with de Villes, or he was annoyed that this well-bred young woman should come into his shop with a pointless request without intending to buy. She was embarrassed.

'I'm sorry. Perhaps I should ask at the Poste. The Monsieur de Ville I am looking for may have a vineyard –'

The man looked astonished. 'My dear Mademoiselle, there is no need to ask at the Poste! A vineyard, indeed! Yes, I believe that may be an apt description. Come with me.'

He came to the front of the shop and led Angel outside. She was too bewildered to argue. Outside in the grey afternoon air, the man pointed to where a lovely old chateau set on a hill seemed to rear up against the skyline. It dominated the area, clearly the domain of a wealthy landowner. Angel felt her mouth go dry, anticipating the *boulangier*'s next words.

'There is the home of Comte de Ville, Mademoiselle. The wine cellars are of the finest, and extend for many miles beneath the hills. If that is not the de Ville you seek, then I cannot help you further.'

It was clear from the pride in his voice that he rode

on the coat tails of the de Villes being in his vicinity.

Angel looked about her for a taxi, but there were none to be hired, only a crowded, clattering bus that took her to the foot of the hills. It was preferable to walking the long distance through the cobbled streets.

She became increasingly nervous. Jacques had given her no idea that his home was so grand, or that he was the son of a Comte. She was filled with misgivings. Coming here to find her beloved was one thing; knocking on the door of a huge chateau and facing someone of the French nobility was quite another.

Some of the young women in her London circle had been dismissive of such aristocratic connections. 'Two-a-penny' had been the phrase bandied about when one spoke of French aristos. But it was a different matter when faced with this vast, turreted mansion, and about to request an audience with the man whom she hoped desperately was Jacques' father!

She shook herself angrily. What was wrong with her? She hadn't come all this way to be demoralised by a house! Nor by the thought that Comte de Ville was so much better than Angel Bannister. Her chin lifted. Her mother would wash her hands of her if she thought Angel was unable to conduct herself properly in these circumstances.

She walked past the arched doors in the hillside that were so similar to those in Jacques' drawing. She took comfort from them. There was a de Ville coat of arms depicted on each door, quietly impressive and understated enough to show that here was a business that didn't need garish advertising to make it successful.

Angel paused for breath when she had finally made the ascent to the imposing gates of the chateau, glancing behind her to take in the sweeping panorama of the town of Bordeaux below and a distant winding river. The chateau was in a magnificent setting. She wondered how Jacques could ever bear to leave it, a thought that made her hands go clammy again.

What would his reaction be at seeing her, if his memory had returned? And if it hadn't, then what had she accomplished in coming here after all?

She wasted no more time on useless surmising, pushed open the great iron gates and approached the massive oak front door of the chateau. 'Two-a-penny' they might be, she thought incongruously, but even minor French nobility had a heritage behind them that was unnerving to ordinary mortals.

A manservant answered the door. Remembering her manners, she asked for Comte de Ville, thinking also that to speak with his father might be better than facing Jacques immediately. He didn't even know she was in France. She hadn't answered any of his letters, and it would serve her right if he refused to see her. The enormity of it all threatened to overwhelm her.

She was shown into a room with costly wall hangings and deep pile carpets and exquisite furniture. It all seemed to separate her even more from the man she had known and loved. His was a different world from hers, and how could she dare to think she could become part of it? She was so upset by the time an elderly man entered the room, she was poised for flight.

'You wished to see me, Mademoiselle?' Comte de Ville said politely, half-annoyed at being disturbed by a young woman so obviously distressed. He sighed. Listening to tales of woe was one of the duties of his position, but this girl was certainly no French peasant. He saw the breeding in her face, despite the twisting hands, and bade her to sit down.

'Monsieur le Comte, please forgive me for coming here unannounced. My name is Angel Bannister. I am English, and have been nursing at the Abbey of St Helene, and have heard about your son. I believe I know him, and we need his identification for our records, and I wondered if he was here –'

Angel babbled on as the thoughts occurred to her, the words dying away as she saw the frown on the Comte's face. Dear God, what must he be thinking? That she was some silly litle ingenue infatuated with Jacques, and seeing this excuse as a way to infiltrate into his home? Her eyes closed with shame, and nausea made her head throb.

'My dear, please drink this.'

Vaguely, she registered that the Comte spoke in English now, and that he held a glass of brandy to her lips. The taste was bitter, causing her to choke a little.

'I'm so sorry. What must you think of me?' she mumbled.

'I think perhaps you are the young lady of whom my son has spoken briefly,' the Comte said quietly.

Angel felt the wild hot colour flood her face.

'Jacques has recovered his memory? He *is* here? Oh, please may I see him?'

The Comte straightened. There was pain in his eyes.

'Of course. But please realise that he is no longer as you will remember him. The crash –'

'So his plane did crash?' Angel's voice was husky. 'The nuns at the Abbey couldn't even be sure that their patient was an airman –'

The Comte gave a slight smile. 'Then you really are from the hospital?'

Angel blushed again. 'I'm sorry. My words were foolish. I hardly knew what to say when I saw you. I've waited so long for news of Jacques, and now I'm scared. Isn't that silly?'

To her horror, tears rushed to her eyes again. This large man with the grave face and the eyes that were the same colour as Jacques' eyes, somehow reminded her of her own father. Comte de Ville was so gentle that Angel felt the wildest desire to weep on his shoulder. But it was not why she had come. She struggled to swallow the feeling of inadequacy, her throat working painfully. Comte de Ville admired the quiet strength of the beautiful English girl, and rang a bell for the manservant again.

'Would you please inform Monsieur Jacques that he has a visitor, Cartier, and that she awaits him in the blue drawing room?'

The man withdrew with a small bow. Angel took sudden fright, and spoke urgently.

'Please tell me. Has Jacques truly recovered his memory? Did he know you?'

The Comte's voice was grave. 'Not at first. It seemed that some instinct drew him here. But thankfully, his own environment and our excellent family physician have done the rest. Yes, he is aware of who he is, my dear. And now I will leave you to be re-acquainted with my son.'

He left the room, and all Angel could hear was the sweet singing of the birds outside in a sudden burst of pale sunshine; the ticking of the ornate clock on the mantelpiece, and the frantic beat of her own heart.

A few minutes later, she heard the low voices of two men outside the drawing room door. And then it opened. And there was Jacques.

Chapter 20

It seemed an endless moment that they stood and looked at one another. Jacques' eyes were incredulous and disbelieving, as if he were seeing a ghost. Angel noted the fading scars down one side of his cheek and neck, disappearing into the open neck of his shirt, and the slight limp in his walk. None of it mattered. If he had been physically only half a man, he would still have been whole and dear to her. She gave a strangled cry as he moved towards her, his arms opened wide. She hardly knew how she crossed the room to meet him halfway. She only knew the glorious feeling of being held in his arms, of tasting his kisses on her mouth, of tears mingling and two hearts beating as one.

It was a while before they could bear to speak and break the spell of just being together, and even then they sat closely on the silk-covered sofa, arms still around each other, faces close, unwilling to break the contact denied them for so long.

'I thought you were dead,' Angel wept. 'And yet I never gave up hope. I couldn't –'

'And when you didn't answer my letters, I thought you didn't care any more. And you're here, in France, and my father tells me you've been at the Abbey of St Helene! God, we could only just have missed each other –'

'I was even closer to you, Jacques, without knowing it. I was at Piersville hospital at first, and I went to Brighton Belle to find you, just after you had been reported missing. It was a terrible, terrible time – but nothing like as terrible as it must have been for you!'

She felt him shudder in her arms.

'How did you find me now, *chérie*?' He resisted any discussion of his crash, and she guessed that it was going to be told in Jacques' own time. She knew from her nursing experience that the deeper the mental suffering, the longer it took to be brought to the surface in actual telling, especially to those nearest and dearest.

She smiled crookedly. 'It was what my mother would call one of life's little coincidences. A casualty at Piersville thought he knew me from one of the drawings done by the mystery man at the Abbey of St Helene. I was certain in my bones that it was you. I wanted to go there at once, but they said you refused to have visitors.'

'I wanted no one outside the hospital to see that poor creature,' he said grimly. 'Least of all you! Did your parents approve of your coming to France? And cutting your lovely hair!'

She laughed naturally for the first time in what seemed like years. 'Of course not! Though I think my mother is gradually coming round to the idea that women are not such feeble things as they once were.'

'And your father? Your wonderful father?' Jacques smiled, remembering how she had put him on a pedestal.

She buried her head against him.

'I don't want to talk about them any more. I still can't believe we're actually together again. I'll have to return in a week's time, but at least I can write to you here –'

'Angel darling.' His voice was quiet, warning her. She stopped, afraid.

'What is it? What haven't you told me?'

She whispered the words, realising as she said them that he had told her little. His mind was closed to reminders of his crash, and the weeks that followed. But there was definitely some purpose in Jacques' eyes now.

'I'm not staying here. I'm well, *chérie*. Well enough to resume flying –'

She was horrified, almost pushing him away from her.

'Jacques, you can't! Don't tempt fate a second time –'

'Airmen are tempting fate every time they fly. Would you want me less of a man than they are? Should I sit at my easel all day long painting portraits of pet dogs for rich widows?' He couldn't hide the bitterness in his voice. 'I expected more than that from you!'

'You expect more than I can give! I don't want to lose you a second time.'

He gave a harsh laugh. 'What confidence you have in me! Deprive me of my ambition and you take away my life. I would be no use to anyone, least of all the woman I want to marry.'

Angel caught her breath. Her throat was tight with tears. If this was a proposal, it was said at the worst of times, when she was so vulnerable from knowing him to be alive, and so terrified of losing him all over again . . .

Jacques caught her to him, and she felt the virility and the strength of him, that not even a near-fatal crash in a flimsy, burning aircraft could quench. His arms could still hold her close, his voice was a soft seduction, and he was still Jacques, whom she loved beyond all reason.

'Promise me that one day we'll be married, Angel. Your promise is all the luck I need to bring me safely through this war. Haven't we survived this far?'

'There's nothing I want more than to be your wife, my love,' she whispered back. And if it was the sweetest kind of blackmail that he used to extract her promise, that didn't matter either. They clung for long minutes, pledging themselves, until a discreet sound behind them made them pull apart.

Comte de Ville smiled benevolently on the English girl who could bring the life back to his son.

'Please do us the honour of staying at the chateau while

you're in Bordeaux, Miss Bannister.' He spoke with continental courtesy.

Jacques stood up with Angel, his arm still around her shoulders. He spoke before she could reply.

'Father, I want you to know that Angel has agreed to marry me, and that of course she will remain here until we leave together next week. Perhaps we could have a small party with a few close friends to celebrate.'

Angel was apprehensive at this bald statement, wondering if Comte de Ville might have other ideas for his son, than marrying an English girl who had arrived unannounced. But she was forgetting Jacques' own mother had been English, and that the family's links with England were strong.

She saw nothing but pleasure in the Comte's face as he raised her hand to his lips in a way both charming and touching.

'My dear, I couldn't be more pleased. I've guessed for some time that my son had met someone very special, and now that I see his choice, I welcome you to our family.'

It was said with such simple dignity that Angel almost threw her arms around his neck and hugged him. But not quite. She didn't know him well enough for that yet.

'Please don't be insulted, Monsieur le Comte, when I say that this must all be unofficial until my parents have been told. My father will want to meet Jacques – although I am quite certain there could be no objection!'

She spoke in some embarrassment at the remotest suggestion that there could be any objection to an untitled English girl becoming betrothed to the son of a French count. But Jacques' father understood.

'Your consideration for your parents does you nothing but credit, dear Miss Bannister, and naturally any formalities must wait until after the war.'

Jacques and Angel did not look at one another. Instead she said warmly, 'Oh please – my name is Angel. I would be so happy if you would use it.'

'Of course. A charming name for a charming young lady. But you must be tired and hungry after your journey. One of the maids will show you to your room, and we will dine in an hour. Press your bell when you are ready, and you will be shown the way to the dining room.'

It all sounded terribly grand, but until that moment, Angel hadn't realised just how exhausted she was. And hungry too. The maid, Marie, showed her to a beautiful guestroom with adjoining bathroom of the utmost luxury, and within minutes, Angel was soaking in blissfully fragrant water, and sending up a little prayer of thankfulness that out of all the world, she and Jacques had found one another again.

She had brought the minimum of luggage, and was suddenly aghast at presenting herself at dinner in this splendid house with two gentlemen of quality, looking less than her best. It seemed such ages since she had thought of silk dinner gowns and the latest fashions, and attending to her manicure and buying jewellery and combs for her hair... a sudden sadness for the loss of all those things swept over her. In three short years, so much of youth had been snatched away from young men and women. Those who died were beyond remembering. Those who were left had been forced to grow up too soon...

She heard a knock on her door while she was still pondering on the better of the few dresses she had brought with her. Marie entered, several dinner gowns over her arm.

'Monsieur le Comte instructed me to offer you the choice, Mademoiselle. They belonged to Madame, and he thinks you are about the same size, and begs that you will not be offended.'

'*Merci*, Marie,' Angel said quickly, touched by his thoughtfulness. The gowns were slightly outdated, but exquisitely made, and the slight bustle on each of them did something quite remarkable for Angel's shape. How elegant those Edwardian ladies must have been, she thought wistfully, and how elegant this shimmering pale rose gown that had belonged to Jacques' mother made her feel.

She was not in the least offended, and when she followed Marie's directions and walked down the long curving staircase, feeling like a queen, it was to find the two handsome de Ville men awaiting her. Jacques took her hand.

'How beautiful you are, *chérie*,' he murmured.

'You do credit to my wife's memory,' his father added, clearing his throat, 'and you will do me the honour of keeping the gowns, Angel.'

'I'm the one who is honoured,' she said, more moved than she admitted. 'I would not insult you by refusing such a very personal gift, Monsieur le Comte.'

Dinner was the gayest meal Angel had enjoyed for months. The talk was kept deliberately light and away from the war. Bordeaux was far away from the Front Line, and although Angel guessed that the Comte would follow its progress with the fervour of every patriotic Frenchman, tonight was not for sombre talk, but a time for reunion and laughter and for relating to Jacques' father the circumstances in which Jacques and Angel had met.

Naturally, neither mentioned the enchanted night they had spent at the Hotel Portland, but glances that met and then looked away, tinges of colour in the cheeks and the constant awareness of one another, told their own story. Through the flickering candlelight across the wide table, their eyes spoke of love, their spirits ached for each other. The wine was the very best from the de Ville cellars, and was potent and heady.

At last, when they retired to the drawing room for strong coffee and delicious minted sweetmeats, it was as if Comte de Ville felt he must break the spell that made the atmosphere between the young couple too emotionally charged.

'You understand that Jacques is to rejoin his squadron next week, Angel?'

It was like a dash of iced water in her face.

'I wish he would not!'

The words were out before she could stop them. She bit her lip, seeing Jacques' frown. She had no right to try and shape his life. Not yet, if ever . . . French wives were subservient to their husbands. Even English women . . . it was such bad form to disobey . . . she could hear her mother's disapproving voice through her senses, and knew she had become emboldened by the wine.

'A de Ville never turns his back on duty, my dear,' the Comte said gently.

'Nor would he wish to be tied to a woman's apron strings,' Jacques added.

'I would never do such a thing. Nor would I want a man who permitted it!' Angel said hotly. To her relief, the Comte laughed.

'I think you and Jacques are well matched, Angel. But a word of advice, my dear. You may as well try to change Jacques' mind as try to stop the sun from rising every morning.'

'I'm not sure that it's admirable to be so intractable. A man should bend but not break.' She stopped in acute embarrassment. It was how Margot had once described Angel. It was hardly the thing to do to censure Jacques for being dogmatic in his own home. He leaned back, blowing smoke into the air from a fragrant cigar, and appeared not to be insulted.

'When one has lost all identity as I had, *chérie*, and then gradually finds it again, it's like a miracle. All the love I had for flying was back, perhaps intensified –'

'Even after what happened to you?'

'Even so. It was wiped out, in a way. I was reborn, and remembering that it was bad luck to have someone permanently filling my chair in the Officers' Mess. Soon I shall fill it again. I'm pronounced fit enough for service, and my unit is delighted to have me back. Apparently they had a little ceremony to reverse the wake they held for me some months ago.'

She shivered at his teasing tone. But there was a mute appeal in his voice too, begging her not to argue with him. He had made his decision. He had survived, so he had to go back, as she might have known he would.

'Then it's lucky I can go back with you at least part of the way,' she said with a great effort at lightness. 'My sister Ellen is at Piersville now. Have I told you that?'

The warmth in Jacques' eyes told her what her words meant to him. If her heart was breaking at the thought of the new danger he would encounter every single day once he rejoined his squadron, she would never reveal it. In time of war, it was not only men who had to be brave and strong.

They spent an idyllic week. She spent hours in his studio, absorbing the smells of turpentine and oils and marvelling at Jacques' artistic talent, wanting to watch him work, and breathing down his neck until he had to tell her laughingly to stop.

He showed her the de Ville wine cellars, musty and cool beneath the hills, the great casks of fermenting juice, and the endless racks of wine already bottled and maturing. There was a fortune beneath the hills, and once he took her to the vast vineyards and explained some of the workings to her, Angel realised just what the Chateau de Ville really meant to Jacques and his family.

When his father died, it would all belong to him. And when Angel became his wife . . . it was a daunting prospect, and one that she had never envisaged. When they were seated inside one of the family cars once more, it was as if he read her mind, and Jacques tipped up her chin with his finger.

'Are you having second thoughts about marrying me, *chérie*?' he challenged.

She shook her head slowly. 'Of course not! It's just that I

had no idea of – all this.' She spread her arms as expressively as any Frenchwoman. 'You seduced me under false pretences, you know. I thought you were just any old officer.'

Her smile belied her teasing words. Never could she think of Jacques as just any old officer, when he stood head and shoulders above the rest, physically and mentally. Her heart beat faster as she saw the new look in his eyes.

'And I have not come to your room since you came to the chateau,' he stated. 'Are you hurt because of it?'

'No. We must respect your father's house, Jacques –'

She was crushed in his arms before she could finish.

'That's not the reason.' She could barely hear the ragged words against her hair. 'My lost memory, my burns, they have all healed. But there are still nightmares, and there is still the fear of not being all that a man should be. Do you understand what I'm saying?'

'Yes,' she whispered. 'But it doesn't matter, Jacques –'

'It bloody well does matter!' She could hear the outrage in his voice as he pushed her away from him. 'I can't expect you to understand. No woman could.'

Tears blurred her eyes. She couldn't bear to quarrel with him. She smothered the pain at his scathing words.

'All I meant was that it takes time for wounds to heal, dearest, mental and physical –' she said carefully, at which he gave a harsh laugh.

'I don't mean to imply that there are any bits missing. Just that they may not be in perfect working order yet.'

She didn't know how to answer so delicate a subject. If she said it didn't matter, he would think she had lost interest in him. If she said that it did, he would think her a shameless woman, only interested in his body. Or worse, keen to ensure that she married into the French aristocracy, now that she was aware of his status.

She gave an involuntary sob. At which, Jacques was all contrition, and took her in his arms again.

'Forgive me. I've become a self-centred bastard since the

crash. One day I'll tell you about it.'

It was the nearest he came to admitting its effect on him, and that alone was strangely reassuring. She hugged him close, without words.

'Let's go home,' he said huskily. 'We're having a party this evening, and I've something very special to give you, my darling.'

A dozen guests were invited to the chateau for the very informal engagement party. Neither Jacques nor Angel had wanted anything more pretentious, although the Comte would have thrown a much more lavish affair for his only son.

But remembering Jacques' recent illness, and the need to be conservative in entertaining during these wartime days, the Comte had given in, to Angel's great relief. She loved parties, but these people would all be strangers, and it would be something of an ordeal.

At the Comte's request, she wore another dress that had belonged to his wife, a deep green dinner gown in rich satin that rippled with every movement, complementing Angel's English rose skin and fair hair, and bringing out the colour of her eyes. Jacques thought she had never looked so beautiful.

Before the guests arrived, he gave her the special gift. Angel gasped as she opened the long velvet box and took out the necklace of fabulous emeralds and the matching ring with a single huge emerald in an antique setting.

'It's too much,' she said shakily. 'It's far too valuable a gift, Jacques.'

He took the jewels from her and fastened the necklace around her neck as she stood in front of the enormous gilt-edged drawing room mirror. The necklace looked perfect against her flawless complexion. Jacques turned her round in his arms and slid the ring on the third finger of her left hand. It was a little large, but not for worlds would she have taken it off again.

'With this ring I ask you to be my wife,' Jacques said gravely. 'The jewels are family heirlooms, Angel, and are entrusted only to those we cherish.'

Her throat was thick at his simple words. He could have been far more flamboyant, but the de Villes had style enough without the need for such ploys.

It was agreed that the jewels should be returned to the family vault for safe keeping before they left the chateau the following day. Angel would never have dared to take them away with her. They would remain at the chateau until she returned here with Jacques as his wife. They were one more talisman to bind them together.

But for tonight . . . they glowed against Angel's fair skin and were the object of much admiration among the evening's guests. Not the least admired was Jacques' betrothed, and Angel wondered how she could ever have been nervous of meeting these charming people.

If only her own parents and sisters could have been here too, she thought wistfully. She had written to Clemence and Fred, unable to leave him out this time, and told them all that had happened. She had also sent an ecstatic letter to Ellen, an equally ecstatic one to Margot Lacey, and a slightly less hysterical one to her sister Louise.

Jacques had written formally to her father, asking for his daughter's hand in marriage in due course, and separately to Clemence, a letter which would surely charm the birds from the trees, Angel thought privately and inelegantly.

The Comte de Ville had sent a letter to Angel's parents too, assuring them of the propriety of their daughter staying at the chateau, acquainting them of his son's position and prospects. And undoubtedly dazzling them with the secure future envisaged for their daughter, Angel chuckled to Jacques, when the Comte had told them of his intention.

There had been no time for replies, but the engagement party went ahead, assuming it was all a *fait accompli*. And tomorrow, the idyll was to end, Angel thought, as the guests drank a toast to the young couple in the oldest and costliest de Ville wine. Tomorrow, they were to return to the war.

But there was still tonight . . .

Angel and Jacques said good night lovingly at her bedroom door. Once inside, she slipped out of the green satin gown, holding its rich fabric against her cheek for a moment before hanging it in the wardrobe, and wondering when she would wear such a garment again. She unfastened the lovely gems from her neck and slid the ring from her finger, placing them reverently in the long case.

She was very tired, but too excited for sleep. A quick bath might help, and afterwards she dried herself with a big fluffy towel in her bedroom. She had turned out the lights and flung open the curtains to let the moonlight flood the room with light, wanting to savour this last night at the chateau with the ghostly shapes of the town below and the hills all around.

She was aware of a small sound. She turned sharply, to see her door handle turn. Her heart beat erratically, knowing it would be Jacques. Wrapped in the towel, she stood very still as he came inside the room, wearing only a dressing robe. He came nearer, and without saying a word, gently removed the towel from her shoulders. She shivered slightly, and he unfastened the belt of his robe and enveloped them both inside it. His voice was a warm, desperate caress against her cheek.

'How can I see you without constantly wanting to touch you? Your very presence is sweet torment to me, Angel. The sound of your voice, the scent of your hair, the longings I've suppressed all these months –'

'Hush, my love,' she whispered back. 'I'm here now, and we're together.'

He lifted her bodily and lay her on the opened bed. The robe slid away from his body, and she could see the silvery patterns of the scars all down one side of him. His hands too, had that strange sheen of new skin, but none of it changed the Jacques she loved. Nor had the sensitivity of those fingers been diminished as they stroked her breasts, swiftly followed by his lips, reviving the exquisite memories of the love they shared.

She felt the growing proof of Jacques' love, and her spirit soared to meet it. Now, the last barrier between them would be removed, and in his own eyes, he would be restored as a man. Angel relaxed as the sweet sensations overwhelmed her, then suddenly she was rudely brought back to reality, hearing Jacques' bitter laugh as he flung himself away from her.

'So much for wishing,' he said harshly. 'If your presence can't make a man of me, then God knows there's little hope left.'

'Jacques, please – it's all right. Let's take a little more time – please –'

He moved off the bed, throwing on the dressing robe and tying it tightly, as if to deny the existence of his manhood.

'We have no time for dalliance, *chérie*.' The word was no longer an endearment but a form of sarcasm. 'We have a war waiting for us, so go to sleep and be ready to leave after breakfast in the morning. I'm sorry I troubled you.'

She was stunned when he had gone. In so short a time, his confidence had been shattered. But he hadn't given it a chance! She wept into her pillow. He had been convinced of his impotence before he even came to her room, and she realised anew what a tenuous hold a man had on his masculine ability. She raged at the only thing she could, relieving her of the anguish she felt. It was all the fault of the bloody, bloody war . . .

At breastfast, Angel could hardly believe Jacques was the same person who had blundered out of her room in the darkness. He was very much in control now. Since informing his unit of his survival, a new uniform had been sent to him, and he looked as dashing and exciting as on the night they had first met, and her heart turned over with love for him.

But she was wiser now, knowing that Jacques must make the next move, and that she dare not taunt him with her sexuality in a way that had become delightfully uninhibited on that last wonderful leave at the small hotel in England.

Today was a sad day for the Comte, as well as a proud one. He had sent his son to war once, and been thankful to see him come home alive, and now he was sending him off again. And this time with a future daughter-in-law in the passenger seat of the car. They were to drive back to Brighton Belle, so that Jacques would have his own transport, and providing he could obtain some petrol, they might manage to meet a few times.

The Comte hugged them both, telling them to take the luck of the house with them, and looking forward to the day when they would return. Neither tried to guess when that might be. In many newspaper reports, the fortunes of war had moved to the sea, but for those involved in continual land and air battles, such speculation gave grim comfort.

'Will you come inside the Abbey, Jacques? The nuns will be so relieved to see you well again,' Angel said, when at last they neared the hospital.

They had been travelling for two days, staying overnight at an inn, where the proprietor gave them separate rooms, to both their secret relief. Angel wept inside that she should feel so, but there was too much tension between them now to risk another humiliation for Jacques.

'Just for a short while,' he agreed. 'I owe them my life, and there are no words adequate enough to thank them for that.'

He didn't tell her that he had more than words to give the nuns. His father had made a generous gift of money to the Abbey of St Helene, and Jacques intended handing it over to the Mother Superior discreetly and without fuss.

So instead, Angel merely heard the nuns scold him for his

desertion but with teasing in their eyes and thankfulness that this handsome young man should have recovered so well. And in all too short a time, they were saying good-bye once more, and it was hard to hold back the tears as they clung together, promising to write, and to meet whenever they could. . .

And then he was gone, and within minutes she was already lonely without him.

Chapter 21

Sir Fred Bannister kept telling himself that this was just an ordinary day. If he said it often enough, perhaps he could believe it. He refused to look at the clock in his office every five minutes, or to leave the factory early. They had a rush of orders to get out, he was a conscientious employer, and for the moment his private life must wait.

Despite the fact that America had now entered the war amid sighs of relief, and were now true allies, there was still an unceasing demand for replacement uniforms and blankets to be sent to the Front, and that told its own story . . .

But Fred was as thankful as any of his millworkers when at last the whistle sounded, and he could feel satisfied that there was no one at Bannister Textiles who could say the boss left early whenever it suited him. He drove quickly away from the red brick buildings, and headed south into the country.

The garden of Beckside Cottage was a riot of hot summer colours. Harriet had always loved her garden, Fred thought, as he finally drove the car neatly around the back of the sturdy little Yorkshire cottage, away from prying eyes. It was a long while since the shock of seeing Angel on the doorstep, but he still felt like some guilty schoolboy every time he parked the car, and it was a feeling he didn't enjoy.

He opened the kitchen door, sniffing appreciatively as he went inside, expecting the usual smells of good cooking to greet him. There were none, and Fred stopped abruptly, sudden fear in his gut. The kitchen was sparklingly tidy. Harriet's cottage was always clean, but never with the irritating fussiness of a spinster's domain. He always thought of it as welcoming and homely. Today, everything seemed different. There was no sign of preparation for the evening meal, no vegetables peeled, nothing simmering on the hob to get his taste buds working.

'Harriet!' He suddenly found his voice, bellowing her name and taking the twisting stairs two at a time. Dear God, don't let anything be wrong, he prayed, knowing in his heart that something must be bloody wrong for Harriet to be missing at the time she knew he'd be coming home.

She was lying face down on the bed. The bed they shared. The bed on which they romped in glorious abandon. Her body was curled up like a foetus. Crumpled somehow. Defeated. The thoughts screamed through his head in little staccato bursts.

'Christ, Harriet, what's wrong?' His voice was hoarse now, his face red from the run up the stairs and the panic in his heart. He couldn't live without her. Nothing else mattered. And she looked so still . . . his senses reeled.

She moved languorously, stretching her arms inch by inch, and the relief was so overwhelming he stumbled towards the bed to kneel down beside her. She had merely been sleeping, and he had thought . . . he had thought . . .

But why the hell shouldn't he have been scared? Harriet never slept in the day. Never went upstairs to bed, unless he turned up unexpectedly, and then it was for a different reason, and neither of them thought about sleeping . . .

He took her roughly in his arms, holding her close to him, breathing in her scent to reassure himself that she wasn't dead. Dear God, it was what he had been thinking, and the imagined sharpness of grief was still in his head. He couldn't get rid of it as he rocked her to him.

'Freddie, you're stifling me!' Harriet started to laugh,

pushing against his chest. 'What ails you, for goodness' sake?'

He stared at her, at the finer lines of her cheeks that had been so full and rosy, and couldn't rid himself of the fear either. But he knew better than to show it.

'What ails *me*, woman? Do you know what time it is? Are we going without dinner tonight?'

She looked at the clock, her mouth dropping open as she saw the time.

'I must have dropped off to sleep! After I'd been to town today, I felt so tired, and thought I'd just lie down for a minute or two, but the hours must have skipped by. And you must be starving, Freddie! I'll get something cooking right away –'

He held onto her arms as she made to scramble off the bed. He could see the traces of tears on her face, and the anxiety in her eyes. She couldn't hide it from him the way he hid it from her.

'Did you think I'd forgotten that it was today you were to see the specialist? What was the verdict?' He was harsh with worry, trying to bore into her mind with his own, wishing now that she'd agreed to let him take her. Even though they both knew it would have been asking for trouble.

Tittle-tattle would have started, and Harriet wouldn't allow it. Not for herself, but for him. For his good name at the factory and his reputation. As if he cared a damn . . . even as he thought it, he knew to his shame that he did care.

'I have to go for tests. They want me in hospital, Freddie. Only for a few days, just to be sure –'

'Sure of what?' Even as he said it, he guessed. He'd been poring over medical books in recent weeks, frightening himself half to death over all the possibilities it could be, and even more afraid to suggest anything to Harriet. It might be just a bad cold, or a lingering bout of influenza . . .

'It's most likely consumption,' she said quietly. As if to underline her words, the dry little cough began irritating her again. She turned away from him quickly, trying not to make it obvious that she was trying to avoid breathing into his face. He folded her in his arms.

'But they don't know for sure?' He grasped on to any straw. 'Most likely' didn't mean 'definitely' . . .

'No, they don't know for sure, and I'm not going to spend my time worrying over summat as isn't certain!' Harriet said defiantly. 'So I'll thank you not to make things worse by looking at me like a gloomy spaniel, Freddie!'

He smiled reluctantly, trying to match her flippancy.

'So that's how I look to you, is it? It's hardly the image of a romantic lover!'

Harriet suddenly looked pink, leaning forward to kiss him lightly on the lips.

'Oh, my love, I can think of nothing more romantic than my man with a spaniel's eyes. But if that's your stomach I hear rumbling, I'm going to insist that we stop talking of illness and miserable things we can't change, and let me get us some food.'

He caught at her wrist. 'Harriet, you know I'd give you the earth if I could –'

'I know it. But even you can't give me back my health, so no more sad faces, Freddie. What do you fancy for dinner?'

'You,' he said simply. 'But I'll settle for taking you out to a restaurant instead. Let's go a little crazy tonight, Harriet. We'll drive up to York and find ourselves a secluded place where nobody knows us. What do you say?'

' 'Tis the best idea yet, Freddie. That's if we can find a restaurant with any food.'

'If you've brass to pay, you can always find it!'

He mimicked her accent. Everyone was aware of food shortages now. There were queues at food shops, scarcely any butter to be found; beans were ground up and mixed with wheat flour to make 'war bread'. Potatoes were in short supply and seed potatoes or peelings were cut up into little pieces for planting. Parks were dug up and planted with food crops. It was good for tightening your belt, if you needed to tighten it . . .

'I'll be ready in fifteen minutes,' Harriet said.

'Make it ten. You've already got your glad rags on.'

They both knew she was in her smartest clothes because she'd been to see the specialist. If her dress was slightly creased from lying on the bed, it didn't matter. The crazy mood took hold of them both. Tonight they would both pretend that whatever tomorrow held, it would never come.

Hours later, Fred murmured into the back of her neck as he held her safely curled against his chest in the comfortable double bed.

'Promise me you'll let me send you to a Swiss clinic if necessary, sweetheart. They can work miracles, and there's no need to worry about the cost –'

She turned round in his arms in the darkness, putting her soft fingers against his lips.

'No, Freddie,' she said gently. 'I wouldn't go to Europe in the middle of a war. Besides, I'd feel as if I were deserting a sinking ship if I left Yorkshire. This is my home. It's where I live and where I'll die, and I don't want to hear any more about a Swiss clinic. If God intends a miracle for me, then He'll send it wherever I am.'

She shifted round again, settling comfortably into Fred's lap, and he felt the unmanly sting of tears on his eyelids. Harriet's was a simple faith. He wished to God he could share it, without ever realising the irony of his thoughts.

Telephone communication between Jacques' unit and the Abbey of St Helene was infuriatingly unreliable. If Angel did manage to get through, it was often to be told that he wasn't there, which made her all the more anxious and certain that he was flying again. It was what he intended, but the possibility of another crash terrified her.

But the Royal Flying Corps didn't turn their backs on good pilots just because they'd once gone down in flames.

Survivors were considered lucky. Angel had to keep reminding herself of that . . .

If he was there when she telephoned, there was so much crackling they couldn't hear one another, or they were inexplicably cut off and the line was out of order for the rest of the evening. It seemed simpler to depend on letters than to phone, but she missed the sound of his voice telling her instantly that he was all right.

They managed to meet a few times, but not as often as Angel had hoped. It had seemed so easy, but Piersville was nearer to Brighton Belle than the Abbey, and now that she was here, the nuns had no intention of letting her go. She had proved her usefulness in translating for the wounded British soldiers, and here she would stay.

In June there was a letter from her mother. Angel smiled, sensing the indignation in Clemence's words.

'Louise is expecting a baby at Christmas. Clearly, it happened almost as soon as they were married, which seems to be indecent haste. Dear Stanley was impeccably correct in such matters, but I suppose the Scots have different ideas.

'One does one's best for one's daughters, but there's no guarantee how they will turn out. That is not meant as a slight to you, Angel dear, but it really is too trying that none of you is at Meadowcroft now, and I do feel the strain of the war is making me feel quite poorly.

'However, your father and I are delighted at your news, and at the very eloquent letters from Jacques and his father, the Comte de Ville. Such a charming man!'

Angel was overjoyed about Louise. How wonderful to carry your husband's baby and to feel the living proof of your love . . . she decided to write to Louise that very night. But the smile on her lips faded as she re-read Clemence's letter.

It was so unlike her mother to be so griping. Clemence was adamant in keeping a stiff upper lip, and never letting anyone see when one felt unwell, or was less than serene in one's thinking . . . to admit that she often felt poorly and that she felt the strain of the war was a little alarming.

From anyone else, Angel could have smiled and made some sharp comment that they should come to a French hospital to feel the strain and horror of the war . . . but from Clemence, she knew that things must be much worse than the words actually revealed.

In her next letter to Jacques, she hoped she didn't sound too anxious over her mother, nor too gushing over Louise, but she needed to feel near him through the sharing of family news, if by no other means.

The war dragged on. Casualties passed through the hospitals like an endless production line. The Germans continued to use mustard gas, the results of which made raving idiots out of men too weak to tear the rotting cloth of their uniforms away from their burning skin.

Hospitals nearer the front line, such as Piersville, simply couldn't cope with the numbers, and instead of caring solely for convalescents, the Abbey was sent increasing numbers of gas cases. Some of the nuns who helped remove the tattered clothes from the pathetic bodies, developed chest troubles and streaming eyes. They as well as the men, became yellow and dazed from the lingering fumes. The blisters on some of the nuns' fingers were huge and seeping, and the war seemed to produce nothing but more proof of cruelty and inhumanity.

Ellen arrived at the Abbey on one of the ambulance night runs, begging a lift as helper with some of the stretcher cases. She sought out her sister as soon as her charges were allocated beds, given half an hour before returning to Piersville.

'It's so good to see you!' Angel said delightedly. Being together again was like finding water in the desert. She never realised how much she missed her family until such times. But Ellen had a special reason for wanting to see Angel.

'I've heard from Mother this week,' she said. 'She's got

shingles, poor thing, and she sounds so distraught. It would almost be laughable if it weren't so awful. Are you due some leave, Angel? Couldn't we go home together and cheer her up? We've both been working nonstop since Easter.'

'I'm sure the nuns would agree to it, especially if Mother's really ill,' Angel said slowly. She glanced at Ellen, knowing that her face was falling a little.

'Darling, I know what you're thinking. The last thing you want is to leave France now, when you've found Jacques again. But I really feel we have to go. You know how pathetic Mother's been on the rare occasions she's been ill. She does need someone, Angel, and Dad's always so damned busy in Yorkshire.'

Angel avoided looking at her. It was so tempting to blurt out the truth. To say bitterly that Fred was too damned busy with his lady love to care what was happening to Clemence . . . but she knew that wasn't strictly true. Fred had always been considerate to his wife. It was Clemence who hadn't wanted the boisterous affections of a loving husband . . .

'Well?' Ellen persisted. 'Will you ask the nuns for leave? I'm getting away the day after tomorrow. I'm sure I can get a lift here, and we can go to the coast together in one of the empty supply wagons.'

'I'll find out right away. Of course we must go if Mother needs us, Ellen.' She pushed all other thoughts from her mind. Clemence's misery was very evident in her letters.

The day after tomorrow. Time enough to let Jaccques know what was happening. No time to see him, though, but she mustn't think of that. When would there ever be time enough to think of themselves, to forget all the terrible things that kept them apart and share the lovely summer days? Once the war was over . . .

She swallowed quickly, leaving Ellen with a welcome cup of hot chocolate while she went to find the Mother Superior. Ten minutes later she was back, a small smile on her face.

'All settled. Day after tomorrow. One week's leave.

Darling, I must try to phone Jacques –'

'It's all right. I've got to go, anyway. See you soon, darling, and keep smiling.'

It wasn't so easy to smile when Angel had finally got through on the impossible telephone link.

'Call me again as soon as you get back, *chérie*.' He had to shout to make her hear, and even then, his voice was so faint. She gripped the wire, as if it would bring him nearer.

'I will. And please take care, Jacques. I'll be thinking of you every moment.'

'You take care too. No risky taxi-cab rides to London, do you hear me?'

She could hear the smile in his voice, and knew that he remembered everything, the way she did. There was nothing missing from Jacques' memory now, and it lifted her spirits just to know it.

'I promise,' she said unsteadily. 'Just you promise me you won't take any undue risks either, darling.'

She waited for his jaunty reply, but the crackling on the line told her they were about to be cut off. The next second the line was dead, and she hung up, biting her lips in frustration. It was childish, but if only she had heard him make her that promise . . . a foolish promise, perhaps, because they both knew he lived with risks every single day.

Jacques banged the phone down on its cradle. Damn unreliable instruments, he swore to himself. But at least it stopped his voice betraying him. His squadron had stepped up their night flying raids since he had returned to his unit. They were dangerous, costly in men and machines, and he hadn't told Angel about them.

He'd been afraid he might have lost his nerve. The first time he had been allocated a replacement plane for his own burnt-out wreck, his hands had been visibly shaking as he took the controls. Thank God his new gunner couldn't see it.

Phil Brakes had perished in their appalling crash, and he missed him.

Even now he had nightmares about the sheer agony on Phil's face, the brilliant flames leaping and gobbling at his skin, shrivelling it into curls of glowing ash and exposing the raw flesh and melting bone beneath. The smell of burnt flesh was one that he would never be able to forget.

How Jacques himself had managed to crawl to the pond nearby and collapse into it, he never knew. Nor how he had survived the bitter cold of the water after the engulfing fireball of his plane. A nameless saviour had dragged him free of the water, and somehow he had been picked up and taken to the hospital at the Abbey of St Helene. And little by little, he had been painfully restored to a kind of normality.

It was all behind him now. His destiny had allowed him to find Angel again, and he had come back to his unit to begin the dawn patrols at 4.30 in the morning with cocoa and biscuits. Then hearing the raucous noise of the aircraft warming up until the formation took off, a soaring of eagles, and he knew the exhilaration of flying again.

Now it was night flying over the enemy lines, the most dangerous of all. Once pinpointed by enemy searchlights, each plane was a silver dart in a beam of light, rocked by the so-called Archie, the ack-ack fire beneath them; mouths dry, eyes strained to bursting. Sometimes the bombardment from below was so heavy it gave a crew nausea, and made the blood scream in the veins as the aircraft rolled and slewed in the air.

There was heavy cloud cover in the summer of 1917. It could be useful to dive in and out of it to avoid the searchlights. It could be a hindrance at finding the targets below. It could be a blessed relief when a Jerry plane appeared out of nowhere and was hot on your tail.

Jacques told Angel little of this. There was a fine line between the charge of adrenalin at flying, cheating the enemy, pitting the wits against the German Aces; and a gut terror at glimpsing the eyes of an enemy pilot hell-bent on your own destruction, and knowing instantly that it was either you or him.

Jacques tried to ignore the fear, as they all did. His new gunner, Chalkie White, was a Cockney, first class at his job and with nerves of steel. Together, they told one another with desperate bravado, they would conquer the skies.

Angel and Ellen reached England with varying feelings as the soft evening coastline came into view. Ellen with a surprising tug of nostalgia; Angel wishing Jacques were here, that it was still that magical night when they met, watching the show at Beezer's Club, and then learning the joy of belonging in the modest little Hotel Portland.

'Let's find a cab,' Ellen said as they were jostled on all sides by soldiers returning home on leave, Red Cross personnel and V.A.D.s., and a few civilians who had decided to get out of France while they still could. Their shrill voices had made no secret of it on the boat. Were the Bannisters ever so stuffy and middle class? Angel wondered. She thought war had changed all that, but not for everybody, it seemed.

'Want a lift to London, girls?' a cheerful voice asked them, and minutes later they were clinging on to the sides of an army lorry taking soldiers away from the ports. At Paddington they had the usual dreary wait for a train, but everyone seemed used to that now too. There was no point in grumbling, because it wouldn't happen any quicker.

But at last they reached Meadowcroft, tired and hungry as a new dawn lit the sky with rose and silver streaks. So beautiful . . . and in the middle of it, men were killing one another in their flimsy machines . . . Angel gave an involuntary shudder, and Ellen squeezed her arm.

'Nearly there,' she yawned, misunderstanding. 'Right now, I don't care if I never go back. All I want is a hot bath and to sleep for ever.'

'Sounds good,' Angel mumbled, her eyes suddenly

stinging, because it sounded so blessedly normal. She should be happy, and so she was, that all the little everyday things were suddenly possible for them again. They were home, away from the fighting and the war, but for Angel, it was tarnished by the thought that she was also away from Jacques . . .

By the time the taxi dropped them at the house, she had composed herself. But the composure slipped a little as the huge door opened and their father came outside to greet them and Ellen gave him an exuberant hug.

Before Angel could think of some way to avoid it, she was enveloped in her father's arms. Just for a moment she was able to forget that she was supposed to be hating him. For a moment she was his best girl once more, and her eyes were damp with sheer exhaustion and the sudden longing for things to be the way they used to be. But they weren't the same, and never could be again.

She slid from his arms and followed Ellen indoors quickly, leaving Fred to pick up the bags and bring them inside. It was Clemence they had come home to see, and Clemence who shocked them both when they saw her so frail and white, and so badly in need of their company. It was pathetic to both of them to see how dependent their self-assured mother had become because of her wretched illness.

'The doctor says it will take time to clear up,' she told them repeatedly. 'It's not a fatal disease or anything ghastly, but oh, my dears, it is just so very miserable! I can't tell you how distressing it is.'

Angel and Ellen avoided looking at one another. The trivia of miserable complaints that would eventually recover, compared with the horrors that both of them had seen, was in both their minds at that instant. But it would have been cruel to say as much to Clemence, who looked so abysmally sorry for herself.

Fred gently led the conversation towards their youngest

daughter's engagement. The letters from Jacques and his father had reassured them both, but they wanted to discuss it further, and it was sweet comfort to Angel to bring his name into the open at Meadowcroft at last. And clearly Clemence was more than happy to know that her daughter was to marry the son of Comte de Ville.

What a difference a title made, Angel thought, with a sly wink towards Ellen. But after the burst of enthusiasm, the talk turned inevitably to Clemence's illness again, and the girls guessed from the small resigned sighs from their father that this was the way of things at every opportunity.

They could almost see their mother shrink into the self-centred shell she had made for herself. Clemence had once been so strong, Angel thought sadly, caring for the wounded at the railway station and diligently organising her knitting circles for the poor soldiers' welfare. Nor could Angel forget her mother's stoicism over poor Hobbs, and she couldn't find it in her heart to censure her.

Ellen felt differently. When they had both recovered from the journey and were sitting on Angel's bed late that evening, she reverted to the old Ellen with amazing ease.

'Honestly, old thing, did you ever see such pathos? I expected to hear the violins playing at any moment. It's only shingles, for God's sake! Nobody dies of shingles!'

'Oh, but Ellen, she does look ill!'

'I'm not disputing that. She seems much better since we've come home though, haven't you noticed? She brightened up once we talked about Jacques and his prospects, even though she only pecked at her dinner. Not that there was much to peck at, mind you. Hospital rations are better than these!'

Angel was thankful that her sister's attention soon changed direction. It was Angel herself who came back to the topic of their mother a while later, when they had agreed on the paltry amount of food on the table at dinner and the privations at home that neither of them had really thought about.

'What should we do about Mother, Ellen?'

'What can we do? You heard what she said. She'll get better in time. You can't hurry shingles, apparently.'

Angel looked out of the window, to where the green summer countryside stretched away into the distance.

'One of us should be here. Louise is so far away –'

'And it's a pity that Dad has to keep skipping off like he does. Not that I blame him,' Ellen said bluntly. She looked directly at Angel. 'So that leaves you and me. Are you suggesting that one of us should give up our jobs at the hospitals?'

'It sounds a pretty awful thing to do. We both know how much we're needed there –'

'And one of us is needed here. There's not really any choice, is there?'

'What do you mean?'

Ellen gave a soft laugh. 'Come on, old girl, do you think I don't know that you'll be itching to get back to France long before the week is out?' She gave a shrug as Angel didn't answer. 'As for me – well, we both know that I went to France as a kind of escape from my own inadequacy. The devil of it is, you can't escape from yourself, darling, no matter how far away you go.'

'So you'll stay, if Mother wants you to?'

'I can't do it just like that. I'll have to go back. But perhaps Mother's doctor will give me a note so that I can get discharged on compassionate grounds.' She chewed her lip. 'Will Sister Yard and her battle-axes think badly of me, do you think?'

Angel's voice was gentle.

'I know they won't. They'll miss you, though. You're solid, remember? We're the solid Bannister girls.'

They convulsed in laughter on the bed, remembering Sister Yard's beetling brows, each glad that the solution had been decided. Ellen would come home just as soon as she could. Angel would go back to stay as long as she was needed, and that in itself was a relief.

It was hard to pretend that there was a normal home life at Meadowcroft now. Despite the pleasure over her engagement to Jacques, Angel was so conscious of undercurrents in the family that had never been there before. Especially between herself and her father, who seemed in a world of his own half the time.

She might morally hate him and still feel the hurt and the bitterness, but she still felt deeply enough to mourn the loss of their once-loving and special relationship.

Chapter 22

Ellen was counting the days now to going home. She had already made up her mind what she would do. The idea had come to her like an inspiration when she had faced Sister Yard with a stomach that felt full of butterflies, and made her request for an early discharge.

'I never thought you were a young woman who would desert her duties, Bannister,' Sister Yard had the knack of looking a person up and down and reducing them to dust. Ellen looked her squarely in the eyes.

'My mother needs me, Sister –'

'I need you. The army needs you. There's so much to be done here –'

'And so much to be done at home,' Ellen said swiftly. 'I don't just mean caring for my mother. There are other ways to help win the war –'

'By marching around London and waving banners, I suppose? I thought the redoubtable Miss Pankhurst had suspended her activities for the duration.' Sister Yard's voice could wither the most noble cause.

'I didn't mean that,' Ellen spoke as evenly as she could, considering the way her temper was rising. 'Nor do I mean to fritter away my days. I mean to join the Women's Land Army. You *have* heard of it, I suppose?'

She couldn't resist glaring at the unbending woman. To her surprise, Sister Yard gave a tightly-stretched smile.

'Well done, Bannister. Always knew you were a good egg.'

Solid, wasn't it . . .? Ellen tried frantically to stop her lips from twitching as Sister Yard overlooked any further objections, promising to arrange that Ellen would be allocated transport back to England as soon as the discharge was approved in the official quarters.

Ellen went weak with relief, and stuttered her thanks.

'Don't thank me. Thank the flood of replacements coming out here. I think the entire youth of England has been hit by a new burst of patriotism since the Americans joined us,' Sister Yard said crisply. Then her eyes flickered a moment. 'We shall miss you, Bannister. You've a fresh, no-nonsense approach to your work. Good breeding always shows.'

She swished away, leaving Ellen feeling more like a pampered cow than a normal, healthy young woman. But it didn't matter. She went at once to phone Angel and tell her the news. She was going home without disgrace, and nothing was going to dim her buoyancy.

But the weeks passed, and there was still no official release for her. August began with incessant rain, and for the first four days and nights it rained without stopping. Reports from the Front were appalling as the wounded were brought in, caked in mud and effluent. Stories of weakened men drowning in their own trenches were common among the survivors. Tales of how they tried vainly to bale out with tin hats and cocoa mugs were pathetic and terrible in their visual impact on those who were forced to listen.

The date of Ellen's discharge was finally arranged for August the 4th. In England it was Bank Holiday Saturday. The journey to the French coast and on to the hospital ship was a nightmare, with the ambulance being bogged down every few yards every mile of the way, and every able-bodied person being obliged to get out and help dig the wheels clear of the mud. They were all exhausted by the time they reached the ship.

So many wounded men were being sent home that the ships were low in the water, and there was a real fear that with the bad weather and the extra weight, they would all end up as fishes' bait. Long before they reached the English coast, the jocular phrase on the soldiers' lips had ceased to be funny.

Ellen had expected to feel jubilant at being back on English soil again, and this time to stay. But she felt nothing. She was numb, and it was a feeling that remained with her long after she reached Meadowcroft. Clemence was glad to see her, even though they were never as close as mother and daughter should be.

Fred was away in Yorkshire, and as soon as she felt she decently could, Ellen reported to the appropriate office in Bristol to join the newly-formed Women's Land Army. Her mother had argued against the idea, but Ellen was adamant, and even Clemence couldn't deny a sneaking relief that the two of them wouldn't be under each other's feet all the time.

'I don't mind where you send me, as long as it's near my home, since my mother's unwell,' she said imperiously to the fussy little clerk behind the desk. 'And as long as it's not on Mr Peter Chard's farm.'

The clerk squinted up at her from behind his owlish spectacles. Some of these girls with the plummy accents thought they owned the world, he thought disagreeably. Probably spent the war years flitting from dance to dance, with never a thought for more serious pursuits. And now they fancied the look of the new country uniforms with their jaunty hats. But her last defiant words had caught his interest. He ran a skinny finger down the list of farms requesting Land Army women.

'Is there any special reason for not wanting to work for Mr Chard? He's on our list –'

'My reasons are my own,' Ellen snapped, her heart jumping. 'Now, do you have somewhere to send me, or do I have to go back to France to be needed?'

The clerk stared at her.

'You've been in France? I have a son there. He was at the

Somme, but I've had no news of him for six weeks. Still, no news is good news, they say.'

He spoke with a dogged refusal to believe otherwise, and the caustic words Ellen was about to say stuck in her throat.

'I'm sure you're right. You'd have heard if anything was wrong.' She closed her mind to the memory of the horrific tales of men stepping on dead comrades and their identities being lost for ever beneath the mud and slime of the trenches.

'I don't want to rush you,' she said more kindly, 'but there are other ladies waiting outside. Can you please tell me where I should report?'

She finally left the little office after being allocated a job on Peartree Farm, for a Farmer Green. It was about three miles from Meadowcroft, and in the opposite direction from Peter's farm. The clerk pointed out the place on the huge wall map, on which he stuck a new pin representing Ellen's appointment. She gave a great sigh of relief. She wanted to work on the land, but never for Peter again. It would have been impossible.

Farmer Green and his wife were large country people, quite happy that the men who had left the farm to go to war should be replaced by the pretty young girls who brightened up the place. There were other three girls beside Ellen, two local ones and Charlotte Prole from Kent, with whom she immediately became friendly. The others, May and Lucy, were pleasant enough, but the girls drifted into amicable pairs almost at once.

If she thought the work was going to be easy, she soon discovered how wrong she was. Farming had taken on a new meaning since the food shortages. Farmer Green and his wife saw to the milking, to Ellen's relief, but there were hens and pigs to be fed and cleaned, and a constant eye kept out for rustlers.

And there was much more back-breaking work to be done. Much of the land was ploughed up to grow produce, and Peartree Farm was as much a market garden as a working farm now. Row upon row of potatoes were waiting to be dug up, and the four Land Girls were set to work almost immediately.

By the time Ellen cycled home to Meadowcroft that first evening, she could hardly crawl into the house. The other girls were billeted at the farm, but she was near enough to go home. Every evening she sank thankfully into a hot bath, feeling as if every muscle cried out in protest.

'It's hardly the kind of work for a young lady, Ellen,' Clemence said disapprovingly, trying not to notice the broken nails on her daughter's hands. 'Couldn't this Farmer Green give you something less physical to do?'

'No, he couldn't, Mother,' Ellen said wearily. 'We do what we're told, so just be thankful that there are women willing and able to do men's work. There'd be fewer potatoes on your dinner plate if it weren't for the Land Army.'

'I know that, my dear girl, and nobody knows better than I do about helping the war effort. But I fear that this war is taking away a woman's most precious gift.'

'And what's that, Mother?' Ellen stifled a laugh. Her mother looked so stuffy, her spirits quickly restored since Ellen had come home, and reverting very quickly to her old autocratic ways, despite the irritation she still suffered from her miserable complaint.

'Why, her femininity, of course!' Clemence looked in amazement at her middle daughter, as if uncomprehending that Ellen could ever have doubted her meaning. Although, of course, Ellen was never as feminine as her other girls . . . her thoughts stopped abruptly, as Ellen's laughter would not be checked.

'Oh, Mother, I promise you that when you're holding a dying soldier's hand and helping him into eternity, the last thing he worries about is whether a woman's lost her femininity or not. Or any other bits and pieces! All he wants is comfort and to feel that somebody cares.'

Clemence spoke distantly. 'You seem to forget that I spent hours at the railway station, doing what I could for the poor boys, but I didn't feel it necessary to look like a hoyden.'

Ellen was weary of this discussion. She pushed a stray lock of hair into its tortoiseshell comb, from where it immediately fell out again. She ached all over. It hurt to laugh, and she didn't particularly feel like laughing any more.

'Mother, I've asked a friend to dinner on Sunday. I hope it's all right. Her name's Charlotte Prole and I'm sure you'll like her. Her family owns a big estate near Deal in Kent.'

Clemence's interest was caught at once.

'I believe I've heard of the Proles. How nice! And where did you meet Charlotte? I know you young people don't seem to care about proper introductions –'

'It hardly seemed necessary to be introduced when we were both mucking out a pig sty at the same time,' Ellen grinned. 'You'd be amazed at the proper young ladies who do menial jobs these days, Mother. So it's all right for Sunday, is it?'

'Of course,' Clemence was cool, but Ellen knew she wouldn't be able to resist meeting Charlotte Prole and gleaning her family connections. Poor Mother, she thought. Neither war nor famine would move her. She was British to the core, and would uphold every patriotic tradition until the day she died.

To her own surprise, Ellen felt an enormous rush of affection for her mother, who couldn't change, any more than Ellen herself could, in certain directions.

It was no longer possible to ignore the fact that she was bound to bump into Peter Chard sooner or later. She hadn't quite decided yet how she was going to deal with it. Their last meeting had been so appallingly stilted, and she could still feel like weeping when she remembered it.

She realised suddenly how alike she and her sisters were, after all. Louise, despite her insipid marriage to Stanley, had blossomed into her own woman once she had met Dougal;

Angel, whose love for Jacques de Ville had never wavered from the first moment; Ellen herself, with her once and only love, whatever the outcome . . .

'I've asked you twice if you'd ring for dessert, Ellen,' Clemence said crossly. 'Really, you seem to be living in a dream world. No one talks to me properly these days. Your father is always eager to be gone again when he makes one of his rare visits home, and I do wish Angel would tell us more about her young man. He's very well-connected, of course –'

'Oh, he is, Mother,' Ellen said, poker-faced. 'Angel will be a countess one day – have you thought of that?'

She was perfectly sure her mother would have thought of it. It was the one bright spot in an otherwise rather dreary life for her. Ellen knew very well how different life at Meadowcroft must be for Clemence, so used to the busy London season and the round of pleasures of the theatre and the opera and the little afternoon charity teas.

'We should throw a party,' she said suddenly.

'Are you mad? There's no food to spare for parties these days, my dear –' Clemence was half-amused, half-annoyed.

'Then why not ask people to bring their own? Everyone must bring a contribution, and Meadowcroft will provide the wine and we'll be the hosts. It would be such a lark, wouldn't it? We'll leave it until you're feeling better, naturally, and until we can be sure Dad will be here. Perhaps at Hallowe'en, then we can deck the gardens up with Chinese lanterns and pumpkins and be real country folk. What do you say?'

'We'll see,' Clemence said noncommittally, but already Ellen could tell that her busy mind was organising just how the invitations could be worded so that people wouldn't think it too demeaning to bring their own food!

Pedalling home from Peartree Farm some weeks later, aching less now than on the first days, Ellen congratulated herself. The idea of a party had been inspired, and her mother had been far more cheerful ever since she'd decided to organise it. In fact, the whole atmosphere in Meadowcroft had been considerably less tense of late.

It helped that Clemence and Charlotte Prole had taken to one another like the proverbial ducks to water. Clemence had spent some time poring over old books to try and trace the background of the Proles of Deal, and had been even more triumphant to find that her own maternal grandmother was a very distant cousin of Charlotte's. Clemence was therefore delighted that Ellen and dear Charlotte should be having such fun working on the farm . . . a comment that had the two girls doubled up with laughter, and wincing in the middle of it with all the aches and pains that came from 'having such fun' . . .

Ellen was still smiling at the memory. The invitations were being prepared, and the Hallowe'en party would at least cheer everybody up from the gloom of the war. There had been shorter letters than usual from Angel lately, the most telling ones being sent to her sister, and not for her parents' eyes.

'We really thought the assault at the Somme was going to end it all, and I don't have to tell you how that ended. Rumours are rife now about the stupidity of the officers letting our boys march slowly to their deaths instead of ordering them to charge at the Germans,' Angel wrote.

'We can't dispute the strength of the German lines, however much the newspaper cartoons try to ridicule it. It's simply terrible, Ellen. The fighting is raging again at Ypres and at Passchendaele, and the wounded must surely outnumber the Allied armies. I sometimes wonder how we can go on.

'The hospitals are stretched to the limits, and I couldn't begin to describe the conditions now. Beds in corridors, the dead taken out almost before they've stopped breathing to make way for the next casualty, and everyone hardened to the dreadful sights while still trying to be as humane as possible.

'I hear so little from Jacques, although we try to make at least one telephone call a week, to reassure each other. I'm so fearful for him, Ellen. I'm sorry to sound such a misery. I hope all goes well at home. Don't let Mother know how depressed I am. She'd be campaigning for my release too, and I mean to stick it out until the end. I have to, as long as Jacques is here.

'My best love, Angel.'

The letter disturbed Ellen more than anything. Angel had always been the brightest one, strong and brave, and now she sounded almost defeated. Ellen cycled along the autumn lanes, head down as she neared Meadowcroft, worrying about Angel.

'I kept telling myself it must be you that I kept seeing, and not a mirage,' a voice that she knew said lazily from a field alongside her.

Ellen almost fell off her bicycle. She had tried very hard and with great success to avoid seeing anything of Peter. And now here he was, just like that other time, startling her, and making her heart leap uncontrollably in her chest at the sight of him.

He leaned on the gate, dark and rugged and thoughtful. She had always considered him to be an intelligent, thinking man, which was one of the things she'd admired most about him.

'Are you always going to make me jump like that?' she snapped.

'If it's the only way I can get you to talk to me, then I suppose I am,' his country drawl, smooth as cream, was more pronounced as he looked her up and down in her Land Army clothes, her boots caked in something unspeakable, smudges of dirt on her face and hands. She felt hot and unkempt and was annoyed with herself for caring.

'What do you want to talk to me about?' she said pointedly, poised like a bird for flight.

Peter leapt the field gate in one easy movement. His slight limp didn't prevent him from being as agile as any man when he chose to be. Nor as handsome and desirable and as damnably dear to her, she thought, with a catch in her throat.

'I met your mother in the village today,' he said calmly.

Oh no . . . even as she heard the words, Ellen guessed what was coming. Her mother didn't know of the rift between her daughter and the young farmer, nor the reason for it, and had presumably just assumed that Ellen had moved on to other pursuits with her usual impatience.

'I've been invited to a party,' Peter went on relentlessly.

'You'll refuse, of course.'

'Why should I?'

She looked at him helplessly.

'Peter, you know why! I should be embarrassed every time I looked at you –'

'You're not embarrassed now, are you?'

She bit her lip. His hand, strong and tanned, was on the handlebar of her bicycle. If she wrenched it away from him, he'd probably lose his balance and go sprawling.

'You know I am,' she said in a low voice.

'I fail to see why. I'm not embarrassed.' He was deliberately blocking out all that had gone before. But she couldn't do that. It was too painful a memory. Ellen had never been afraid to look the truth in the face before, and she despised herself for doing it now. She was also furious with Peter for forcing the words out of her.

'I can't forget that you know what a fool I made of myself, that's why. You know my shame, and that's something I'm not willing to share with anyone. I've got too much pride, Peter, and I'd be glad if you'd let me go, please!'

This time she did wrench the bicycle away from him, straddling it with shaking legs, her long skirt threatening to catch in the wheels where she had neglected to hitch it up properly. Her eyes stung blindly as she pedalled furiously. His voice followed her.

'I'll see you at the party, Ellen.'

He couldn't be such a cad as to be there after all that, she thought! Had he guessed at her feelings for him from her strangled words? She couldn't bear it if he had. He was playing with her, like a cat with a mouse, and if it was a way of punishing her for being lower than the pedestal he had put her on, then he was succeeding very well.

She marched into the house, seeking out her mother. There was a new intake of four billeted soldiers that day, and Clemence was busily organising their sleeping quarters with the housekeeper. As soon as she could get her alone, Ellen stormed into her.

'Mother, how could you invite Peter Chard to the Hallowe'en party without asking me?'

'My dear girl, what an extraordinary question,' Clemence said mildly. 'I thought Mr Chard was a friend of yours. We're inviting everyone from the surrounding farms, so we could hardly leave him out! Besides, he's been most generous with his offers of fruit and cream for the day. It will have to be a buffet table, of course, we couldn't have anything grander, but I'm sure everyone will be delighted with the result. I thought we might raffle a few things as well, and send the money we raise to the Soldiers' Comfort Fund. What do you think?'

Ellen was speechless. Clemence was right back on form with her organising abilities, dismissing the question of whether Ellen wanted Peter Chard at the party or not as one of minuscule importance. It was just that to her, of course. It was only to Ellen herself that the humiliation of seeing Peter here at Meadowcroft again was beginning to assume gigantic proportions.

She knew how foolish she was being. She should be able to brush aside all memory of the episode with Andrew Pender.

With a start, she realised she could hardly remember his face. It wasn't the shame of being so gullible that haunted her. It was the fact that Peter knew. Peter had witnessed it, and it was Peter that she loved, and she wanted his respect above all things.

How conventional she was after all! And how little one knew about oneself until faced with unexpected situations. Who ever would have thought Louise would defy Clemence, when she had been so much under her mother's thumb? Who would have expected Angel to become so excellent a nurse and ambulance driver, and journey across France to find the man she loved?

'I wish I could be at the Hallowe'en party,' Angel wrote when she heard about it. 'It sounds such fun, Ellen, and just like the old days. I shall be thinking of you all, and envying you. Mother sounds so much better, and I know we have you to thank for that. She never says it in so many words, naturally, Mother being Mother, but her letters are full of how helpful Ellen is, and how hard Ellen works at Peartree Farm, and how she met Farmer Green's wife in the village and heard how much they think of Ellen – and all the other girls, she adds, as an afterthought! But it's clear that Ellen is quite the little heroine, darling!'

Ellen smiled ruefully. To hear her and Clemence wrangling sometimes, no one would think Clemence was glad to have her at home. But yes, her mother *was* better. She had less time to think about herself with the party to arrange, and the day was almost on them. They prayed for fine weather, but if rain was threatened, there was the old marquee to erect.

It was decided to put it up anyway, just in case, and the billeted soldiers assisted cheerfully. And long before the party began, Ellen resolutely decided that as far as she was concerned, Peter Chard was just another guest at her mother's party. This was Clemence's day, and even Fred, who came down from Yorkshire especially, was loud in his praise at all the hard work his wife had put into it.

The party was to be held in the afternoon. There couldn't be lighted lanterns and fireworks in the evening, which may alert enemy aircraft, however distant and sleepy the Somerset countryside seemed. Clemence was cross that the Germans should ruin their party in this way, but it hardly mattered. The atmosphere was one of gaiety, almost like pre-war days, except for those in uniform sprinkled among the guests.

The billeted soldiers had helped Ellen and Clemence and Fred make the Jack-o'-Lanterns to string up in the marquee. They were made from hollowed out mangel-wurzels with faces carved on them and with candles placed inside. There was plenty of Somerset cider as well as Meadowcroft wine. The raffles for some of Clemence's good pieces of china and the lowlier fruit cakes contributed by farmers' wives, were conducted with good nature and produced outrageously rewarding amounts of money for the Soldiers' Comfort Fund.

'I say, we've been sent to the wrong farm, haven't we?' Charlotte nudged Ellen in the ribs as the two of them finished their fish paste sandwiches that disguised the fact that there was only a smear of butter on the bread.

Ellen followed her glance. Peter had arrived late, and she had thought he wasn't coming. She didn't know whether to be glad or sorry to see him. He nodded at her briefly and then turned his back on her as the music for dancing began.

'Excuse me, old thing,' Charlotte said enthusiastically. 'If I don't manage a dance with that handsome chap, then I'm not half the girl I think I am!'

Ellen watched her weave her way through the crowds. Charlotte was as outgoing as she, and together they made a good pair. But not today. Ellen was tongue-tied at the sight of Peter, and spent the next half hour rehearsing what to say when he asked her to dance.

She watched him cavorting clumsily around on the patch of grass left free for dancing. First with Charlotte, then with his own Land Girls who had arrived before him. He danced with May and Lucy, and several of the older ladies. He asked Clemence to dance, and was graciously accepted.

By the end of the party, everyone said what a splendid time they had had, and how generous it was of Lady Bannister to arrange it. Everyone was far too excited at this pleasant interlude in the middle of a war to notice that the main instigator of the party had a hard job not to cry as the Bannister family finally waved their guests good-bye.

It was just too ridiculous to be so upset, Ellen thought furiously, as she went to her bedroom to kick off her shoes and change out of her finery into something less constricting. For a moment she caught sight of herself in the mirror, and couldn't miss the misery in her eyes before she looked quickly away.

He had danced with everyone else but her, she raged. As if to show the world, and Ellen Bannister in particular, that he cared nothing about her at all.

Chapter 23

'Angel, can you hear me?' Jacques swore silently at the inefficient phone. As well as the poor service, the air around Brighton Belle seemed to rock with aircraft noise, and there was an impatient jostling behind him for others waiting to use the one available telephone.

'Not very well!' Her voice was faint and edgy. They had been waiting hours to get a call through to each other, but with Christmas looming in a few weeks, everyone else was trying to do the same thing.

'I said I can't get leave until the New Year. Can you get over here at all, even for a couple of hours?'

'Oh, Jacques!' Frustration made her even edgier. She had so hoped that they could spend part of Christmas together. 'I'll see what I can do, but supposing I get there and you're on duty?'

'If you come in the afternoon, I'll be damned sure I'm free. Just let me know which day and I'll meet you. Look, I'm sorry, Angel, but I'll have to go. There's a stream of chaps behind me wanting to use the phone. Let me know, all right?'

'All right. Jacques, I love you –'

Her voice dwindled as she realised she was talking to thin air. He had either hung up or they had been cut off as usual. Angel slammed the receiver down in a fury, tears smarting her eyes. It seemed an eternity ago that they had left the chateau in Bordeaux so gloriously happy, newly-engaged, and with the feeling that they had the world at their feet.

Now, Angel sometimes felt that the whole world was conspiring to keep them apart. The Germans, the entire Allied forces, the nursing system, all made outrageous demands on their time and their energies. Like everyone else, she was war-weary, and wondering, like all those who dared to put it into words, if it was ever going to end. And if it did, what it was going to solve.

The only certainty was that there would be thousands of broken homes, wives without husbands, mothers without sons, girls without sweethearts . . . she shivered. There would also be families without daughters, she thought fearfully, knowing that she was in the grip of the first real attack of nerves she had experienced for some time.

'Are you going to cling on to that phone all day, Bannister?' a voice said crossly, as another nurse pushed past her.

'I'm sorry, Moss.' She answered like an automaton, moving away without being aware of her feet touching the ground. For a moment she was lost, living among people with no real identities. She felt like shouting it to the world. This is *me*. I'm alive. I have a given name. I'm *Angel*, with the special, beautiful name chosen for me by my father . . .

Her own choking tears were suddenly the only sound in her head. She felt a great wave of nostalgia for her father, for things to be the way they had always been, before the holocaust of the war, before she had discovered that her father had feet of clay like everyone else, when there was still time for gentleness and beauty and love . . .

'I say, Bannister, are you all right?' Moss had abandoned her attempts to make her phone call, and was holding onto Angel's arm. Angel felt the tightening of the capable fingers as though they were pincers. She tried to focus on the girl, and the face became a mist, all eyes, rounded and angular shapes, gaping mouths that swirled and then merged into nothing.

She awoke in her own bed, with Sister Therese holding her pulse and tut-tutting severely.

'You're a foolish girl for not eating properly,' the nun said in the *patois* of her native southern France. 'What use are you to the patients or the Abbey if you don't have the strength to carry on, Bannister?'

She spoke the name with a grand flourish at the end. Bannis*terre* . . .

'My name is Angel. Angelique,' she mumbled ineptly. The nun smiled.

'Then in private, I shall call you Angelique. Such a pretty name. But why do you not eat properly?' Sister Therese persisted in the stupid questioning. Didn't she know why Angel couldn't eat! It was perfectly logical.

'The patients need nourishment. I leave some of my food, and they can have more. I don't need it.'

Perhaps an old-fashioned novel would call her lovesick. Unable to eat because she was pining over her lover . . . such sentiments were enough to make Angel cringe, and anyway they were untrue. She had always had a hearty appetite. It wasn't only the meagre rations that made her refuse the food. It was the appalling feeling of nausea whenever she was faced with it. She couldn't rid herself of the thought that while she was eating, men were dying, unable to swallow one mouthful.

'My dear, you do need it. You are helping no one, least of all yourself. There are various names for your condition –'

'I know the nurses' favourite one. Sitophobia!'

'So you have suspected it for yourself –'

'Sister Therese, I do not have a fear of food,' Angel said carefully. 'I'm not mad in the head –'

'Of course not,' the nun spoke soothingly, as if to a child. 'You've merely been neglecting yourself in your wish to help others. It's admirable, Angelique, but it cannot go on.'

Angel stared at her. 'What do you mean?'

The nun looked at her thoughtfully. Angel was more

slender than when she had arrived at the Abbey, seemingly as fragile as though a strong breeze would snap her in two.

'Nurses who succumb to your condition are usually sent home.' Sister Therese's calm voice was suddenly crisp and unrelenting, reminding Angel of Mother Superior's stern manner on her arrival. Reminding her of Sister Yard at Piersville. Strong women all, when they needed to be.

Angel gasped, struggling to sit up, her voice jerky. 'You can't send me home! I'm useful here. I must stay!'

'A nurse who collapses through her own stupidity is not useful. Make an effort within the next week, Bannister, and your situation will be reviewed. Otherwise –'

She shrugged expressively, her eyes showing no emotion. Even nuns, Angel thought angrily, were bound by the rigid needs of wartime. There was no place for sentiment or for people who didn't pull their weight. No place for Angel Bannister if she didn't do something about it. She spoke sarcastically.

'Perhaps I should begin now. I'll have smoked salmon and caviar, followed by fresh Cheddar strawberries and clotted cream, all washed down with a bottle of vintage champagne, naturally.'

If the thought of it curdled her stomach, she gritted her teeth and didn't show it.

Sister Therese laughed gently.

'I'll see what I can do. Though don't be surprised if it's cold meat and bread, washed down with cocoa. A tray will be sent up immediately, and you will stay here for one week.'

'Oh, but –'

'One week to decide your future, Nurse Bannister.'

She went out of the room silently, and Angel was left in no doubt that it was now up to her. She closed her eyes. Sitophobia. It was a long-winded name for a condition that had unexpectedly affected many nurses who were caring for the wounded. She knew several who had been sent home because of it, but it was the very last thing she wanted.

And now she was stuck here in bed, not even able to arrange to meet Jacques. Perhaps she could turn this to her advantage, she thought hopefully. She would surely be allowed one extra day, and she could use it to go to Brighton Belle . . . to her absolute chagrin, her request was left in the balance until she had proved herself. Of course, she thought bitterly, they would need her back on duty as soon as she was well.

A new and fierce battle at Cambrai had been in progress for nearly two weeks, and with the new influx of casualties everywhere, the hospitals were operating a kind of shuttle system between them. It was just like the trains pulling into Temple Meads station, Angel thought. Walking wounded to the front, middling to the middle, stretcher cases to the rear. Only in this case, those who had desperate need of medical attention were sent to hospitals nearest the Front, the lesser wounded went to hospitals like the Abbey, walking and convalescents went to the clearing hospitals or onto the ships for short leaves in Blighty before returning to be shot up all over again.

And if she didn't want to be joining them, to return home ignominiously, then she had to jolly well eat something and ignore the threat of disgorging in her stomach. She forced down the cold meat and bread and swallowed the cocoa as quickly as she could, remembering the words of another sufferer when Angel had been curious to know the symptoms and the remedy.

'The best way is to pretend you're not actually eating anything. Tell yourself there's nothing being pushed past your teeth and into your growling stomach. Keep your mind fixed on other things and fool your body into thinking it's not being bombarded with nourishment it doesn't want, and you gradually overcome the food phobia and begin to enjoy the taste again. That's the theory, anyway. It doesn't work for everyone.'

To Angel's enormous relief, it worked for her. As she ate a

reasonably good breakfast on the last day of her enforced confinement to her room, she knew that it wasn't only the other girl's advice that had helped her. It was mostly due to her dogged determination to remain in France where she could make contact with Jacques.

Mother Superior was to see her that morning, to decide whether she could return to duties or not. Angel was filled with impatience as she waited. Days began very early at the Abbey, and it was still barely light on the cold December morning when the door of Angel's room opened.

'So, Bannister, you've decided it's not worth while starving yourself, after all,' the nun greeted her.

'Mother, I'm quite well now. I must have put on pounds in weight in the past week! And you were going to tell me if I may have today free.' She held her breath.

'So you think you are ready to resume work?'

Angel's heart gave a jolt.

'Of course! I was stupid, that's all, and I shan't do such a silly thing again.'

'I hope you will not. There are enough deprivations nowadays without self-inflicted ones.'

'And – about today, Mother?'

The nun smiled slightly.

'Yes, you may have today free. I would not wish for a repeat performance to alarm our patients. They must always be our first concern, Bannister. A nurse who cannot fulfil her duties is best occupied elsewhere.'

'I understand –'

'Please do.' After the warning, her expression softened. 'My dear, the man we knew as Papillon – Monsieur de Ville – was under our care for a long time, and I appreciate your wish to be near him. But there are other ways if the work here becomes too testing for you. Munition factories, packaging food supplies for the soldiers –'

'No!' Angel shook her head violently. 'I'm proud to be a nurse, and it's what I shall continue to be.'

The nun nodded as if satisfied, and suggested that if Angel wanted to spend the day away from the hospital, she must see about her own transport.

It was all the incentive Angel needed. Once alone, she washed and dressed, and despite being in her room for a week, felt considerably stronger than before. She rushed downstairs to the phone and left a message with the batman who answered, letting Jacques know that she hoped to be there that afternoon.

There was a bus service of sorts that went part of the distance. Once before, she had been able to hire a bicycle for the rest of the way. It was all very haphazard, but she was unable to ask Jacques to meet her at the bus-stop with his car, and determination gave her an extra charge of adrenalin. She would reach Brighton Belle if it took all day . . .

'I've been so worried about you!' Jacques said, when at last they found a quiet corner of the officers' mess, and were discreetly left alone by the others. 'I tried to phone twice this week, only to be told that you were unwell, and I couldn't get away to see you –'

'It was nothing,' Angel said shakily. 'A touch of 'flu or something. I'm fine now.'

She felt suddenly too ashamed to admit that she'd been so foolish, and thankful that the nuns hadn't revealed the truth to Jacques. Looking back, she could see that starving herself hadn't accomplished anything.

'Don't let's talk about it, Jacques. I can't stay more than an hour. I must get to the St Helene bus before dark.'

'I'll borrow a truck. We can throw the bicycle in the back and I'll return it once you're on the bus. I shouldn't have asked you to come. It's far too risky, *chérie*.'

In the distance, she was aware of the sounds of battle, much nearer here than at the Abbey. She had become used to them at Piersville, but after some months away from it, she was suddenly afraid. She clung to Jacques, warmed by his protective arms around her, and all the things she had been determined not to say came tumbling out.

'Oh, Jacques, I'm scared that I'm losing my nerve,' she stuttered. 'It's a terrible admission to make, and I hate myself for it –'

She felt his lips on her cheek, and the steady beat of his heart against her own.

'It's human, *chérie*,' he said gently. 'Do you think you're the only one who ever felt afraid? There's no achievement in being brave if you have nerves of steel. It's the people who manage to overcome their fears, who are the courageous ones.'

She looked into his face, the silvery scars that were the banners of his bravery fading more and more. He was her dear, her very dearest love . . .

'Like you?'

'Like me, if you wish. Did you think I was never afraid?'

She nestled closer. It didn't make him less of a hero in her eyes. She understood exactly what he meant. Without fear, one had nothing to overcome. It made it all slightly easier to bear.

'Do you want to take a walk? It's cold outside, but you're well wrapped up, and we can't be alone any more, Angel.'

She realised that the door had opened and a group of officers had come in, still wearing their flying suits, faces shining and blackened with oil, eyes glinting with exhilaration.

Angel stood up at once. She didn't want to hear of their exploits, their dare-devil risks, their closeness to oblivion as they raced across the sky with an enemy plane marking them as its next target. Let Jacques hear it all later . . . she stumbled ahead of him to the door, unaware that his feelings echoed hers precisely.

For just a little while, she wanted to pretend that the two of them were merely taking some exercise, walking briskly over the crisp wintry ground, arms around each other to keep warm, in the lee of the buildings and into one of the empty aircraft hangars where they could be unobserved.

Jacques took her in his arms, just holding her for a long while before he kissed her. His skin was cold on her cheek, slightly unshaven and tinglingly fresh. She was overwhelmed with love for him, as she was every single time they met. Their bodies were pressed close, and against her softness, she knew that Jacques had recovered his abilities as a man.

'You see what your nearness does to me, my darling one?'

He murmured huskily against her mouth. 'God, but I'm so impatient for all this to end, so that we can begin our life together. It's what drives me on, and what I suspect drives many men on.'

'More than patriotism?'

'We don't fight only for the glory of our country, *chérie*, we fight for the right to be ourselves, for the freedom of being with those we love. Now you have my admission, my Angel. Is it more terrible than yours?'

'Not to me,' she whispered. 'It's the most beautiful and honest thing I've heard yet about this dreadful war. It makes some sense of it. Do you think the Germans feel the same way?'

He was tempted to condemn all Germans as inhuman monsters. They had killed his best gunner, and burned countless friends and acquaintances. They had killed Margot Lacey's brother and been responsible in a way for blowing up Louise's husband. They had committed every atrocity known to man . . . but he had glimpsed the naked fear in a German pilot's eyes, and he knew how frighteningly it matched his own.

'Even the Germans have wives and sweethearts,' he said grudgingly. 'Ordinary men and women must want the war to end as much as we do.'

Angel shivered in his arms. 'Not as much as you and I do, my love –'

Jacques gave her a very private smile, holding her closer,

as if he would never let her go.

'But who would ever dare to call you and I ordinary people, my Angel?'

Thoughts of home were in everyone's mind as Christmas Day approached. There were special services in the Abbey, the nurses holding candles high and singing carols in the holly-decorated wards. They sang in English and in French, but the meanings were the same, the personal memories and the lumps brought to every throat were the same, and it could have been any hospital anywhere in the world.

Angel had managed to make a long-distance telephone call home on Christmas morning. Ellen answered, and the two of them wasted precious seconds crying into the phone at the sound of each other's voices.

'Darling, I must tell you quickly. Louise had a baby boy in the early hours. Isn't she clever to have such good timing? They're going to call him Christopher, naturally. It was either that or Noel, and that would have been too ghastly –'

'What wonderful news!' Angel said excitedly. 'Oh, Ellen, do call and congratulate her for me. And thank-you all so much for the presents and cards. They arrived more or less intact –'

'Good-oh. I'll have to go, old thing, Mother's hovering to talk to you. Chin up, darling, and write soon.'

'You too –'

Clemence came on the line, too delighted at the thought of being a grandmother now to waste emotions on recriminations for Louise's undue haste in producing a child. Angel listened to her enthusiastic plans for inviting the three of them to Meadowcroft as soon as it was reasonable for the baby to travel, and was filled with a fierce longing to be home, in the midst of all this . . .

'Angel?' Suddenly it was her father's bluff voice on the phone, and her own unaccountably caught in her throat. 'Happy Christmas, my dearest girl.'

'Happy Christmas, Daddy.' Tears blinded her, remembering other years at Meadowcroft and at Hampstead. The rituals always the same, with love overflowing among family and friends as they gathered for the day. The huge glittering tree, almost weighed down with tinsel and baubles, presents piled excitingly high beneath, the tantalising aroma of the goose sizzling for hours, the spice of the hot mince pies and the wine flowing freely . . .

'Come home soon, Angel. We shall drink a toast to our absent loved ones this afternoon. You'll be with us in spirit, darling girl, never fear.'

Fred's words were meant to be tender, but they acted like a dash of cold water in Angel's face. Absent loved ones for Sir Fred Bannister would presumably also mean Harriet Garth and Angel resented the very idea of being included in the same thought as that woman. A curt reply hovered on her lips, but before she could make it, she heard Ellen's voice again.

'I can't let the old folks hog the phone without telling you some more news, Angel. Margot Lacey's engaged! She called last week and asked for your address, but I couldn't wait to let you know. She's getting married in a few weeks' time.'

'Good Lord!'

Angel hardly knew what to say. She felt ridiculously let down, and guiltily resentful that Margot had got out of France and was now apparently marrying and settling down as if the war wasn't happening at all. Somehow, other people still led comparatively normal lives. And then she remembered young Eddie Lacey and felt even more shamed by her own thoughts.

'I'll leave Margot to write and tell you the rest,' Ellen laughed. 'We'd better stop talking, Angel. We're off to church and Mother's glaring at me already. Have the best time that you can, darling!'

'I will. Good-bye –'

They were cut off, and it was Angel who had the lump in

her throat now, and had to make a great effort to conquer it. It didn't do to be down-hearted on Christmas Day. Not when there was a hospital full of wounded soldiers all missing their loved ones, and hoping to have a bit of cheeky banter with a nurse or two as a kind of compensation.

Some of the men grew extraordinarily attached to their nurses. Small wonder, really, when the nurses knew them more intimately than wives or mothers ever could. It was a relationship that was unique, closer than love, freer than air when the man was finally discharged. Any nurse foolish enough to think it went deeper than that was wasting precious emotion.

But on days like Christmas Day, any could be forgiven for transferring their affections to the one nearest, even if it wasn't the one who was dearest. Angel put up with it all, with as much good nature as the rest of the nurses.

'Come on, Nurse Angel, give us a kiss!'

'A quick cuddle would be even better –'

'Nobody's going to notice if you slip the curtains round us for five minutes, Nursie – I've got a tasty bit of apple pie we can share –'

She laughed down at them, teasing them back, trying not to let her mouth water at the thought of hot apple pie and cream. Her appetite was fully restored now, and she still felt a small shock at a cutting from *The Times* newspaper her mother had sent her, listing the food shortages at home, now that strict rationing was in force.

Sugar, butter, tea, margarine, lard, dripping, milk, bacon, pork, condensed milk, rice, currants, raisins, spirits, Australian wines . . . many of the quoted items were unrationed, but were in such short supply that the government was being ridiculed for bothering to appoint a Minister of Food at all.

Everything had changed. Even to the poor royal family being pressured to change from the old German name of Saxe-Coberg-Gotha to Windsor, a fact that had caused

Angel's mother to write her own outraged letter to *The Times* on the humiliation of demanding such a thing from their beloved royalty.

Angel's attention was caught again by a soldier begging a kiss for Christmas from Nurse Moss, which she laughingly refused, saying cheekily that he'd do better with a cup of cocoa to dampen his ardour, since he couldn't do much about it!

Nurse Moss grinned at Angel, who silently agreed. They had all inevitably become freer with words in the uninhibited atmosphere of the hospital wards, despite the presence of the nuns, but they didn't have to be so free with their kisses.

Besides, the only kisses Angel wanted were Jacques', and there was still the best part of another week to go before they both had a blissful three days' leave, and they were going to spend it somewhere in the country. They were going to be Mr and Mrs Anonymous.

It couldn't be so wrong to want to spare a little time for themselves, when all her waking hours were spent in putting men back together for other women to love . . .

He picked her up at the Abbey in his small car. This was going to be Christmas and New Year and everything wonderful rolled into one. Angel was bubbling inside, hardly daring to believe that this day had come. That they were driving away from the Abbey, away from the danger of the Front Line and the sound of guns and the orange glow of burning in the sky. Now at last there was a little time for love.

They found a small country hotel, half-hidden by trees, en route from St Helene to Paris. It was a secluded place, which suited their mood. Christmas festivities had been modest, the New Year yet to be celebrated that night by the proprietors and the few other guests.

There were no bells chiming to greet the new year of 1918, no wild fireworks exploding, no dancing in the streets. But there was music and kisses, and a fervent hope in everyone's heart that this would be the last new year under siege, that the dawn of 1919 would be celebrated in freedom, a sentiment echoed by all who drank the toast with Monsieur and Madame Alphonse.

And then there were just the two of them in the small hotel bedroom with its typical French furnishings, heavy ornate bedposts and floral wallpaper. It didn't matter. It could have been a palace or a hovel. The only thing that mattered was that Jacques was holding her in his arms, and saying all the things she most wanted to hear, speaking the words of love of which she had been so starved.

'God, but I love you, my *chérie*. I've spent so many nights longing for you and aching for you, and wondering if we would ever be like this again.'

'I know,' Angel mumbled against his skin. 'Because it's been the same for me, Jacques. I've missed you so much. I've wanted you so much.'

His body was warm against hers beneath the cool sheets. She knew every part of him, as he did of her. They belonged, in the sweetest, deepest meaning of the word. Theirs was the God-given joy of love, and it was their right to glory in it.

She felt the caress of his hands on her body, as if reminding himself anew of each soft rounded contour like a blind man. His sensitive artist's fingers, feather-light on each responsive area of her flesh, sent waves of sheer pleasure rippling through her.

No thought of impotency ever entered their minds. This was not a night to think of failure. This was the new year, a time of beginning, the forging of new bonds, and love flowed between them like a molten river. Seconds before he sank into her and became part of her, Angel felt brief tears on her eyelids at this most intimate knowledge of the strong and beautiful source of all life, and the ecstasy sent her spirit soaring to meet him.

Chapter 24

There was a New Year's Eve dance in the village hall near Meadowcroft. Fred said dryly that the Bannisters lent a bit of class to the proceedings, at which Ellen called him a terrible snob. They both laughed, knowing that the biggest snob was Clemence, who took the remark perfectly seriously, and agreed with it.

It was the usual boisterous affair, with much larking about by young men in uniforms, fresh-faced farmers and flushed village girls, all eager to have some fun and collect a few kisses when the church clock struck midnight and announced the arrival of 1918.

Charlotte Prole had gone home for the holidays. Ellen watched the other girls prancing up and down in time to the music without partners, only half-heartedly wondering whether to join them. Clemence would definitely disapprove, and for once, Ellen had to agree with her. It looked ungainly, and somehow sad. Women without partners . . .

'Dancing alone is hardly the same thing, is it?' She heard Peter Chard's voice, and it was as though he had read her thoughts. She had watched his slow progress around the room, pausing to chat to everyone he knew. Ellen was quite ready to snub him, saying coolly that it was better than to risk having one's toes stepped on by a blundering farmer.

And then he looked straight into her eyes and held out his arms, and there was nothing in the world that could have stopped her moving into them. They didn't speak, and if Ellen knew she was allowing the occasion to fill her with magic, there was nothing she could do to stop it.

They heard the chimes of midnight. Cheers and laughter filled the village hall as it was plunged into darkness. Still held in Peter's arms, Ellen felt the sudden roughness of his skin against her cheek, then the warmth of his mouth on hers.

Just as quickly, it was over. Couples broke apart in the sudden intrusion of light, turning to other people, hugging and kissing and wishing them a happy new year. And when Ellen looked for Peter again, he had gone.

With every mile that Angel and Jacques travelled back to St Helene, depression crept over her, like the soft snowy flakes blanketing the ground. The three-day idyll was over, the memories locked away in her heart.

And Jacques wanted them to be married as soon as possible, without the pomp and ceremony on which both families would undoubtedly insist after the war. The joy of it made her answer an instinctive yes, but practically it wasn't so easy.

Angel wasn't of age until the end of February. Until then, she needed her father's permission to marry. They intended keeping the marriage a secret until it was a *fait accompli*. There would be so much fuss, otherwise. Angel could imagine Clemence, planning and organising, forgetting that there was a war on, and that such lavish occasions were out of place . . .

Undeniably, Angel felt a pang of regret too, for herself, and the lovely day she would willingly forgo; for her mother, who would be so disappointed . . .

But the thought of being Jacques' wife, together or apart, was the sweetest, most desirable thing in her mind from that moment on. It softened the moment of parting, just a little . . . it gave them something to hope for.

There was a letter for Angel from Margot when she got back to the Abbey.

'The most *Wonderful* thing has happened, darling. I'm getting married to the dearest, most charming man on earth, and I'm *Absolutely* the luckiest girl.'

Margot's superlatives had returned, Angel grinned, marvelling at the coincidence, and yet not really, for they had frequently done things together, knowingly or not.

'The wedding's on February the third, and Angel, *Darling*, you simply must be there. *Please* say that you will. I'm sure the nuns will let you go – incidentally, what a lark, working with nuns. Is it too peculiar? All those soldiers' salty remarks!

'*Write back Immediately*. You can stay with us the night before. We're back in London now, and life must go on, despite all. By the way, my fiancé's name is Basil. *Ghastly*, isn't it? I call him Baz. You'll *adore* him – well, not too much, I hope! I trust you and J are still flourishing.

'Your devoted Margot.'

Angel felt weak, reading it. It was vintage Margot. And she dearly wanted to be there. She read the letter again, her heartbeat quickening. While she was in England, she could pop down to Meadowcroft and get hold of her birth certificate.

With that in her possession, her date of birth would be undisputed. Once she was officially of age, she could marry without written permission. God bless Margot, she thought.

She wanted to phone Jacques right away, but decided to put it all in a letter, since it would take too much precious time explaining.

She was filled with sudden confidence. It was all going to work out beautifully, and she wrote back to Margot as soon as she had begged five days' leave at the beginning of February, promising to work every spare minute to be sure she got them.

She dare not tell anyone about her own plans. Superstitiously, Angel felt that even to tell her best friend might break the run of luck she was sure was going their way. And Jacques' response was all that she had hoped for.

'I'll be counting the days until you are my wife, my dear one, even though you will never be closer to me than you are already. But knowing that I have my wife waiting for me, will make the dark days a little easier to bear, and for that I bless you with all my heart.'

It was a letter to make her throat thicken, and the tears to fall, until the ink was smudged and she had difficulty in reading it. But the essence of it remained with her through the impatient days until she was back in England again, and Margot was greeting her in London with excited cries, and drawing her into the Lacey home. And it was all like being in the midst of an old familiar tableau.

The house, so elegant and comfortable; Mrs Lacey, excited over her daughter's wedding; bravely determined not to let young Edward's death overshadow Margot's day; and Margot herself, as bubbly as a schoolgirl again as the tall young naval officer arrived to be introduced to Margot's dearest friend. And Angel saw from the glances they exchanged, that Margot was no longer the spoilt child she had often seemed, but a woman in love.

For Angel, there were other, special memories. The last time she had been inside this house was almost three years ago. After leaving it, she had been caught in a shower of rain, and in leaping for a taxi-cab, a man's hand had closed over hers on the door handle, and she had looked into the face of the man who was to be her destiny.

'No ghosts, old thing,' Margot said quietly, not understanding the look, and Angel realised she had been staring unseeingly at the flames in the fire.

'Of course not!'

'Good. We must be happy, for Mother's sake. She's lost

Eddie, but now she'll have Baz, and she couldn't be happier at my choice of husband.'

She linked arms with the naval officer as she spoke, and Angel could almost feel the love between them, strong as an electric current. Baz had done a considerable time at sea, but now he had a home posting at Portsmouth, and probably wouldn't be sent on active duty again. Lucky, lucky Margot . . .

The wedding day was bright, the small service performed with dignity at the local church. There were less than thirty guests, since they had felt it wrong to have too big a show, remembering Eddie. Angel was mightily relieved that Margot was rid of the strange obsession over her brother's death. If she had nothing else to thank Baz for, she thanked him silently for that.

After a small reception at an hotel, the couple went off for a few days' honeymoon at a secret destination. Mrs Lacey's sister had moved in with her, so as soon as Angel decently could, she got away and took the train west. The family knew she was coming, and Ellen met her at Temple Meads station, amid hugs and kisses and a few tears.

'You look different,' Angel said, as they sped off in a taxi, and Angel had given her a quick resumé of Margot's day. 'And I don't just mean the fetching Land Army outfit!'

Ellen gave a grimace.

'Do I? Perhaps it's the strain of wondering if my secret intended intends anything towards me or not!'

'For a girl who speaks her mind, that's the most obscure sentence you've ever made! Say it in plain English, darling.'

'I don't know if Peter is interested or not. Is that plain enough for you? And short of asking him outright, which would make Mother disown me, I find it bloody frustrating to twiddle my thumbs and play the little milkmaid!'

Angel laughed, hoping the taxi driver wasn't shocked by such language from a well-brought-up young lady!

'I can't quite see you in that role, Ellen.'

'Can't you? You should see me mucking out the pigs and clucking at the hens by name, like a blasted idiot!'

'It's all good practice for being a farmer's wife,' Angel said lightly, trying to jolly her out of her gloomy mood.

As soon as they arrived at Meadowcroft, Clemence wanted to know every detail of Margot's wedding, sighing with pleasure at the thought of the lovely white dress and veil. She eyed her two younger daughters with some sorrow.

'I suppose one of you will give your father and me as happy a day when it suits you?' Clearly, she dismissed any idea of Ellen getting married and turned to her youngest. 'Angel, we shall depend on you. I'm sure Comte de Ville will expect something splendid for his son. I wonder if we shall all have to go to France? I should hope not. A bride's family always chooses the location –'

'I really don't think you need worry too much about that yet, Mother,' Angel's voice was unnaturally high. 'There's still a war to be won, and Jacques and I are both involved in it.'

'So there is, and there are still plenty of couples who refuse to let the Kaiser dictate their personal lives for them!'

Ellen saw that there was going to be an early clash between them, and intervened quickly.

'It's a shame you missed Dad, Angel. He was here last week, but he had to get back to Yorkshire on urgent business.'

'I'll bet,' Angel couldn't help muttering.

'*What* did you say?' Clemence stared at her daughter. 'What an extraordinary remark to make about your father, Angel!'

Angel felt the heat in her cheeks. The words had slipped out, and now she had to try to justify them without making her mother suspicious. It wasn't the sort of flippant comment that Clemence would appreciate.

'I just meant that it's a shame Daddy's always away these days, that's all. I know Bannister Textiles does important work for the war effort, but it's hardly the same as Jacques flying over enemy lines, is it? Or the soldiers fighting and dying in horrible mud in the trenches. Or even nursing, like Ellen and Margot and I did. I mean, making cloth and turning it into uniforms and blankets just seems so – so *ordinary*!'

She floundered on, seeing Clemence look more outraged by the minute.

'How dare you speak so scathingly about your father's business, Miss! I'm ashamed of you. Your precious soldiers wouldn't have uniforms to wear, nor blankets for their beds, if it wasn't for home industries such as Bannister Textiles. You've obviously got above yourself, since becoming engaged to the son of a count, and I'd remind you that it's your father who'll be paying the bill for your wedding, distasteful though such talk is to me, and his despised industry that will make a society affair of it. And now you'll excuse me. I feel one of my headaches coming on, and I shall lie down until dinner time.'

She swept stiffly out of the room, a lady to her fingertips, and Angel collapsed onto one of the sofas with Ellen open-mouthed beside her.

'Good Lord, what brought all that on?' Ellen said. 'That was a spectacular homecoming, darling!'

'I don't *know*. I didn't mean her to hear. It's all too silly.' But it had shaken Angel, especially her mother's hints about Angel's society wedding, realising that the truth was all going to be such a disappointment to Clemence . . .

'Why did you say it? Don't you think Dad's got urgent business in Yorkshire? There's no other kind of business going on, is there?' Her voice pooh-poohed the very idea.

Angel shrugged, immediately on her guard.

'Hardly! I told you. It just slipped out. It didn't mean anything. Mother always takes things so literally, Ellen. You know that!' The need to defend herself made her irritable.

It annoyed her even more that she was in effect defending her father now, an accessory after the fact . . . and it was something she had never wanted to be. She jumped up, prowling about the room with arms folded across her chest, more upset that she let Ellen know.

But she knew one thing. As soon as she and Jacques were married, they must let both families know. It would be cruel to let Clemence go on planning a big occasion in her mind, when none of it was going to happen. Angel felt sorry for her mother, but this marriage was too important to her and Jacques to change their minds now.

'Don't let it worry you, love,' Ellen said sympathetically. 'Mother gets over things quickly. She'll simply put it out of her mind and pretend it never happened. Anyway, we've got something to show you. It only arrived yesterday, and you're expected to go all sloppy over it.'

She reached into a sideboard drawer and brought out a large envelope containing several photographs. A smiling Louise and Dougal on one, an enormous close-up of a tiny baby on another, the three of them together in a stiff awkward pose, as if they were about to drop the infant Christopher at any minute.

Angel didn't need prompting to go all sloppy. The photos brought a lump to her throat. Louise looked fulfilled and happy, and so different from when she was married to Stanley. As for the baby, round-faced, with a tiny mouth and clear blue eyes . . .

'He's wonderful,' she said softly, imagining how it would feel to hold such a mite in her arms. Imagining how a child of hers and Jacques would look . . . his father would paint wonderful pictures of him, of course. Oil paintings of the most beautiful child in the world . . .

'Have you finished going gaga over them?' Ellen grinned. 'I'd better put them away. Mother's going to get them framed, and dear Louise is very much back in favour now!'

On her second day home, Angel asked her mother casually for her birth certificate. As Ellen had prophesied, Clemence had put the unpleasant episode right out of her mind, and they sat amicably together over afternoon tea. Ellen was back at Peartree Farm, and Angel was glad of this time alone with her mother.

'Why on earth do you want it?' Clemence asked at once, but Angel was prepared for the question.

'You know what officials are like. Even the nuns have to abide by rules now that the Abbey is virtually an army hospital, and Mother Superior is insisiting that everyone produces their birth certificate to prove where they were born, to be entered into the Abbey records. Idiotic, isn't it?'

As she had anticipated, Clemence took it seriously.

'Not at all! It makes very good sense. One never knows who one is working with these days. Any of the doctors or nurses could be Germans. And imagine what they could do in a hospital full of helpless wounded men. The nuns are quite right to take every precaution.'

'Oh well, I suppose so,' Angel said, hating the deception now, with Clemence looking so self-righteous. 'So can I have it, please, Mother?'

'What? Oh, it's not here, dear.'

'Not here? But you said you were bringing the box here for safe keeping!' She tried not to let the shock show on her face, and hoped her mother couldn't hear how sickeningly fast her heart was beating.

'So I did, but our solicitor needed to see some documents relating to Louise's house, and your father took the box back to London. It's in the safe at home. I don't imagine the Germans will drop any bombs on Hampstead after all this time.' She dismissed them as incompetent fools.

'So I can find it there?' Angel persisted.

Clemence looked at her dubiously. 'You'd go back there alone, my dear?'

Angel's laugh was brittle. 'Oh, Mother, I've travelled half across Europe alone! I'm not a child, and the Joneses are still there, aren't they?'

'They go in every day,' Clemence nodded. 'They moved in with their daughter when her husband was killed.'

'Oh.' Angel swallowed. So many things had happened at home that she didn't know about. She remembered the Joneses' daughter Penny, bright and perky, and now she was a young widow, like Rose Morton . . .

'I'll telephone Mrs Jones when you're coming, Angel. She'll air your bed for you –'

'I shan't stay there, Mummy. I'll pick up my birth certificate and get the train for Dover. In fact, I really should leave tomorrow –'

'But you've only just got here. I was going to invite some of my ladies round for afternoon tea tomorrow –'

'I'm sorry. But it's a long journey.' And she wanted to be back in France, where her heart was. 'Will you telephone straight away?'

Clemence looked at her daughter, seeing the new strength in her face, the character that had emerged in the last two years, and felt something that was almost a birth pang.

'I hate to lose you. It seems I'm always losing one or other of my daughters.'

It was an unexpectedly emotional remark from Clemence, and Angel put her arms around her mother.

'You'll never lose us, Mummy. Our ties are too strong. We always come back, don't we? Louise will come back someday, and bring that lovely baby with her.'

Clemence brightened, moving away from Angel's embrace.

'He is beautiful, isn't he? One would expect him to be, naturally. Good breeding always shows, and I suppose

Dougal's quite good-looking, in a Scottish way, of course.'

Angel felt the laughter gurgling inside her. Nothing would change Clemence. It was suddenly a comfort. Countries may fall, and governments may tumble, but the splendid spirit of the English lady would always remain intact.

Angel left Meadowcroft early the next morning. The train to Paddington was crowded as usual, but the sense of camaraderie was still undimmed among the khaki-clad veterans returning to the Front, with swaggering tales to tell the raw recruits. It gave one a strange feeling to be a part of them, to recognise the names of battles and hospitals, and an even stranger feeling to know that experiencing this war would be told to countless children and grandchildren.

She felt buoyant as she left Paddington station and caught a tram to Hampstead. It was a very long while since she had seen her real home. Meadowcroft would always be a delight to visit, but Angel was city-born, and loved every stick and stone of their London house. She felt a great sense of thankfulness as she walked the short distance towards it after leaving the tram. The house was still intact, solid and welcoming.

She revised her ideas. Perhaps she would stay tonight. Just for one night, pretending everything was the way it had always been. She would be the schoolgirl Angel again, youngest daughter of Sir Fred and Lady Bannister, on the brink of adult life with none of its responsibilities. She would stay in her old room, with its remnants of childhood all around, and just for a little while, she would pretend there was no war, no deaths . . .

'Miss Angel!' The door was thrown open, and the plump housekeeper emerged, smiling delightedly. The next second, Angel was enveloped in her arms. 'How well you look. And such a young lady now, though I do miss your lovely long hair. Such a beautiful golden colour! Your father knew what he was doing when he named you, my duck!'

'Oh, Jonesey, it's so wonderful to see you!' Angel almost wept at the extrovert welcome, far less inhibited than her own mother. She hugged the housekeeper tightly as she went indoors. Mrs Jones was exactly the same as she remembered her. Everything here was the same, as if the family had just stepped out of it.

The house smelled of the same beeswax furniture cream and the faint odour of Cardinal polish, and Angel guessed that in her own words, Mrs Jones had treated the house to a right royal doing-over, in honour of Angel's arrival. The thought made tears prick her eyes.

'How are you and Jones and Penny? I was so sorry –'

'We're middling,' Mrs Jones nodded. 'Our Penny's shown what she's made of, and that's the main thing. Can't do more for King and Country, can you? 'Cepting for brave young ladies like you and your sisters, o' course, and we're very proud of you, ducks.'

Angel bit her lip. The honest pride in the woman's eyes, for her bereaved daughter, and for the daughters of this house, made her want to weep.

'Hold on now, no tears! There ain't much food to be had, but I'm preparing a nice bit o' fish for your dinner tonight, and a bit o' fresh winter cabbage Jones has grown in the shrubbery. Your dear Mama 'ould have a fit if she knew, but you and I ain't telling her, are we?'

Angel laughed between her tears. She was the same old conspiratorial Jonesey, making a pet of the youngest girl, her favourite.

'You're a darling, Jonesey!'

'And your bed's aired, all ready. I'll put a nice hot bottle in it before I go back tonight.' She looked anxious. 'You'll be all right on your own? If you want me to stay –'

'Of course not, Jonesey. Your family needs you. But how did you know I'd stay? Didn't Mother tell you I'd be leaving straight away?'

Mrs Jones chuckled, her head on one side like a bright-eyed little sparrow.

'Always knew you better than your own Mama, didn't I? 'Course you'd stay, once you saw the dear old place. You go and get reacquainted with everything, ducks, while I make us a nice cup of tea. The Kaiser ain't started to blow up tea plantations yet, thank Gawd.'

Angel was still smiling as she wandered through the house, breathing in its familiar aura. This was home, and it was good to be back. More than anywhere else, the battle-grounds of Europe seemed a million miles away from here. It struck her as very strange, when this was London, and according to all the panic reports in the newspapers, she should feel an imminent sense of danger. But she didn't. She was surrounded by too many years of love and happiness, and nothing could take away the special memories of childhood.

The adornments in her room were a mixture of those old carefree times and the post-college days, before the war had stopped most of her mother's plans for her younger daughters. She wandered in and out of the other rooms, feeling the essence of her parents and her sisters wherever she went.

She tested the water in the new modern bathroom Fred had installed with its ornate tub. Mrs Jones had had the gas heater going, and there was blissfully hot water, and she decided to bath before her evening meal. There was plenty of time to find the birth certificate, and she would relish this time on her own.

It occurred to her that it was a rare event. The house had always been bustling with people, and in her head, the echoes of other times came and went like a half-remembered melody.

Later, she dressed in one of her old frocks that was a little dated, but suited her nostalgic mood. But there was one important thing she must do right away. In her father's study, she opened the safe and found the precious document she needed. This was the key to her new life . . . she put it safely in her bag.

That was for tomorrow. For tonight, she would be gay and bright, and enjoy Jonesey's excellent fare, cooked with all the ingenuity of a housekeeper faced with the challenge of preparing something nourishing out of nothing. The fish had some kind of sauce that tasted only faintly of cheese; the cabbage contained a filling of other vegetables, and a minute helping of potato completed the dish. It tasted wonderful, and Angel was told to leave the clearing-up for Mrs Jones to do the next day.

'No arguments now. It'll be like old times, fussing around after you. Now, you're sure you'll be all right?'

'Quite sure. Give my love to everyone, and take care of yourself, Jonesey.'

'No fear of that, my duck. Me and Jones'll still be here after we've finished with Kaiser Bill!'

Much later, when it was growing dark, Angel went to her room and closed the door. She pulled the heavy curtains across tightly, remembering the regulations, before she turned up the gaslight to a flickering softness. She found a suitable gramophone record, put it on the turntable, and wound up the machine. The tinny sound of bright dance music filled the air. She grabbed her pillow and held it like an imaginary partner, and danced around the furniture.

Breathless when the first tune ended, she put on less robust records, dancing with dreams in her eyes, imagining that it was Jacques that she held close, Jacques with whom this night would end . . .

How long she danced, she couldn't have said. As each record ended, she put on another, wound the handle, and drifted into her dream world again, loth to lose the feeling of magic.

She couldn't have said what made her catch her breath and feel the sudden pounding of her heart. A small sound, perhaps. This house was well back from the road and isolated from neighbours, and Angel was sure she had locked the doors. And yet there was something, she was sure of it.

She opened her door cautiously. The rest of the house was in darkness, but there were definitely small noises coming from the direction of her father's study. She felt a rising panic. She should send for the police, but to use the telephone in the hall downstairs would surely alert the intruder.

The walls of the house were solid. The burglar wouldn't have guessed anyone was there, since her door had been shut, and the gramophone music wouldn't have penetrated. She was sick with fear and indecision.

And then a sort of angry calm swept through her. How dare this person violate her father's private sanctum? Snooping around her home, prying into personal things . . . she looked around quickly. There was a heavy iron poker in her little fireplace. She had grown strong during her months of lifting the soldiers. She was no coward, and perhaps faced with someone in the house, the burglar would take fright and flee.

Angel crept downstairs, her fingers around the poker damp and clammy, nerves fluttering in her throat as she neared the study. Her legs shook, despite her resolve.

The door was open, the curtains still pulled back. Pale moonlight lit the room. She could see Fred's heavy oak desk, the candlesticks and pen-and-ink stand, the silver-framed photographs and ornaments seemingly still in their places. She noted all these things in an instant. What stopped her moving forward was the searing shock of seeing the slumped figure seated at the desk, his unmistakable outline silhouetted against the light from the window.

But the shock came not so much from the sight of him as the sounds he was making. He sat with both elbows on the desk, face cupped in his large capable hands, and great wrenching sobs seemed to be torn from his soul. It was obvious that something terrible and private had happened. Angel forgot everything else.

'Daddy!' Angel croaked his name in a dry, fractured voice. The poker dropped to the floor with a heavy thud as Fred's head jerked up, and within seconds she was around the other side of the desk and kneeling at his side, her arms around him.

Chapter 25

In those first few minutes, Fred's mind was totally unable to take in that the warm and pliant body in his arms was his daughter, Angel. He had believed her to be in France, not here at their old home, where neither of them was meant to be. If Angel had had a shock at seeing him, then his own shock was none the less traumatic. Neither of them could speak for long minutes, and Fred had also to fight down his own shuddering loss of self-control, knowing to his shame that his best beloved daughter had witnessed it.

'What are you doing here, Angel?' The words seemed to be dragged out of him. Even to himself, he sounded like a shuffling old man, dazed and senile. It was so ludicrous, because he was feeling totally unlike the way he had expected to feel on this day. He should be dancing on tables . . .

'Daddy, what's happened? Tell me, *please*! I can't bear to see you like this. I know it must be something awful!'

Angel mumbled into his shoulder. When she raised her face against his in mute sympathy, he could feel the moist warmth of her lips, and the soft melting tears on her lashes. He was reluctant to break this spell. If it was some kind of miracle that had brought her here tonight, then he never questioned the existence of miracles. It was the second miracle today.

At the thought, bile rose in his throat. He couldn't help it. Hale and hearty though he was, good news or bad had always had the same effect on him, and it was frequently only due to his iron will that he kept it inside his gut and not spewing out of him. Right now, though, he felt in danger of losing that particular battle, and made a supreme effort. Angel felt his limbs go rigid, and mourned for whatever loss he had suffered.

'Please tell me, Daddy,' she whispered, still holding him. 'Share it with me, like you always used to say to me.'

She brushed everything else aside. Old hurts didn't matter, compared with this . . . to her horror, she felt him relax against her again, so swiftly that she was almost unbalanced from her kneeling position. Heavy sobs racked Fred's body again, and furious with himself, he knew the words had to be said.

'I'd share my dreams with you if I could, my Angel,' the words seemed ground out of him like chips of ice. Feeling the brittleness in him, she realised she was breathing shallowly to catch every word. 'But I lost that right when you discovered that my dreams weren't high and mighty like you'd always imagined. You put me on a pedestal, and then I toppled –'

'It's not important now –' she was more distressed than she could say. Didn't every daughter put her father on a pedestal, believing him superior to every other man?

'Yes it bloody well is!' Fred's voice was harsh with the pain of pent-up feelings. 'It's Harriet I love more than life, and it's Harriet whose name I can never mention to another living soul, and I can't possibly make you understand how that feels. How can you know the torment to a man living his life with a frigid wife? The gradual breaking down of his confidence, and his very masculinity? And then to meet a warm, caring woman who makes him feel he's ten feet tall every time he walks through the door? You wouldn't understand how it feels to be suddenly alive again, after years of being the so-called master of my own home, when that farce stops at the bedroom door. And I'm sorry if it shocks and offends you, my darling, and I shouldn't be talking to you like this, but the relief of today has taken all the stuffing out of me, when it should be the other way round. I should be getting drunk and celebrating, and instead, I'm a rag doll blubbering like a baby, and God knows why –'

'Daddy, for pity's sake stop treating me like a child and tell me what's happened.' Angel's voice was a thin thread of sound. She couldn't bear this torrent of words. None of it shocked or offended her. To her own surprise, not even the mention of Harriet's name did that on this particular night. She could only feel supreme sadness to see her father so disorientated when he had always been so strong.

Fred looked down at her upturned face as if seeing her for the first time. He felt a lump in his throat. She was so young and beautiful, his Angel. She was everything he had ever imagined her to be when he had named her with what Clemence called that impossible name. He had always known she would be special to him, and God knew he needed that special closeness between them now.

'I thought Harriet was going to die,' he was still hoarse with emotion. 'For months we've lived with the fear of it. I could see her slipping away from me, and I could do nothing about it. The doctors couldn't discover what was wrong with her. They strongly suspected consumption, yet they couldn't be sure. She's been in and out of hospital for test after test, and it's been a nightmare. And then, quite suddenly, she began to put on a little weight, and her face started getting rosy again, and we finally got the verdict today that she's in the clear. My Harriet's going to live. She got the miracle she always wanted, and I just wish to God I had her faith so that I didn't feel so bloody guilty for ever doubting it –'

He leaned against Angel, and supporting him, she could feel the dampness of his tears on her cheeks. She ached to find the right words, but somehow there were no words. She rocked him close as if he were the child, and compassion and love for him overcame everything else.

'Daddy, I do understand,' she said quietly, one thought

illuminating everything else. 'When I thought Jacques had died, I wanted to die too. And the memory of times we had spent together sustained me more than anything. I *do* understand.'

She couldn't say more. This was her father, and propriety still prevented her from actually admitting that she and Jacques had been lovers. But perhaps he would understand too, in that peculiar bond they had always shared, and which seemed miraculously restored to them now. If nothing else, the barriers had been broken down, but Angel knew she must do one more thing to prove it to him.

'This is a fine way to celebrate Harriet's good health!' She forced a more cheerful note to her voice. 'Can't we find some wine in the cellar and cheer ourselves up? The house is cold now, but there's a fire in my room. Let's take the wine in there and play some music and pretend I've just come home from college and you want to hear everything that's happened!'

With one great leap she bridged the gap that had existed between them. Taking them back into the realms of a happier past, but with the shared knowledge of the present. Accepting and forgiving the flaws in each of them. Fred drew her to her feet and held her close.

'Your place will always be in my heart, darling girl. No one could ever usurp it.'

'I know it,' she said simply. 'It just took me a little time to realise how alike we are.'

They were determinedly bright for the rest of the evening, talking long into the night by the leaping flames of the fire in Angel's room. Fred needed to talk about Harriet, and Angel let him. It no longer seemed strange or a betrayal, because it was obvious that it was a dear and special relationship her father had with Harriet, and it didn't touch anything else. Clemence would always be Lady Bannister, and Fred's daughters would still be his girls.

Angel had secrets too. Everyone did. And not even to Fred in that sweetly intimate atmosphere did she reveal her own plans for marrying Jacques.

Even Louise had secrets, Angel discovered, finally asking what Fred was doing in London, when they had all thought he was in Yorkshire. Mellowed with the wine, he gave a short laugh.

'Louise wants to sell the house, lock, stock and barrel, and you know what a fuss your mother would make about that. She still thinks fondly that Louise and Dougal will move back there after the war, near enough so that when we all return here, she can see her grandson whenever she likes.'

'Poor Mother,' Angel murmured, thinking that eventually she and Jacques would probably settle in France, and the family would be split even more.

'Poor Clemence,' Fred agreed. 'But you girls must lead your own lives, and Louise is quite adamant that the house must be sold, so I'm seeing to the details for her. Once it's all settled, I shall inform your mother.'

Out of all the mass of words said between them on that emotional night, Angel remembered those particular ones. Weeks later, they were still uppermost in her mind. 'You girls must lead your own lives.' She remembered them as she stood beside Jacques in the cool dark interior of the tiny church in St Helene, lit only by the early spring sunlight pouring through the stained glass windows and dazzling the altar with iridescent splinters of coloured light.

She remembered little of the brief ceremony. The man of God solemnly intoning the words that bound them together until death did them part; the two strangers asked to be witnesses, because she and Jacques wanted this marriage to be as private as possible; the vows and responses; the coolness of the gold ring sliding onto her finger; the knowledge that this was an irrevocable step, and one that she wanted to take above all else in the world. And the only real moment,

Jacques' kiss on her lips, the first kiss as man and wife.

She hardly noticed hands shaking hers in congratulation, or the document that they signed, proof that they now belonged in the eyes of God and man. It was all unreal, a day so longed for that it seemed almost an anti-climax when it actually happened. And she was so perfectly attuned to her father's reaction over Harriet's good health that she was humbled by the thought.

But if the day was a little unreal, then the night was everything that Angel had anticipated. They had one night to share together. The demands of the war denied them the pleasures of a normal honeymoon. But that night in a small hotel in the town of St Helene, a stone's throw from the Abbey, might have been in a different world. Together in the deepest sense of the word, at last they truly belonged.

'If this was the only night we had, my dearest one, it would be enough,' Angel whispered into the bronzed bare flesh of her husband. She heard Jacques' low rumbling laugh as he leaned over to kiss her breasts.

'It would never be enough for me, *chérie*. If we had a lifetime, it would never be enough. So since we have only this one night, let's not think of sleeping. I've waited too long to call you my wife.'

Angel thrilled to the music of the words. This was her husband, the man she had vowed to love and cherish, and would do so until the day she died . . . but this was not a night to think about dying. Tonight was theirs, for love and comfort, and the end of all parting . . . she pushed aside the thought that the morning would be here all too soon, and theirs was a love that seemed destined for parting . . .

Eventually they drifted into sleep, still entwined in each other's arms. And when Angel awoke in the pale early light of day, it was to find Jacques studying her face as if to imprint every pore of it on his memory.

'Don't look at me so intently. I'm a sight first thing in the morning –' she begged smilingly.

'And such a beautiful sight. You have a vagueness about you before you're properly awake that is totally enchanting, my Angel. I love that soft, sleepy look on your lovely face. It's very sensual, *chérie*.'

'Is it?' She looked up at him provocatively, half-closing her lids again. 'Perhaps I should practise it then, to tempt my husband –'

His answer was to pull her into his arms, where the soft warmth of their skins melted together. His reply was teasingly fierce, loving every part of her. His fingers traced around her mouth and down the smooth slender throat until they met the warm swell of her breasts. Beneath the cocoon of the sheets, she felt the sharp sweet excitement begin, seeing the sudden passion in Jacques' eyes, feeling the proof of it in his young body.

'You need do nothing to tempt me, darling wife. Everything about you is a temptation, and a delight. Sweets for the tasting –'

'And you have such a sweet tooth, dear husband!'

She breathed the words, unconsciously seductive, winding her arms around him as the familiar pattern of their love-making began, each new sensation the source of a glorious and abandoned pleasure.

Angel delayed writing home, knowing that eventually the news must be told. She had considered telephoning, but the thought of her mother's reaction quickly prevented that idea. Clemence would be very upset, outraged and undoubtedly furious to know that Angel was married, but her father's words still rang in her ears. 'You girls must lead your own lives.'

And so she had . . . so she had . . .

She still hadn't written home two weeks later, when Mother Superior sent for her. Angel's face whitened.

'Mother, I didn't ask for this!' she stammered.

The nun looked at her with some impatience.

'I understood from Sister Yard at Piersville that you were very keen to take on ambulance duties, Bannister.'

'But here in France! Not in England!' Tears of frustration studded her eyes. 'You can't send me back there!'

'Don't you have a family, Bannister? You have a sister, I believe, and you seem to receive plenty of letters –'

She was tempted to say that she also had a husband, but they had decided to tell no one at Brighton Belle or the Abbey of their recent marriage. Angel wore the wedding ring on a chain around her neck, safely inside her high-necked dress.

'I also have a fiancé,' Angel said shakily instead. 'And I want to be near him, Mother.'

The nun put a cool hand on Angel's tense arm.

'I do understand, my dear, but you've been here for some while, and nurses get battle-fatigued as much as the men. There was a time when we were quite worried about you –'

'You know I'm quite over that episode!' Angel said heatedly. Then she stopped, her shoulders sagging. The nun's face was implacable. Why were these people looked on as being so compassionate, Angel raged!

'When are you sending me away?'

'My dear, don't look on it like that! It won't be for another month yet, but I thought you would like to know.'

Another month. It would be early May by then. A beautiful time in England when everything would be green and fragrant with blossom . . . but she felt so strongly now that her place was in France, with Jacques . . .

'I don't want to go!' She was near to tears as she clung to Jacques, the next time they managed to snatch a few hours together.

'*Chérie*, it cannot last much longer, and we will be together for always. Would it help if you told the nuns that you're married to a Frenchman?'

She shook her head. 'It wouldn't help at all! We had a married girl at the Abbey a while ago, and she was sent straight back. They're so strict about it, and it's so stupid. As if a married woman can't tie a bandage as competently as an unmarried one!'

'That's not the reason, is it – ?'

'No. They think the married ones will go to pieces thinking that every casualty brought in is going to be their husband! I thought they'd seen what I went through to know that it makes no difference when someone's in love. Married or not doesn't change the emotions one feels –'

She stopped, biting her lips and realising the truth in Mother Superior's words. Battle-fatigued. Was that true of her after all? She had been here so long. It was something one didn't recognise in oneself. She knew that only too well.

'I have some news as well,' Jacques said.

'They're not sending you to England too, are they?' She spoke with false hope, knowing it was very unlikely.

She knew well enough that squadrons flew every day, on recce raids and bombing raids. Day and night, until the pilots were punch-drunk with flying . . . and it would go on until the war ended, unless Jacques applied for training instructor duties, and Angel couldn't imagine that. Not until he could barely see to fly any more . . .

'You've spoilt the surprise.'

She looked at him in astonishment, and he grinned.

'No, *chérie*, it's not quite as you think. But the old plane they gave me is falling apart, and I'm to get a replacement one very soon. Now that the new command is officially called the Royal Air Force, things are changing slightly. I'm to take my old crate back to England, collect my new one and fly it back. If we can wangle it for the right time, you could be my passenger.'

Her heart nearly stopped. She had never stepped inside an aircraft before. The thought of it was both exciting and unnerving. She didn't know which was uppermost in her mind at that moment. But the idea had evidently caught Jacques' imagination. He seized both her hands, caressing the palms with his fingertips.

'Why not, Angel? You already share half of my life. Fly with me and share the rest of it,' he said urgently.

She sensed that this was somehow important to him. She felt the pressure of his fingers on hers, and knew that she would follow him to the ends of the earth if he asked her to.

'Yes!' she said, ignoring the hammering of her heart. 'But how can we possibly arrange it?'

'Leave it to me,' he said with supreme confidence. 'Just let me know the date you get your travel pass. You'll have some leave when you get to England, I take it?'

'Just a few days before I report to the convalescent home in Essex. I'll be driving back and forth between there and the hospital ships at Dover.' She stopped, because he wasn't really listening to her last words.

'I daresay I can manage a few days as well, before I return to Brighton Belle,' he said, falsely casual. 'That is, if you're interested in spending them together – ?'

Her answer was in the sudden blaze of happiness in her eyes, and the widening of her smile, and it was ridiculous, but it hadn't even occurred to Angel before. Until that moment, she had been too incensed at the blow fate was dealing her to think about anything else.

Clemence didn't waste time with a letter. There was a message for Angel to telephone Meadowcroft immediately. Her heart sank, knowing what to expect. Comte de Ville had sent a telegram of congratulations on the marriage, but Lady Bannister's reaction was predictably quite different.

'How could you do this to us, Angel?' Mingled hurt and fury seemed to ooze out of Clemence. 'Your father and I are terribly upset, and I'm very, very angry with you!'

Angel felt her throat begin to tighten. 'I thought Daddy would understand –'

Clemence seethed at this. 'Don't think you can wind your father around your little finger this time, Miss, the way you always do! I know now why you wanted your birth certificate. Such lies and deceit! Is this all the gratitude I get? Heaven knows I've done my best to bring you up properly –'

Angel held the receiver away from her ear as Clemence's voice rose. Her heart beat sickeningly, knowing she deserved all this and more, and helpless to stop her mother's tirade.

'What on earth will people think? It's scandalous to get married in this hole and corner fashion. I'm not sure if it's even legal, or if it's not possible to get it annulled –'

'You can't do that, Mother,' Angel couldn't let this go on. Her voice shook. 'Jacques and I are married. It's perfectly legal, and it would be an even bigger scandal to try to get it annulled, because of – uh – certain things that have happened between us –'

She was overcome with the most awful attack of nerves and embarrasment, feeling the hot colour flood her face. Clemence had always been such a stickler for etiquette and proper behaviour, and everything happening in its correct order, and her outrage threatened to swamp Angel. She had flaunted everything her mother stood for, and knew it, and the guilt didn't make this awkward conversation any easier. The small silence told her that Clemence understood exactly what she was saying.

'Well, of course, that was to be expected,' she said freezingly, implying that a young woman who showed such disregard for finer feelings, and a hot-headed continental, would naturally give in to animal lust.

Angel tried again, her voice still trembling. She wanted to be strong, but it was the most difficult moment of her life.

'I didn't want to hurt you, Mother, truly I didn't! But Jacques and I needed to know that we belonged, in case – well, in case anything happened. Surely I don't need to make it any clearer, do I?'

'What does Jacques' father have to say?' Clemence ignored the plea.

'He sent a telegram of congratulations. I'm sure he'll be

writing to you and Daddy. He understands –'

'Well, I'm sure that I don't,' Clemence snapped. 'But it seems to me that my feelings never counted for very much as far as you girls are concerned. Louise seems settled enough, though I'm displeased that she's selling her London house – something else that I wasn't told until afterwards! And Ellen's as much of a trial as ever, not knowing what she wants to do half the time, and I suspect that as soon as the war is over, she'll be waving banners again for the Women's Movement!'

Her attention was diverted for the moment from the shock of her youngest daughter's indiscretion, and Angel seized the moment to divert it still further.

'Mother, I've got some news to cheer you up. I'm being posted to England sometime in May, to a convalescent home in Essex. I'll be able to see you more often, and there's every hope that the war won't last much longer.'

'We heard that the new spot of trouble at the Somme was over,' Clemence said, slightly less fraught. 'And it's a relief to know you'll be on English soil, even though the damage has been done, and it seems there's nothing we can do to reverse it.'

'Nothing at all, Mummy!' she said solemnly.

The wild urge to laugh was tempered by her mother's brief reference to more bitter fighting at the Somme during March and April. There had been heavy losses again, the British outnumbered by an estimated three to one. The Germans had advanced twenty-five miles, enough to begin panic waves, and it had taken desperate defensive measures for the British Tommies to stand firm under Field Marshall Haig's command, despite many of their battalions being wiped out. By April 18th the battle was over, with enormous losses on both sides, the hospitals filled to overflowing, and nothing conclusive gained.

Yes, Angel thought wryly, you could refer to it all as a spot of trouble . . .

'Your father wants to speak to you.' Angel heard the muffled voices at the other end of the line, and her hand gripped the cord more tightly. She needed Fred's approval. All that had happened before was as nothing to the longing to be still his best girl.

'We wish you both all the happiness in the world, my darling girl,' Fred said. 'Your mother's naturally disappointed not to be planning a society wedding, but we'll make up for all that when the war's over. We can still celebrate once we're all together again, and that's the most important thing. Take care of yourself, and come home safely.'

'Thank-you, Daddy.' She was choked, aware of Clemence's annoyance in the background, but Fred was giving his daughter his full support, and for that, Angel was eternally grateful.

Ellen wrote an elated letter, telling her she was a clever old thing. Margot was slightly affronted at not having been told, but she and Baz wished her best luck. Louise and Dougal sent an elaborate card of congratulations, with a smudged scrawl that was supposedly young Christopher's fingerprint.

Following his telegram, Comte de Ville wrote at more length, welcoming Angel into the de Ville family, adding that there must be nuptial celebrations when they were all free citizens again, and that he hoped all her family would be the Comte's guests at the chateau when the time came. A remark that would surely lift Clemence's spirits . . .

Angel lay gritty-eyed in her bed, exhausted and yet unable to sleep, after a late evening ward duty, assessing the reactions of all those important in her life. Alone in her room at the Abbey, above the cloisters that now housed row after row of sick beds, it all seemed totally unreal.

The messages from her family and friends; the final acceptance from her mother that she and Jacques were married, and nothing was going to change it; the endless day-to-day routine of hospital life; the waiting for her transfer to England . . .

And none of it was as important as the fact that she and Jacques were one. Joined in the sight of God and of man. And but for the piece of paper that made it legal, they might as well have been at opposite ends of the earth. Marriage was for the mutal comfort and benefit of each for the other . . . or words to that effect . . . and for each of them, those words were farcical.

Jacques was somewhere among the myriad stars in the night sky, flying with danger, and probably over enemy lines at that very moment. While she, despite being in the midst of a hospital buzzing with noise and activity, a bride of just a few weeks, had never felt more alone and lonely.

Chapter 26

Angel finally left St Helene in the middle of May. Leaving the Abbey itself tugged at her heart more than she had expected. She had grown used to the nuns, to the harshness of their unwavering faith, and to their rules and demands.

She knew the Abbey well, felt the strength of history in its cloistered walls. Strangely, she could still sense the ghosts of the legions of wounded men who had been tended there. It was a sad parting in many ways. She would have clung tearfully to several of the nuns if it had been permitted.

Dignity prevented such a thing, and instead she had to be satisfied with solemn good-byes and a head held high as the ambulance lorry took her to the bus stop north of the town. She had asked to be set down there, saying that she intended to visit a friend before making her own way to the hospital ship bound for the south coast of England.

It was the most calm and beautiful day, sweet-scented with flowers of early summer. Perfect for flying, Angel told herself over and over to quell the way her stomach turned at the thought. No one at the Abbey knew that today she was to make the most exciting journey of her life . . . she had to keep repeating those words to herself too . . .

Jacques looked anxiously at the sky. His artist's eye briefly acknowledged its beauty. Azure blue and corn gold, the great orb of the sun dazzled the eyes . . . Common sense of the practised flyer took over. It was just the setting for the

German planes to hover, hidden between the British planes and the sun, waiting to pounce. A pilot would hear nothing but the throb of his own engines, the flap of canvas and the judder of metal, until out of nowhere came a sudden raucous whine of an alien engine, a flash of gleaming metal, a spitting of red fire from the weapon in the hands of a Jerry gunner . . .

Jacques unclenched his hands, unaware until that moment that they had been tight with tension. Was he mad to have suggested flying to England with Angel as his passenger? If danger threatened they would have no defence. They would be shot to pieces, the way his first plane had been shot down, burning, burning, screaming towards the ground in its death-throes, the earth leaping to meet them before they exploded in a wild eruption of flames.

Memories of that time surged into his mind with their usual nightmare proportions. He could still see Phil Brake's skin shrivelling in front of him, the flesh curling, the stink more abominable than hell. He could hear Phil's cries, mingling with his own, the sounds nothing short of demonic. Jacques' blasphemy had been savage and unrelenting then, denying a God who had put this hell on earth, and begging Phil to die quickly.

He had longed for death for himself, as he had crawled from the inferno of his plane with every inch of his skin on fire, abrasive with the shock of blisters bloating his body, his eyes raw and splinter-dry. And then the new, almost unbearable shock of finding himself at the edge of a lake, of plunging in and feeling the sweet icy water soothe him for an instant, before the new pain enveloped him.

Such pain was inhuman . . . he gave up the struggle, letting himself float face-down and waiting for death . . . ragged and drowning, he suddenly screamed as hands that were not his own began dragging him out of the water.

Hands that ripped the ravaged, tender flesh from his arms, and voices that shouted at him in his native language. Hold on, hold on . . . but couldn't they see that he hadn't wanted to hold on? He'd wanted to let the freezing water suck him down, soothing him into oblivion . . .

He had wanted so much to die, and ever since, he had carried the memory of that thought inside him like a penance. It was wrong to seek death from a God who had given him life. His very upbringing condemned him for it. But if it was wrong to want death for himself, how much worse was it to spend every waking hour in senseless killing?

Jacques had finally been forced to stop questioning things to which there were no answers. He was part of the machine of war. He had to go on, like everyone else, until one side or the other was the victor.

But did he have to do this? It had seemed so simple an idea. To take Angel with him, and try to convey to her without words his own deepest feelings, never nearer to whatever god existed than when he was soaring high into the heavens, part of a great eternal universe.

Was he right to risk taking her into danger, or feeding his own ego while he still searched to find himself out of the muddle of spent emotions since the crash? Even worse, was it just crass foolhardiness?

He gave a grim smile. He preferred to think it was something he had in common with the great dare-devil air aces who were the products of this war. The exploits of them all were imprinted on every pilot's brain. He could recite them parrot fashion, if asked . . .

The inspiration of the RFC 2nd Lieutenant Albert Ball, fearlessly leading an SE5 squadron, was last seen flying into a cloudbank in May of 1917. Later found dead at his controls, badly mutilated when his plane crashed, not yet aged twenty-one . . .

The brilliant German von Richthofen, shot down just last month. When his plane was found, it was rumoured that he was frozen to the controls. The leader of the great 'Richthofen circus' was dead.

News of each death had struck Jacques as oddly

comparable, symbolic of the love of flying. And like many of his fellow pilots, he was unable to separate in his mind the bravery and the loss of ally or enemy.

He shook himself. The bus from St Helene was rattling along the dirt road towards him, scattering a fine yellow dust from every wheel. He had made the plans, and must stick by them. And not for a second must he reveal the fear that sometimes still crawled over his gut, as if to remind him that he was not invincible. He slammed shut the door of his car as he stepped outside it, shielding his eyes against the flurry of dust.

As if through a mist, he saw Angel step through it, and just as instantly, his heart seemed to settle into its proper place. His brave and beautiful wife was here, and at the brief uncertainty he glimpsed in her eyes, followed immediately by a look of love and confidence in him, Jacques felt a fierce protective strength return. He had vowed to love and keep her, and he would do so until eternity.

'Isn't it a wonderful day?' Angel said, taut with excitement when they had hugged and kissed, and he had stowed her baggage in the back of the car. 'Oh, Jacques, I can't believe we'll actually be in England in a few hours!'

He laughed, her exuberance lifting him.

'I promise you it will be an unforgettable experience, *chérie*! Just remember to do exactly as I tell you. Don't move too quickly to left or right and rock the plane, and wear your goggles at all times. Don't be tempted to take them off to wipe away the oil and grime they collect, or you'll have stinging eyes for the rest of the day.'

She listened, wide-eyed, half amused at the seriousness in his voice, teasing him in return.

'Yes, sir! I didn't know I was going to get a lecture!'

'You'll thank me for it, Angel –'

'Is there anything else I should know?' she asked laughing, yet with a sudden catch in her breath. The journey ahead of her was so awe-inspiring to the uninitiated. It was something she had tried not to think about too deeply.

Jacques laughed too. 'Don't fall out! I want to get you home all in one piece.'

Home. It was a word she hadn't even thought of as yet. The transfer to England had been more a frustration than anything else. Being away from the proximity of Jacques' unit. Leaving the Abbey with which she was now so familiar.

But now she swallowed hard. She was going home. The war wasn't over yet, but for Angel at that moment, it almost seemed as though it was. Her throat felt thick, and it seemed as if Jacques was reading her mind. His voice was gentle.

'This is only *au revoir* to France, *chérie*. After the war, we'll both return, and see it all with different eyes.'

'But it is all so changed,' she said sadly, scanning the countryside. Yet here, the waving grasses of the fields were still lovely, giving no hint of the carnage that was such a short distance away in the valley of the Somme and the Western Front.

'France has survived all through history, dearest,' Jacques spoke without expression. 'She'll rise again, like a phoenix from the ashes, you'll see.'

There was a catch in Angel's voice. 'But she'll have lost so much, just like Britain and all the Allied countries. So many young men who will never grow old beside their wives. So many grieving young women –'

She shivered, and it was as if a cloud had passed over the sun, even though the day was still sparklingly bright. Jacques brought the car to a halt on the grass verge, switched off the engine, and turned to her. There was a great and gentle quiet about the countryside now, as if no threat of killing existed. He took her in his arms.

'Listen to the silence, *chérie*. Can't you hear that France and all the world is waiting for the miracle that will come soon? These fields will echo to the voices of children singing again, free to gather wild flowers and roam where they will.

And for you and me, there will be time to grow old together, my Angel. Never doubt that.'

'And all those others?' For some reason, she couldn't rid her mind of their ghosts. 'Will we forget them so soon?'

'The world will never forget. I guarantee it.'

It was as solemn as a vow. Two people who had so far survived a war kissed and clung, almost sensing the grateful sighs of all those lost comrades in the shimmering soft green grasses of France.

'It looks so flimsy!' Angel exclaimed, when at last they stood beside the tiny plane. The car had been safely stowed away until Jacques' return, and Jacques had given her brief instructions as they prepared to climb into the open cockpits.

Angel's mouth was dry as bone, her limbs soft as jelly. It was all going to happen, and she could do nothing to stop it. She wore the smallest size flying helmet, the fragrant scent of the leather wafting into her nostrils. She adjusted the goggles to sit securely on her nose. A young man in overalls was preparing to spin the propeller, and Jacques was holding out his hand to her.

She felt his fingers curl around her own, and his dark eyes looked steadily into hers. She gave a brief nod, and let him help her clamber into the impossibly tiny seat. Jacques seated himself behind her. He shouted something to the mechanic, the propeller spun as the engine jerked into life, and Angel thought all hell had been let loose.

Everything rattled and shook, and she grasped the sides of her seat for dear life. Struts vibrated, spurts of oil were flung into her face, she could hear the air whistling through the flapping canvas, her heart thudded faster than the engine noises, and if there had been time to assess her exact feelings at that moment, she would have admitted to a feeling of pure terror . . .

'Hold tight!' Jacques yelled at her above the roar of the

engine. 'This is the worst bit –'

All of it was the worst bit, Angel thought hysterically. How could anyone be obsessed with flying, when it was so unbelievably frightening? All the romantic notions she had harboured, along with everyone else, disappeared in a flash.

The ground was rushing alongside and beneath them as the plane gathered momentum on the rough grass of the airfield. Then there was suddenly nothing below, only a great tipping void, echoing the way her stomach was plummeting downwards . . .

She gritted her teeth as the plane lurched and dipped, the span of the wings hiding the ground one minute so that they were adrift in a great ocean of blue . . . and the next, revealing the ground still terribly close, although the tiny buildings of Brighton Belle were becoming toytown miniatures below.

And then there was a feeling of sudden calm as Jacques reached the correct height for cruising, and levelled the plane. As he did so, Angel's stomach stopped somersaulting and stayed more or less in its proper place. Jacques yelled at her to breathe deeply, and wasn't the air like heady wine, and clearer than anything she had ever breathed before?

She smiled weakly, trying to make her breathing less erratic. And gradually, she had to agree with him. Despite the undisputed smell of oil from the engine, there was a purity in the atmosphere that she had never sensed before. Compared with the appalling smells of the hospital, this was truly like heaven.

Angel shouted back to tell him so, and her voice was carried away on the wind screaming through the struts, mingling with it like a strangely heavenly chorus.

She heard his rich warm laugh drifting towards her, and with it, all fear seemed to float away. Here they were, the two of them, in a private world of their own, untouched by the war.

'I never imagined it would be like this!'

They both had to shout against the engine noise, but even

that seemed to have a secure rhythm about it now, taking them home . . . taking them home . . .

In place of the fear, Angel began to feel a wild elation. Below them, there was nothing but the fields of France, a patchwork of green, interspersed with clusters of mellowed buildings and scattered farmhouses, and the snaking blue of the rivers. Above them was the infinite blue of the universe, the sun dazzling, the faint pale arc of the moon just visible when she was forced to tear her eyes away from such brilliance.

'It's all so beautiful,' she said raggedly. 'It's the world in a way I never thought to see it –'

'This is only a fraction of it, Angel,' Jacques shouted back. 'One day airmen will conquer the rest of it. They'll even get to the moon, you'll see!'

She was the one to laugh at such absurdity now. It didn't matter. It was a day for making impossible statements. Up here, away from all the reality, you felt you could say anything . . .

'Jacques, I do love you!' she shouted, feeling the wind snatch away the words, elated to know the pleasure of saying such things aloud, yet in total privacy.

'And I love you, my dearest Madame de Ville,' he shouted back. She saw him point downwards to their left.

She looked, and there was the shining blue water of the English Channel, a million diamond points sparkling on its surface, the steady progress of ships ploughing across it no more than toy boats on a pond below.

How could she ever have been afraid of this, Angel wondered? It was the experience of a lifetime . . . and she had no idea that Jacques was thanking God or fate or whatever guardian angel watched over them, that they had come thus far in perfect safety, with a fair breeze blowing them from France to the distant coast of England.

When Angel saw the first hint of land, it gave her an odd, choking feeling. They were almost home, yet she loved

France with almost as much fervour as her native England. It would be no hardship for her to settle there after the war – if that was what Jacques intended. It was something there had been little time to discuss or even consider yet. All they had wanted was to belong, and to be together.

The little fields of England were greener than she remembered, or perhaps it was just the perspective of them from this height. They soared over the great monuments of Stonehenge as they circled towards Salisbury Plain and the airbase where Jacques was to report. He turned off the engine and guided the plane down on its own momentum.

The early evening sunlight was becoming lower in the sky now, and the only sound was that of the wind in the spars and rigging. Angel felt she knew exactly how it must feel to be a bird, to drift on the breeze, to coast gently down to earth, soporific and relaxed . . .

A sudden lurching and bumping jolted her, and she realised they had landed. Jacques turned to her, removing his goggles, and she laughed out loud at his comical black face, knowing hers would be the same once the goggles were removed. There was a question in his eyes.

'Well, *chérie*?' he said softly. 'Did it live up to your expectations?'

'It did far more than that! It was something I shall never forget.'

'That's what I hoped.' He jumped down, and lifted her down after him. 'I'll report in, then we'll get cleaned up a little, and find the hotel near Calne where we stayed before, when you drove up with Margot.'

'That sounds fine,' she said, trying to be casual, though in truth her nerves were beginning to jump again. Delicious, tingling nerves, but nerves all the same. They had had so little time together since their marriage, just brief afternoons and occasional night passes since then.

And now they had three whole blissful days before Jacques flew back to France, and Angel took the train to the convalescent home in Essex. Three days that were to be their true honeymoon . . .

She was shown the way to the women's quarters where she could wash her face with special soap made to clean away grime and oil, and didn't do much for delicate skins, Angel thought ruefully. But in little more than half an hour she and Jacques were together again, and to her relief he had cadged them a lift in an air force truck fetching supplies.

'I was afraid we'd have to walk,' she whispered, embarrassed to talk too loudly with the fresh-faced Air Force personnel in the truck, and feeling very much out of place in her civilian clothes as well as being the only woman.

Unconsciously her hand went up to tuck a stray wisp of hair in place. War devoured the femininity of women, but for three days and nights, she was going to be all the woman Jacques desired. Her spirit soared. She was Jacques de Ville's woman . . .

Before leaving France, she had taken the wedding ring from its customary chain around her neck, and now wore it proudly on her finger. It felt cold and unfamiliar and infinitely dear against her skin. Tonight there would be no need to remove it.

The staff at the hotel welcomed them as old friends, remembering them from the last time they had stayed there. Angel felt a blush rise in her cheeks. They had been lovers then. They were lovers still, but there was an undefinable sweetness in knowing that now they truly belonged. They were honeymooners, but to the staff they were merely the dashing Captain de Ville and his lovely wife, paying them a second visit.

'The fare we have to offer is more frugal than before,' the hostess apologised. 'The war, you know – but then, I don't have to tell you that, do I?'

They murmured politely, and told her that she didn't. Whatever she prepared, they would enjoy immensely, and a glass or two of wine before the meal would help their appetites enormously . . .

They smiled into each other's eyes, because the food didn't matter, and the wine only served to heighten their desire for each other.

They had been given the same room as before, a fact that charmed them both. They closed the bedroom door behind them and shut out the rest of the world. Jacques held out his arms to her and she went into them, as close as though his heart beat within her breast.

He reached up his hands and pulled the pins from her hair. It had grown long again, and she normally wore it in a neat bun at the hospital, but now it cascaded in silky, shimmering waves over her shoulders. Jacques held a handful of it in his fingers and pressed it to his lips. Her heart tightened at the love in his eyes.

'Don't ever cut your beautiful hair again, Angel. This is how it was on that first night, and I had never seen anything so lovely. My lovely, golden girl –'

She buried her face in his shoulder, because her love for him was almost too unbearable to contain. She wished that she could hold every moment, and capture it in a container, so that the light of love would never be dimmed. She brushed the thought away fearfully as a portent of disaster, and tonight was not a night for such thoughts.

'Come to bed with me, my love,' Jacques whispered against her cheek.

She felt his fingers on the buttons of her blouse, and stood mutely, allowing him the lingering pleasure of seeing her revealed to him, bit by bit. Blouse, skirt, shift, all cascaded to the floor, to stay where they fell until he scooped her up in his arms and lay her between the sheets to await him. He turned the gaslight down low, so that only a flickering rosy glow lit the room, intimate and warm, and Angel watched as her husband and lover discarded his own clothes and slid into bed beside her.

They had been together so few times that each time was like the first time, the best time. His hands caressed her like a blind man learning his way around a beloved piece of porcelain by sensitive and delicate touch. Her own fingers sought and found every responsive part of his body, and she thrilled anew that a touch or a kiss from her lips could bring this powerful man to high passion in moments.

'I can't wait another second to make you mine, *chérie*,' she heard his throaty voice against her flesh as he kissed her breasts.

'I was always yours, Jacques,' she whispered, the charged emotion in the room too deep to spoil with any but the softest words. 'It's what I was always intended to be, from that first day, when your hand touched mine in a London taxi –'

'And now you're my wife. My own adored wife, and neither war nor continents will keep us apart –'

As if to underline his words, she felt the beloved weight of his body cover hers, poised for a moment on the brink of a union so sweet that she was dazzled with the magic of it. And then she opened up to receive him, and he soared inside her, a flame lighting her life, completing the perfect being.

Angel lay awake long into the night, not wanting to sleep and lose the wonder of such closeness. Jacques' lovemaking had been ardent and inexhaustible, and at times, both of them felt the pleasures of love almost too emotional to bear.

He was sleeping now, and in the faint glow of moonlight from the curtained window, she could see the strong Gallic profile, relaxed in sleep, more dear to her than she had ever dreamed another human being could be. These three days were an oasis in time, and she wanted to savour every second.

She moved her lips against his cheek, tasting the salt of his skin, and felt him stir slightly in sleep and hold her more tightly. She was safe and warm and loved, and there was nothing in the world that anyone could ever want that was more important than that.

The idyll was over, and they sat on a crowded country bus that would take them to the nearest railway station. Angel would take the train from there to report to her new duties in Essex. There was a sudden unbearable constraint between them. So much to be said, so much left unsaid. Fears that were best left unvoiced, words of love that had no place here among the countrywomen and noisy children who glanced briefly at the handsome airman and the beautiful girl by his side and then ignored them.

They held hands tightly, and with every mile, Angel felt as though she and Jacques were already slipping apart. Actual distance didn't matter. It was the inexorable knowledge that she was on her way to one duty, while he would soon be going back on another. And now that the fascination of her own flight was receding in her memory a little, she was beset with worry for the dangers of his chosen life.

'We're here, *chérie*,' Jacques said quietly, and she felt her heart jolt. So soon, so soon . . .

The railway station was crowded, and as the train came lurching along the line like a giant caterpillar spitting sparks and cinders in its wake, she felt her eyes sting. She must be brave, she thought desperately. She mustn't break now, when Jacques needed her to be strong.

The train surged to a halt, and smoke and steam enveloped them, and it hardly mattered that tears smarted in her eyes, for no one noticed in the general flurry of greetings and farewells. They clung desperately, and then she broke away, for to drag out the parting only increased its intensity a hundredfold.

She found a seat between several servicemen, and watched Jacques through the grimy window. A whistle blew. Doors slammed. She saw him run alongside the carriage window for a last glimpse of her, until the crowds frustrated him, and he was lost in the midst of them.

Angel sat back, closing her eyes, and trying not to let the tears force their way through, incongruously imagining her mother's voice at that moment. 'A young lady never betrays her feelings in public . . .'

'Cheer up, ducks,' she heard a voice say. 'It'll be all over soon, so they say.'

She smiled wanly at the Cockney soldier smiling cheekily at her. Needing desperately to believe him, because it was the only thing she could do. It was what they all did, constantly. Gave each other false hope that the war would all be over soon . . .

Chapter 27

Angel discovered that the convalescent home was a fairly cheery place. The men wore blue uniforms, signifying that they had been honourably wounded, and although some remained in the depths of misery about their lot, most of them showed remarkable resilience to whatever injuries they had suffered.

Some were horrific, of course. The amputees were the ones that Angel found most heartbreaking; the empty sleeves, the ending of a body at the hips; the frustration of men with no fingers wanting to do the simplest, basic things for themselves with human dignity, and having to rely on young nurses to do these for them.

She was not involved in these things now. Her role was to drive ambulances to and from the channel ports to deliver the wounded to the home, and take back those fit enough to resume military life. She sometimes wondered if any of them knew what real life was any more. The old world they had known four years ago seemed part of a distant age. Yet people still went to dances, visited the picture shows, made love . . .

Jacques wrote to her as often as he could. She lived for his letters, for each one meant that he was still safe, still alive, still coming back to her. She wrote to him frequently, wanting him to breathe her essence through the words she wrote.

He sent her sketches of beautiful things, butterflies and

flowers and the calm wash of the ocean on sunlit days, and she treasured them in a scrapbook, and told herself it was something to show their children. She thought of it as a little omen, knowing she had something to keep for them, and their shadowy future images didn't seem so impossible.

She had telephoned her family to let them know she was now in England, and was warmed by their ecstatic reaction. Even Clemence seemed quite choked to hear her daughter's voice, and to know that she wasn't far away in France.

'We had such a terribly anxious time in the spring, Angel,' Clemence said on the telephone in her quick, efficient well-bred tones. 'Everyone thought the Germans were going to win, and some people made tentative arrangements to flee to Canada. I don't think any of them actually went in the end –'

'How is everyone, Mummy?' Angel cut across the beginnings of pomposity, more interested in her own family than strangers at the moment. She was surrounded by strangers, and felt a great need to hear about those dear to her.

'Louise is well, and the baby is apparently thriving. We haven't seen him yet, since Dougal doesn't want them to travel until the war is over.' If Clemence was the snorting kind, she would have snorted then. 'I know he's thinking of his family, but it seems rather odd to be so pedantic when half the country seems to be travelling back and forth to France the entire time!'

'Dougal saw enough of the war, Mummy. He's thinking of Louise's safety,' Angel defended her. 'And what of Daddy? It seems so long since I've seen any of you!'

'Your father's well,' Clemence said. 'Business still keeps him away for much of the time.' She resisted adding that relations between them were probably better because of the little time they spent together. It was something one didn't discuss with one's children.

'And Ellen?'

Angel sensed that her mother paused.

'I'm not sure what to say about Ellen. She's mellowed a little in past months, and she seems to enjoy this appalling farming life. She's as forthright as ever in her views, but somewhat secretive in many ways.'

'Does she see anything of Peter Chard?' Angel said the words casually, dying to know.

'She never tells me, though she can hardly avoid him in a place this size. Anyway, my dear, I shall have to cut this conversation short. My ladies are coming this afternoon, and we're still knitting furiously. Oh – and how is Jacques?'

It was an afterthought, and Angel answered evenly.

'He was well the last time I saw him, thank-you. We came to England together in his airplane, as a matter of fact –'

'*What*? Angel, how could you be so reckless! Didn't you think of the danger –?'

All she could think of was the soaring blue of the sky, the feeling of oneness with God and nature and Jacques, the empathy with Jacques' passionate love of flying . . .

'I'm here, aren't I?' she said edgily. 'Mother, I'll let you go. I know you have a million important things to do. Give my love to everyone. 'Bye.'

She put the instrument down, suddenly stifled by her mother's indignant voice. Clemence still saw her girls dressed in juvenile frilly frocks attending garden parties with their parents in the eternal round of London's social life. To Clemence, the girls had never grown up, nor ever would, despite Louise being widowed, remarrying and having a baby; Ellen involved in a near-disastrous love affair; Angel going through a war and growing up in the process, and finding love . . .

She felt a brief pity for Clemence, knitting diligently, offering dignified succour to victims on the railway station, and yet still somehow remaining virtually untouched by war. Almost everyone would emerge at the end of it, marked in some way. Clemence would merely resume the old life as if four years of war had been merely a hiccough in her ordered routine.

Angel caught her thoughts up short. She was thinking as though the war was nearly over, but everyone was talking of it that way now. She had gone through an anxious time at the end of May when the Germans attacked the French lines on the Marne. The long-range guns were firing shells into Paris, and Angel was desperate with worry for Jacques.

There was no news from him for several weeks until at last she heard that he was well. At the same time, the military news improved, with the Americans taking a key role in halting the German advance, the British counter-attacking alongside them. The Allies had a triumphant victory, and everyone at home breathed more easily again.

The weeks passed quickly by. June merged into July and August . . . another summer came and went, while it seemed as if the whole of Britain held its breath for the end of all hostilities. It was a tormented and tantalising time, when muddled reports promised that the end was near, then another battle would flare up, and hopes would be dashed. Still the wounded came home, were patched up and sent back to fight again.

And still Angel Bannister de Ville drove her ambulance between the ports and the convalescent home, until she could have driven the routes blindfold, and felt that she never wanted to hear the whine of an engine again, nor to feel her eyes so tired and strained from lack of sleep that she could have crawled into the nearest ditch and remained there until the Armistice.

Newspapers reported every new development of the war with screaming headlines, implying that victory was just around the corner, and that each new day brought peace a little nearer. The waiting was almost unbearable, the rumours becoming wilder and more unreliable.

But at last there was great rejoicing, when on August 8th fresh news from France became known. In dense fog, the German front lines were pushed back relentlessly. Even though they still fought fiercely, they were unable to resist the combined tank assaults of Canadian, Australian and British troops, brought together in a massive show of strength.

'We're almost there!' Sir Frederick Bannister said jubilantly, scanning the latest newspaper headlines in the small Yorkshire cottage. Harriet looked at him fondly.

'You'd like to have taken part in this war, wouldn't you, Freddie?'

He grinned sheepishly. 'Is it so obvious?'

' 'Tis to me! Why else would you get so uppity when things have gone wrong? You'd like to have been in France with the young 'uns beating hell out of the Jerries!'

Fred laughed out loud, giving her a squeeze, and revelling in the fact that there was more flesh on her bones than in months past. She fitted more comfortably against him now, in the old sweet way that was familiar and loving.

'It's no comfort to know that you're too old to go to war, sweetheart. I could hold a rifle with the best of 'em, and stick a bayonet where it hurt most –'

'And probably die of a heart attack in the process,' Harriet said with dry Yorkshire perception. 'You do your bit for the war effort, Freddie, providing cloth for uniforms and blankets, and don't ever think otherwise.'

He wasn't a particularly religious man, though there had been times when he'd prayed to God for Harriet's recovery, and God had answered his prayers. There were other times when he remembered fragments of old scriptures, and twisted them to suit his mood. This was one of them, for his Harriet truly restored his soul, he thought irreverently . . .

The battle begun on August 8th raged on. Newspaper reports played down the enormous waves of casualties produced, and concentrated instead on the furious efforts of the Allied forces to break down the famed Hindenburg line, the hugely successful German fortification. Tremendous battles were fought along its length, until in early September it was at last pierced and the defences broken. Surely now at last, victory was imminent . . .

Celebrations were begun far too early in some towns and villages. Without waiting for official confirmation as to whether the war was over or not, people celebrated in their own way, with small parties and mutual congratulations on the ending of four years of hardship and anxiety. They waited impatiently for the final declaration of peace to be signed, and for their men and women to come home. Some wept silently for those who would never return. And still the final news didn't come . . .

Ellen Bannister was as anxious as anyone for the war to end. She was still undecided what to do with her life once it was all over. But of one thing she was certain. She had to get back to London. She adored the country with a fervour that constantly surprised her, but it would be impossible for her to remain in Somerset, knowing that she loved Peter Chard.

If things had been different, she would have stayed so willingly, so gladly . . . but as it was, it was far better to cut her losses with the entire country scene, and get back to the bright lights again. Perhaps join the campaigning work for the Women's Movement once more, which was sure to resume activities again soon. It was a thought that would once have inspired her, but which, guiltily, she now found depressingly hollow.

But once she was back in smoky old London, Ellen thought desperately, everything would fall into place again, and she could forget this madness of ever thinking Peter Chard could love her too . . . Wasn't it some clever theorist who said there was never one so dogmatic in resolution than the one most opposed to it in the first place?

Which was merely a pedantic way of saying that to a woman who had never expected to fall in love, the reality was even more all-consuming than she could have imagined in her wildest dreams. And to find that love unreturned, the most devastating blow to her self-esteem . . .

At the end of September, while the weather was still mild and balmy, there was to be a village street party that was being organised partly by her mother, the vicar, and the other village bigwigs. It was to be a cautious celebration in honour of certain victory, and a way of raising funds for the comforts still needed by bereaved families and wounded heroes about to return.

In Ellen's opinion, it was taking things far too much for granted, but the village was swept along on a wave of having something to do that was cheerful and positive, and bunting was hung from shop doorways, Union flags fluttered from every window, and one might think that peace had already come to one sleepy little Somerset village . . .

And naturally Peter was there on the day, dressed in his Sunday corduroys and polished boots, and the Land Army girls had put aside their businesslike uniforms, and dressed in bright summer frocks. After the drabness and itchy wool of the dark green clothes, Ellen felt strangely light and feminine in soft yellow muslin.

There was a surprising amount of country fare on long trestle tables, and an even greater quantity of scrumpy cider and home-made wines. If the occasion didn't make everyone slightly tipsy, then the alcohol consumed certainly did.

Music was played on an old squeeze-box, and there was lusty singing of patriotic songs. Far down the length of the tables, Ellen saw Peter watching her in a way that made her heart thump. He began moving towards her, and it was as though she watched him in slow motion.

It was as if he would never reach her, as if they were both caught up in one of those awful dreams, where the person one wants the most is forever out of reach . . . she had felt like that before, only this time, Peter did reach her side, and she felt the grasp of his hand on hers. His voice was slightly aggressive, but when he spoke, she found herself obeying.

'I have to talk to you, but not here. Let's go somewhere private.'

She could smell the sweet fragrant scrumpy on his breath but it didn't offend her. If anything, it stirred her blood into a kind of pulsing excitement. Peter pulled her along with him through the winding streets until they reached the edge of the village and the ancient church.

Everyone was busily enjoying themselves elsewhere, and Ellen found herself almost bundled inside the church. It was cool and dim, and she was suddenly very calm, as if she had a presentiment. If it was so, then this was the sweetest moment of her life, and for once she wasn't going to throw it all away . . .

She knew Peter was slightly drunk, and perhaps if he hadn't been, he would never have smothered his pride to do as he did. One minute they were merely facing one another. The next, she was pulled roughly into his arms, and his mouth was on hers, kissing her as though he were making up for a lifetime of wanting her, and she was kissing him back with every ounce of passion in her nature.

When they broke apart, she expected some soft declaration of love from him, but she should have known him better. His eyes flashed almost aggressively down at her.

'All right. That tells me everything I wanted to know. So when are you going to stop wearing the trousers, Ellen Bannister, and settle down to becoming a good farmer's wife?'

She gave a small gasp, her chin lifting in a way that reminded him briefly of her sister, Angel. Only briefly, for there was really no one else in his mind and his heart but the impossible woman in his arms.

'When some good farmer asks me properly!' she managed to blurt out, her eyes flashing back the same aggressive signals.

He began to laugh, the sound vibrating richly in the solemn interior.

'Oh, my dearest Ellen, do we really need the words that other people do?'

'Yes!' she replied with a fierce need to hear him say them. To know she was loved and desired, the same as every other woman who ever wanted a man so badly that it hurt . . .

'Then please will you marry me, Ellen, because I love you so much I can't imagine spending the rest of my life without you, and why we've gone through this farce of keeping apart all these months, I can't think –'

He couldn't say any more, because she swayed into his arms, leaning her head against his chest, the breath in her throat a little sigh of pure happiness.

'Yes, I'll marry you, Peter. Yes, yes, yes! As soon as you like –'

'And live here in the country, buried away from civilisation? I insist on a proper wedding, so as not to offend our country neighbours, and you'll wear a long white dress and veil, and none of your radical thinking –'

'I can think of nothing I want more.'

Ellen spoke breathlessly, slightly awed to find that she didn't think it in the least sloppy to know that the least-expected Bannister sister of all would be the one to have the conventional village wedding . . . it all depended on love, she thought. Love changed everything . . .

In October, it was reported amid much confusion that the Germans had already asked for an Armistice. Their army was breaking up. There was mutiny in their navy, revolution in Berlin, and panic everywhere. The Kaiser had fled to Holland for his own safety, and on November 9th, Germany was proclaimed a Republic. Two days later, at 11 a.m., the Allied armies agreed to grant an Armistice.

Jacques de Ville's reconnaissance flight took him over enemy lines at the exact time that news was released to the German soldiers, and the sight he saw below was an extraordinary one. The Germans came out of their trenches, waving the red flags of the Republic, shouting and singing, still unaware of the true humiliation of their leaders, and believing the Armistice had been agreed because of revolution in their country. Grenades were tossed about, and deeper into the lines ammunition dumps were being exploded.

'What d'you reckon's happening, Cap?' Jacques' gunner, Chalkie White, shouted to him.

'Lord knows, but they're in danger of blowing themselves up if they don't take more care,' Jacques shouted back grimly. 'We'd better get back to base and find out.'

Reasons hardly mattered. Four terrible years of war were officially over, and if the weary British soldiers were too exhausted to show such outward joy as the Germans, that didn't matter either. The only thing on everyone's mind now was how soon they could go home, and home was suddenly the sweetest word in any language.

Angel had been kissed by so many excited patients, she began to think her cheeks would be permanently bruised. She had telephoned her parents as soon as she could, though waiting for a line to be free had been agonisingly slow. Ellen had broken into the conversation, saying that she and Peter had decided to be married before Christmas, and her sister's joy was almost tangible. Angel herself felt in a strange kind of limbo.

There had so far been no word from Jacques for some days, and an unspoken fear gripped her. It would be the most cruel twist of fate if anything had happened to Jacques at the very end of the war, when everyone was on the brink of normality again.

When she wanted him so much, and missed him so much, and loved him so much . . . reunions were happening every day. Women were arriving to take their menfolk home, lights in the cities were turned on again, and the sense of freedom was as heady as wine. And still Jacques didn't call or write . . .

She found herself wondering how the end of the war would affect her own family. She and Jacques would presumably live at his family home, but whereas before she had thought of the idea with pleasure, now she was afraid to plan anything, in case it was tempting fate.

Louise's future was assured, and now, astonishingly, was Ellen's. Clemence and Fred . . . there was no doubt in Angel's mind that her father's liaison with Harriet Garth would continue, and after the scene between them at the Hampstead house, she could only feel sympathy for him.

And it wasn't taking anything away from Clemence. She still had her husband's name, and his family loyalty. Clemence would continue in the same stoic way she always had, doing Good Works, being a pillar of society, and four years of war would not have ruffled her confidence one bit.

Everyone was secure, except Angel herself . . .

Three days after the Armistice, she was preparing to leave the convalescent home. Regular staff were returning, and those under war orders could be relieved of their posts as soon as convenient. And she wanted to go home. To be within the comfort of her family, at Meadowcroft or in London, to have their support in the growing dread that she felt.

'There's a telegram for you, in Matron's office, Angel,' one of the orderlies called out to her.

Her heart felt sick. Her footsteps hardly touched the ground as she went to the small office. She wasn't aware that she moved at all, until Matron thrust the little envelope under her nose. She was terrified to open it, and yet she must. She must know . . .

'Disbanding at once. Arriving London tonight. Book a double room Hotel P. All love, Jacques.'

Tears blinded her eyes and relief flooded through her, as

searing in its way as a knife edge. He was alive. He was coming home . . .

'Drink this, my dear.'

She felt the coldness of a glass at her lips, and tasted the stinging bite of brandy, swallowing obediently. The mists cleared, and she saw Matron watching her uncertainly. Her lips formed a trembling smile, when she had begun to believe she would never smile again.

'It's all *right*! My husband's safe. He's coming home. I have to leave at once to be with him –'

The scalding tears overflowed, and she felt herself rocked in the woman's arms. When she had recovered, she was released from her duties at once, and telephoned the Hotel Portland. To her enormous relief, they had a room available. It was a dreary little hotel, but Jacques had promised that one day they would return there, to see the lights of London once more, and it was a promise they had to keep together.

She managed to catch a train to town, and all the way her feelings were in turmoil. The train was as crowded with passengers as ever, naturally with more jubilation than before, and despite the rain that was falling when she reached Fenchurch Street, Angel was swept along in the wave of patriotism surrounding her.

She hailed a taxi, and climbed inside it thankfully, but long before it had taken her through the mean little back streets of Soho to the Hotel Portland, she realised just what a crush of people were filling the streets. Victory was several days ago, but here in the capital, the celebrations went on and on . . .

The taxi-cab was jostled alarmingly every time it crawled to a stop. People shouting for transport rapped on the windows, shouting at her to stop being a toff and share it with them. Angel became quite frightened, and recognising a street very near to the hotel, she told the taxi driver she would get out there and walk the rest of the way.

'Are yer sure, Miss? Yer might get squashed –'

'I didn't get squashed in France, so I'm not too worried about a crowd of merrymakers,' she said with some spirit.

Once outside in the cool November air, the drizzle still falling, she wasn't so sure. There were people everywhere, some the worse for drink, and she began to wonder frantically if she had survived the years of war only to be crushed to death in the first days of peace. She was finding it hard to breathe . . .

She had turned the corner of the street, and the lights of the Hotel Portland were ahead of her. Only a little farther. She stepped into the road to avoid a crowd of drunken revellers, and was almost immediately snatched back to the pavement again.

'Are you trying to get yourself killed?'

The familiar voice sent waves of nostalgia rushing through her. The same words, the same voice, that she had heard a lifetime ago . . . she twisted round, and was clasped tightly in Jacques' arms, the crowd pushing them even closer together. She tasted his mouth for a sweet wild moment, and then he was protecting her from harm with his embrace.

'I've been watching out for you from the entrance. Let's get inside quickly, Angel.'

They raced across the road, and entered the small hotel. It might have been cheap and none too savoury, but to the two of them it seemed as though they had just reached heaven. The tired receptionist gave them their key without bothering to look up. They moved upwards in the clanking lift, hands held as if afraid to let one another go.

'She probably thinks we're here on a clandestine night out,' Angel murmured, fighting the urge to weep all over this man who was her husband, because the joy of their being together at last was almost too much . . .

'Like the last time?' Jacques said softly and deliberately. He tipped up her chin until her eyes met his. She ached at the love she saw there.

'Last time was a promise for the future, *chérie*. Tonight is forever.'

She kept that thought in her mind as they reached their room. For one blissful moment, they leaned against the closed door and kissed and clung, and then Jacques moved towards the window, his arms still around her, and pushed the curtains aside.

They stood with arms entwined in the darkness of the hotel room, but outside, the city was bathed in triumphant light. A tree dismally flapped its branches against the window, but not even the sadness of falling leaves could dim the revitalised splendour that was London.

Jacques spoke with restrained emotion. 'I promised that we'd come back here and see the city as it should be, Angel. This is for you, *chérie*. This, and all the love in the world.'

She turned into his arms. Pressed close to him, she could feel the beat of his heart that was also her heart.

'I need none of it but your love, Jacques,' she whispered. 'All I want is you. All I ever wanted was you.'

He held her tight, love blazing between them as brightly as a flame. When he would have closed the curtains again, she stopped him, her voice tremulous, hoping he wouldn't think her words over-dramatic. But she couldn't quite forget all those others . . . not yet . . .

'No, don't close the curtains, Jacques. I want to see the lights shining in on us, giving us their blessing. We deserve it, don't we?'

'We all do . . . the survivors, and all the others who gave everything they had,' Jacques agreed quietly, and she knew instantly that he understood everything she couldn't find the words to say.

Jacques lifted his wife in his arms, and lay her on the coverlet, gazing down at her for long moments before her arms reached out to him. Somewhere in the night, the joyful muted sounds of celebratory singing went on. Life went on . . .

The momentary sadness drifted away from them. Thoughts of countless lovers who would never again know the ecstasy of moments like these, flitted briefly through their minds and out again, with a gentle, loving grace.

Tonight was theirs, and surely no silent ghosts could begrudge them all their tomorrows.